FRANCINE PASCAL'S

SWEET VALLEY

Twins

TEACHER'S PET

Also by Francine Pascal

Sweet Valley Twins®

Sweet Valley High®

Sweet Valley University

Sweet Valley Confidential

Fearless®

My First Love and Other Disasters

Save Johanna!

Little Crew of Butchers

La Villa

Also by Nicole Andelfinger

Power Rangers Universe with Simone Ragazzoni

The Dragon Prince: Bloodmoon Huntress with Felia Hanakata

A Thief Among the Trees: An Ember in the Ashes Graphic Novel with Sabaa Tahir & Sonia Liao

A Spark Within the Forge: An Ember in the Ashes Graphic Novel with Sabaa Tahir & Sonia Liao

Also by Claudia Aguirre

Hotel Dare with Terry Blas

Lifetime Passes with Terry Blas

SWEET VALLEY Twins®

TEACHER'S PET

Created and story by
Francine Pascal

Adaptation written by
Nicole Andelfinger

Illustrated by
Claudia Aguirre

Colors by
Sara Hagstrom

Letters by
Warren Montgomery

RH
GRAPHIC

NEW YORK

Text copyright © 2023 by Francine Pascal
Cover art and interior illustrations copyright © 2023 by Claudia Aguirre

All rights reserved. Published in the United States by RH Graphic, an imprint of Random House Children's Books, a division of Penguin Random House LLC, New York.

RH Graphic with the book design is a trademark of Penguin Random House LLC.
Sweet Valley Twins is a registered trademark of Francine Pascal; used under license.

Visit us on the web! RHKidsGraphic.com • @RHKidsGraphic

Educators and librarians, for a variety of teaching tools, visit us at RHTeachersLibrarians.com

Library of Congress Cataloging-in-Publication Data is available upon request.
ISBN 978-0-593-37650-8 (trade paperback) — ISBN 978-0-593-37651-5 (hardcover)
ISBN 978-0-593-37652-2 (library binding) — ISBN 978-0-593-37653-9 (ebook)

Designed by Patrick Crotty

Printed in Canada
10 9 8 7 6 5 4 3 2 1
First Edition

A comic on every bookshelf.

To Molly Jessica Wenk

—F.P.

For the best pack of teacher's pets I ever
did know: Karisa, Katrina, and Amber

—N.A.

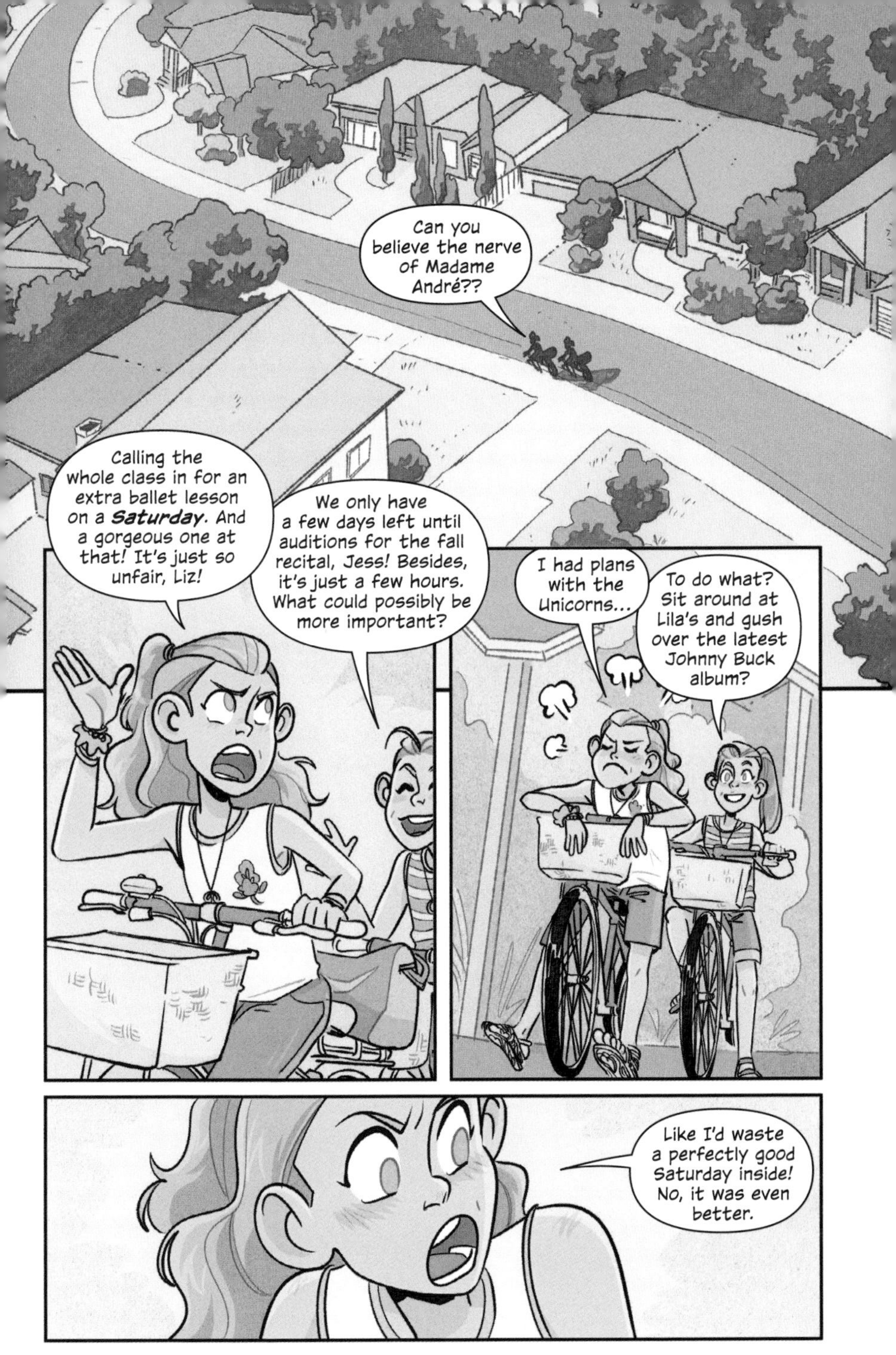
Can you believe the nerve of Madame André??
Calling the whole class in for an extra ballet lesson on a ***Saturday***. And a gorgeous one at that! It's just so unfair, Liz!
We only have a few days left until auditions for the fall recital, Jess! Besides, it's just a few hours. What could possibly be more important?
I had plans with the Unicorns...
To do what? Sit around at Lila's and gush over the latest Johnny Buck album?
Like I'd waste a perfectly good Saturday inside! No, it was even better.

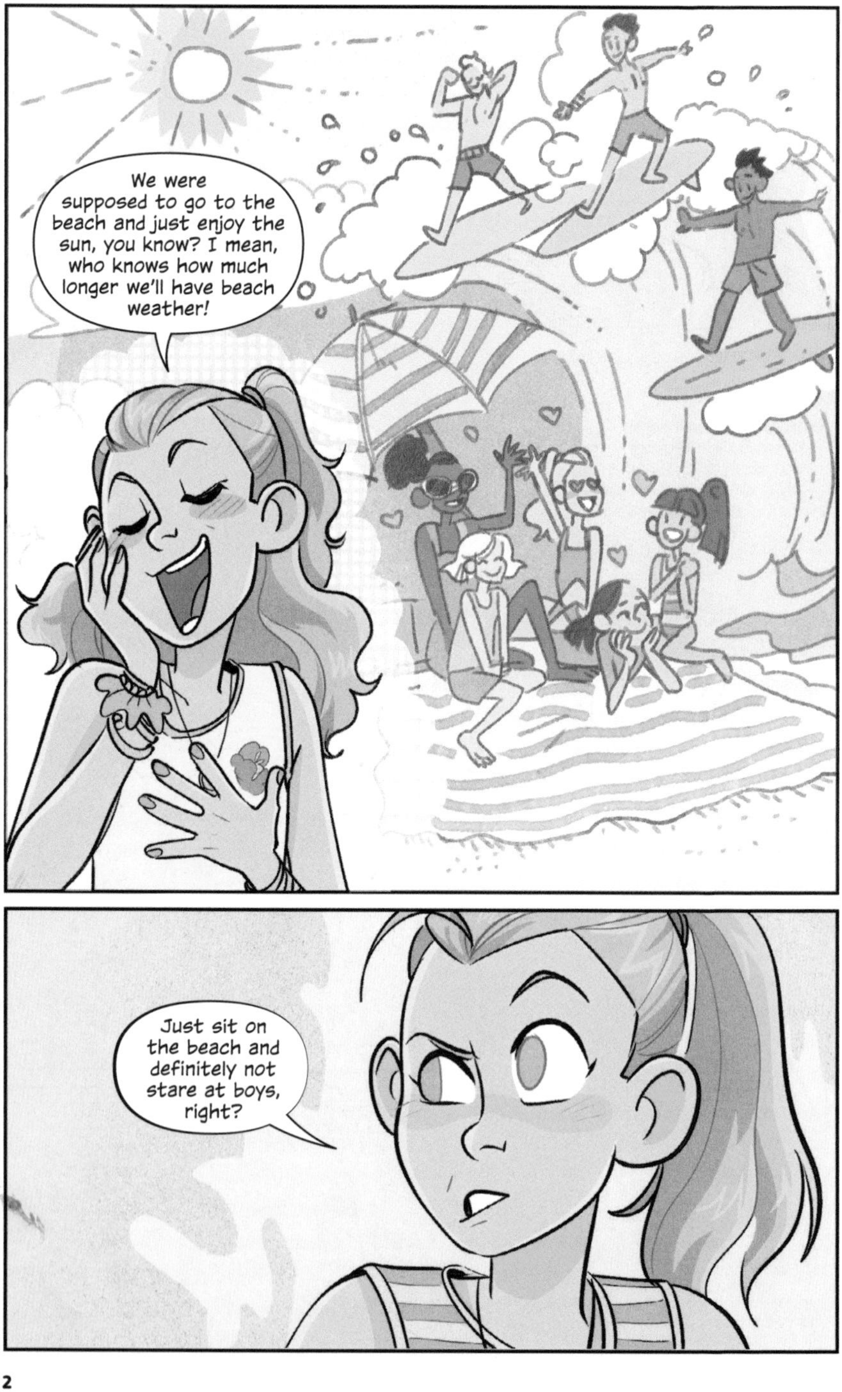
We were supposed to go to the beach and just enjoy the sun, you know? I mean, who knows how much longer we'll have beach weather!
Just sit on the beach and definitely not stare at boys, right?

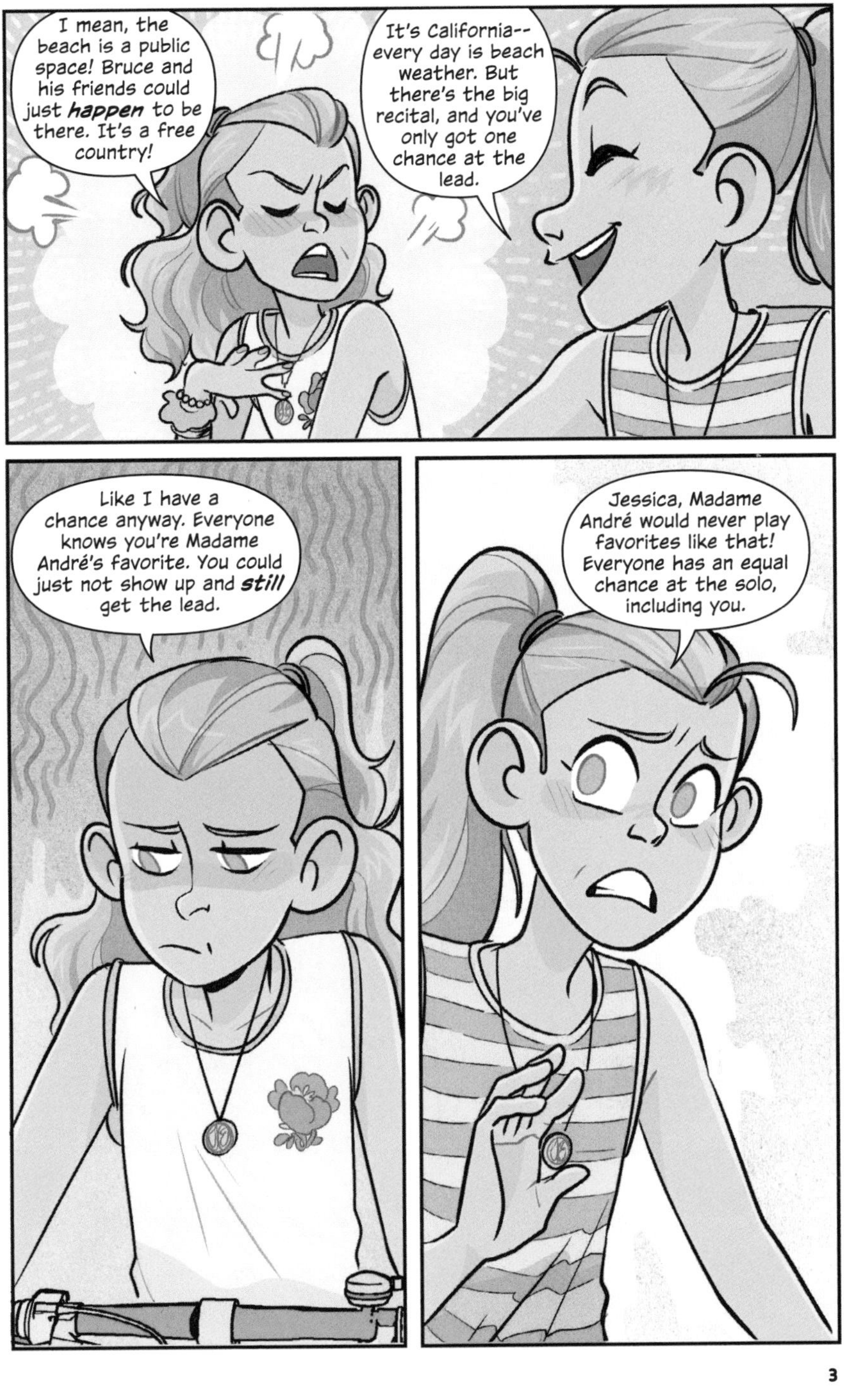
I mean, the beach is a public space! Bruce and his friends could just ***happen*** to be there. It's a free country!
It's California--every day is beach weather. But there's the big recital, and you've only got one chance at the lead.
Like I have a chance anyway. Everyone knows you're Madame André's favorite. You could just not show up and ***still*** get the lead.
Jessica, Madame André would never play favorites like that! Everyone has an equal chance at the solo, including you.

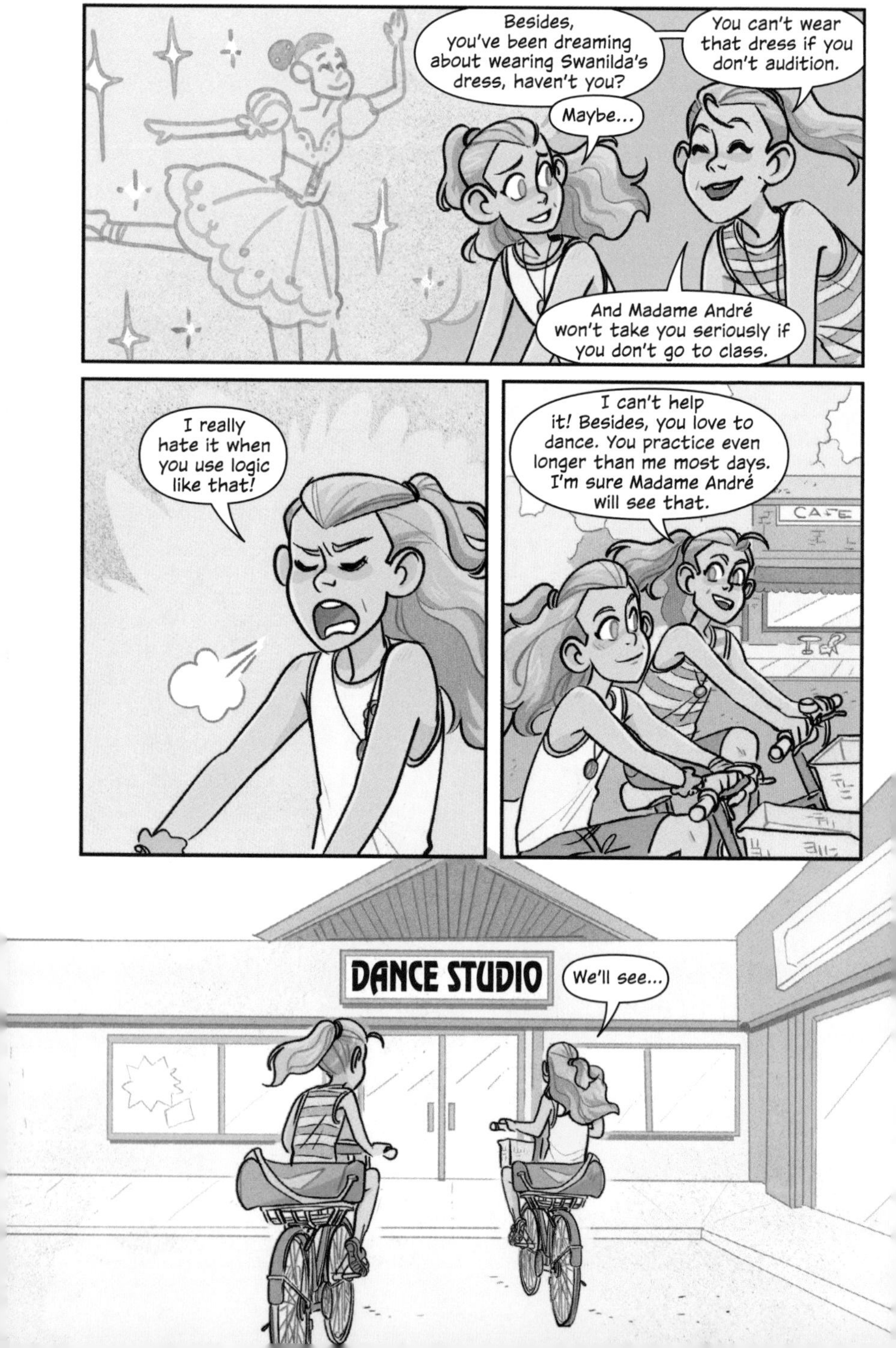
Besides, you've been dreaming about wearing Swanilda's dress, haven't you?
You can't wear that dress if you don't audition.
Maybe...
And Madame André won't take you seriously if you don't go to class.
I really hate it when you use logic like that!
I can't help it! Besides, you love to dance. You practice even longer than me most days. I'm sure Madame André will see that.
CAFE
DANCE STUDIO
We'll see...

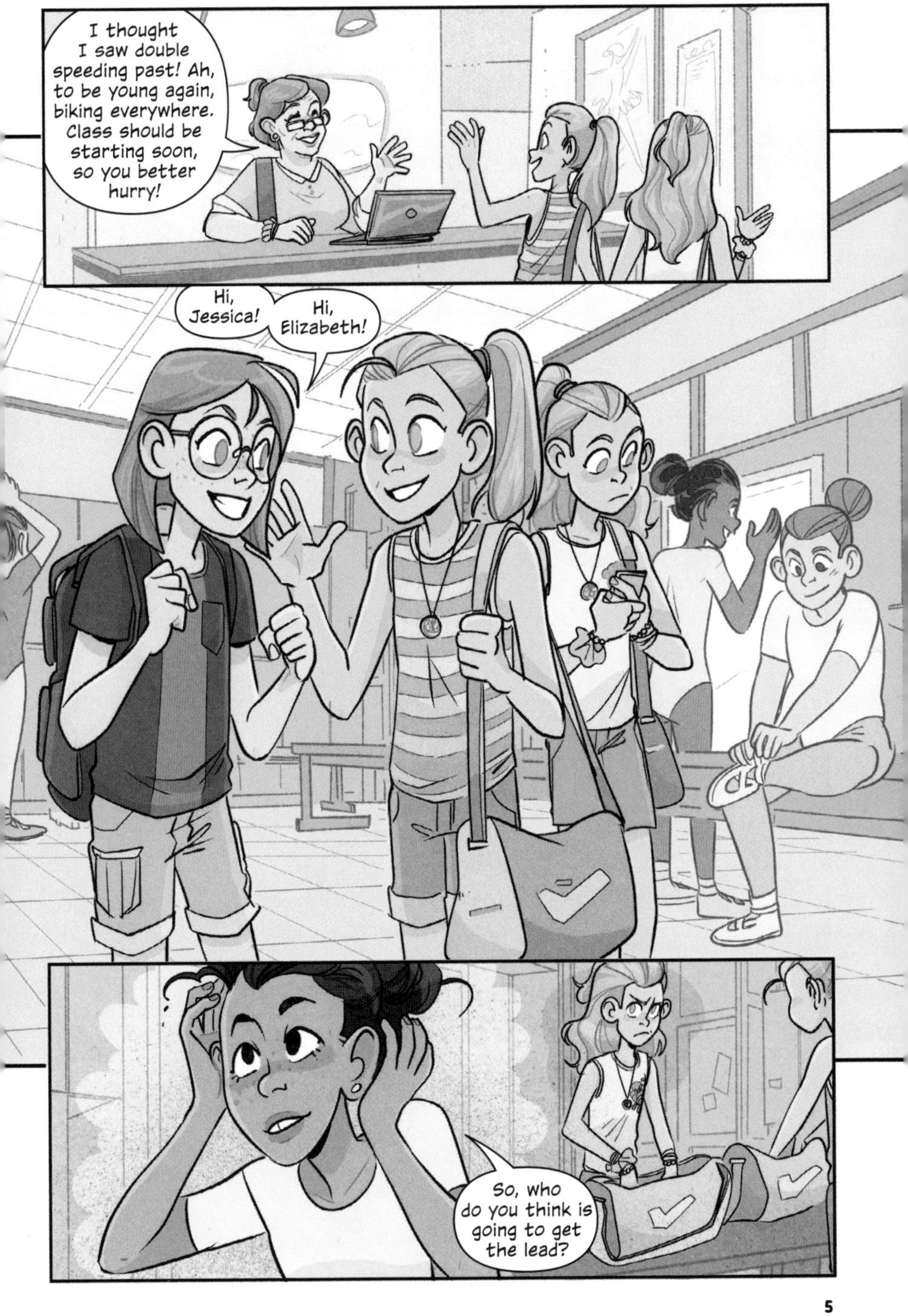
I thought I saw double speeding past! Ah, to be young again, biking everywhere. Class should be starting soon, so you better hurry!
Hi, Jessica!
Hi, Elizabeth!
So, who do you think is going to get the lead?

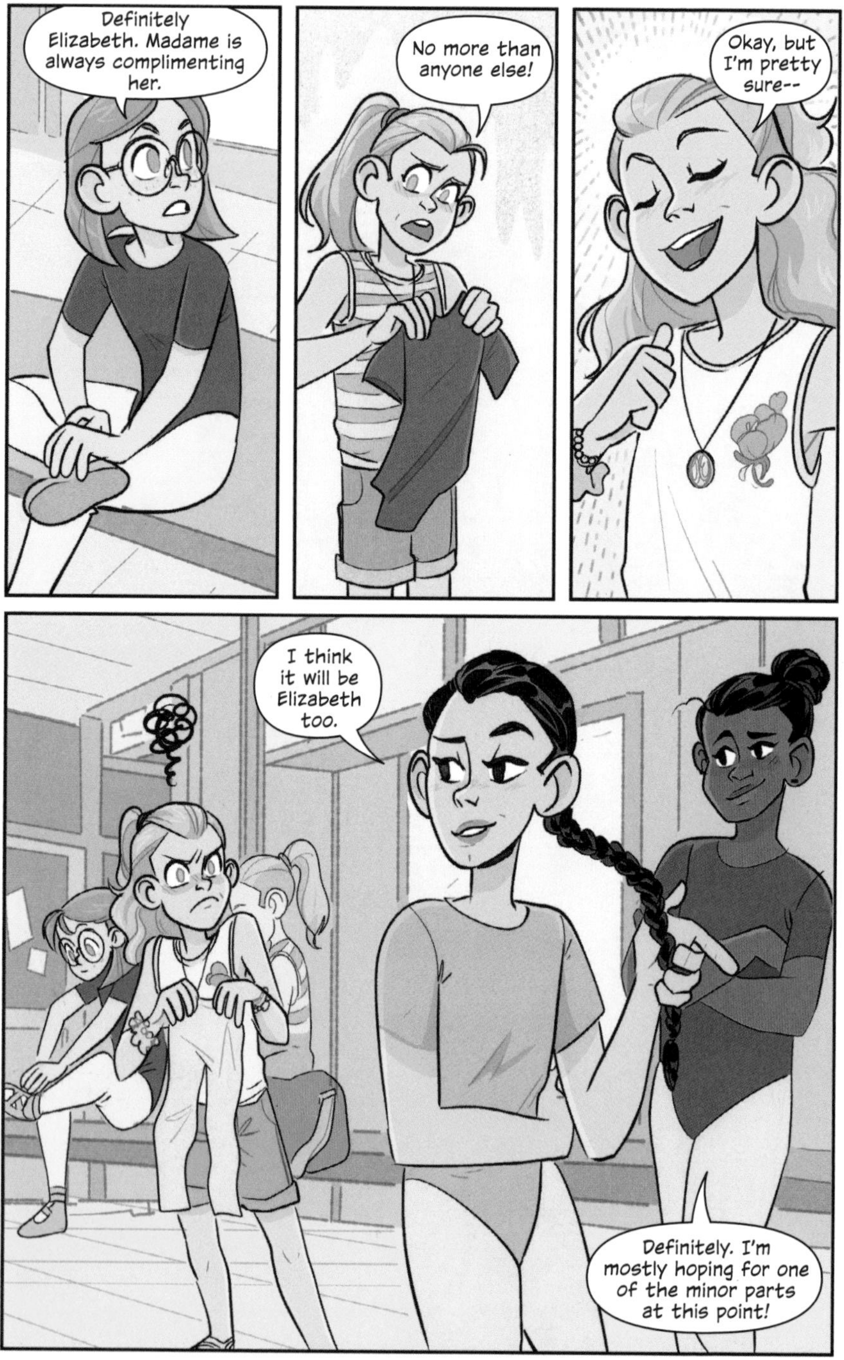
Definitely Elizabeth. Madame is always complimenting her.
No more than anyone else!
Okay, but I'm pretty sure--
I think it will be Elizabeth too.
Definitely. I'm mostly hoping for one of the minor parts at this point!

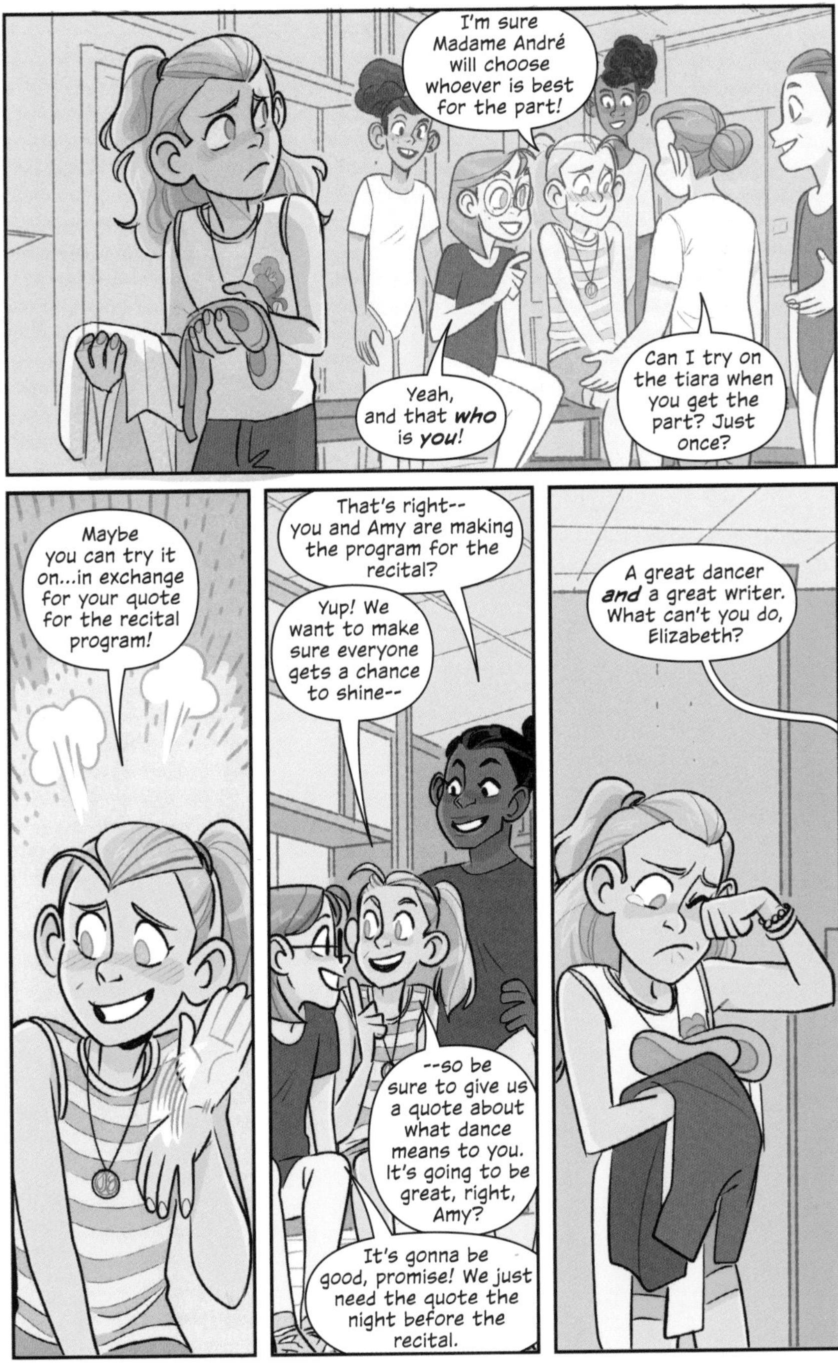
I'm sure Madame André will choose whoever is best for the part!
Yeah, and that *who* is *you*!
Can I try on the tiara when you get the part? Just once?
Maybe you can try it on...in exchange for your quote for the recital program!
That's right-- you and Amy are making the program for the recital?
Yup! We want to make sure everyone gets a chance to shine--
--so be sure to give us a quote about what dance means to you. It's going to be great, right, Amy?
It's gonna be good, promise! We just need the quote the night before the recital.
A great dancer *and* a great writer. What can't you do, Elizabeth?

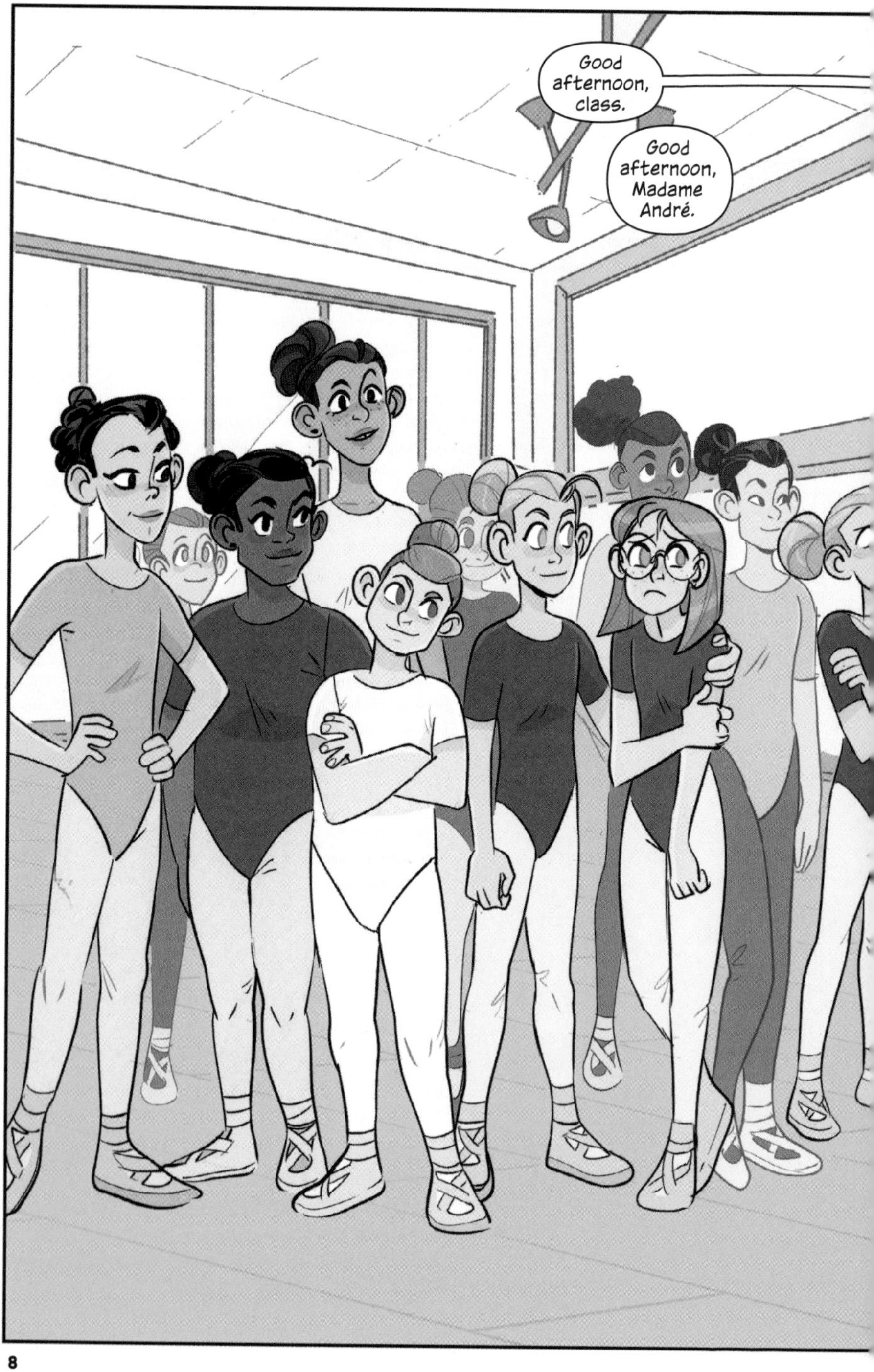
Good afternoon, class.
Good afternoon, Madame André.

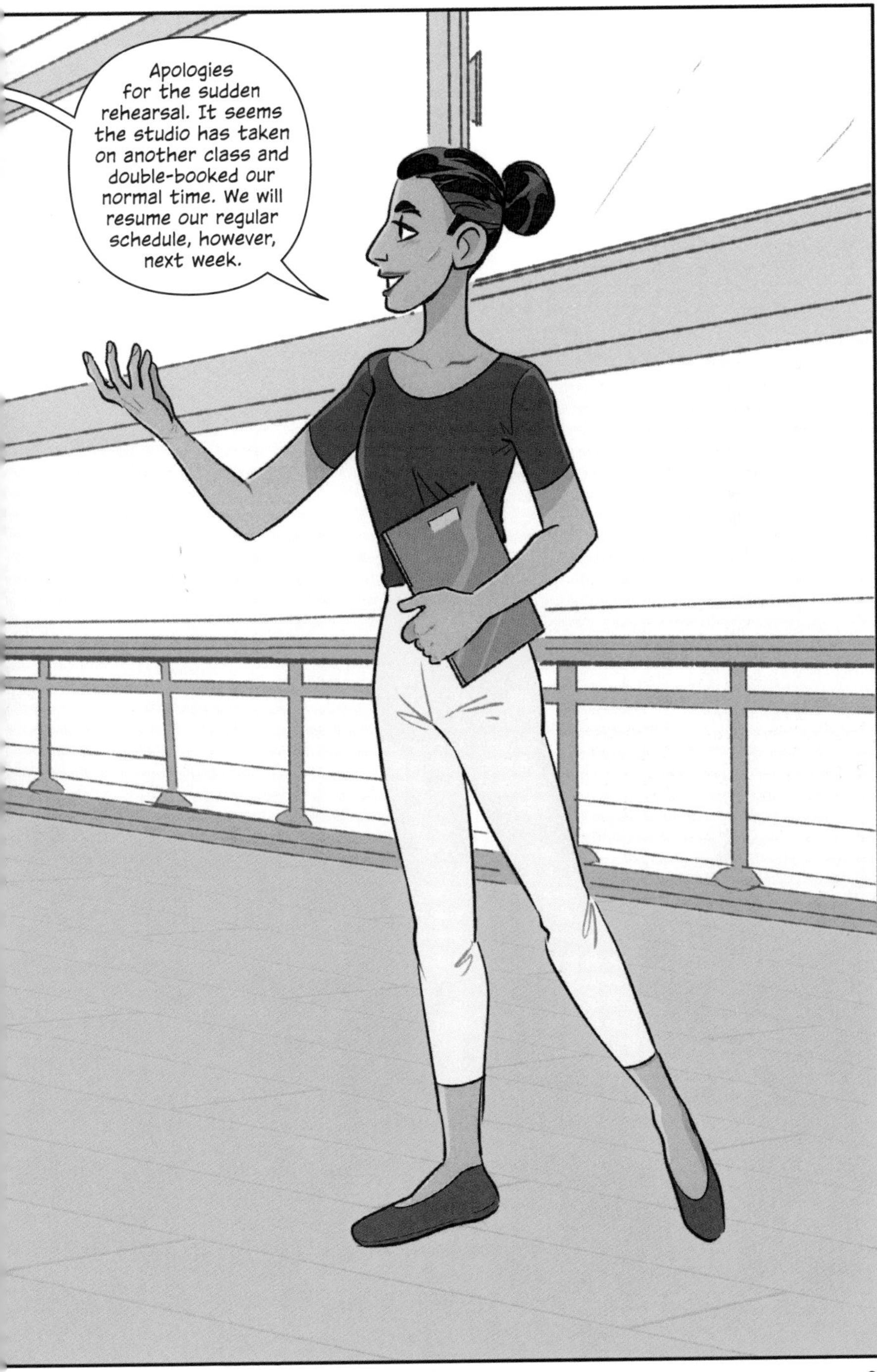
Apologies for the sudden rehearsal. It seems the studio has taken on another class and double-booked our normal time. We will resume our regular schedule, however, next week.

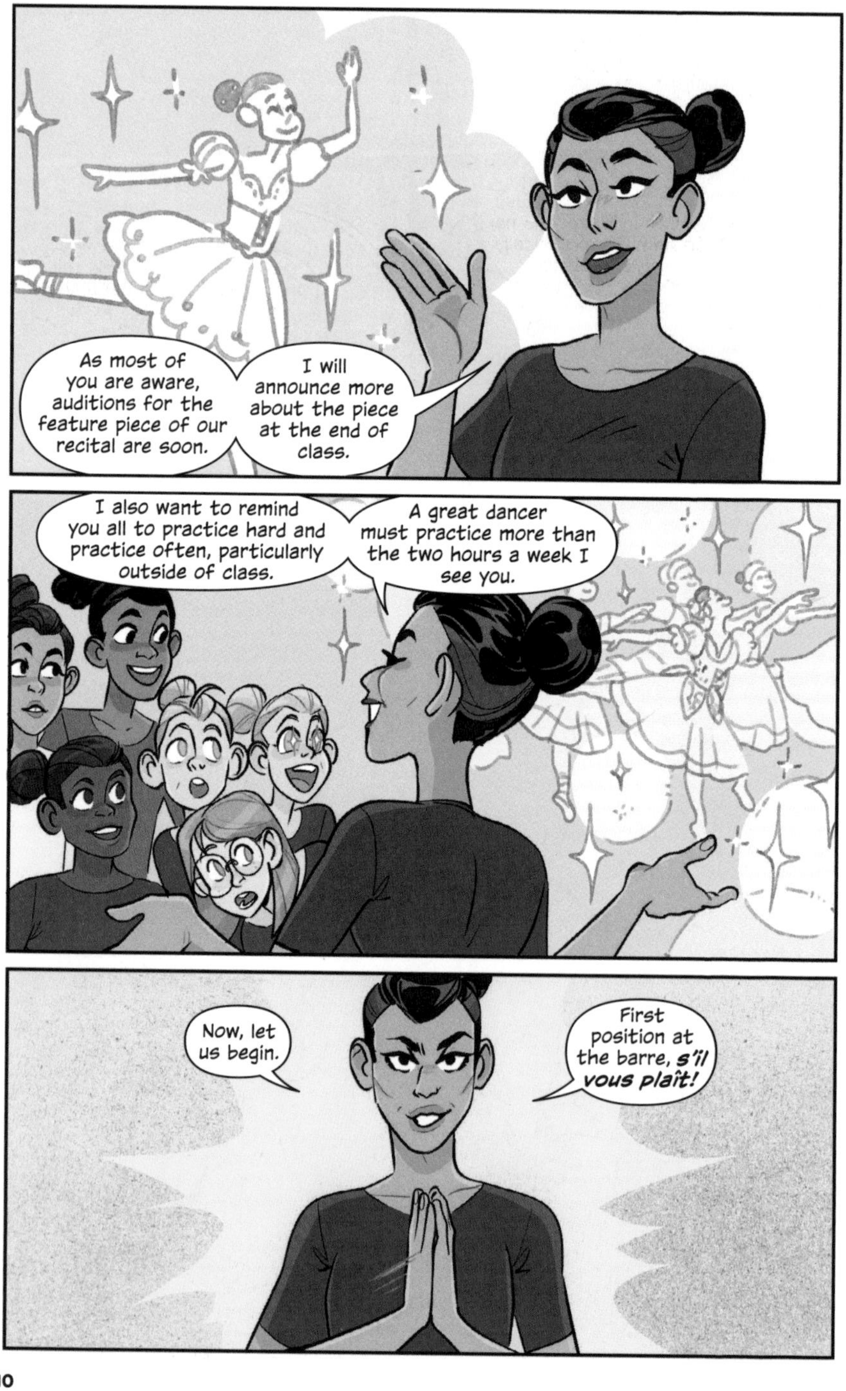
As most of you are aware, auditions for the feature piece of our recital are soon.
I will announce more about the piece at the end of class.
I also want to remind you all to practice hard and practice often, particularly outside of class.
A great dancer must practice more than the two hours a week I see you.
Now, let us begin.
First position at the barre, ***s'il vous plaît!***

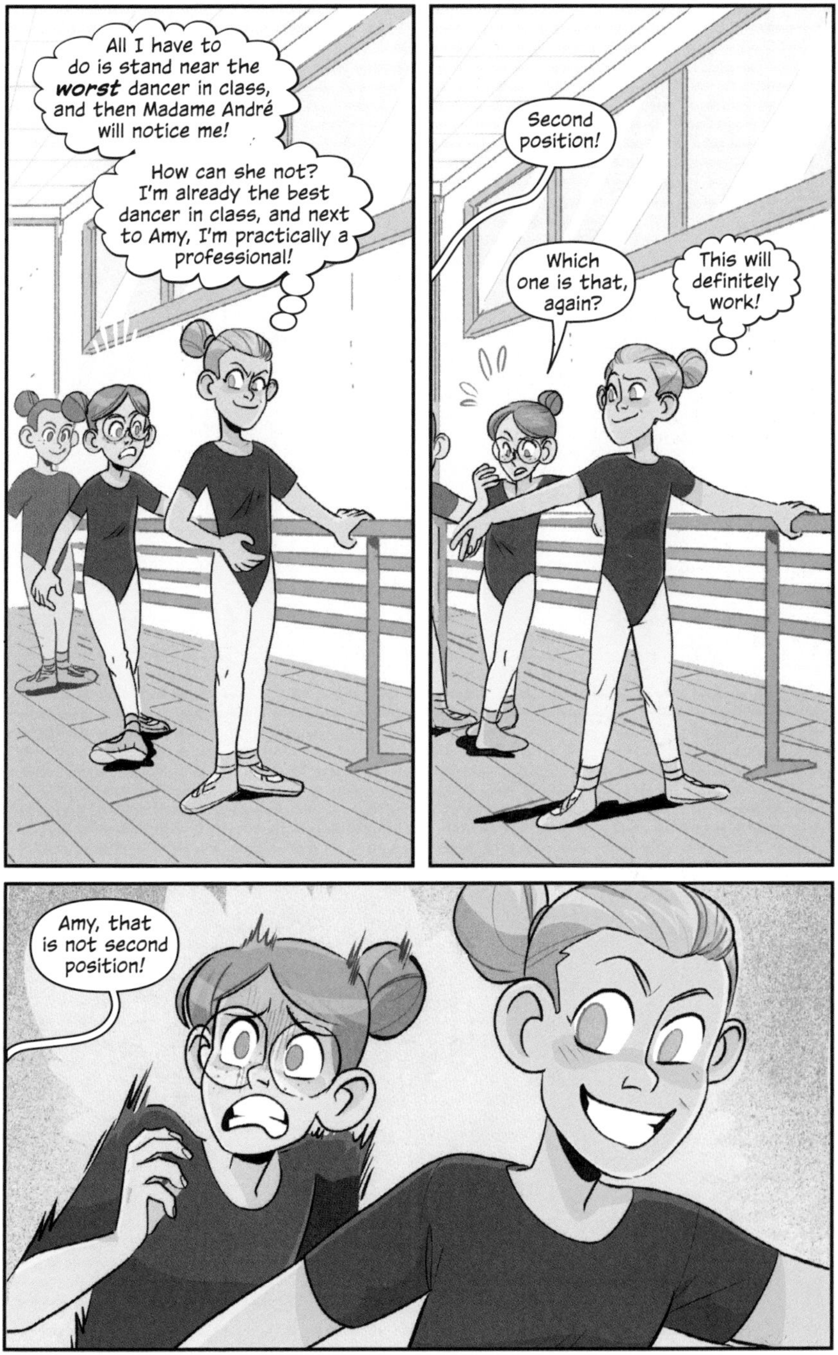
All I have to do is stand near the ***worst*** dancer in class, and then Madame André will notice me!
How can she not? I'm already the best dancer in class, and next to Amy, I'm practically a professional!
Second position!
Which one is that, again?
This will definitely work!
Amy, that is not second position!

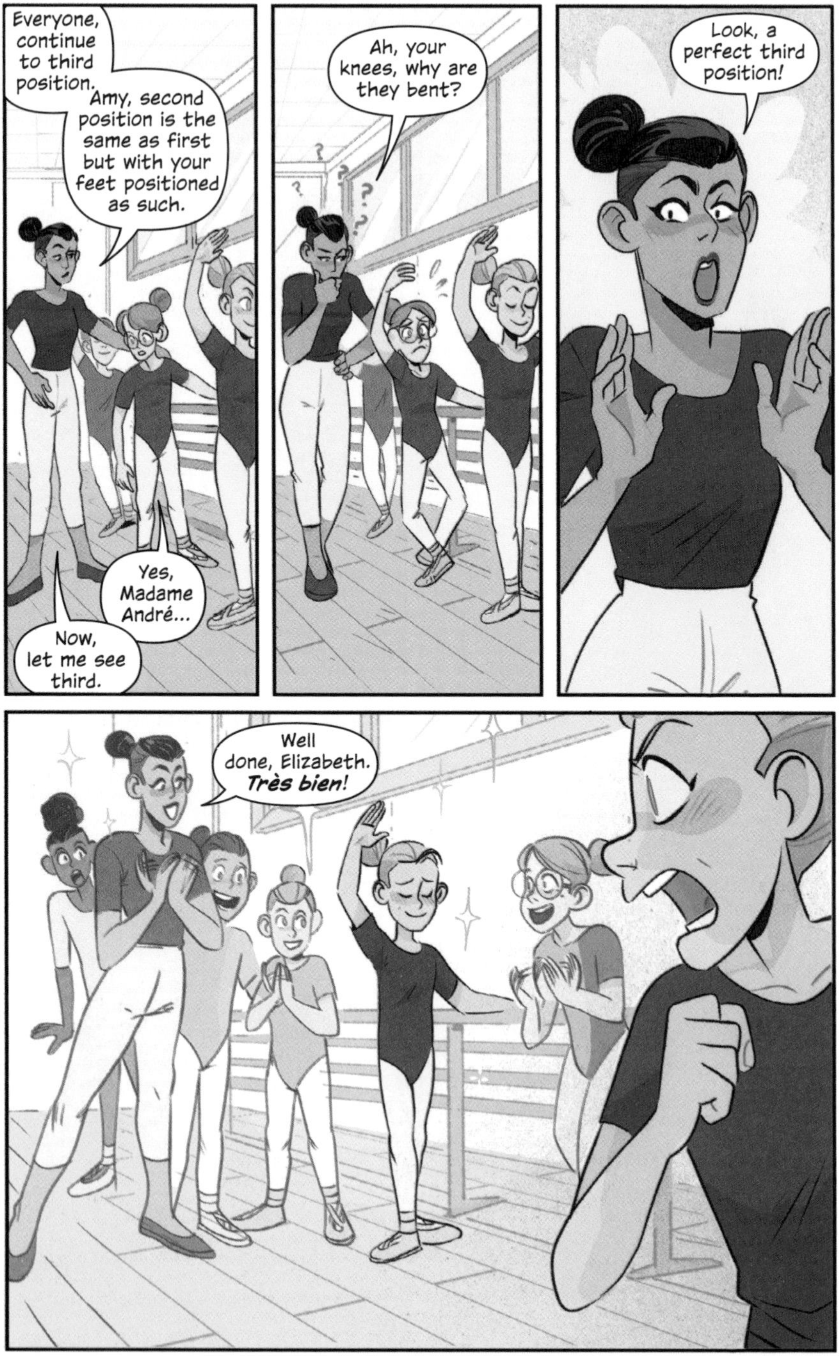

Everyone, continue to third position.
Amy, second position is the same as first but with your feet positioned as such.
Yes, Madame André...
Now, let me see third.
Ah, your knees, why are they bent?
Look, a perfect third position!
Well done, Elizabeth. ***Très bien***!

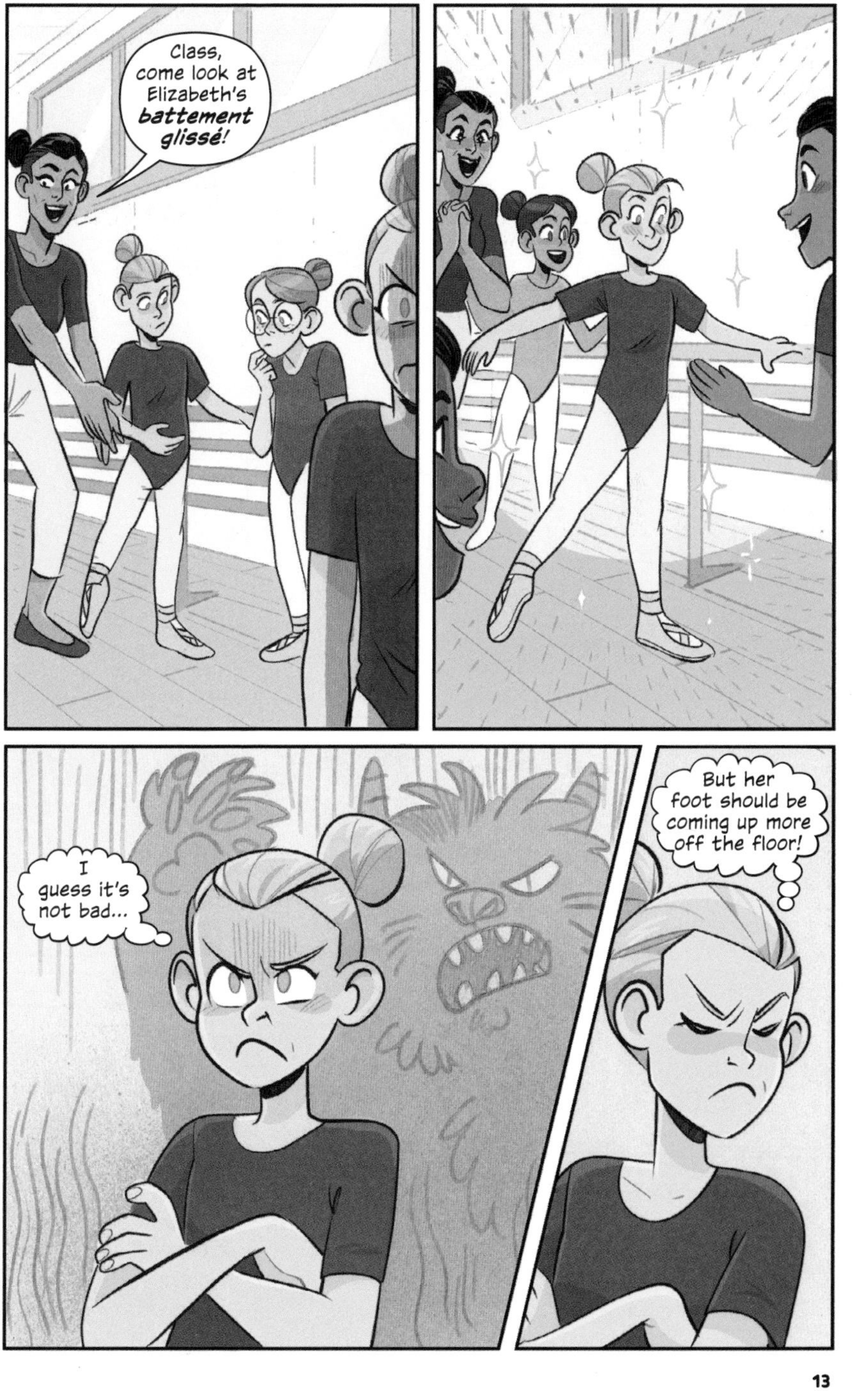
Class, come look at Elizabeth's ***battement glissé!***
I guess it's not bad...
But her foot should be coming up more off the floor!

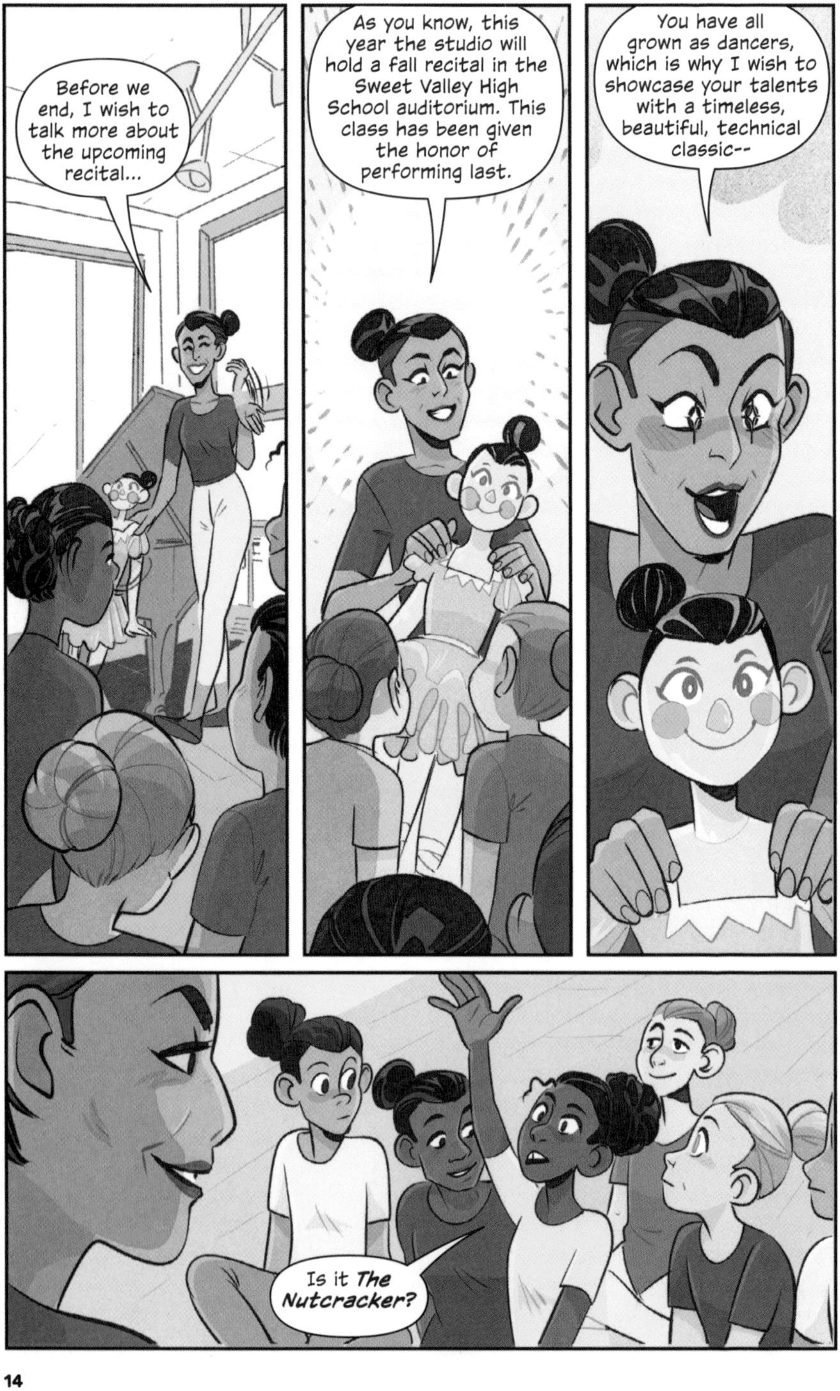
Before we end, I wish to talk more about the upcoming recital...
As you know, this year the studio will hold a fall recital in the Sweet Valley High School auditorium. This class has been given the honor of performing last.
You have all grown as dancers, which is why I wish to showcase your talents with a timeless, beautiful, technical classic--
Is it *The Nutcracker?*

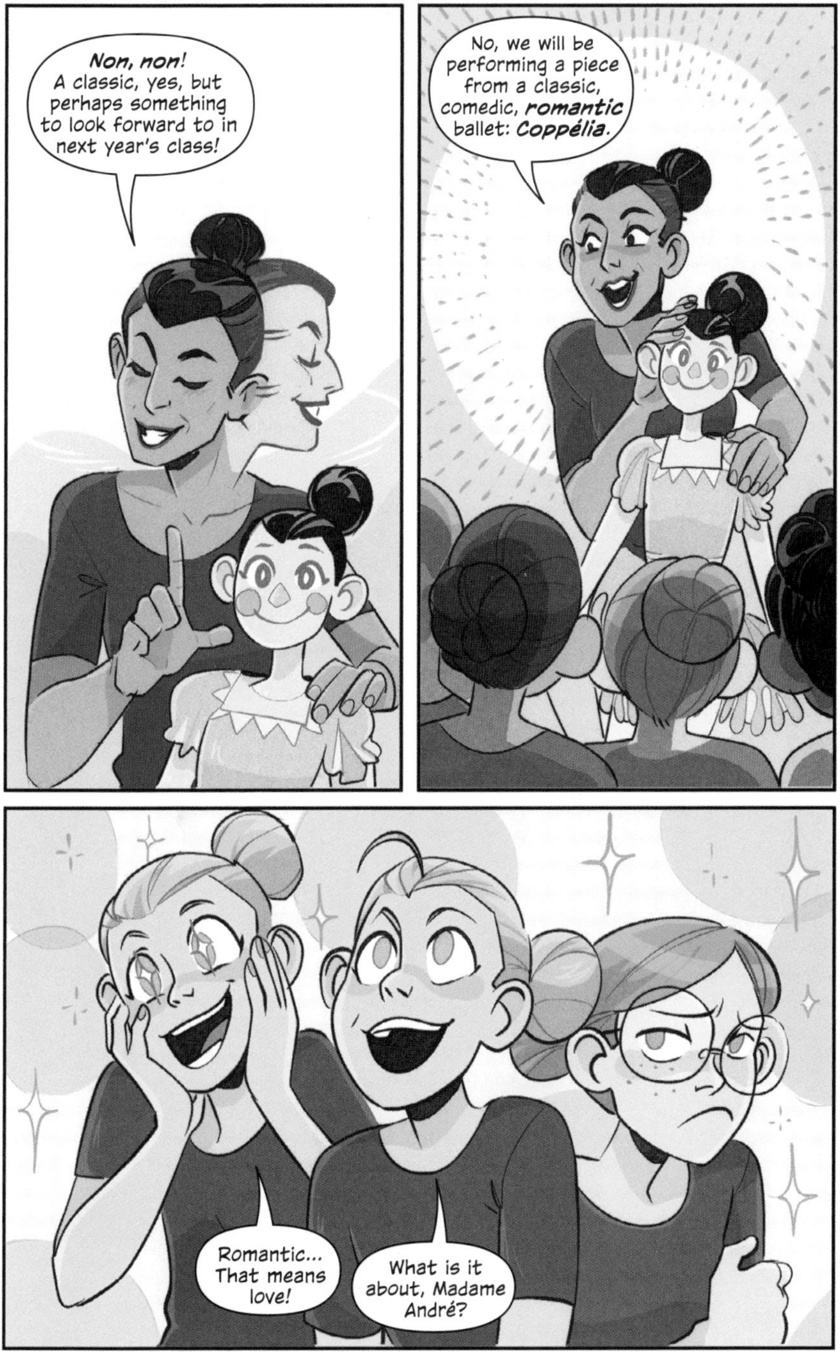

Non, non! A classic, yes, but perhaps something to look forward to in next year's class!
No, we will be performing a piece from a classic, comedic, **romantic** ballet: **Coppélia**.
Romantic... That means love!
What is it about, Madame André?

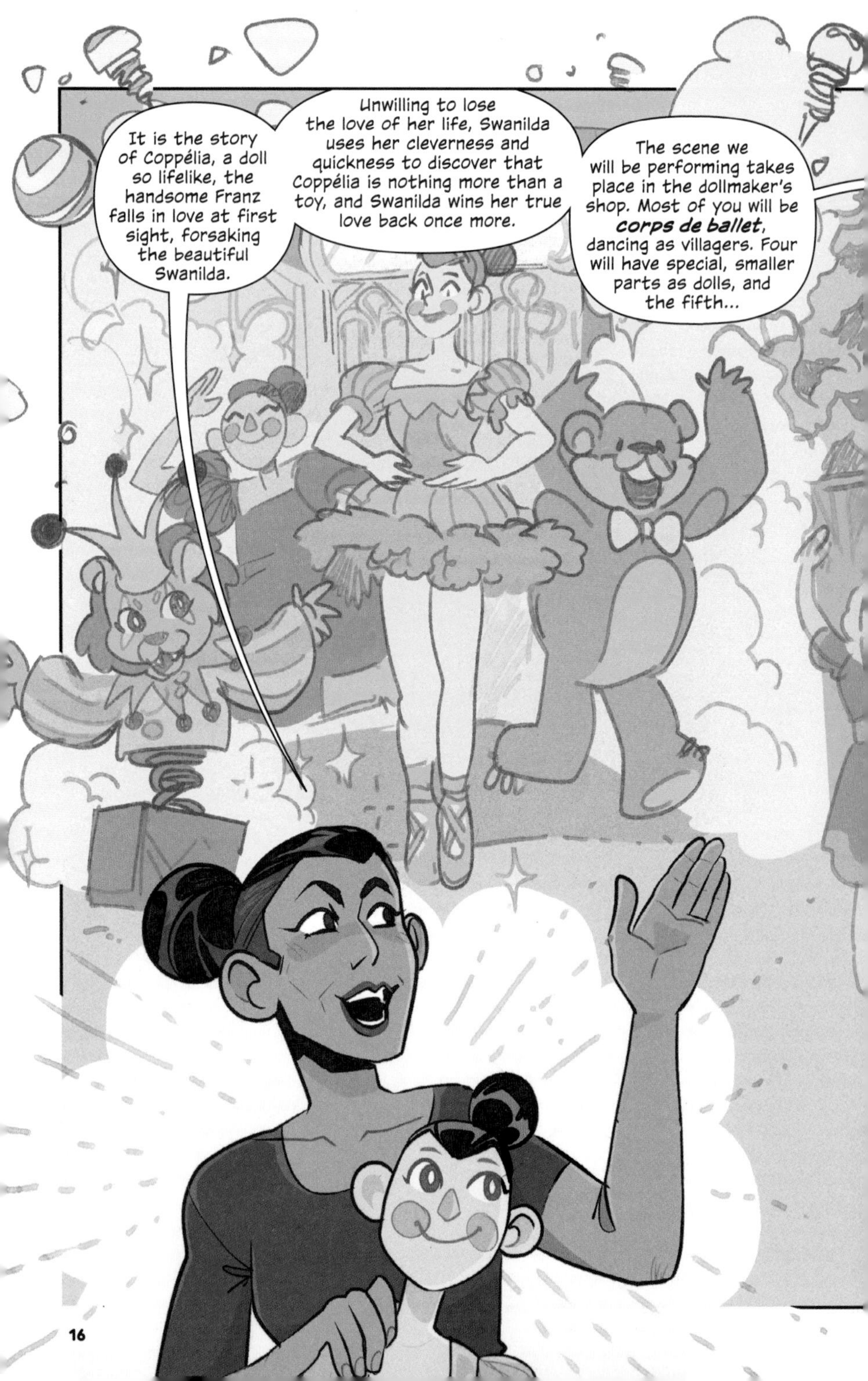
It is the story of Coppélia, a doll so lifelike, the handsome Franz falls in love at first sight, forsaking the beautiful Swanilda.
Unwilling to lose the love of her life, Swanilda uses her cleverness and quickness to discover that Coppélia is nothing more than a toy, and Swanilda wins her true love back once more.
The scene we will be performing takes place in the dollmaker's shop. Most of you will be ***corps de ballet***, dancing as villagers. Four will have special, smaller parts as dolls, and the fifth...

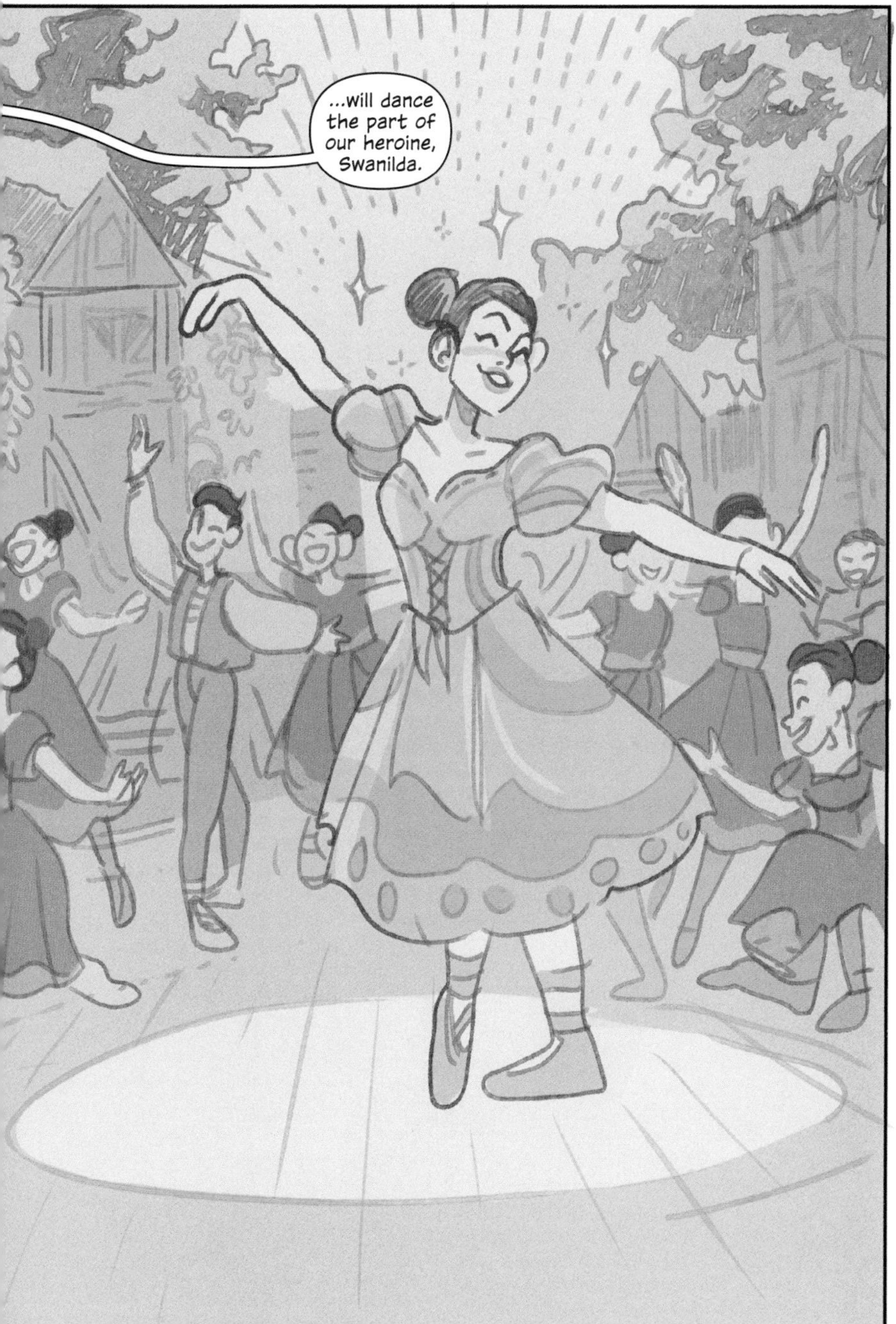
...will dance the part of our heroine, Swanilda.

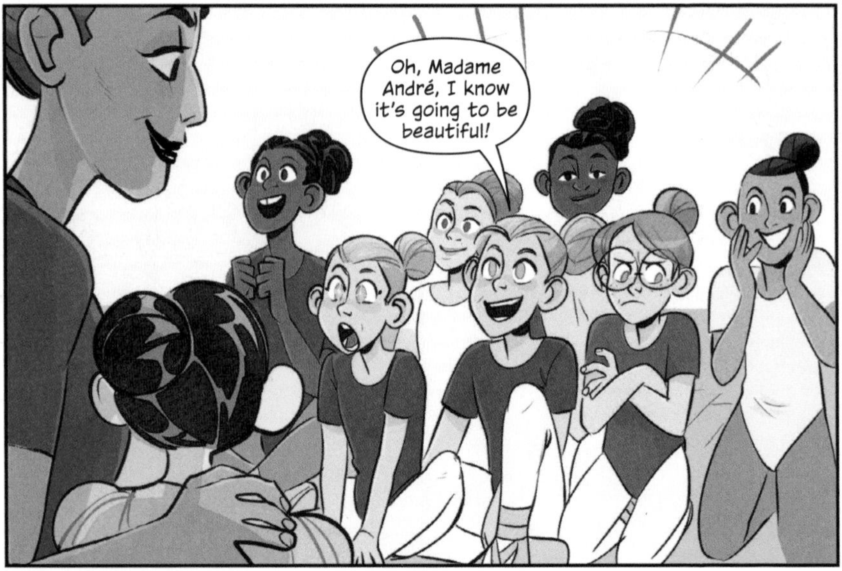
Oh, Madame André, I know it's going to be beautiful!

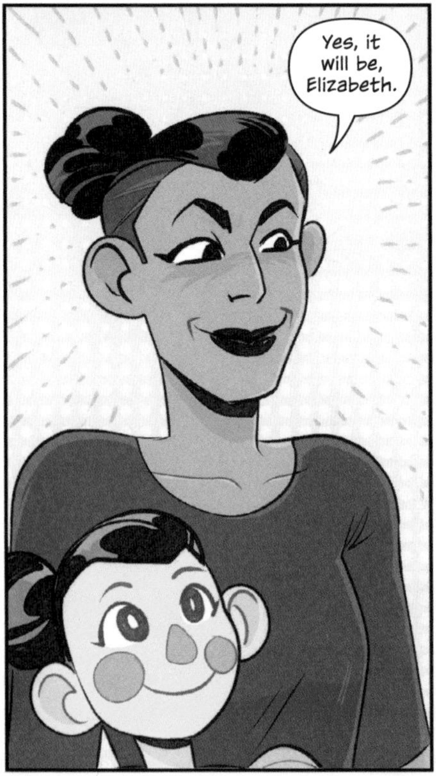
Yes, it will be, Elizabeth.

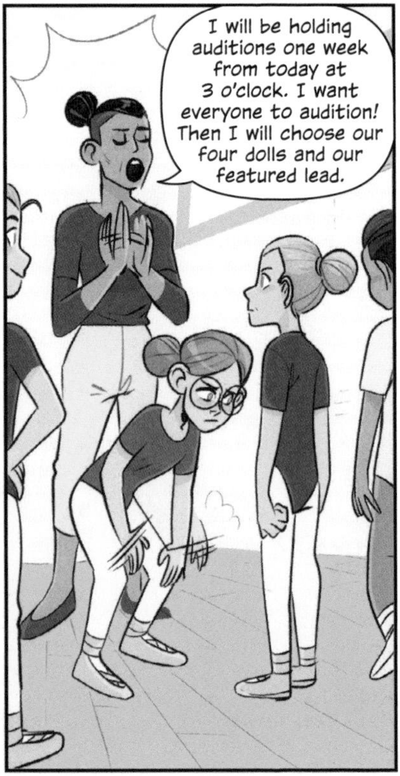
I will be holding auditions one week from today at 3 o'clock. I want everyone to audition! Then I will choose our four dolls and our featured lead.

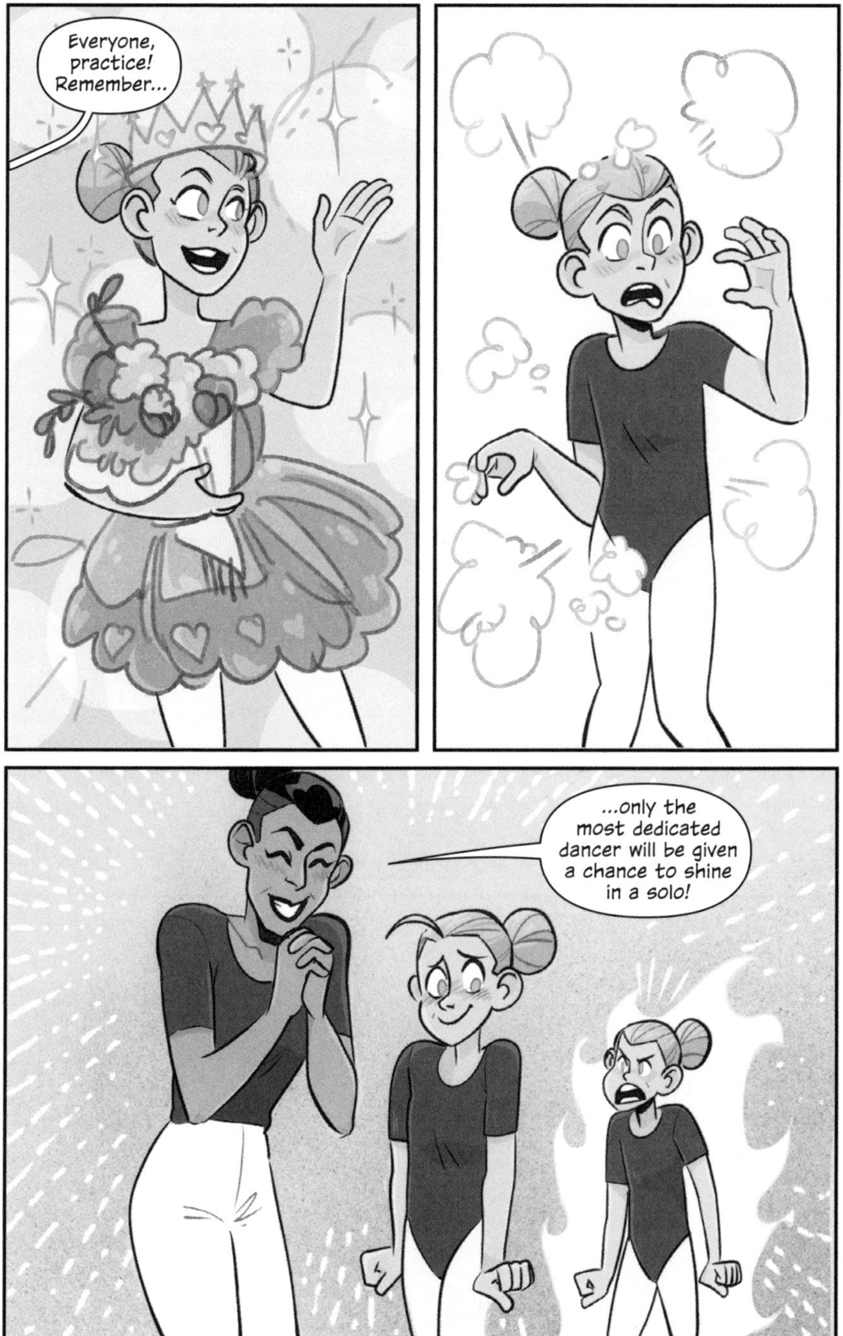
Everyone, practice! Remember...
...only the most dedicated dancer will be given a chance to shine in a solo!

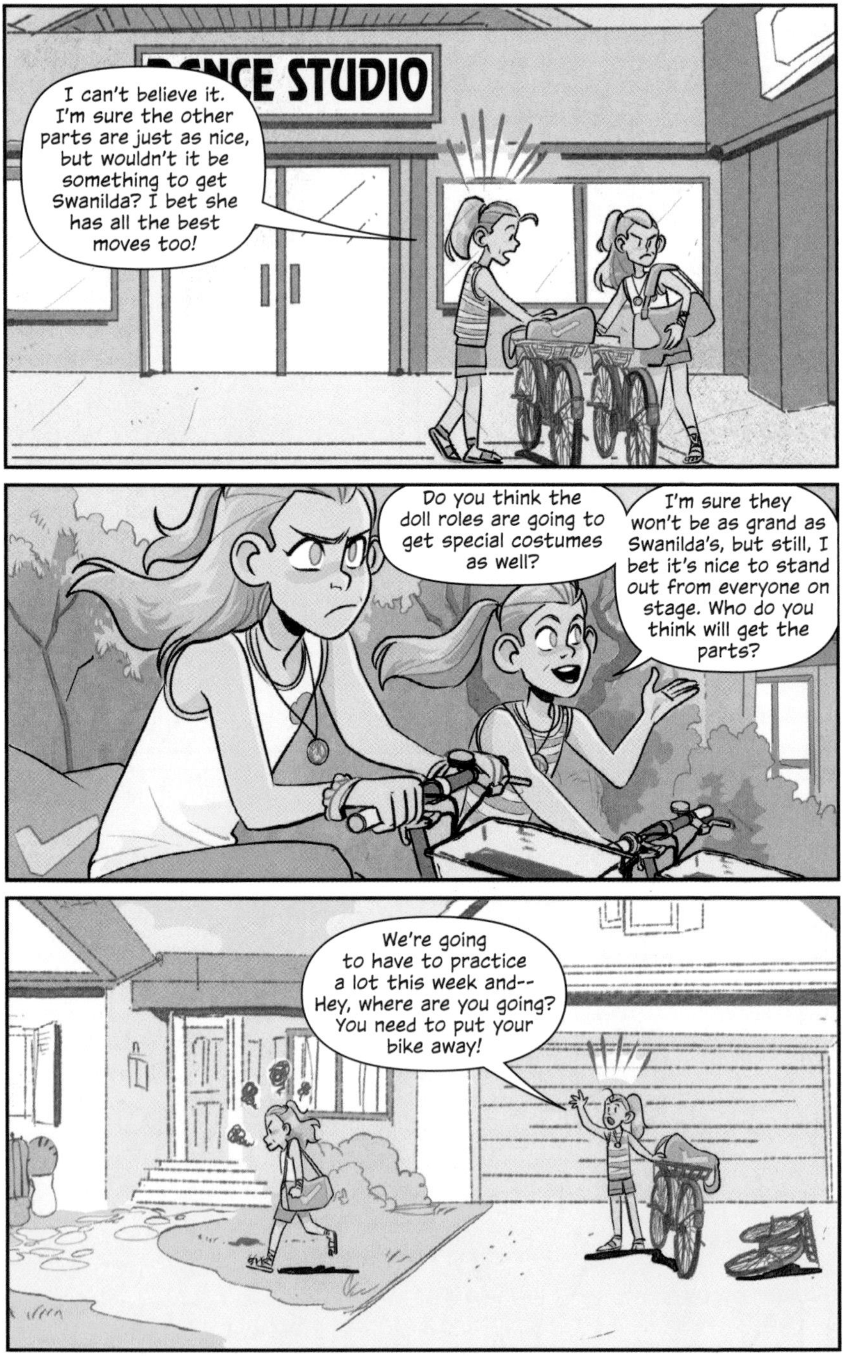
DANCE STUDIO
I can't believe it. I'm sure the other parts are just as nice, but wouldn't it be something to get Swanilda? I bet she has all the best moves too!
Do you think the doll roles are going to get special costumes as well?
I'm sure they won't be as grand as Swanilda's, but still, I bet it's nice to stand out from everyone on stage. Who do you think will get the parts?
We're going to have to practice a lot this week and-- Hey, where are you going? You need to put your bike away!

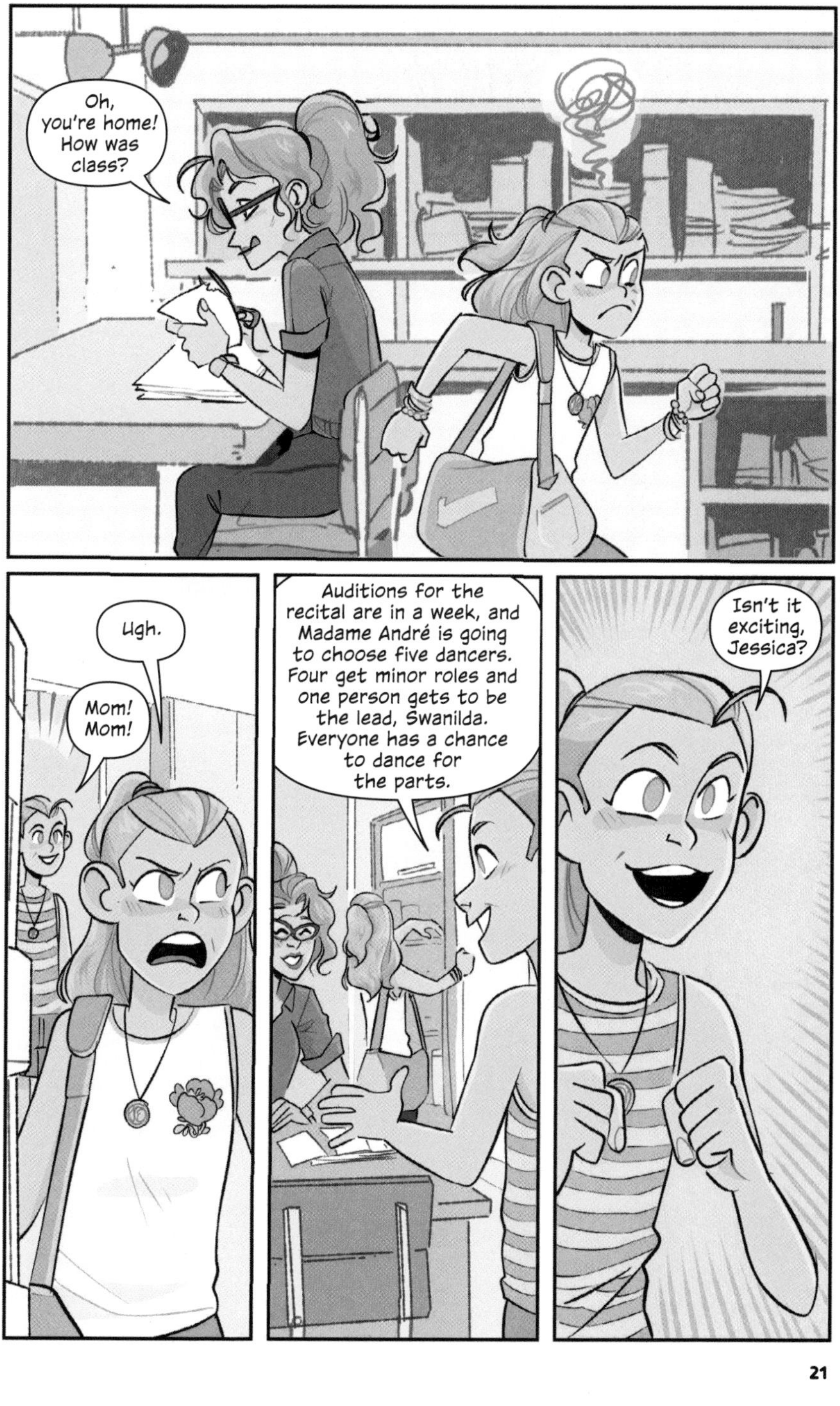
Oh, you're home! How was class?
Ugh.
Mom! Mom!
Auditions for the recital are in a week, and Madame André is going to choose five dancers. Four get minor roles and one person gets to be the lead, Swanilda. Everyone has a chance to dance for the parts.
Isn't it exciting, Jessica?

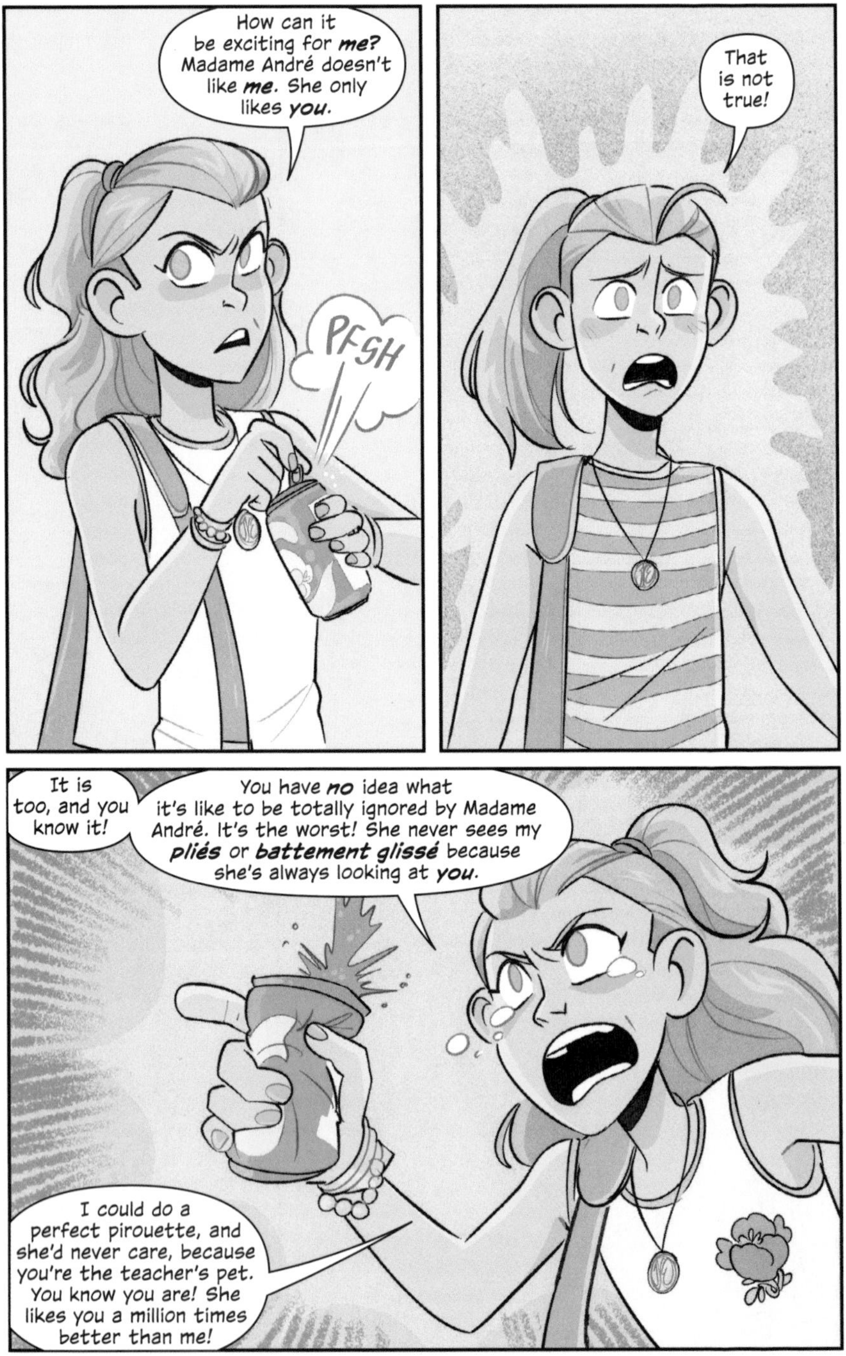
How can it be exciting for ***me?*** Madame André doesn't like ***me.*** She only likes ***you***.
PFSH
That is not true!
It is too, and you know it!
You have ***no*** idea what it's like to be totally ignored by Madame André. It's the worst! She never sees my ***pliés*** or ***battement glissé*** because she's always looking at ***you***.
I could do a perfect pirouette, and she'd never care, because you're the teacher's pet. You know you are! She likes you a million times better than me!

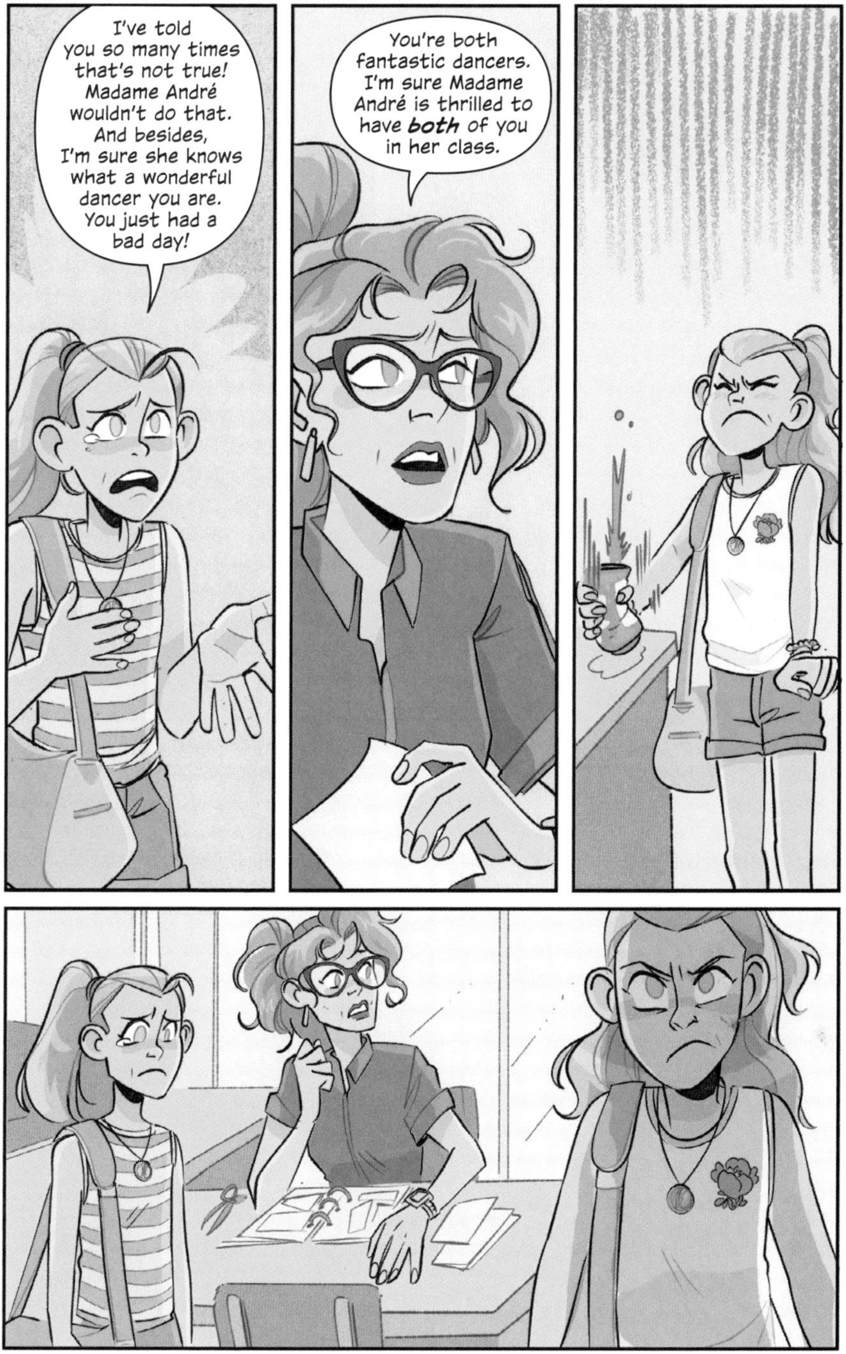
I've told you so many times that's not true! Madame André wouldn't do that. And besides, I'm sure she knows what a wonderful dancer you are. You just had a bad day!
You're both fantastic dancers. I'm sure Madame André is thrilled to have **both** of you in her class.

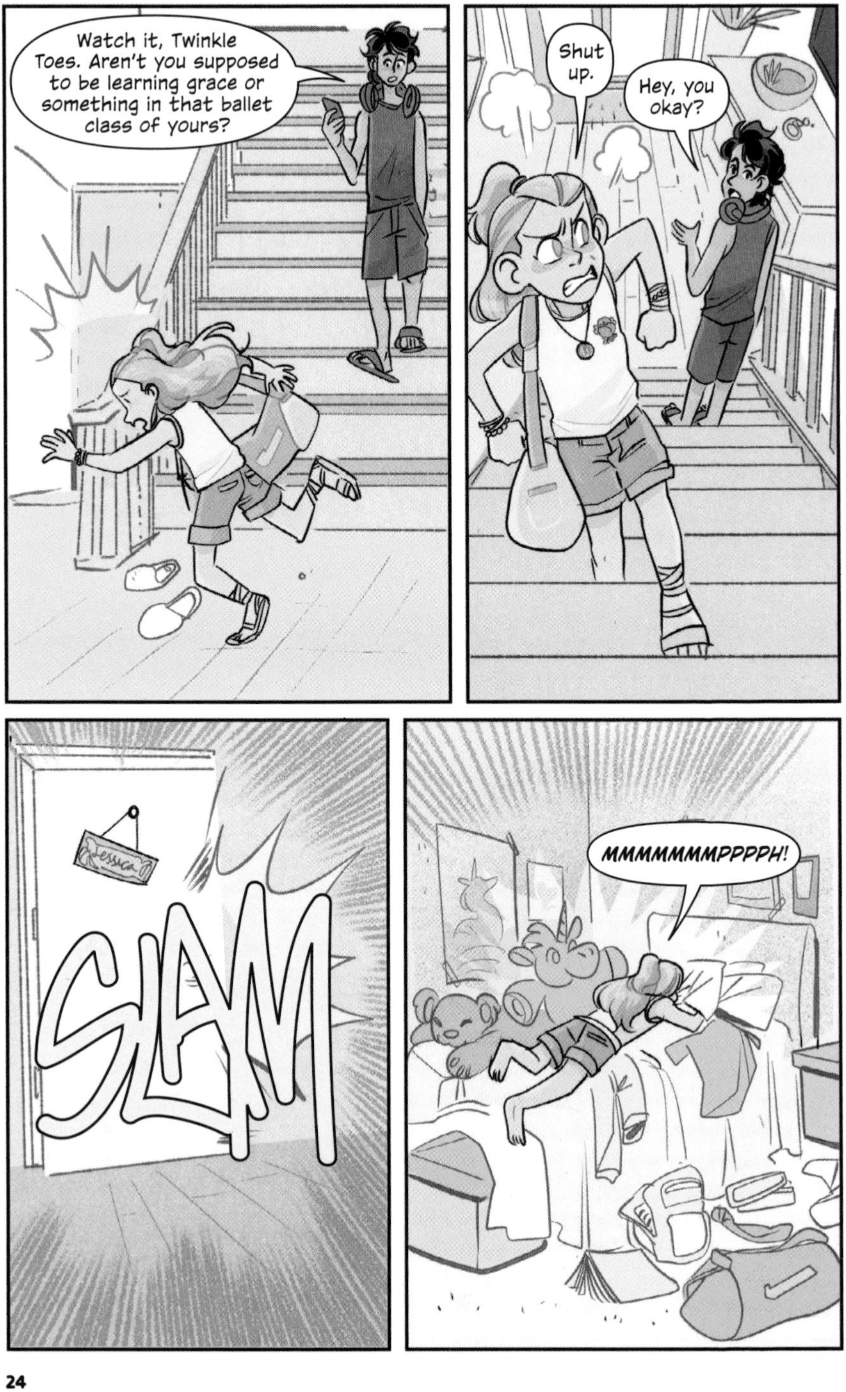
Watch it, Twinkle Toes. Aren't you supposed to be learning grace or something in that ballet class of yours?
Shut up.
Hey, you okay?
Jessica
SLAM
MMMMMMMPPPPH!

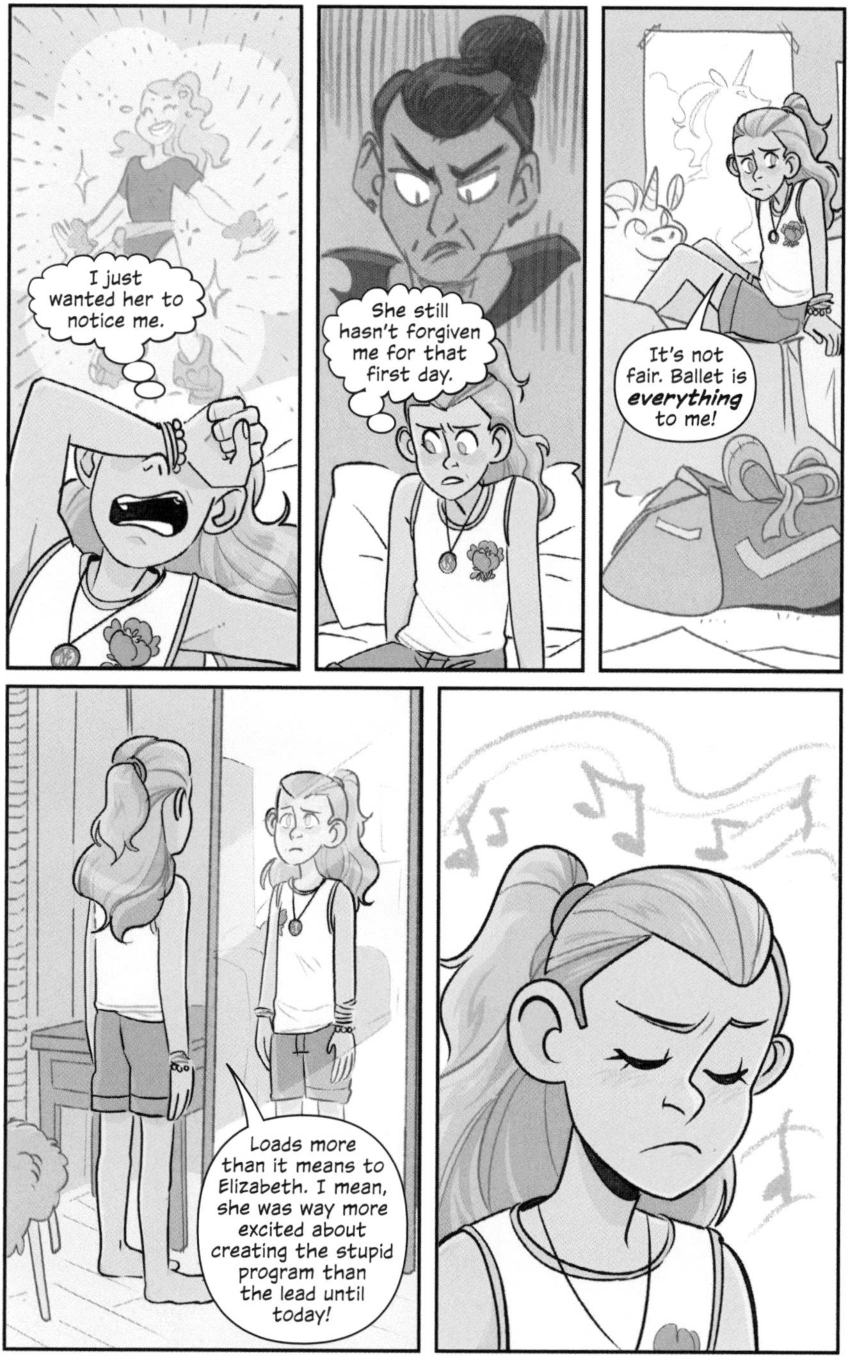
I just wanted her to notice me.
She still hasn't forgiven me for that first day.
It's not fair. Ballet is ***everything*** to me!
Loads more than it means to Elizabeth. I mean, she was way more excited about creating the stupid program than the lead until today!

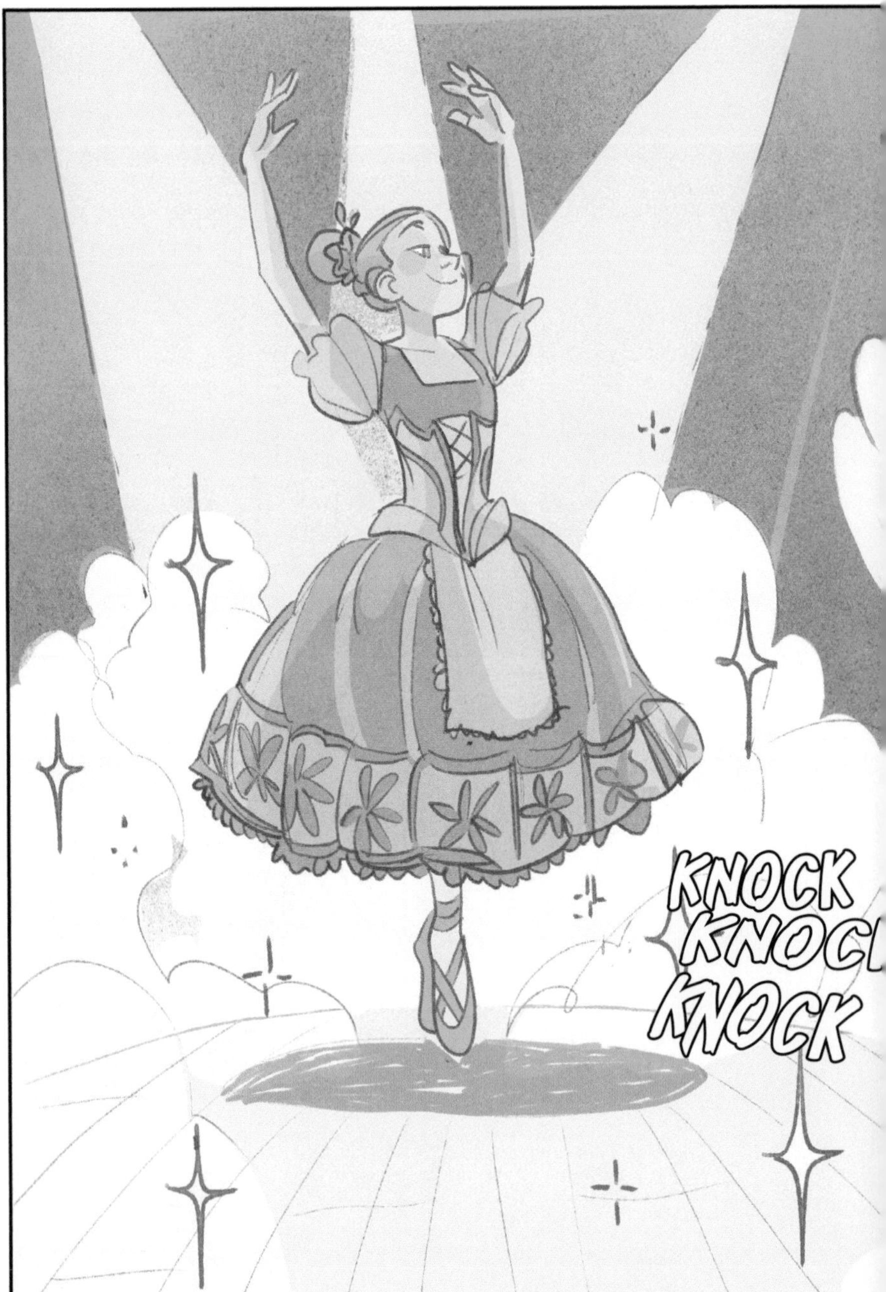
KNOCK
KNOCK

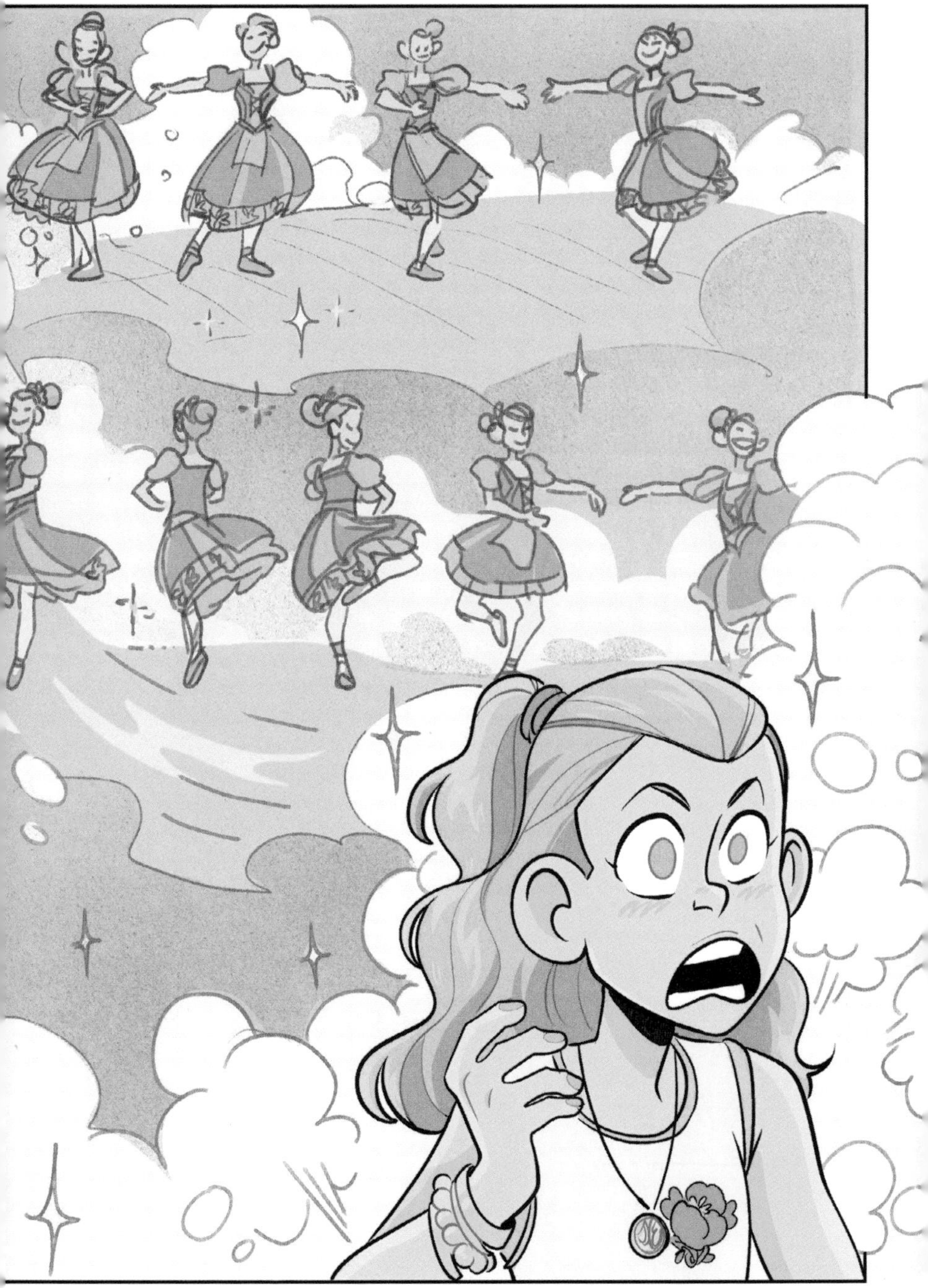

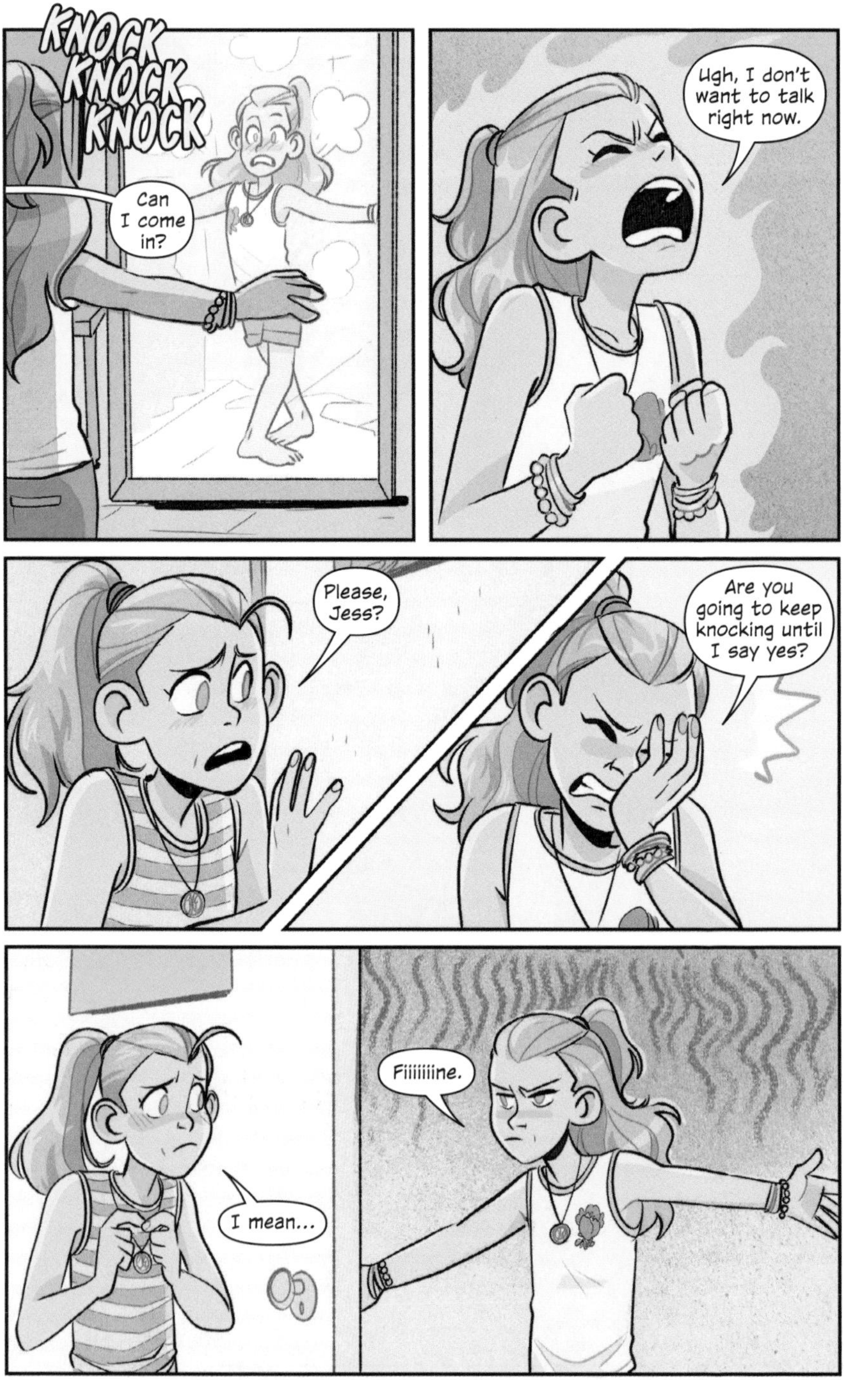
KNOCK KNOCK KNOCK
Can I come in?
Ugh, I don't want to talk right now.
Please, Jess?
Are you going to keep knocking until I say yes?
I mean...
Fiiiiiiine.

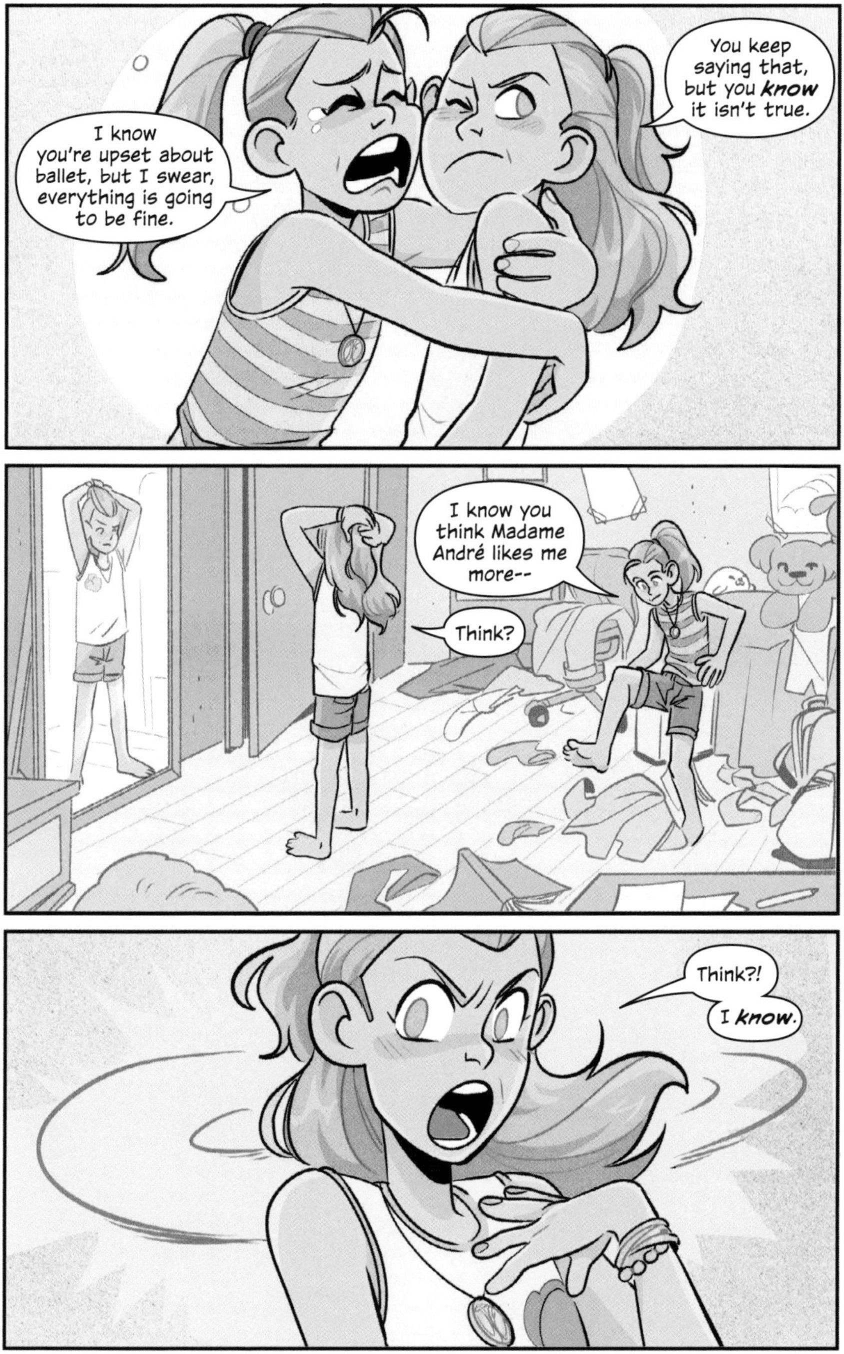
I know you're upset about ballet, but I swear, everything is going to be fine.
You keep saying that, but you *know* it isn't true.
I know you think Madame André likes me more--
Think?
Think?!
I *know*.

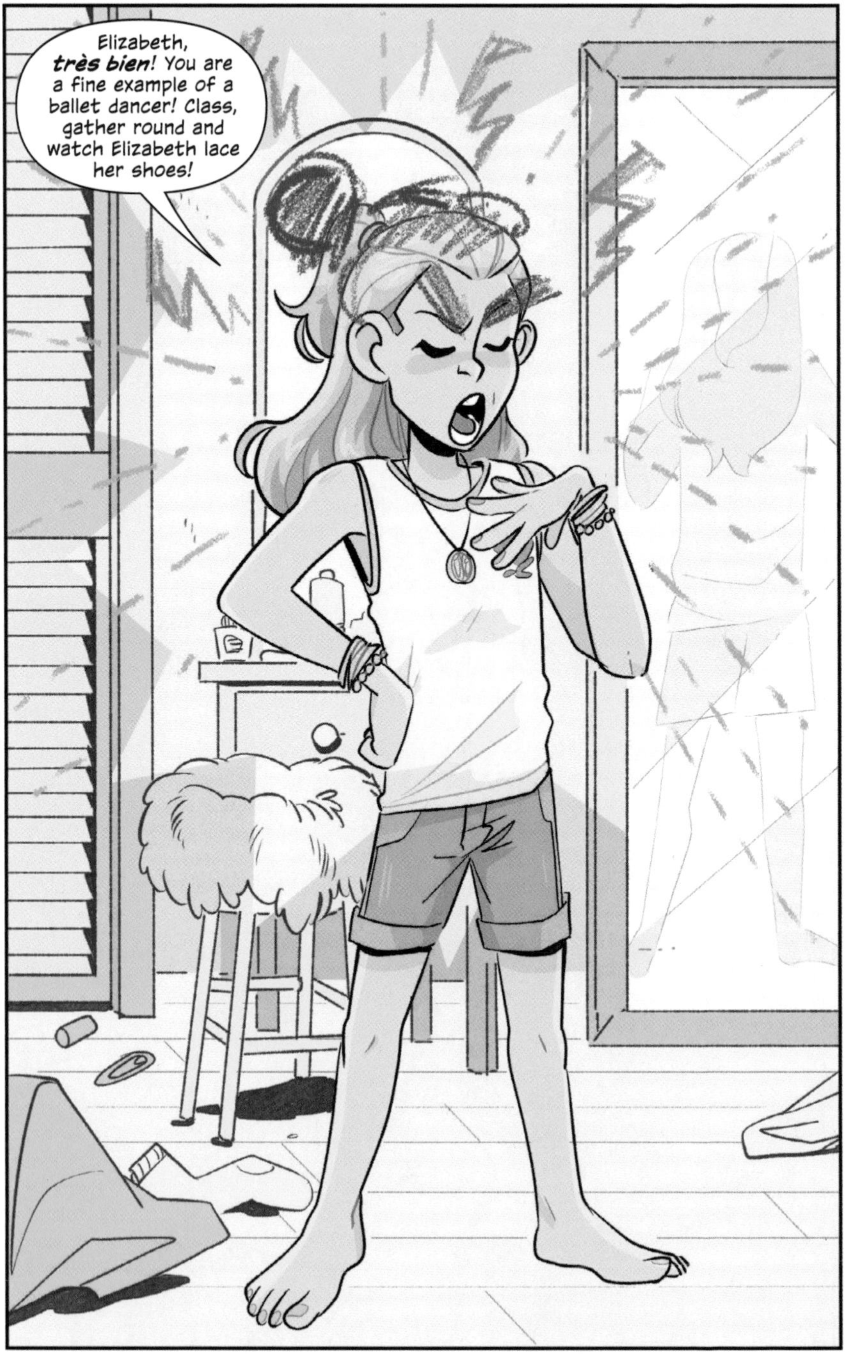
Elizabeth, ***très bien***! You are a fine example of a ballet dancer! Class, gather round and watch Elizabeth lace her shoes!

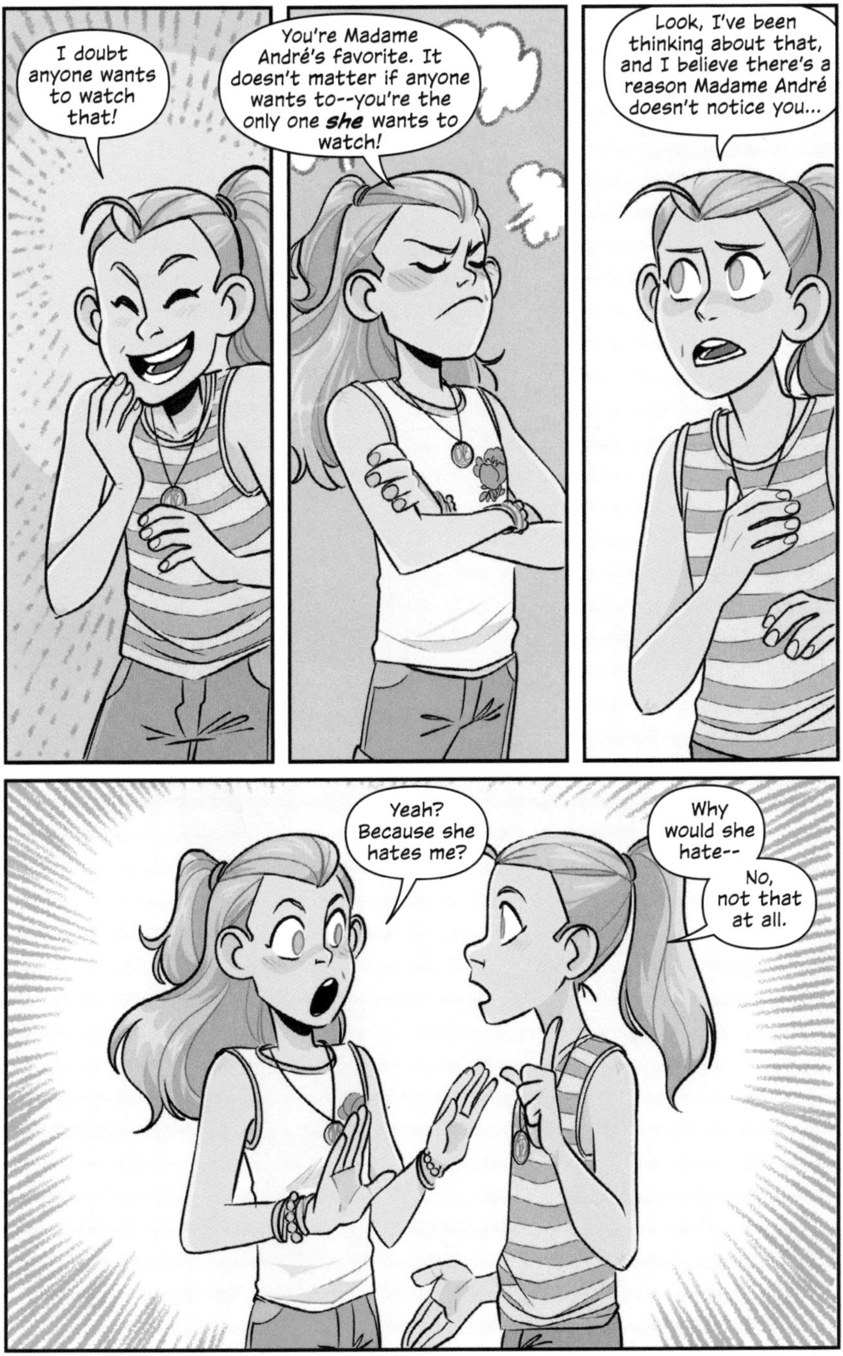
I doubt anyone wants to watch that!
You're Madame André's favorite. It doesn't matter if anyone wants to--you're the only one **she** wants to watch!
Look, I've been thinking about that, and I believe there's a reason Madame André doesn't notice you...
Yeah? Because she hates me?
Why would she hate--
No, not that at all.

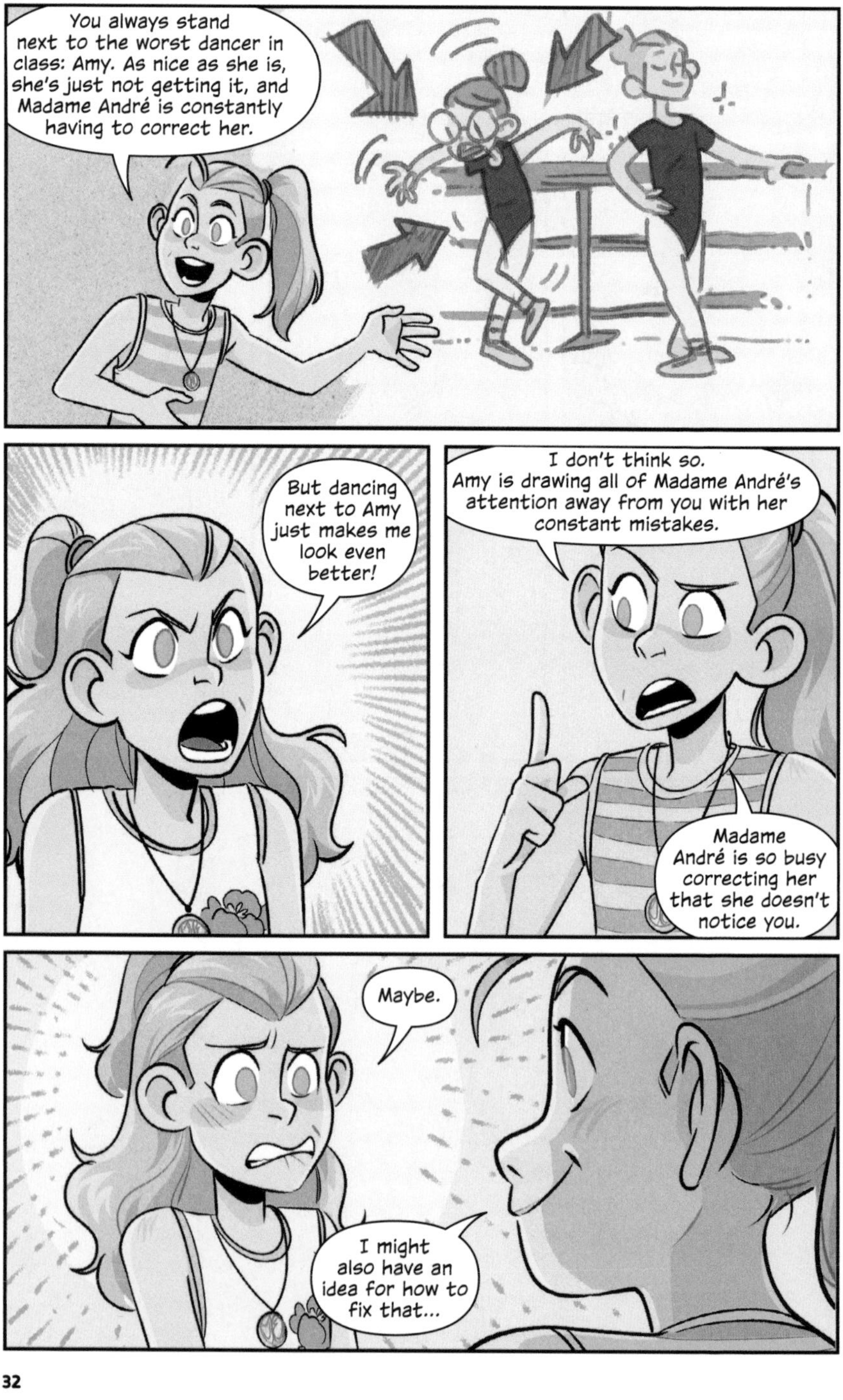
You always stand next to the worst dancer in class: Amy. As nice as she is, she's just not getting it, and Madame André is constantly having to correct her.
But dancing next to Amy just makes me look even better!
I don't think so. Amy is drawing all of Madame André's attention away from you with her constant mistakes.
Madame André is so busy correcting her that she doesn't notice you.
Maybe.
I might also have an idea for how to fix that...

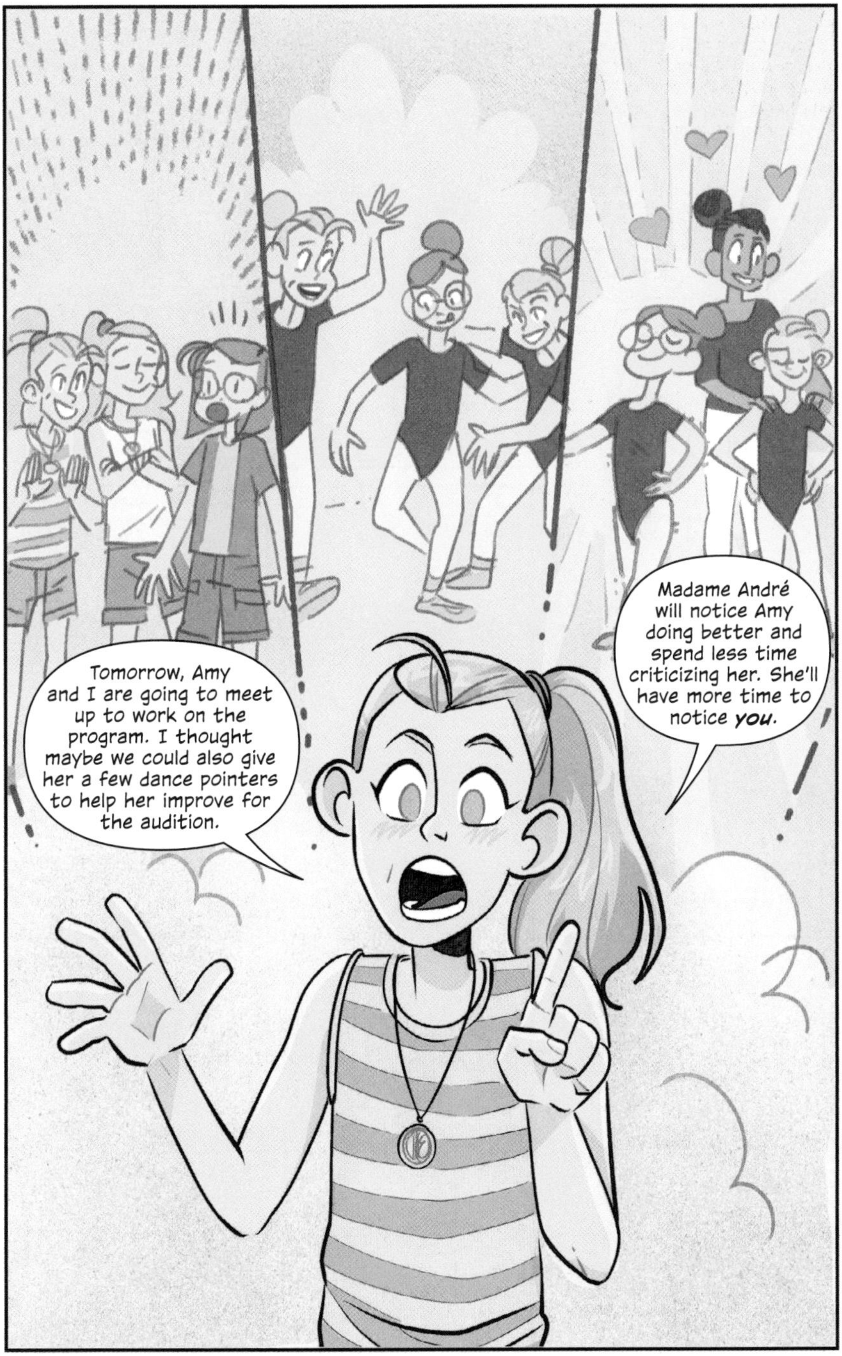
Tomorrow, Amy and I are going to meet up to work on the program. I thought maybe we could also give her a few dance pointers to help her improve for the audition.
Madame André will notice Amy doing better and spend less time criticizing her. She'll have more time to notice ***you***.

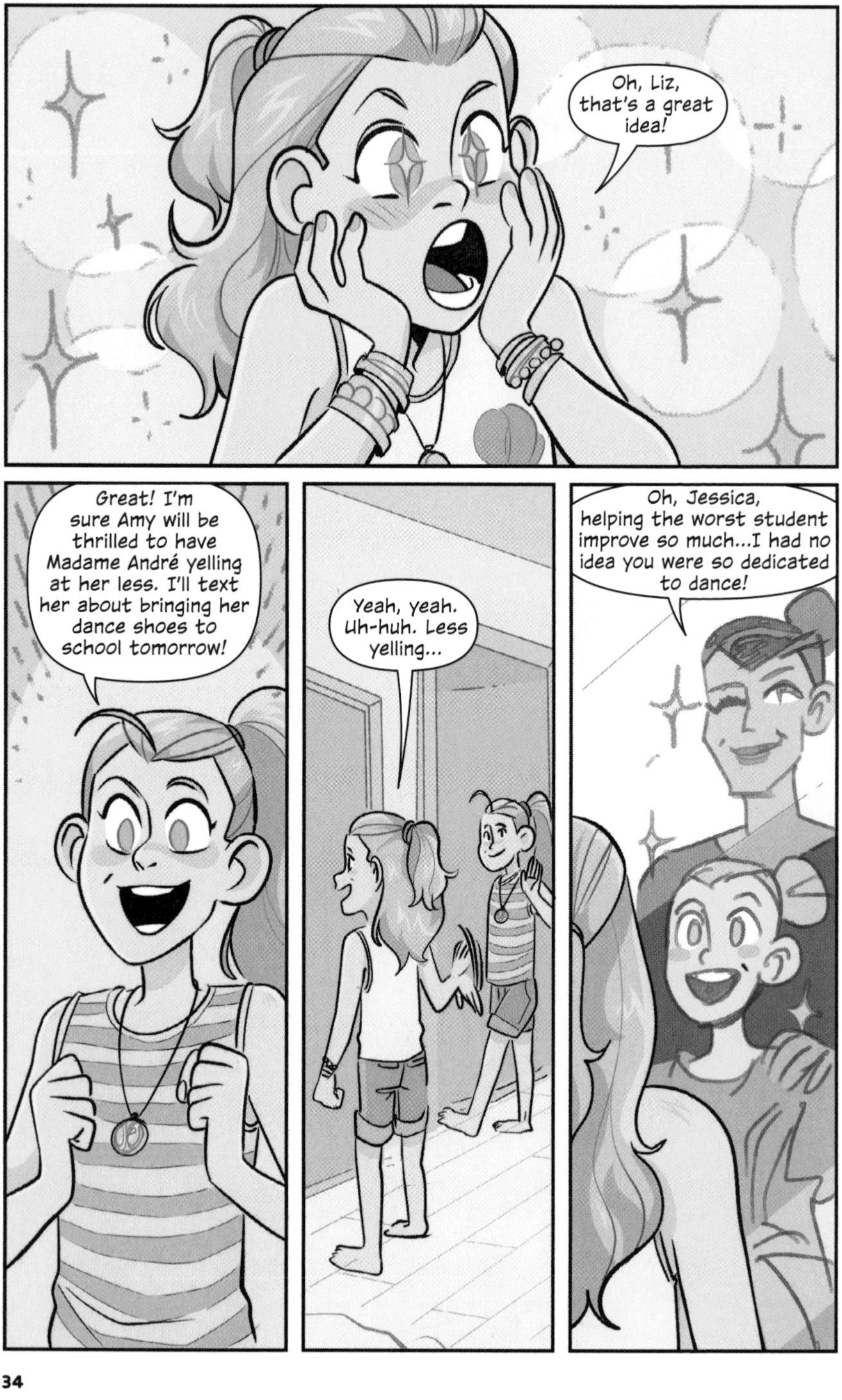
Oh, Liz, that's a great idea!
Great! I'm sure Amy will be thrilled to have Madame André yelling at her less. I'll text her about bringing her dance shoes to school tomorrow!
Yeah, yeah. Uh-huh. Less yelling...
Oh, Jessica, helping the worst student improve so much...I had no idea you were so dedicated to dance!

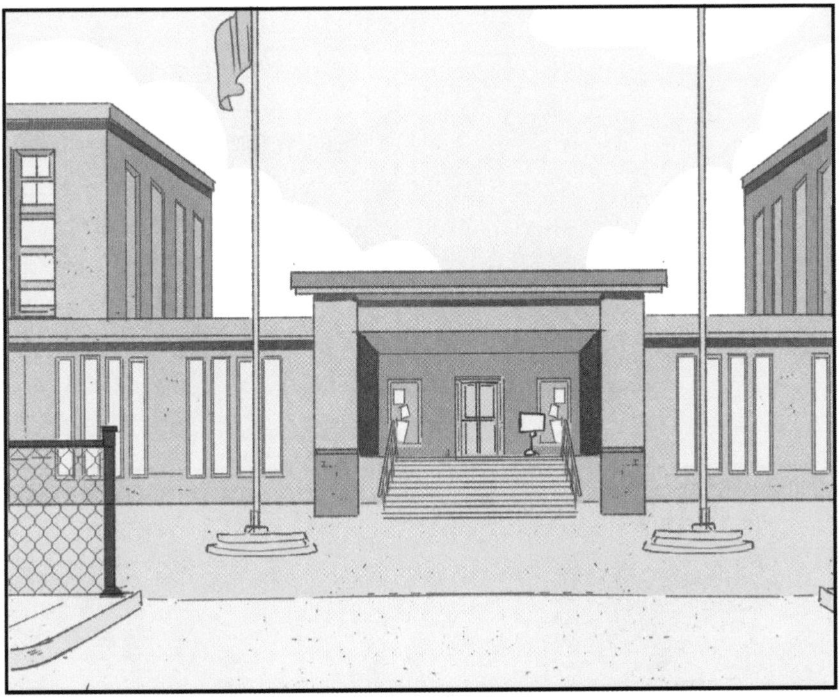

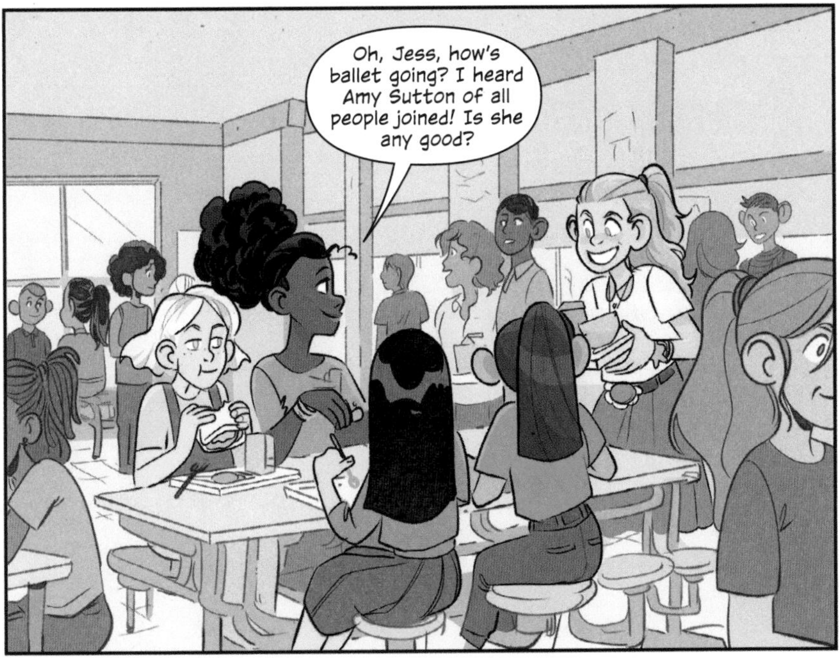
Oh, Jess, how's ballet going? I heard Amy Sutton of all people joined! Is she any good?

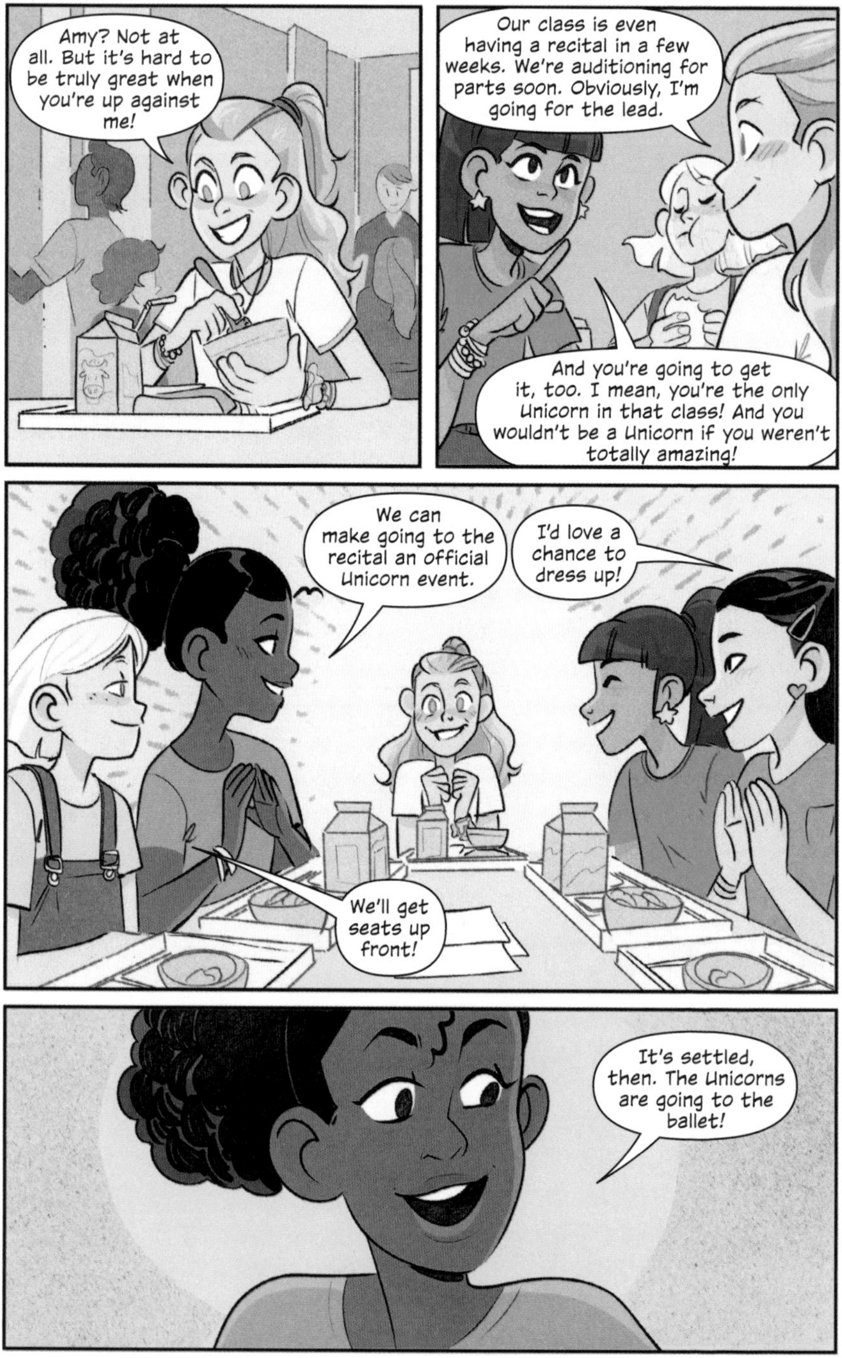
Amy? Not at all. But it's hard to be truly great when you're up against me!
Our class is even having a recital in a few weeks. We're auditioning for parts soon. Obviously, I'm going for the lead.
And you're going to get it, too. I mean, you're the only Unicorn in that class! And you wouldn't be a Unicorn if you weren't totally amazing!
We can make going to the recital an official Unicorn event.
I'd love a chance to dress up!
We'll get seats up front!
It's settled, then. The Unicorns are going to the ballet!

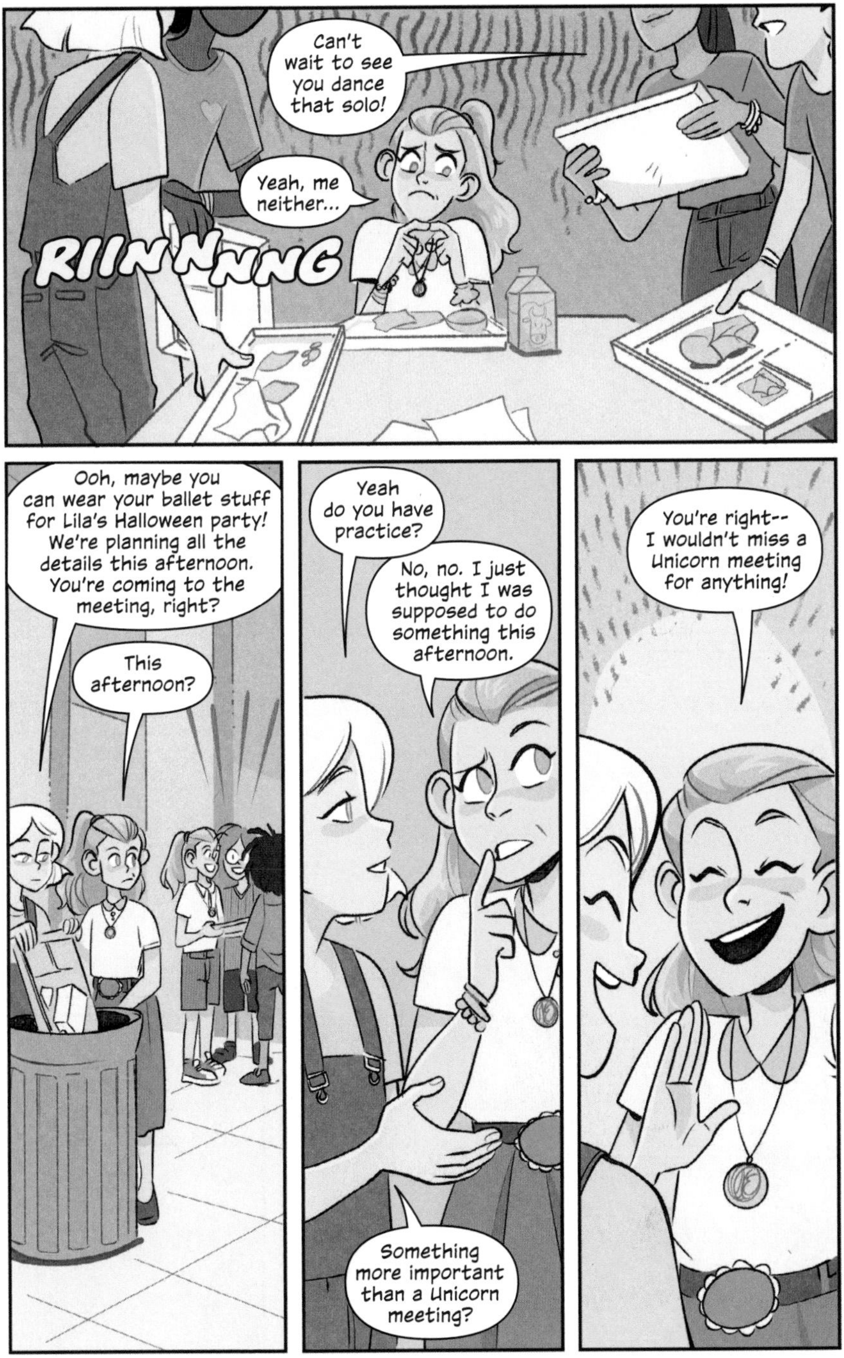
Can't wait to see you dance that solo!
Yeah, me neither...
RIINNNNG
Ooh, maybe you can wear your ballet stuff for Lila's Halloween party! We're planning all the details this afternoon. You're coming to the meeting, right?
This afternoon?
Yeah do you have practice?
No, no. I just thought I was supposed to do something this afternoon.
Something more important than a Unicorn meeting?
You're right-- I wouldn't miss a Unicorn meeting for anything!

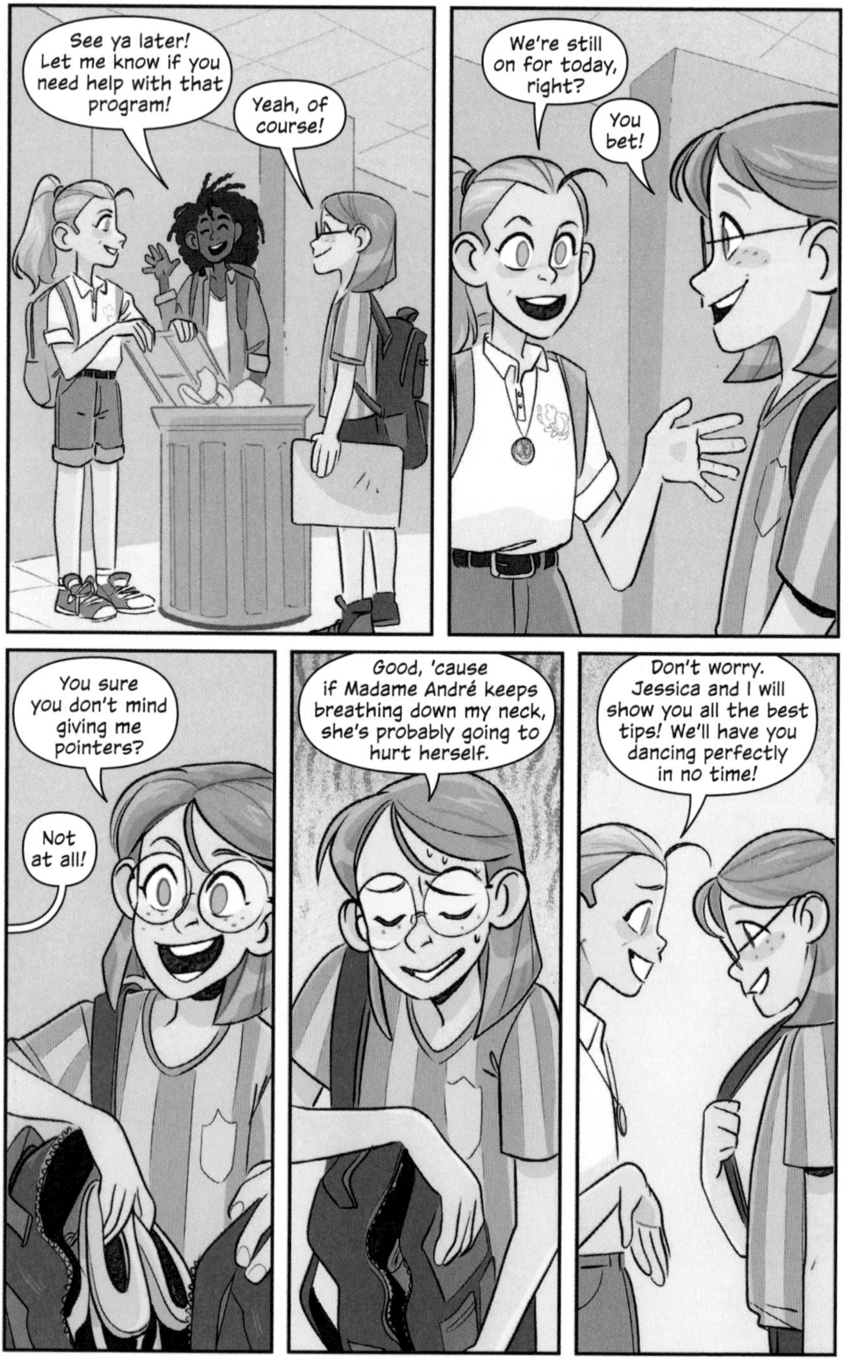
See ya later! Let me know if you need help with that program!
Yeah, of course!
We're still on for today, right?
You bet!
You sure you don't mind giving me pointers?
Not at all!
Good, 'cause if Madame André keeps breathing down my neck, she's probably going to hurt herself.
Don't worry. Jessica and I will show you all the best tips! We'll have you dancing perfectly in no time!

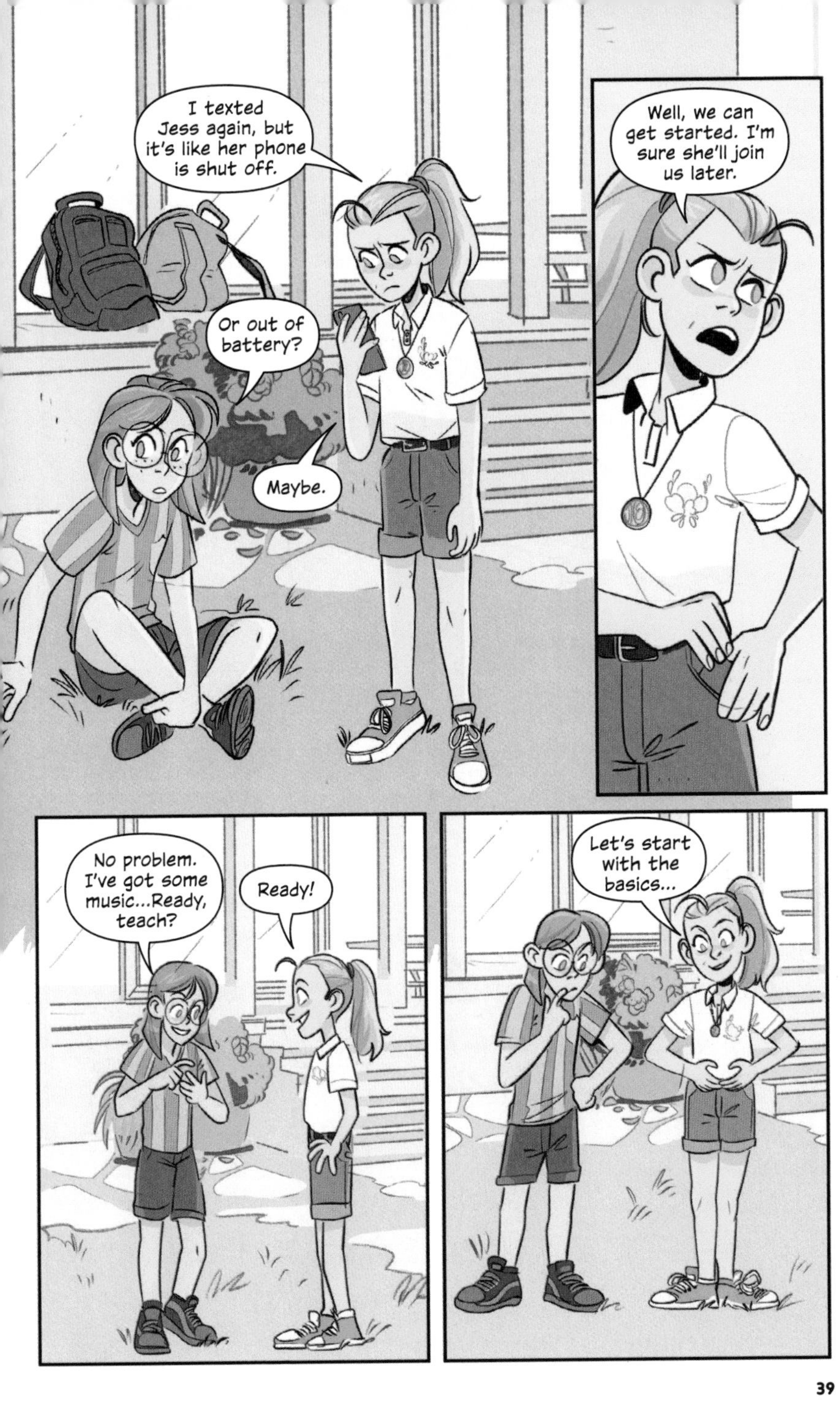
I texted Jess again, but it's like her phone is shut off.
Or out of battery?
Maybe.
Well, we can get started. I'm sure she'll join us later.
No problem. I've got some music...Ready, teach?
Ready!
Let's start with the basics...

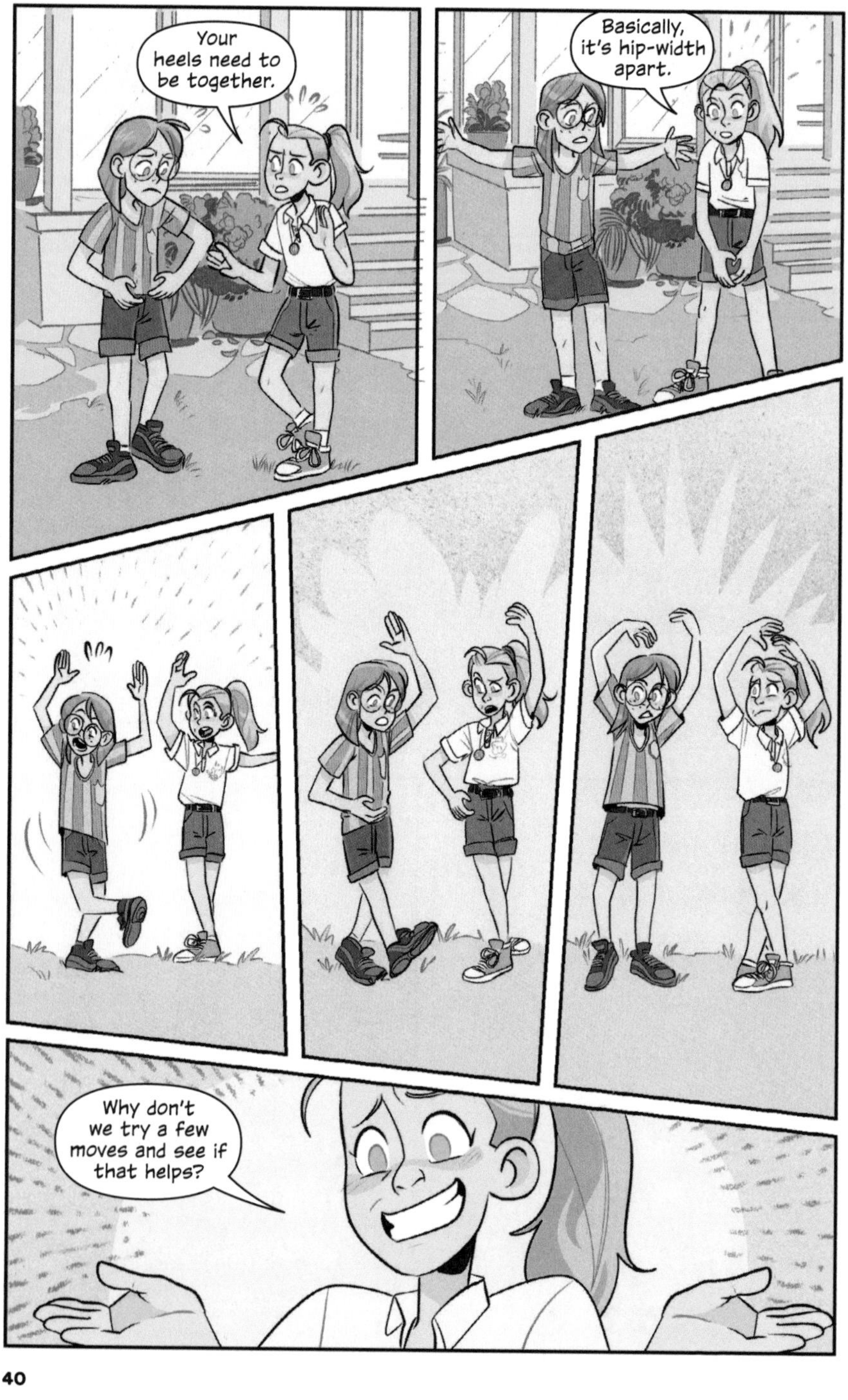
Your heels need to be together.
Basically, it's hip-width apart.
Why don't we try a few moves and see if that helps?

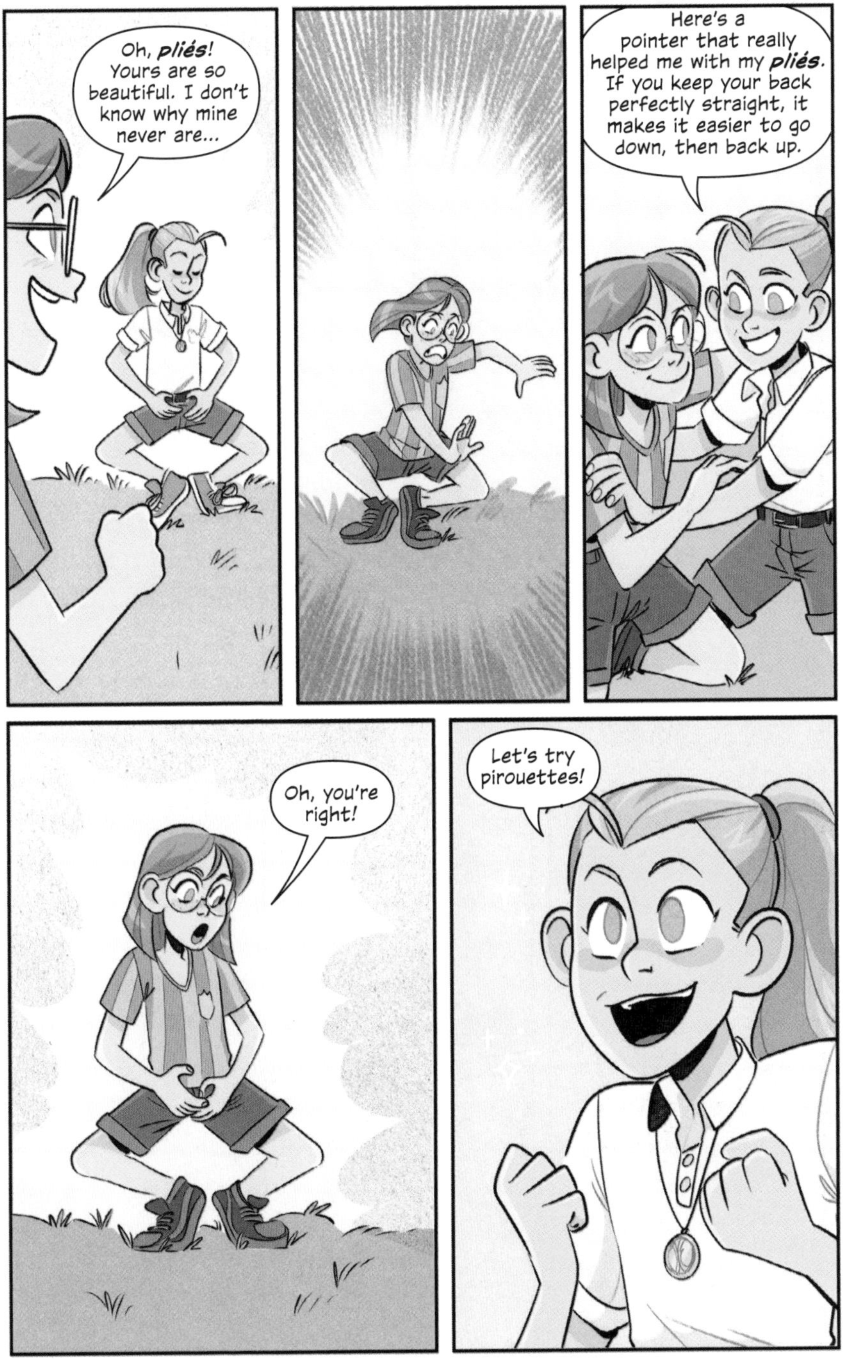
Oh, *pliés*! Yours are so beautiful. I don't know why mine never are...
Here's a pointer that really helped me with my *pliés*. If you keep your back perfectly straight, it makes it easier to go down, then back up.
Oh, you're right!
Let's try pirouettes!

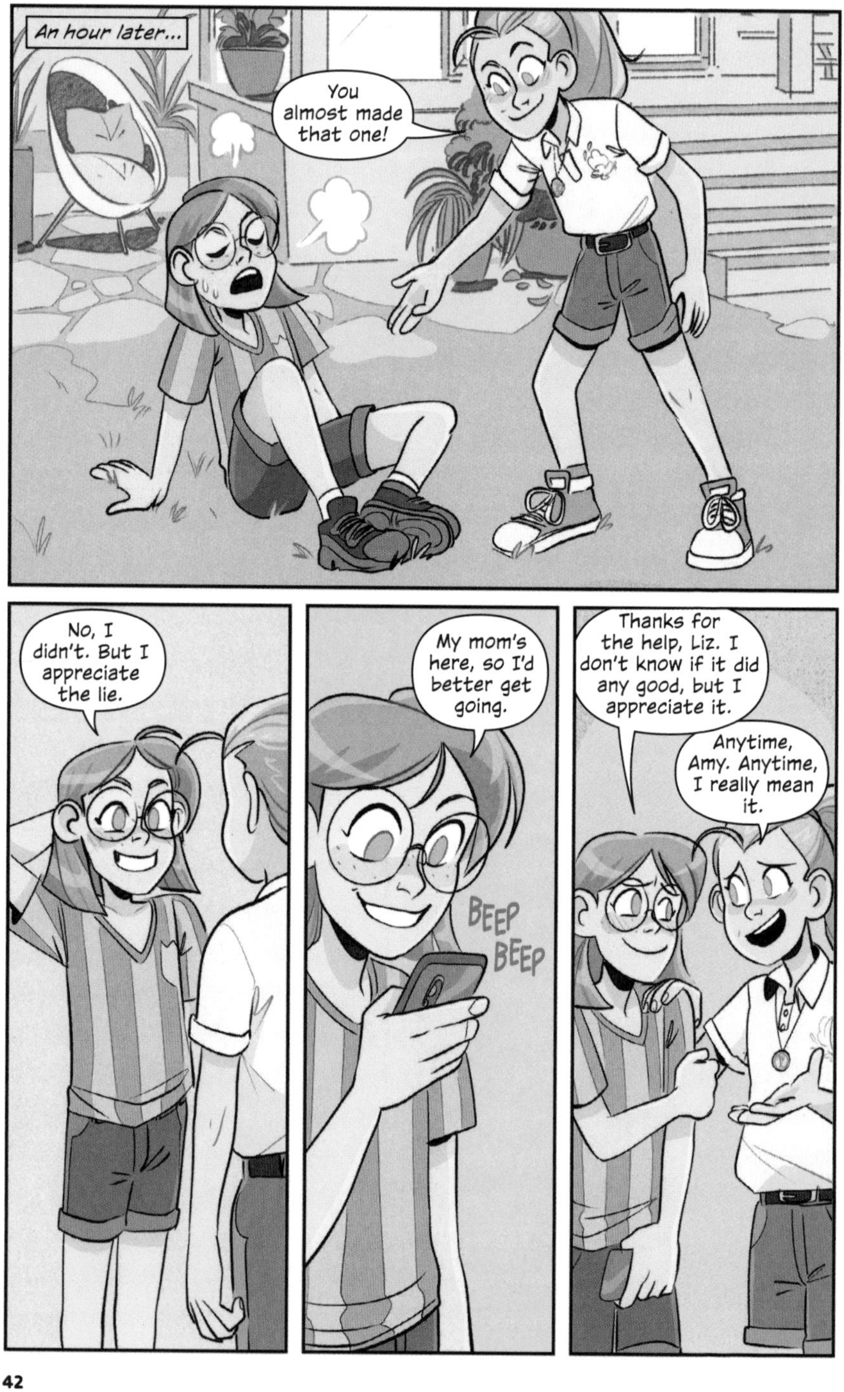
An hour later...
You almost made that one!
No, I didn't. But I appreciate the lie.
My mom's here, so I'd better get going.
BEEP BEEP
Thanks for the help, Liz. I don't know if it did any good, but I appreciate it.
Anytime, Amy. Anytime, I really mean it.

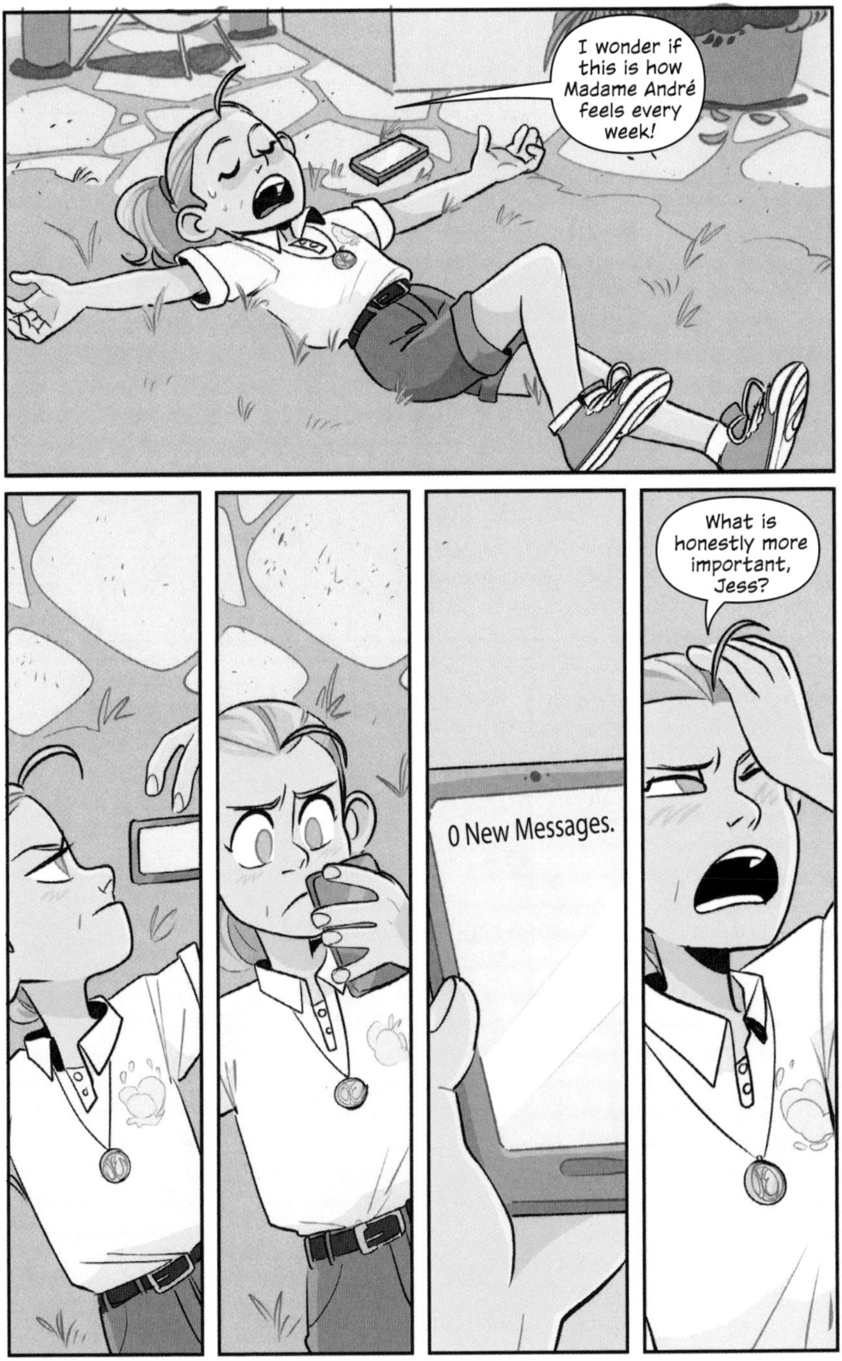
I wonder if this is how Madame André feels every week!
0 New Messages.
What is honestly more important, Jess?

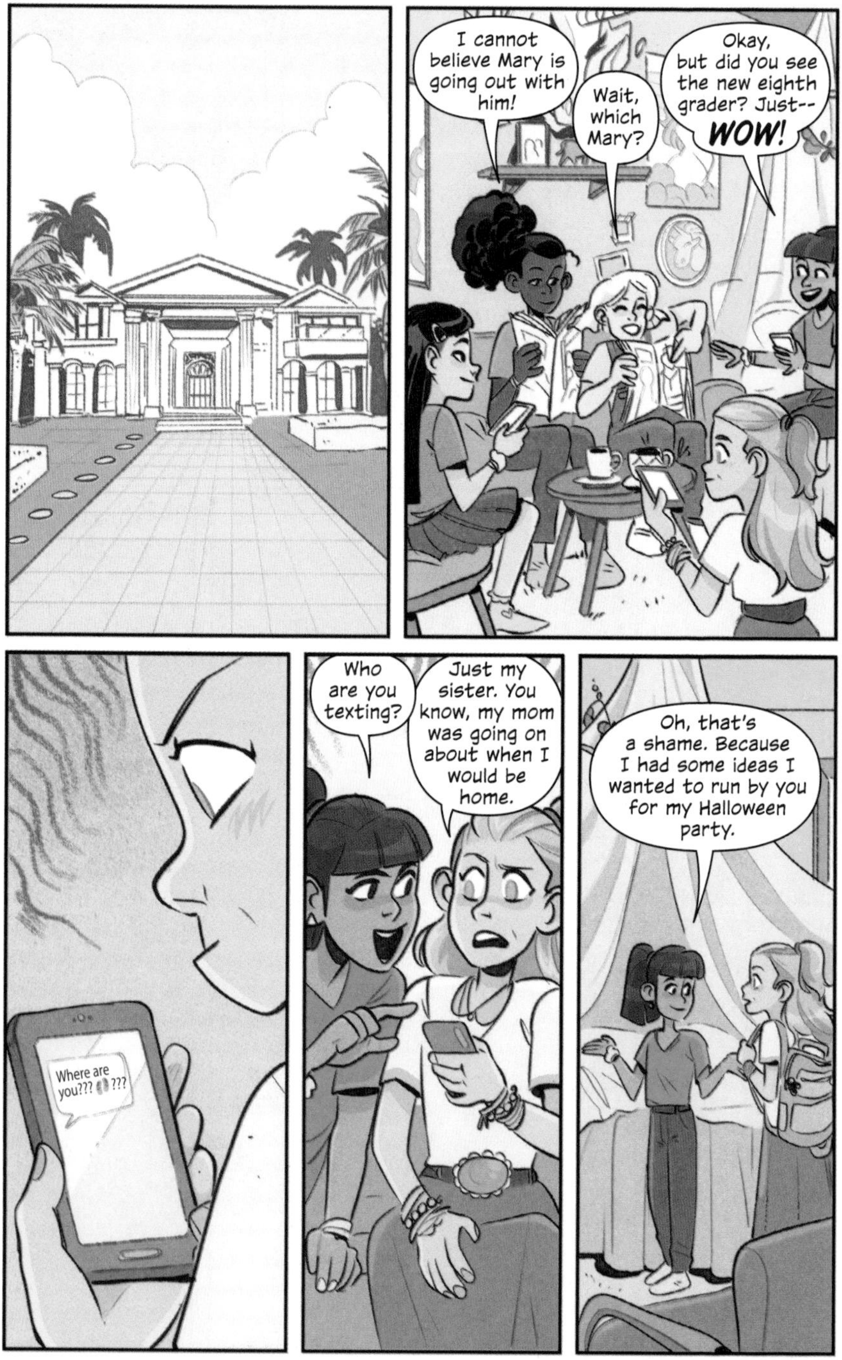
I cannot believe Mary is going out with him!
Wait, which Mary?
Okay, but did you see the new eighth grader? Just-- WOW!
Where are you??? ???
Who are you texting?
Just my sister. You know, my mom was going on about when I would be home.
Oh, that's a shame. Because I had some ideas I wanted to run by you for my Halloween party.

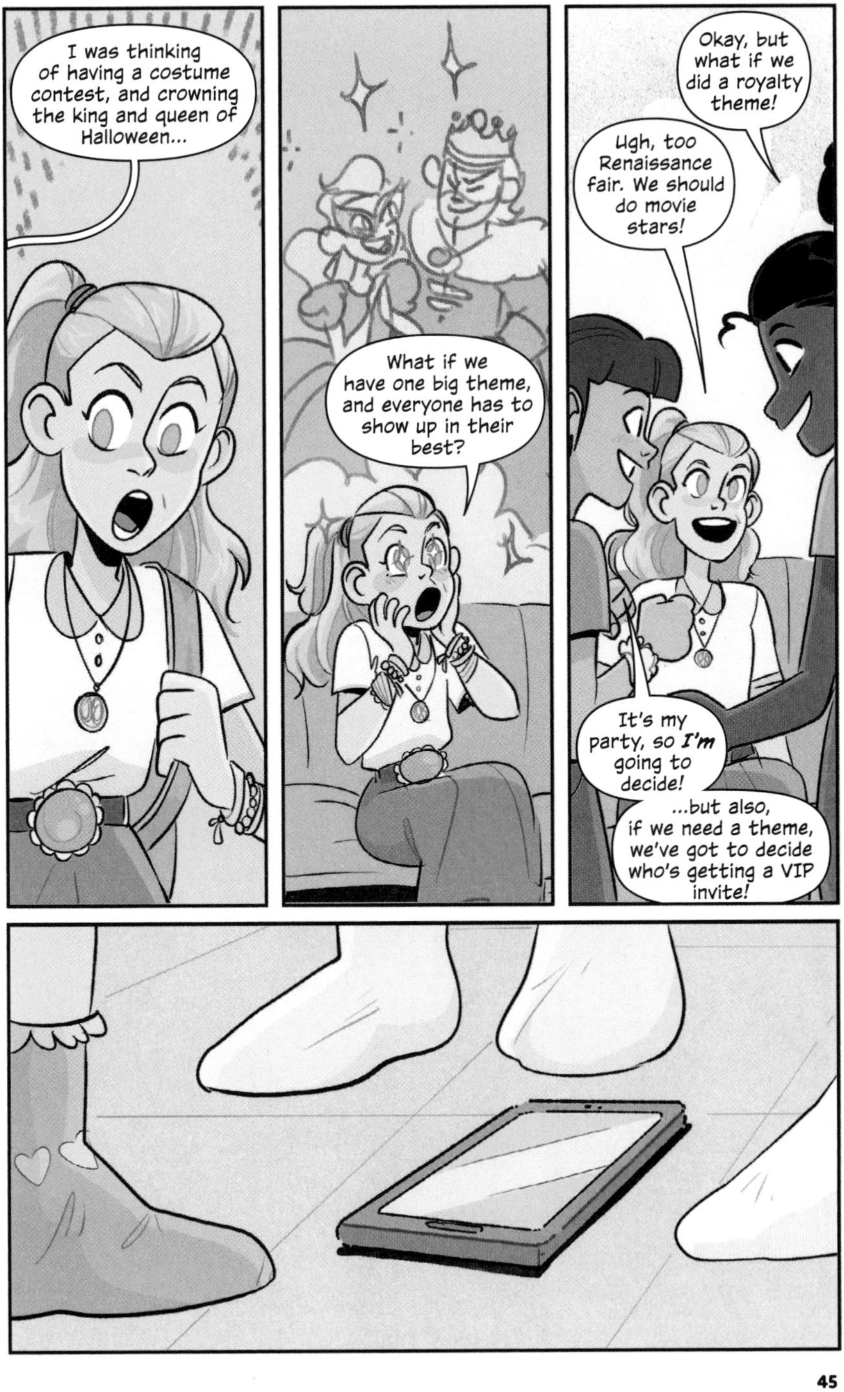

I was thinking of having a costume contest, and crowning the king and queen of Halloween...
What if we have one big theme, and everyone has to show up in their best?
Okay, but what if we did a royalty theme!
Ugh, too Renaissance fair. We should do movie stars!
It's my party, so ***I'm*** going to decide!
...but also, if we need a theme, we've got to decide who's getting a VIP invite!

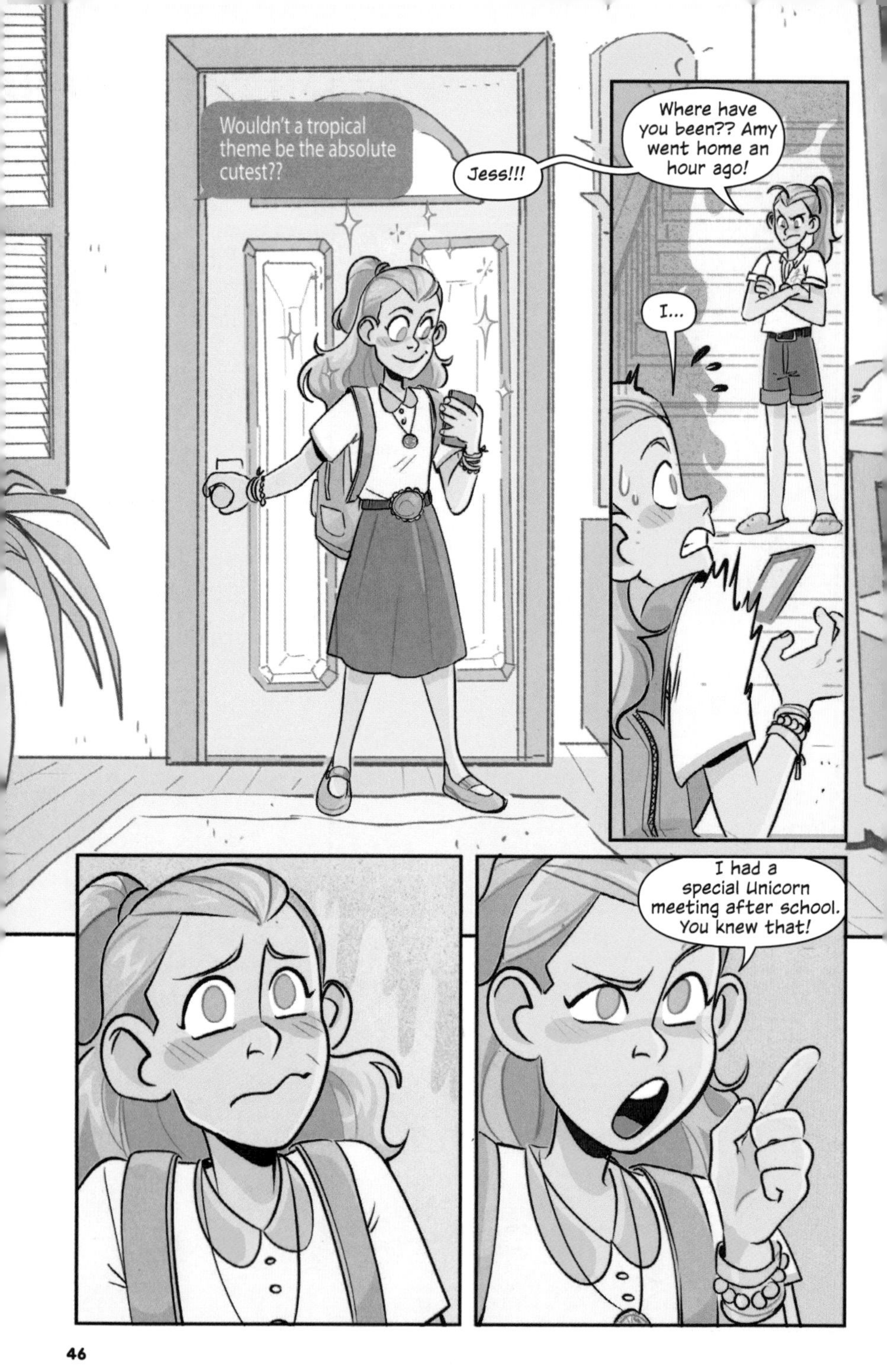
Wouldn't a tropical theme be the absolute cutest??
Jess!!!
Where have you been?? Amy went home an hour ago!
I...
I had a special Unicorn meeting after school. You knew that!

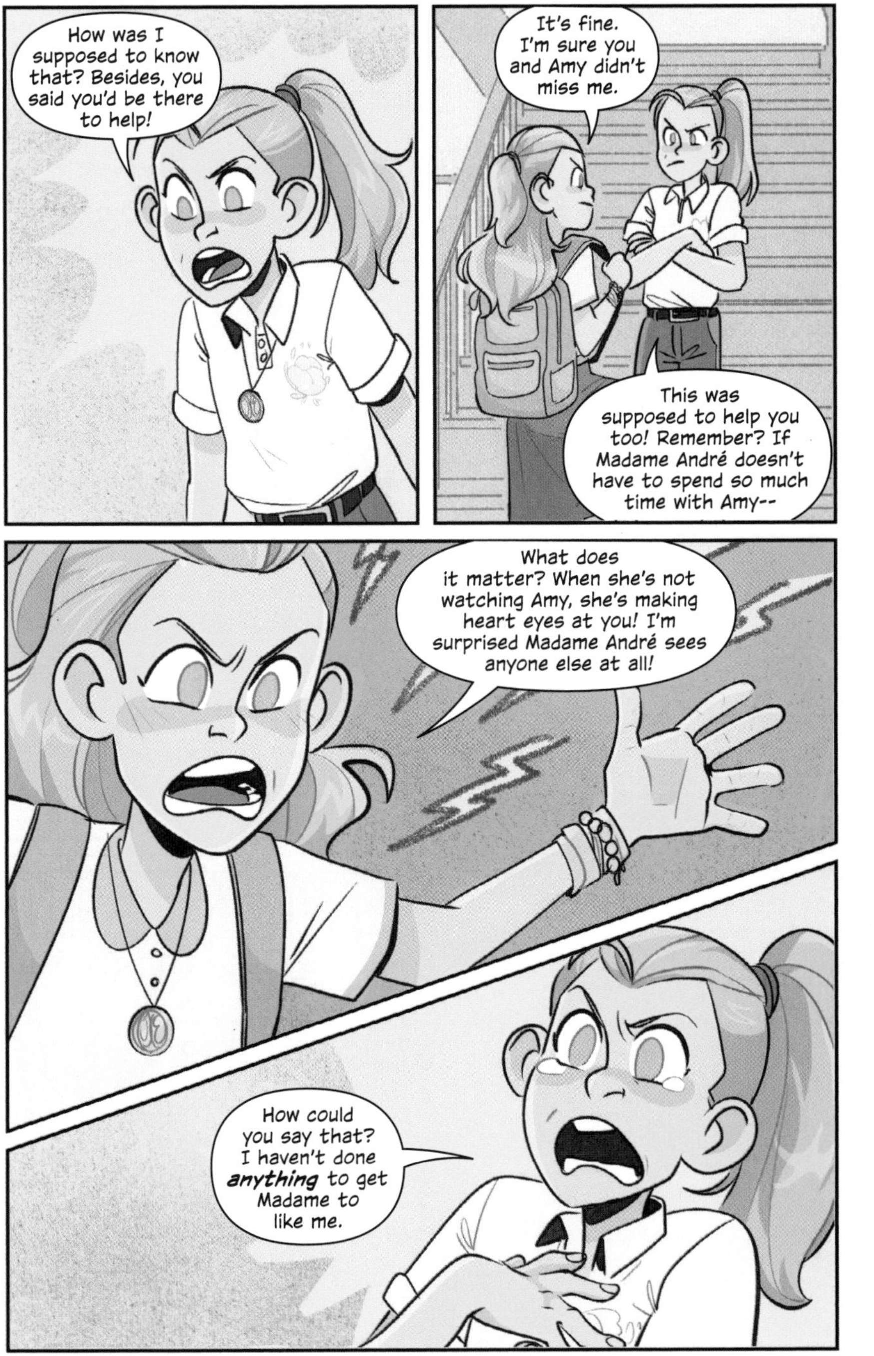
How was I supposed to know that? Besides, you said you'd be there to help!
It's fine. I'm sure you and Amy didn't miss me.
This was supposed to help you too! Remember? If Madame André doesn't have to spend so much time with Amy--
What does it matter? When she's not watching Amy, she's making heart eyes at you! I'm surprised Madame André sees anyone else at all!
How could you say that? I haven't done ***anything*** to get Madame to like me.

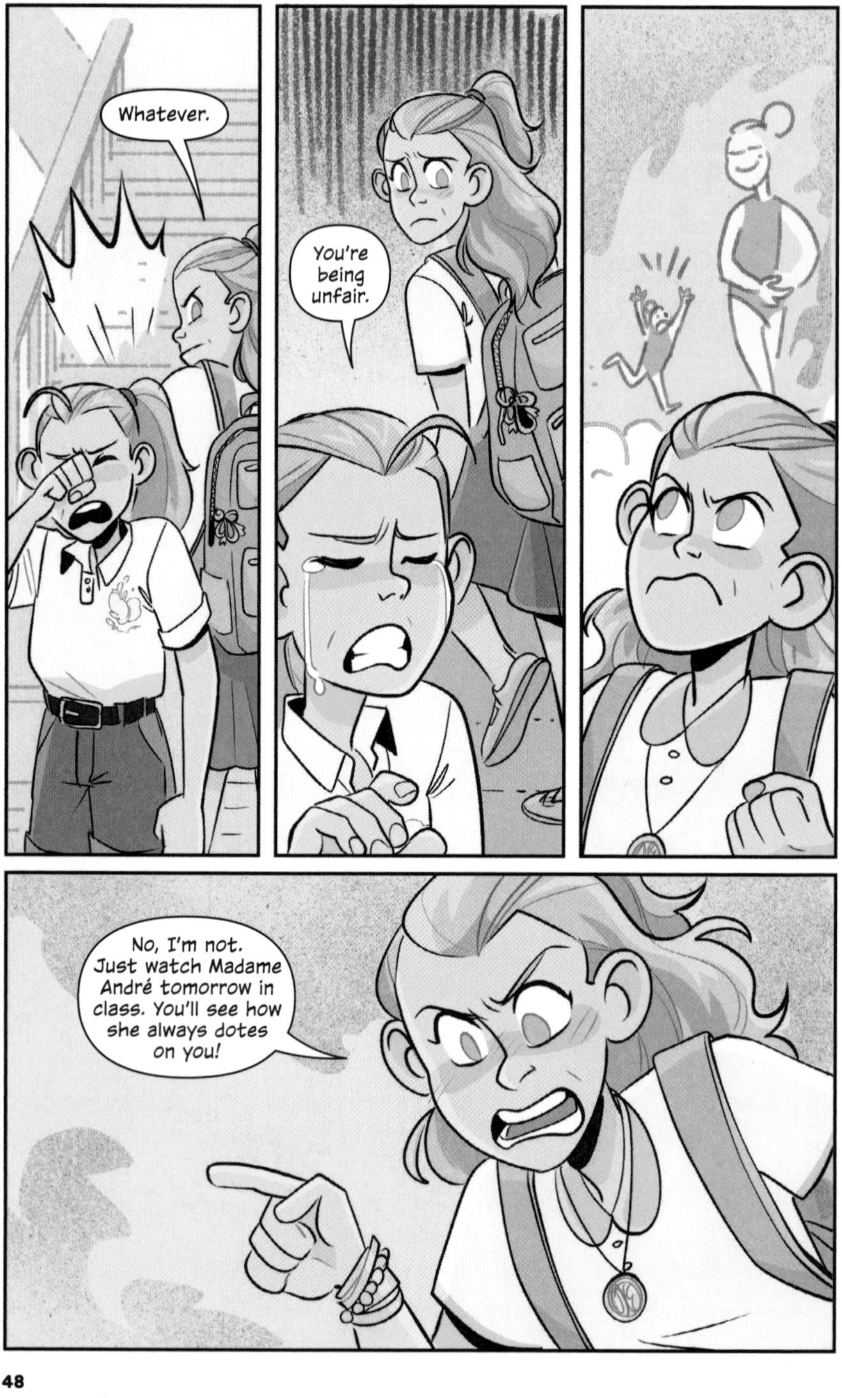

Whatever.
You're being unfair.
No, I'm not. Just watch Madame André tomorrow in class. You'll see how she always dotes on you!

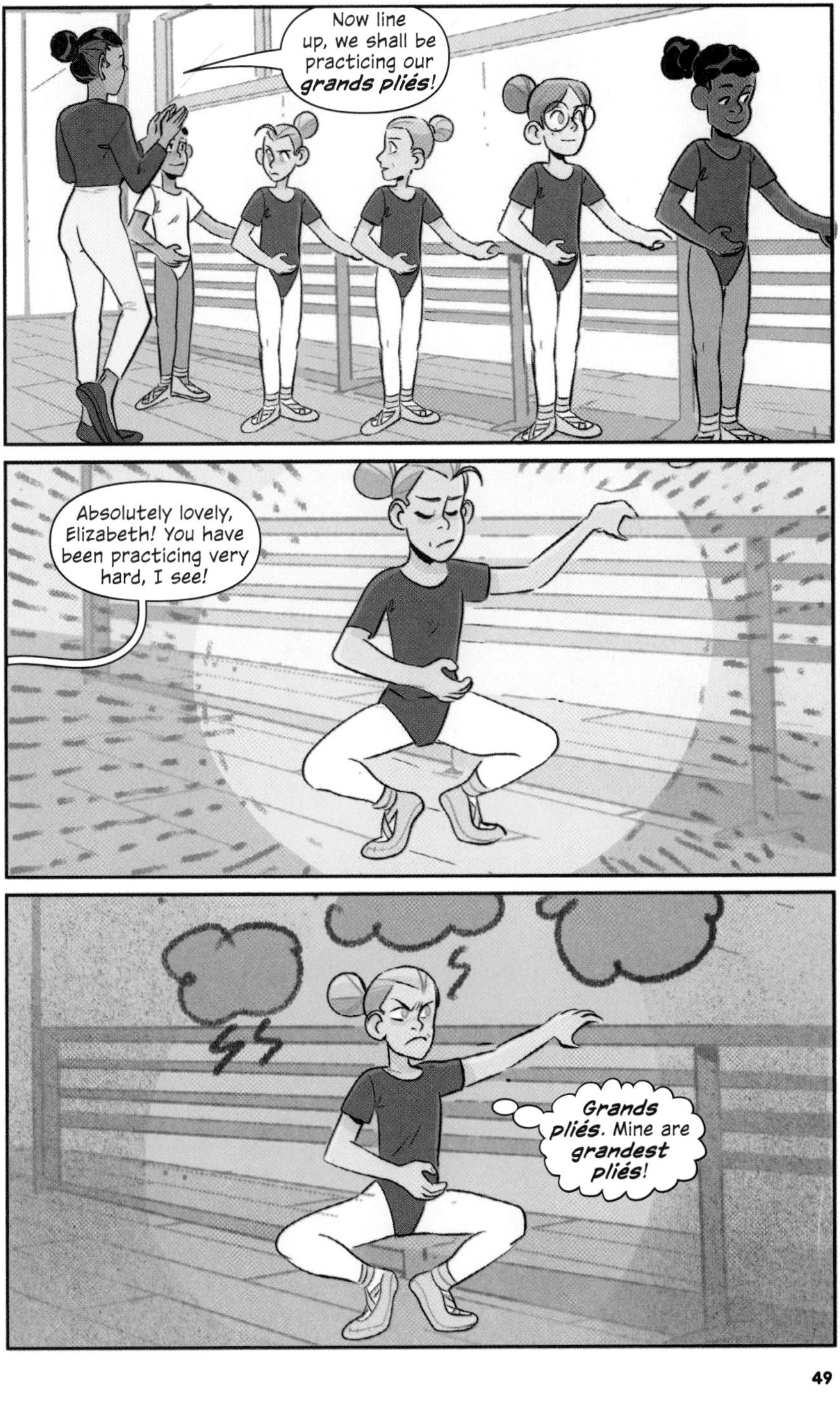
Now line up, we shall be practicing our ***grands pliés***!
Absolutely lovely, Elizabeth! You have been practicing very hard, I see!
Grands pliés. Mine are ***grandest pliés***!

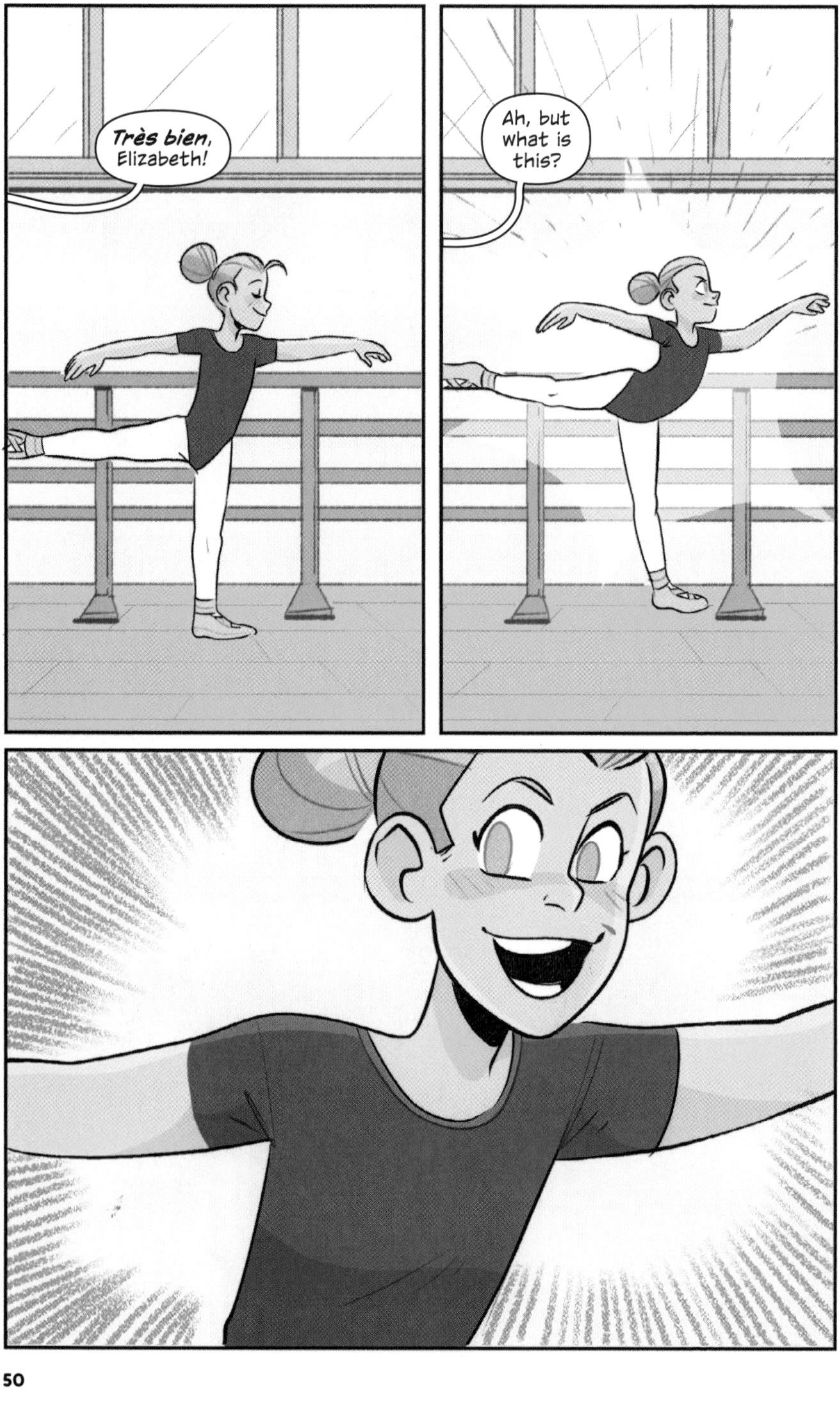
Très bien, Elizabeth!
Ah, but what is this?

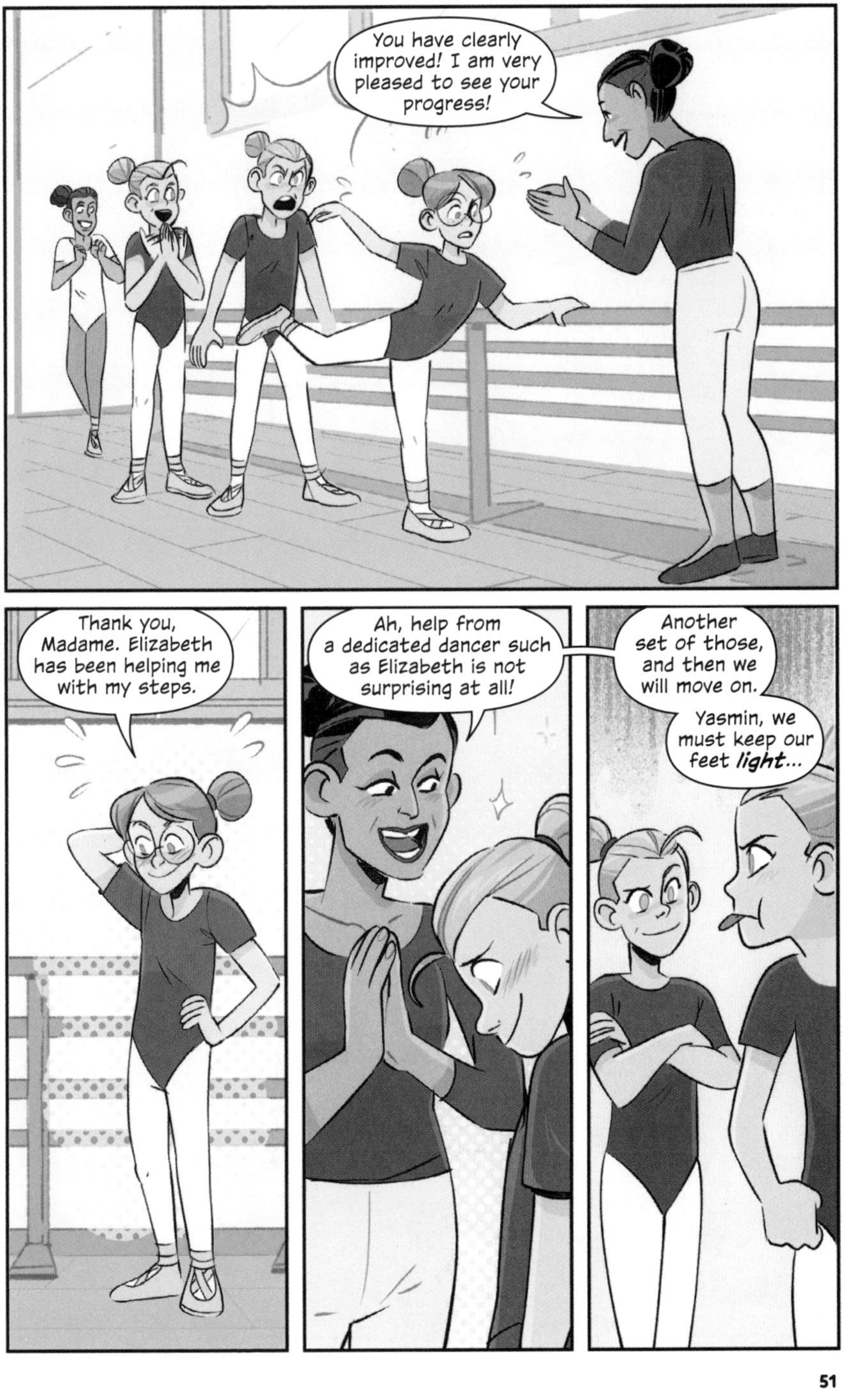
You have clearly improved! I am very pleased to see your progress!
Thank you, Madame. Elizabeth has been helping me with my steps.
Ah, help from a dedicated dancer such as Elizabeth is not surprising at all!
Another set of those, and then we will move on.
Yasmin, we must keep our feet *light*...

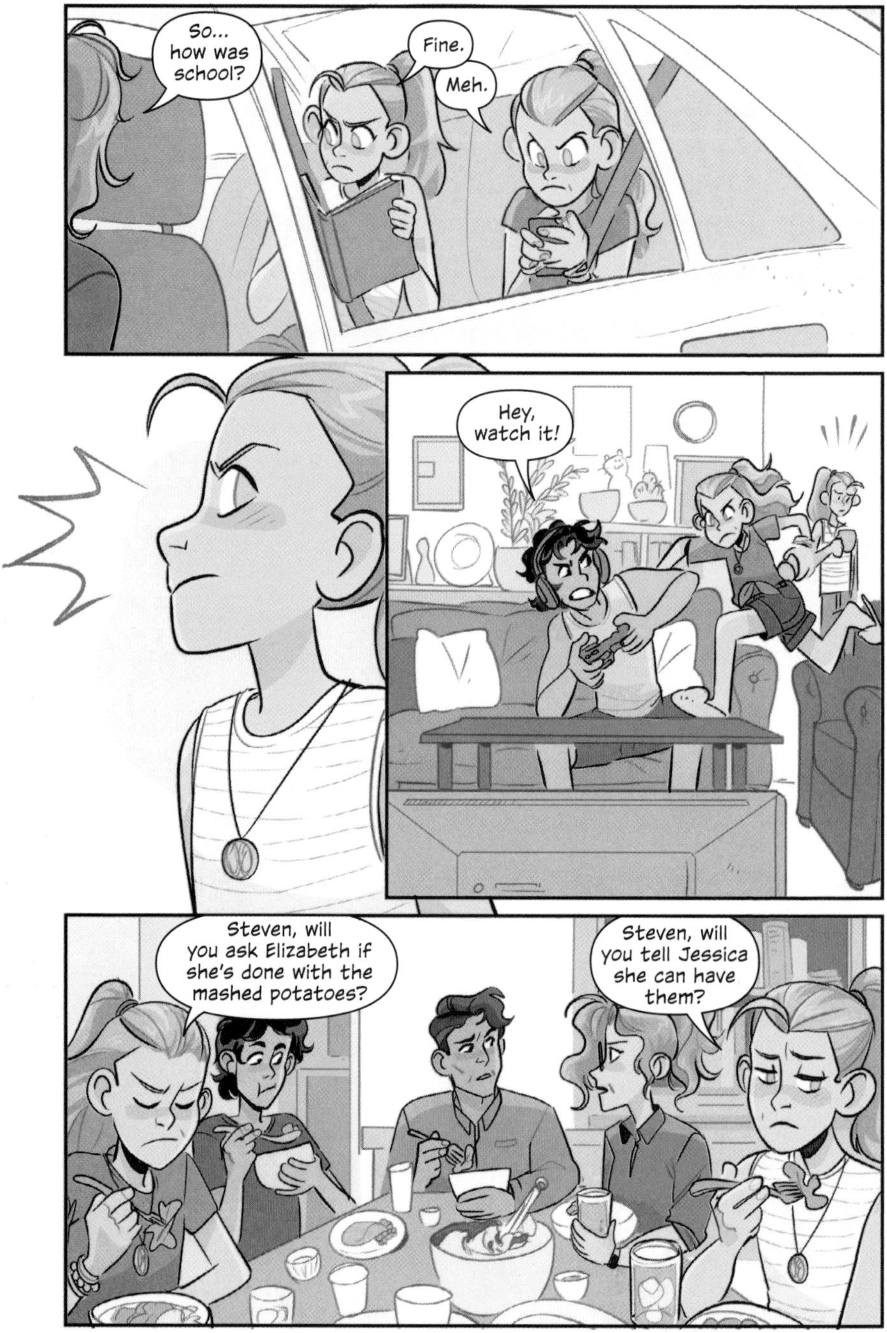
So... how was school?
Fine.
Meh.
Hey, watch it!
Steven, will you ask Elizabeth if she's done with the mashed potatoes?
Steven, will you tell Jessica she can have them?

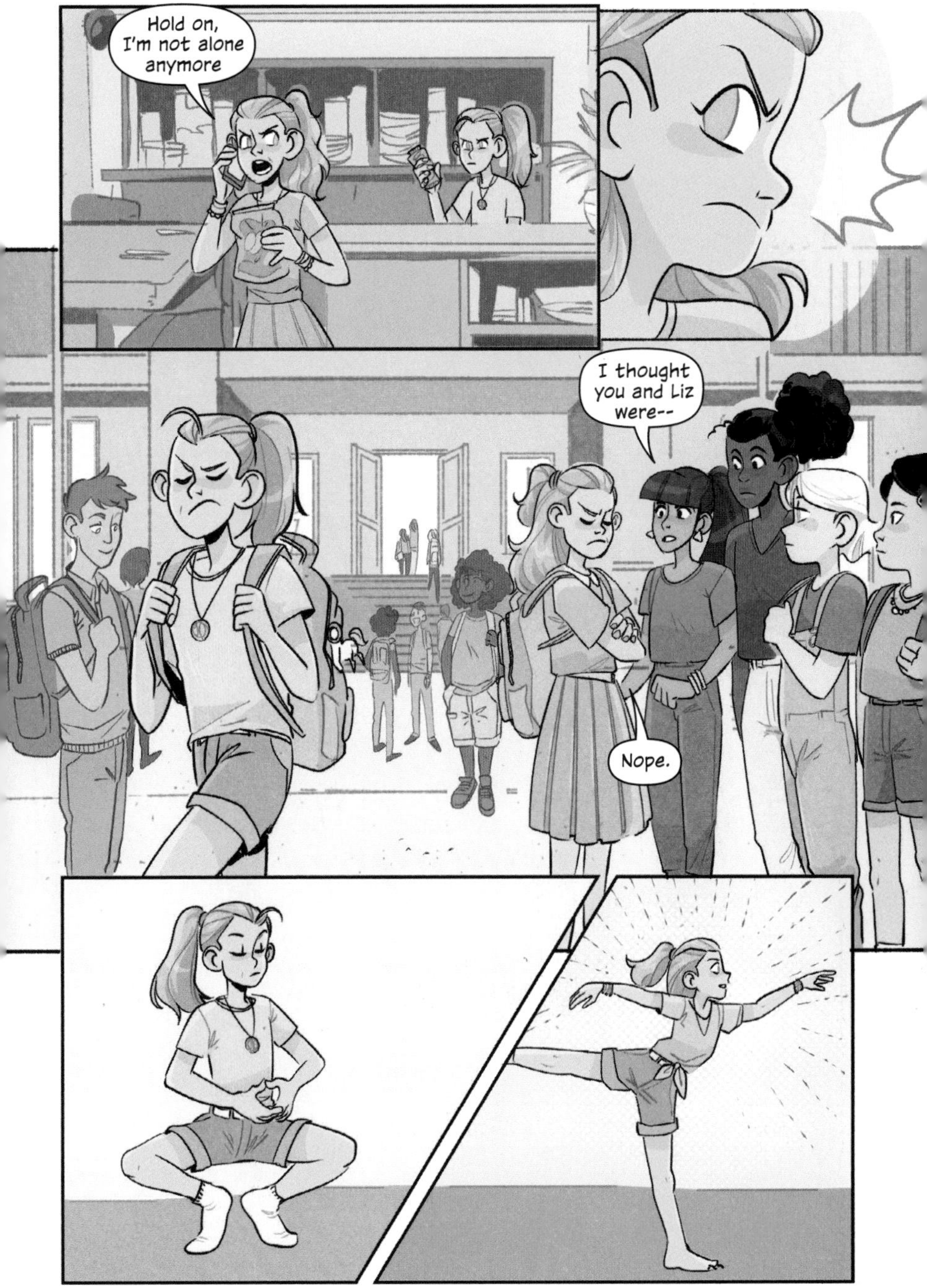
Hold on, I'm not alone anymore
I thought you and Liz were--
Nope.

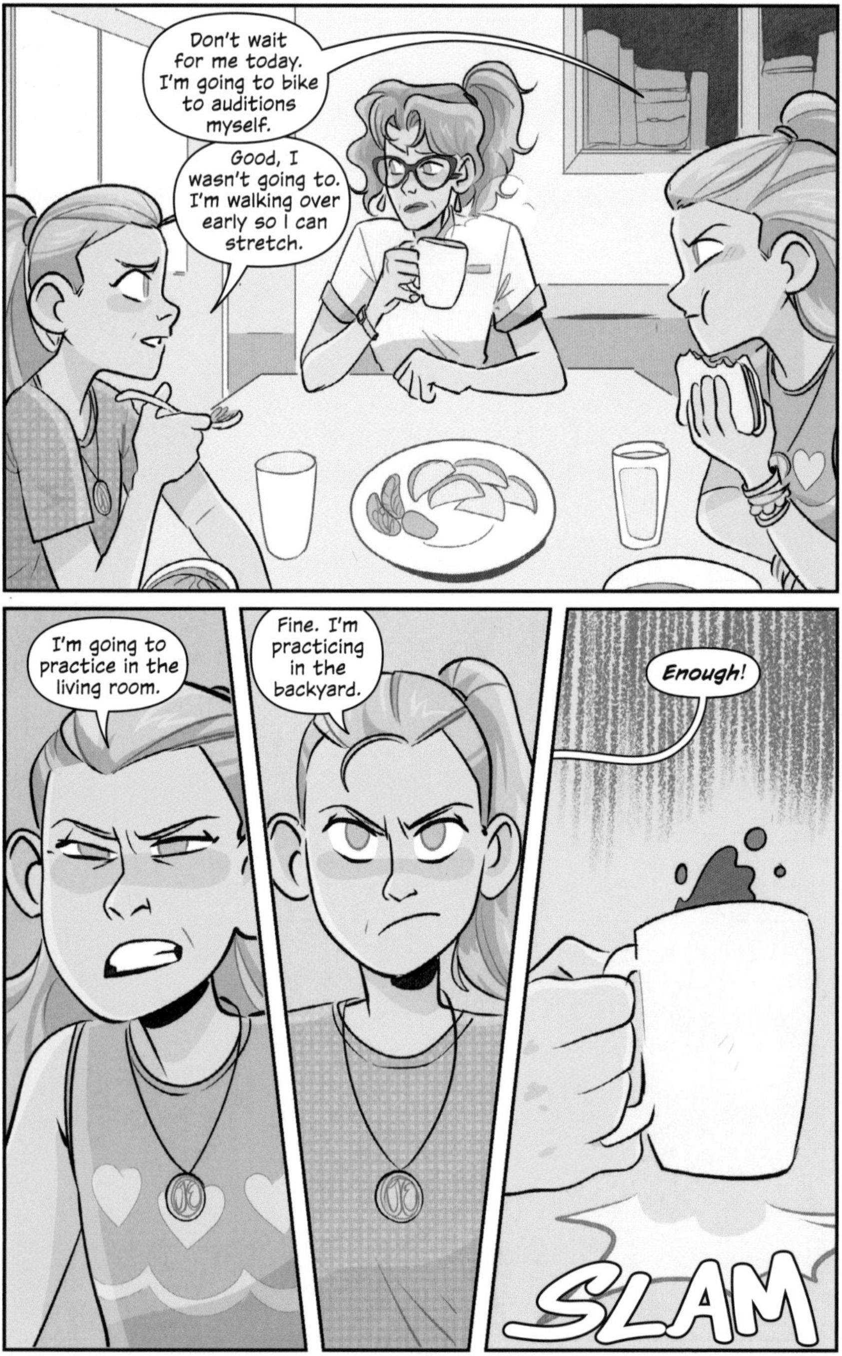
Don't wait for me today. I'm going to bike to auditions myself.
Good, I wasn't going to. I'm walking over early so I can stretch.
I'm going to practice in the living room.
Fine. I'm practicing in the backyard.
Enough!
SLAM

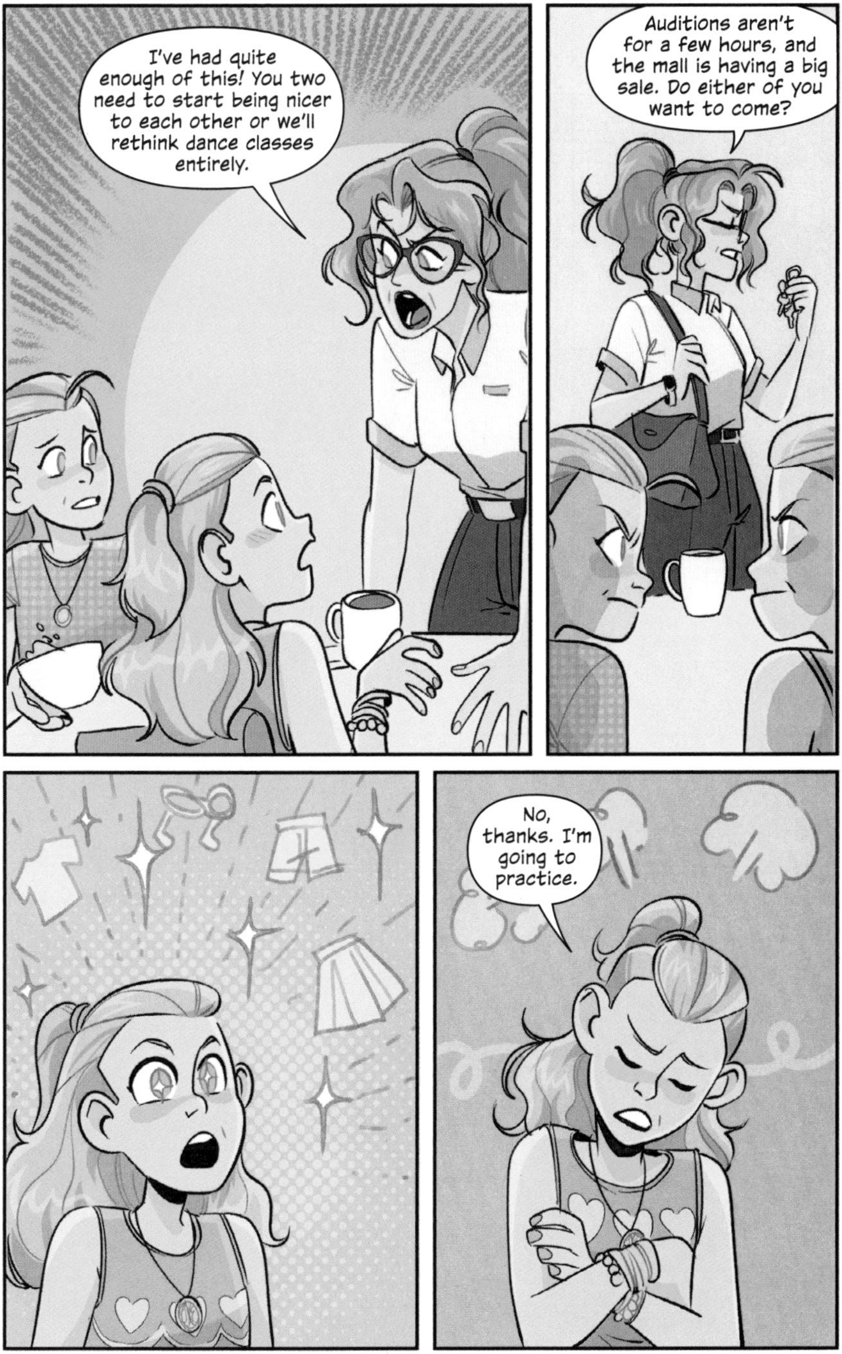
I've had quite enough of this! You two need to start being nicer to each other or we'll rethink dance classes entirely.
Auditions aren't for a few hours, and the mall is having a big sale. Do either of you want to come?
No, thanks. I'm going to practice.

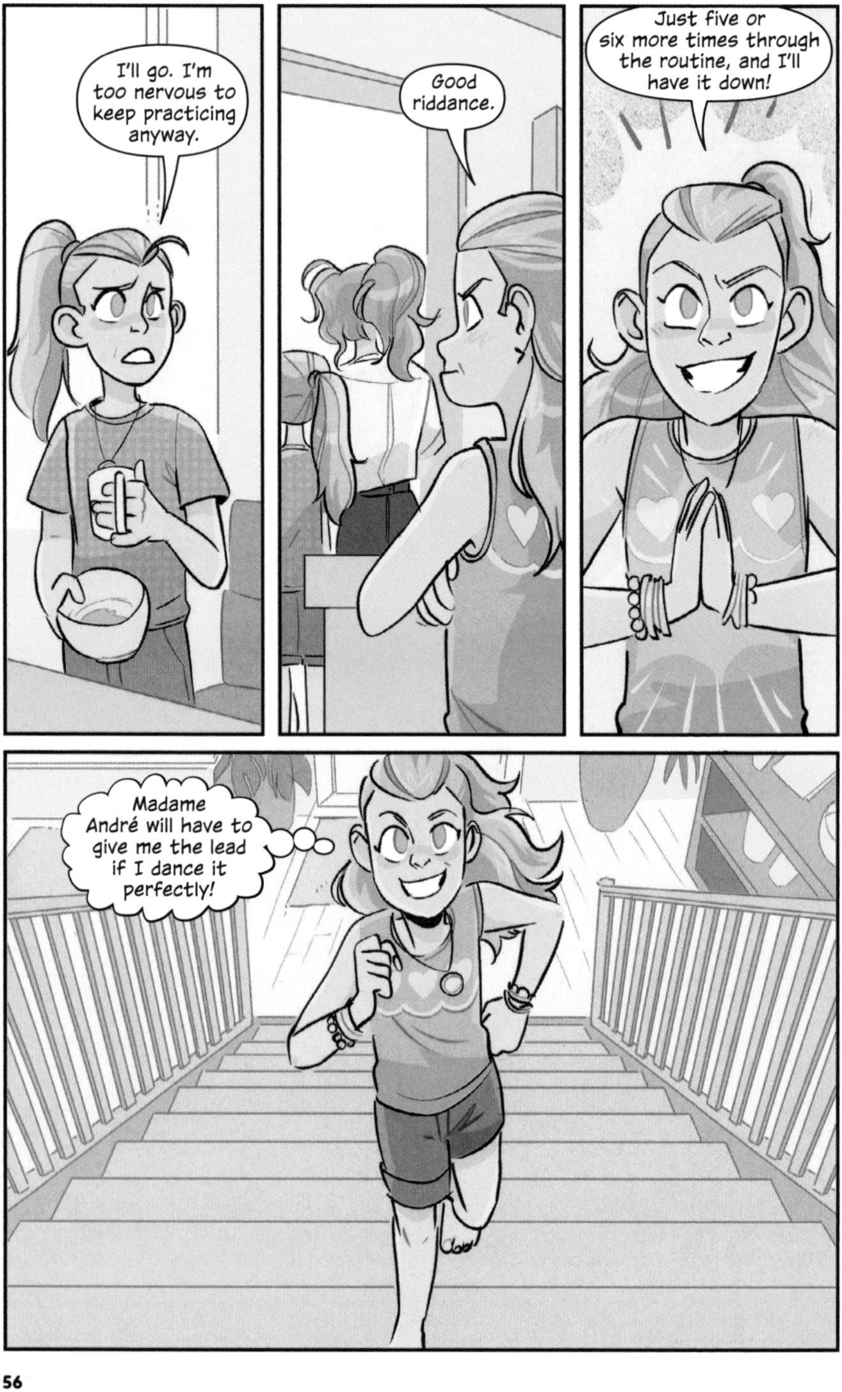
I'll go. I'm too nervous to keep practicing anyway.
Good riddance.
Just five or six more times through the routine, and I'll have it down!
Madame André will have to give me the lead if I dance it perfectly!

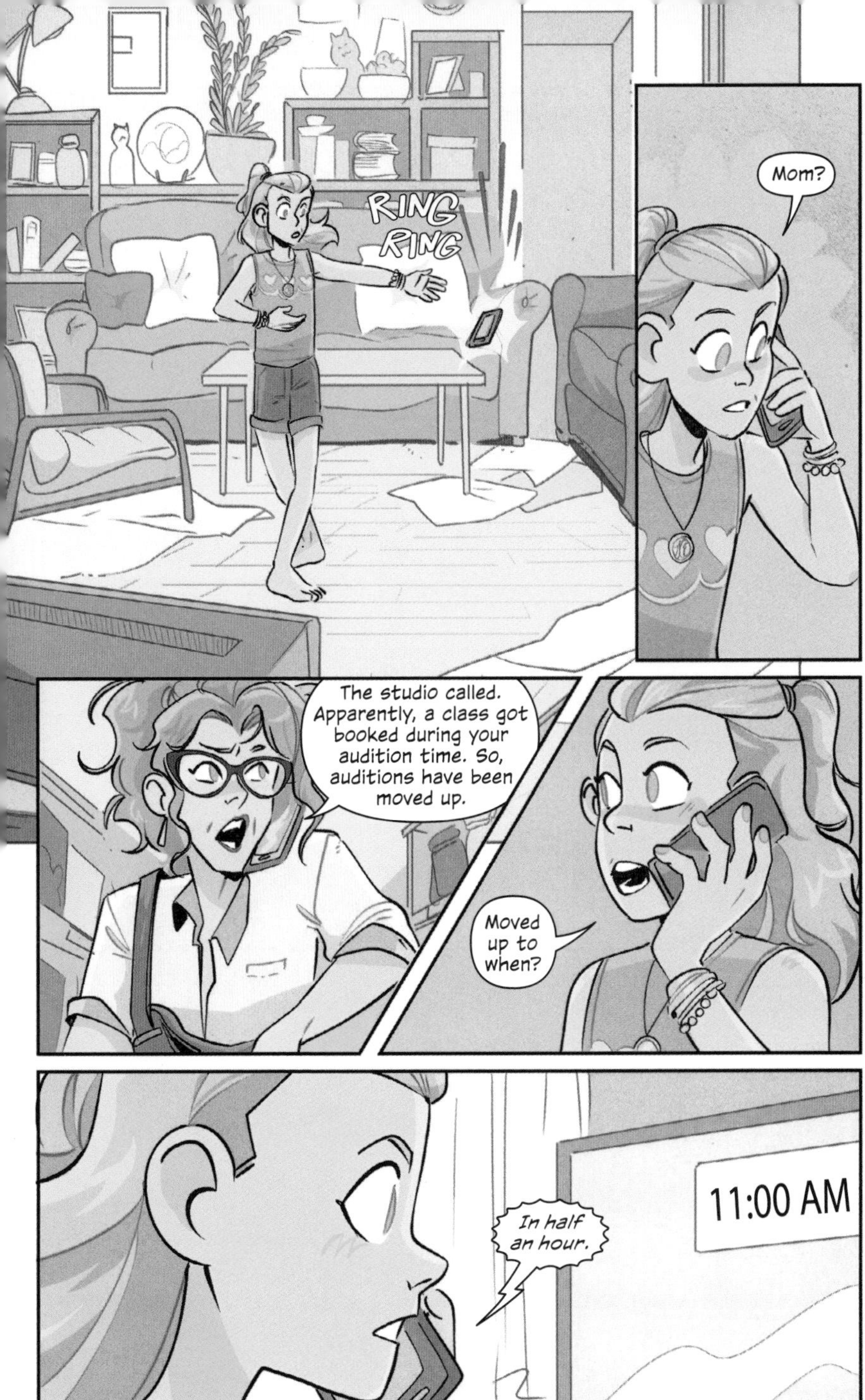
RING
RING
Mom?
The studio called. Apparently, a class got booked during your audition time. So, auditions have been moved up.
Moved up to when?
In half an hour.
11:00 AM

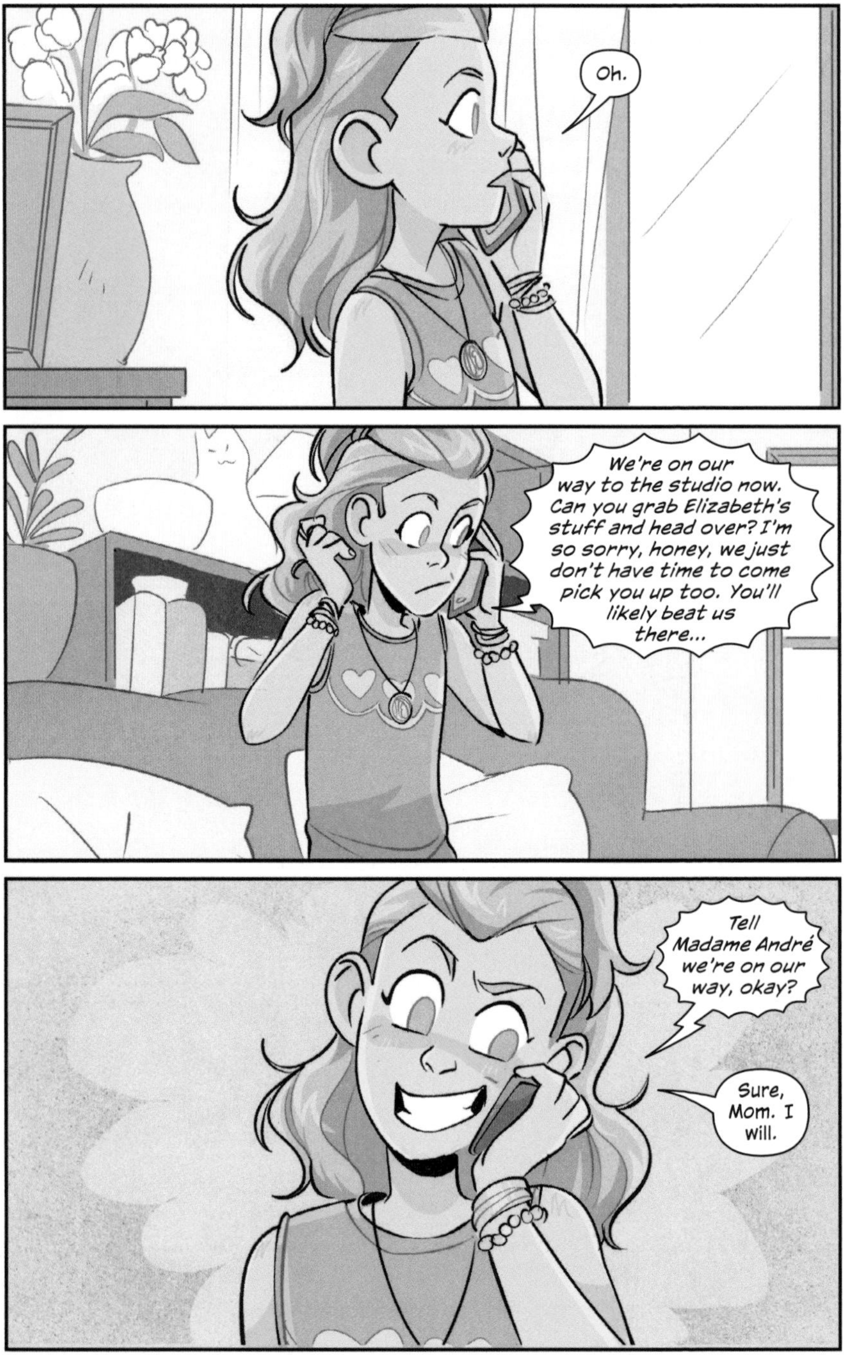
Oh.
We're on our way to the studio now. Can you grab Elizabeth's stuff and head over? I'm so sorry, honey, we just don't have time to come pick you up too. You'll likely beat us there...
Tell Madame André we're on our way, okay?
Sure, Mom. I will.

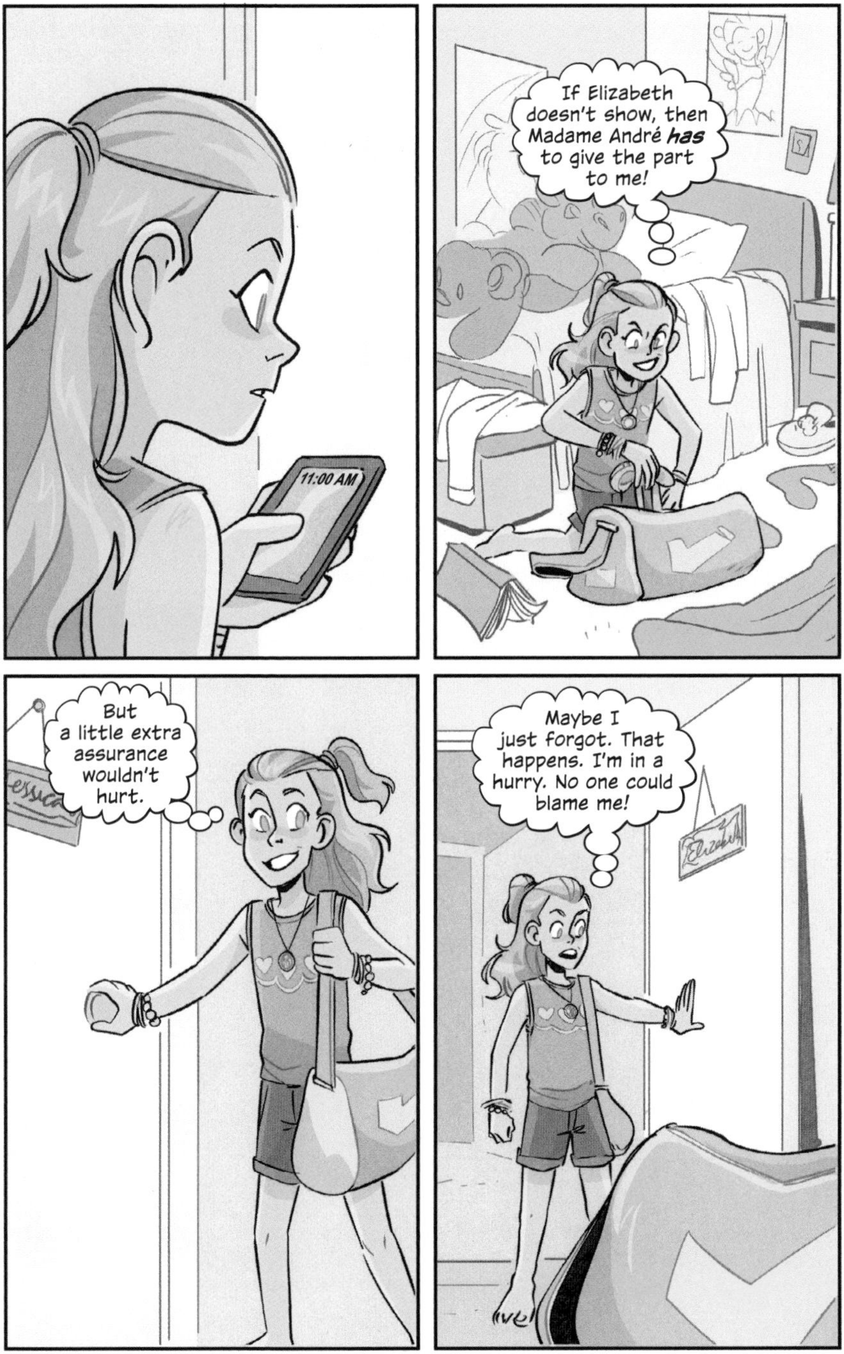
11:00 AM
If Elizabeth doesn't show, then Madame André ***has*** to give the part to me!
But a little extra assurance wouldn't hurt.
Maybe I just forgot. That happens. I'm in a hurry. No one could blame me!

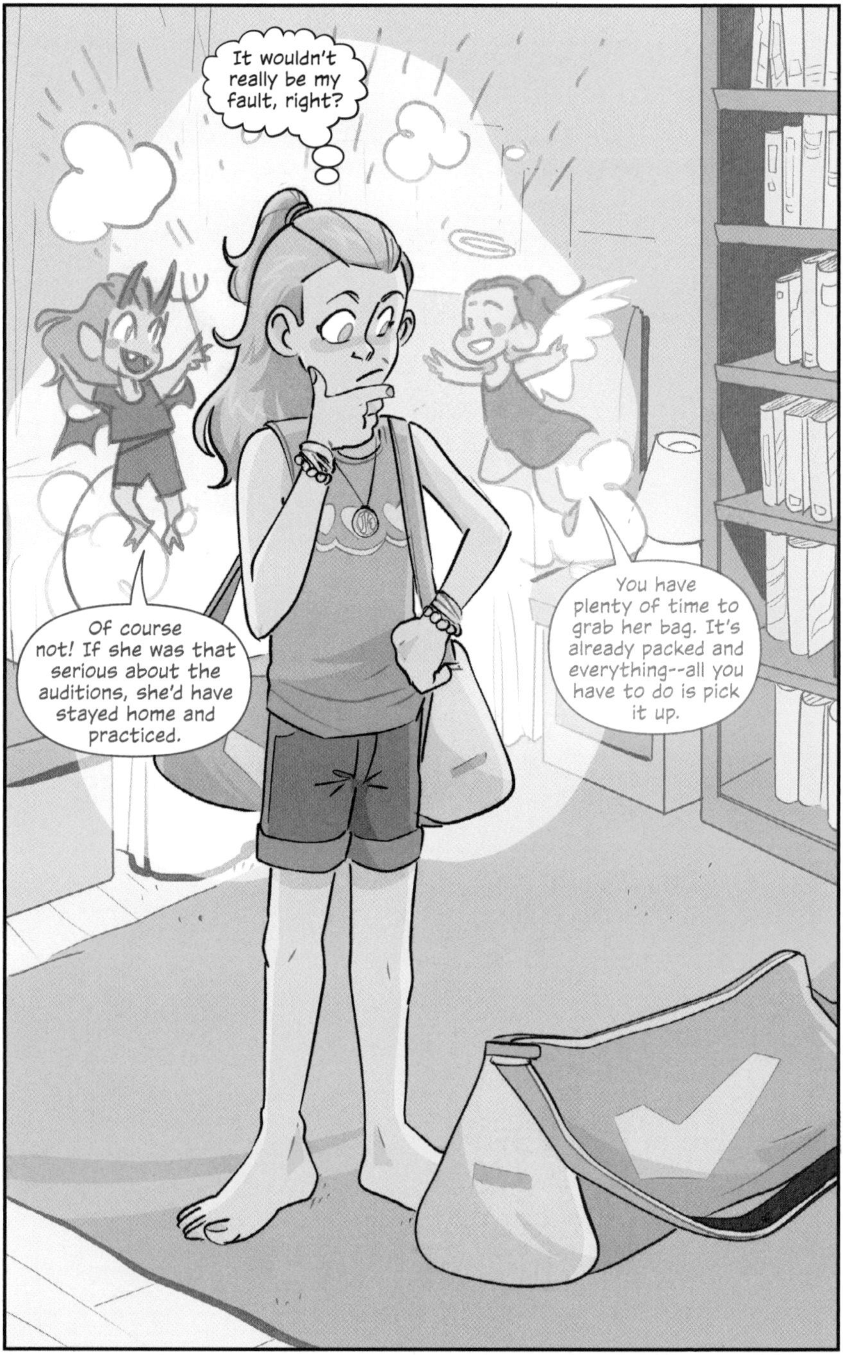
It wouldn't really be my fault, right?
Of course not! If she was that serious about the auditions, she'd have stayed home and practiced.
You have plenty of time to grab her bag. It's already packed and everything--all you have to do is pick it up.

Ugh, *FINE.*

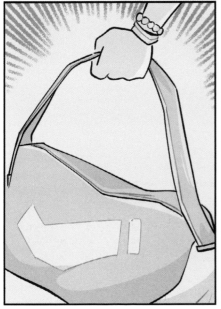

You owe me big, Liz!

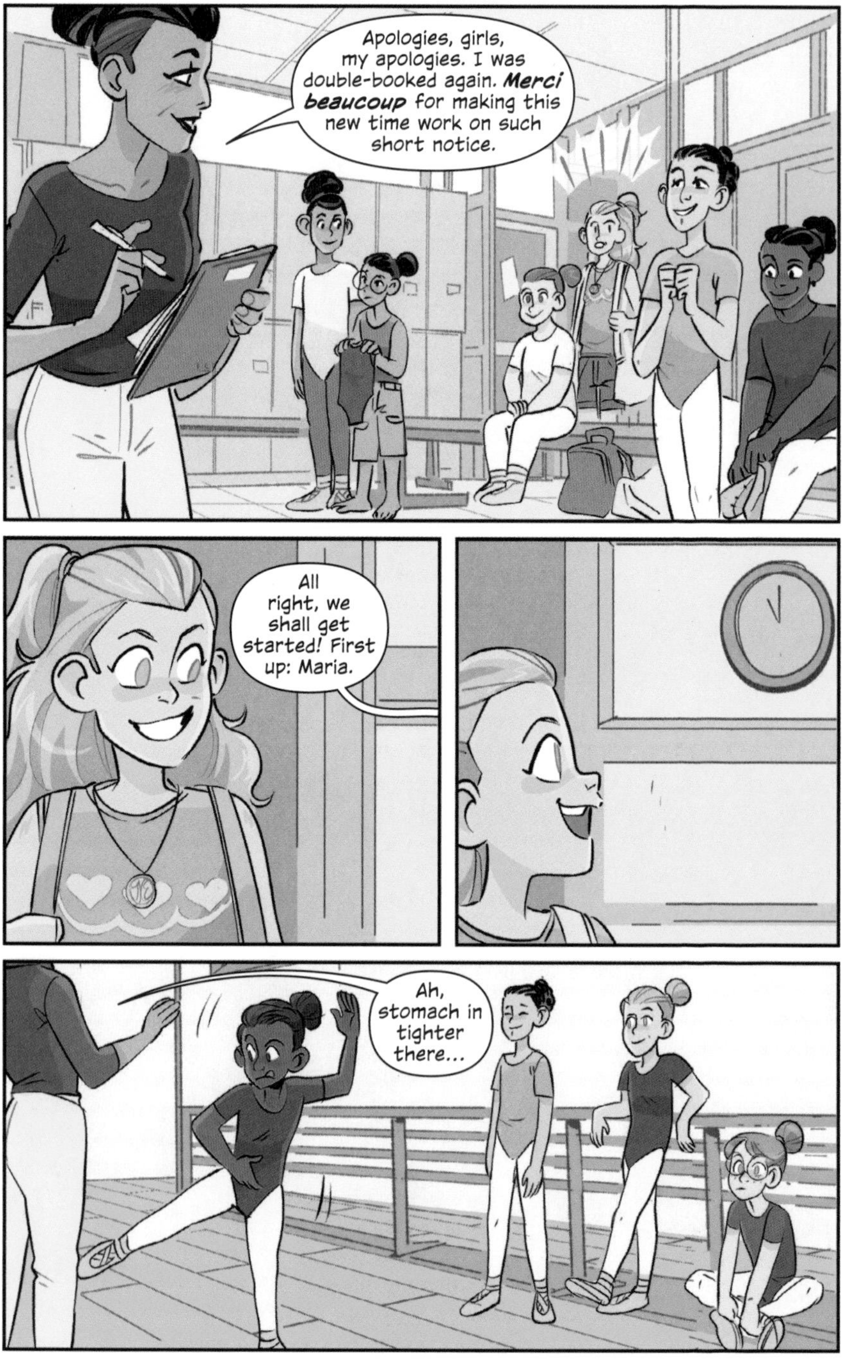
Apologies, girls, my apologies. I was double-booked again. ***Merci beaucoup*** for making this new time work on such short notice.
All right, we shall get started! First up: Maria.
Ah, stomach in tighter there...

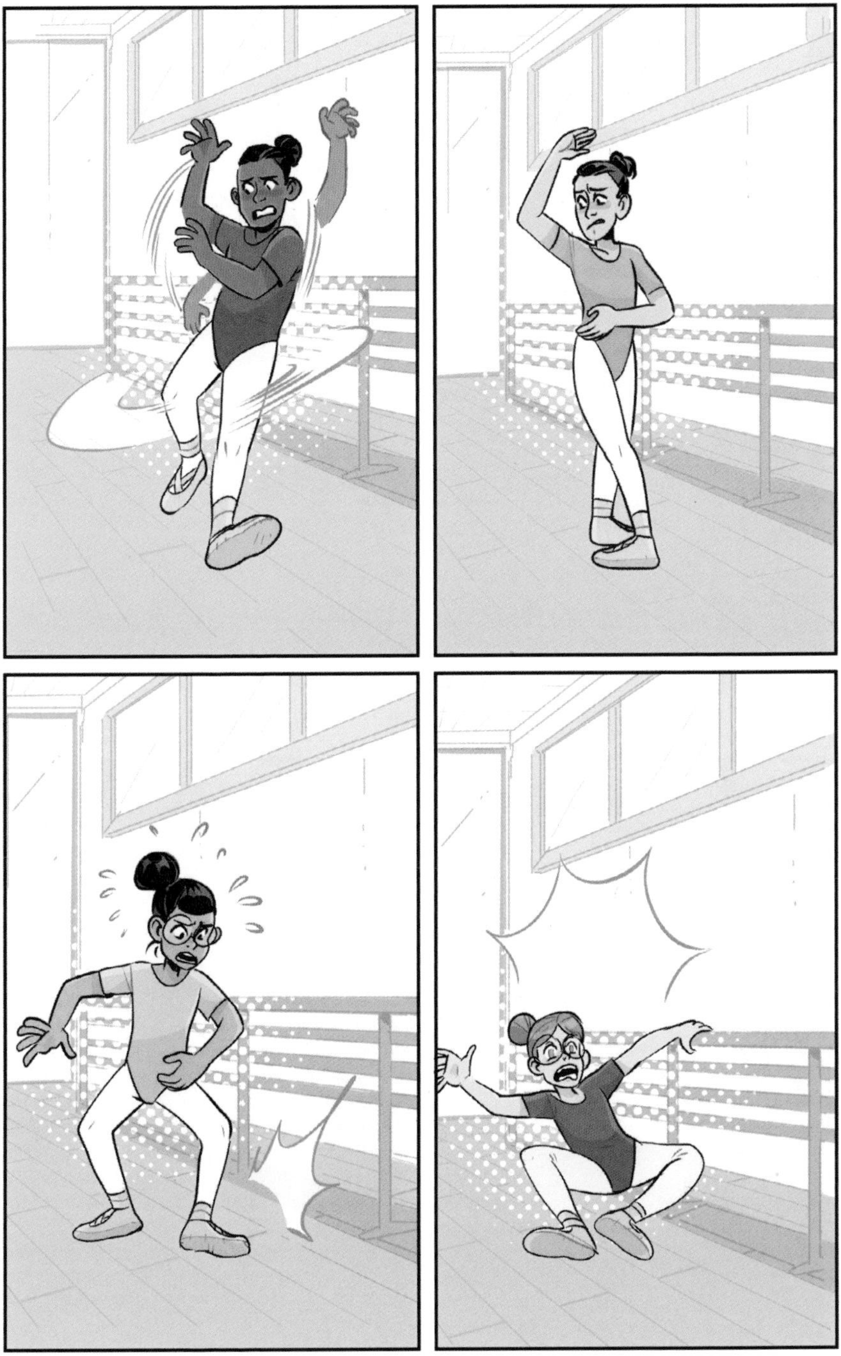

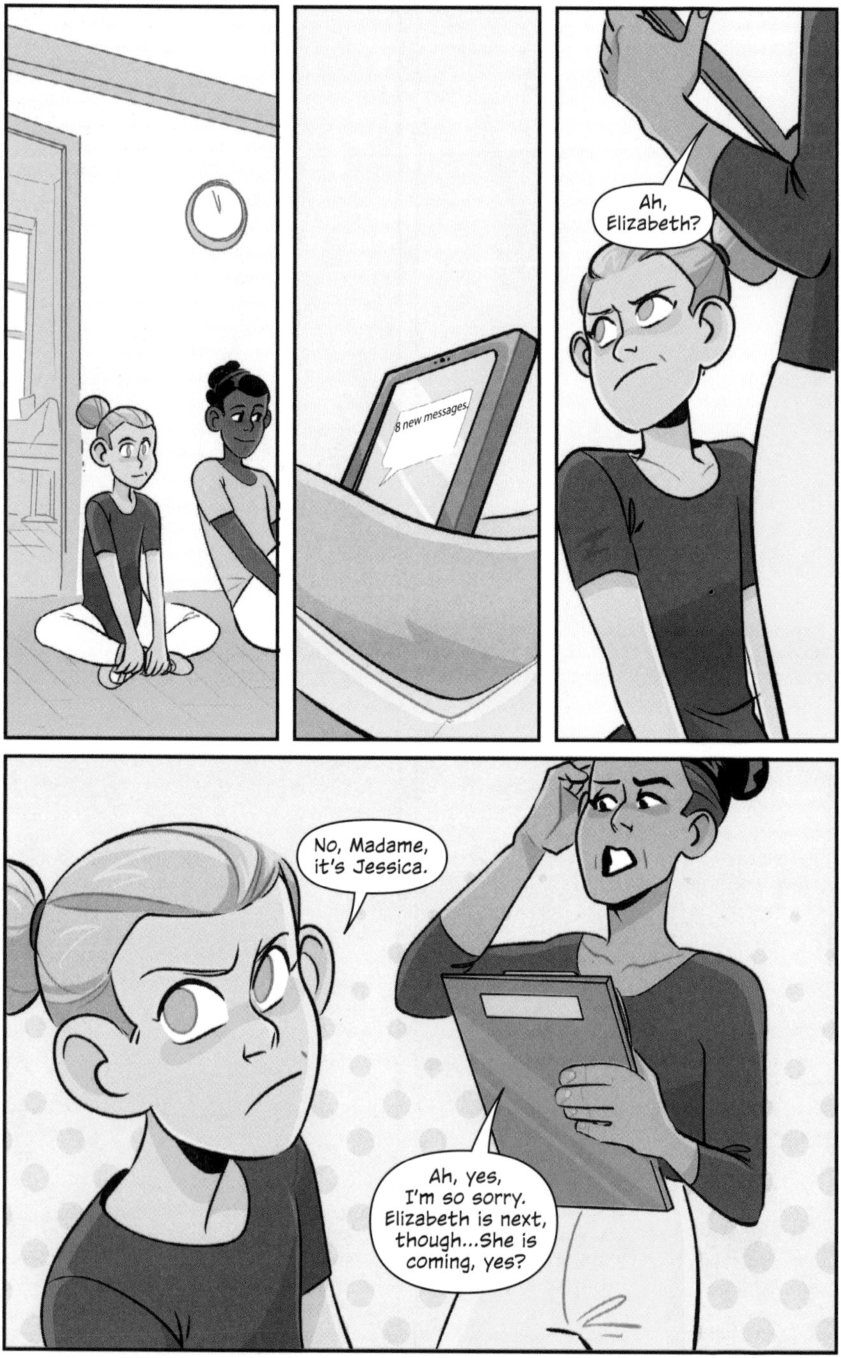
8 new messages.
Ah, Elizabeth?
No, Madame, it's Jessica.
Ah, yes, I'm so sorry. Elizabeth is next, though...She is coming, yes?

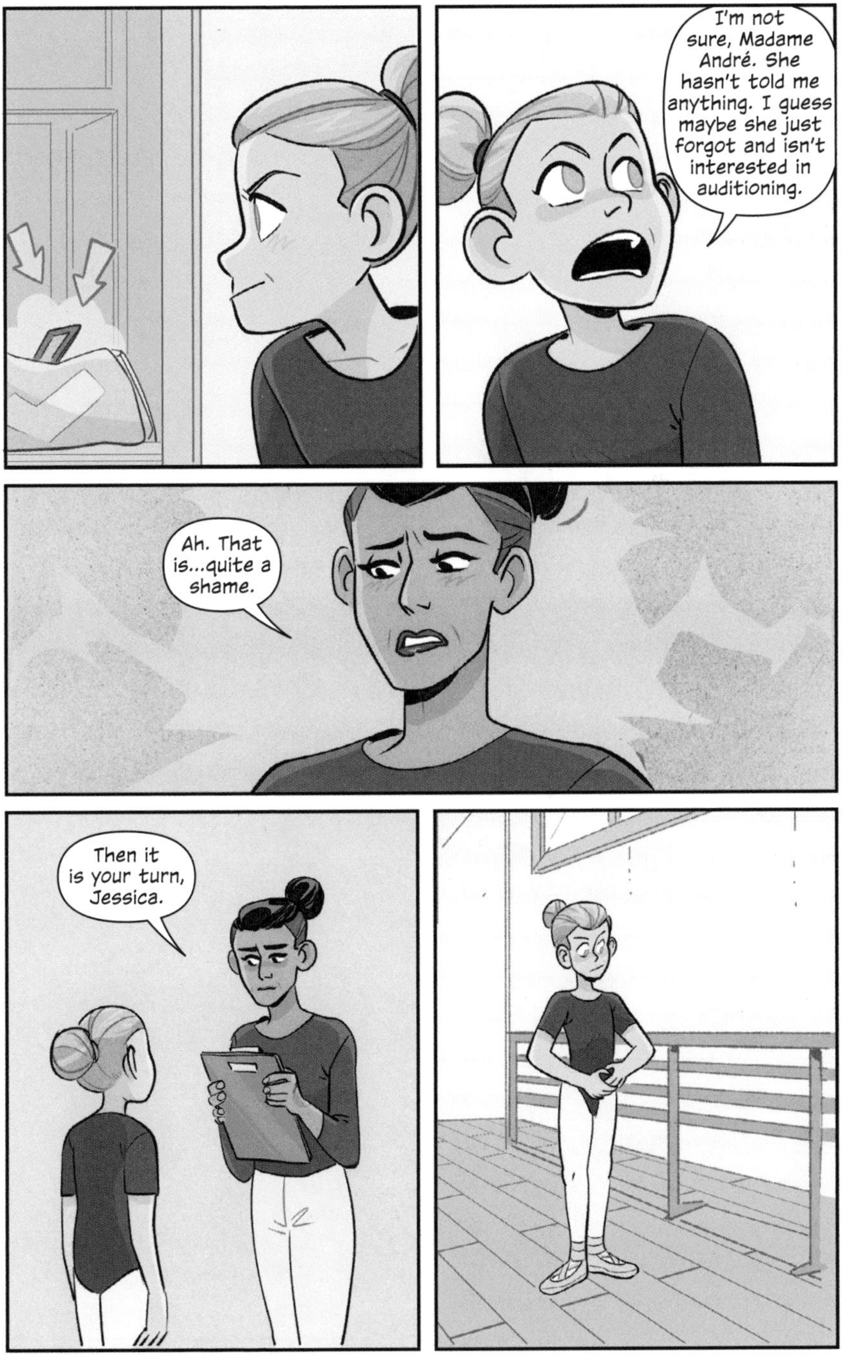
I'm not sure, Madame André. She hasn't told me anything. I guess maybe she just forgot and isn't interested in auditioning.
Ah. That is...quite a shame.
Then it is your turn, Jessica.

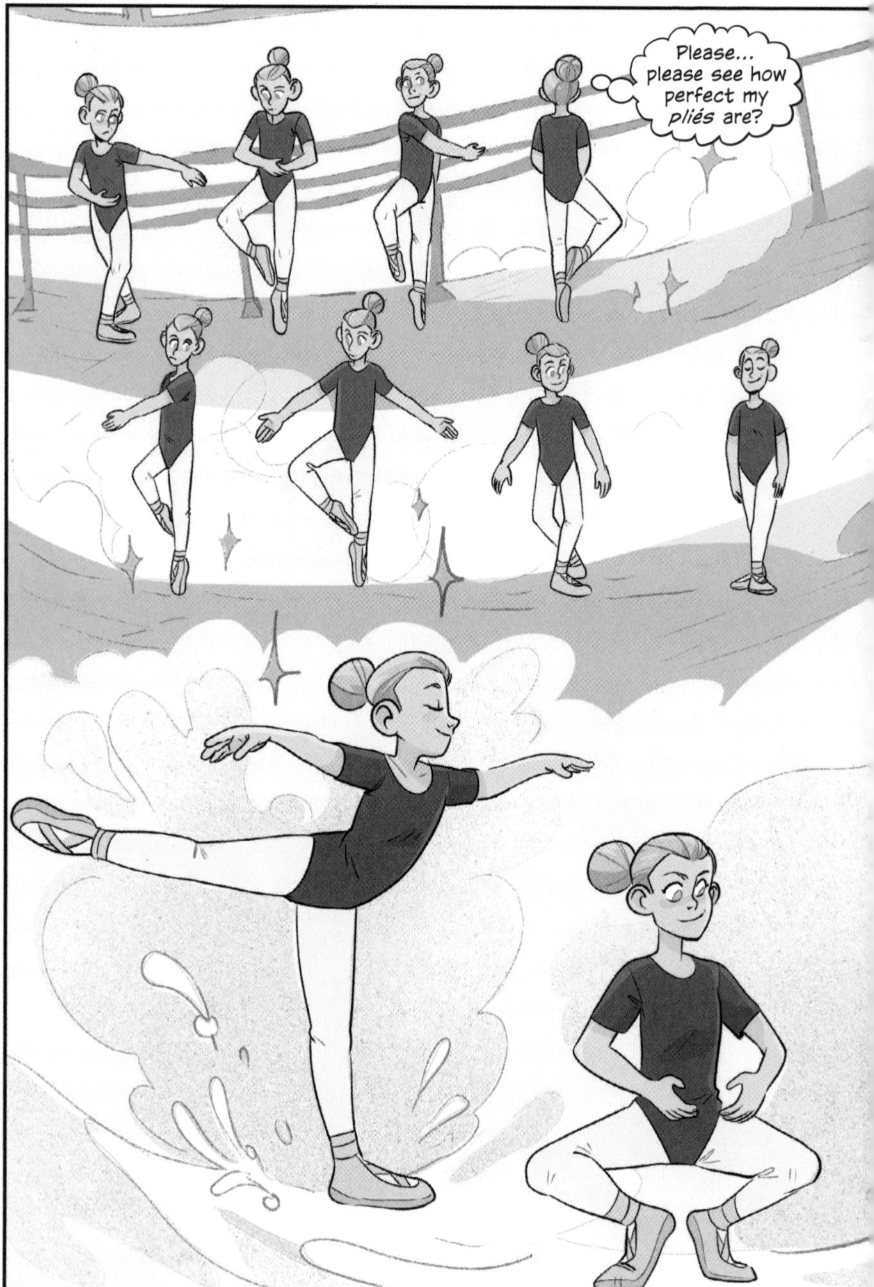
Please... please see how perfect my *pliés* are?

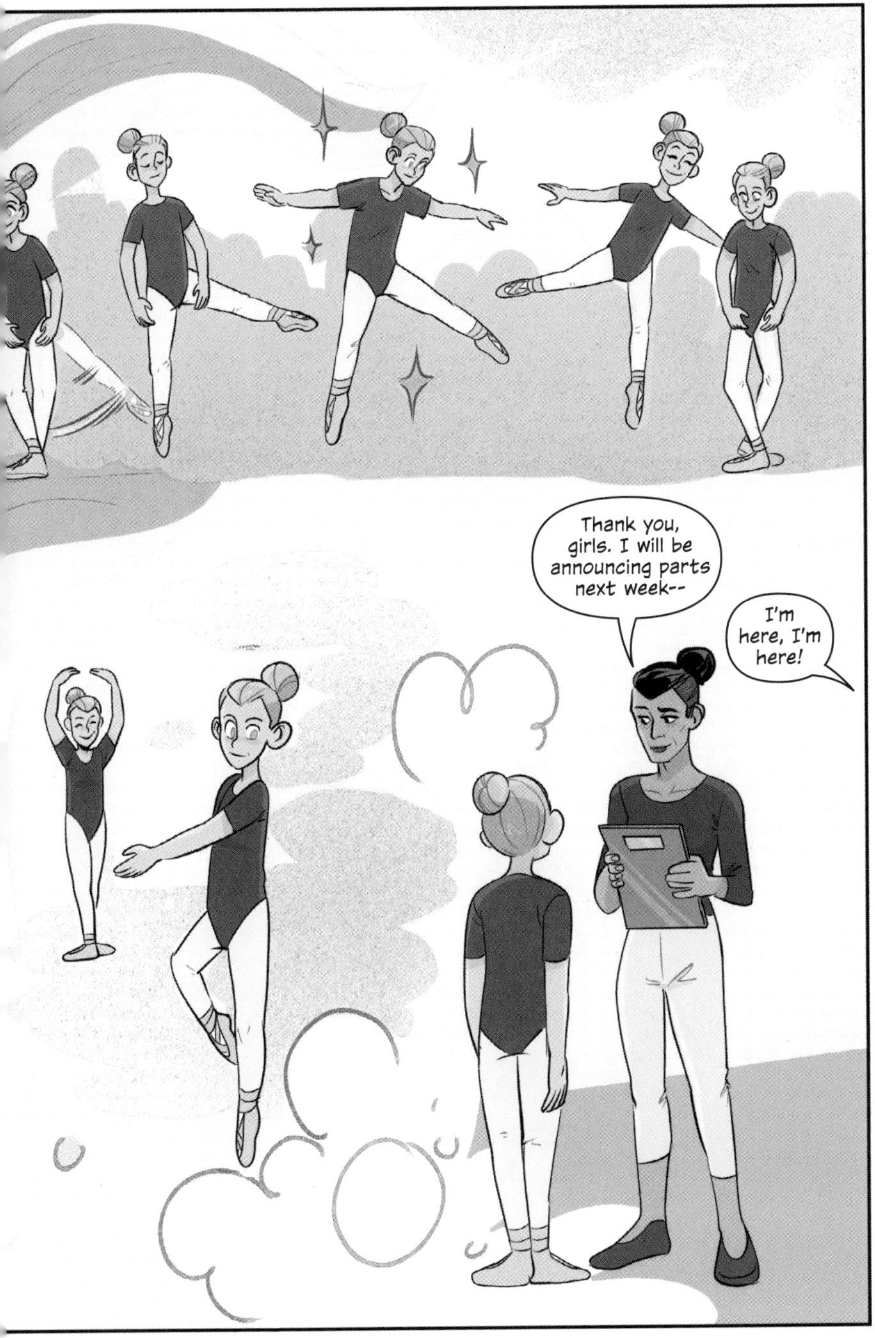
Thank you, girls. I will be announcing parts next week--
I'm here, I'm here!

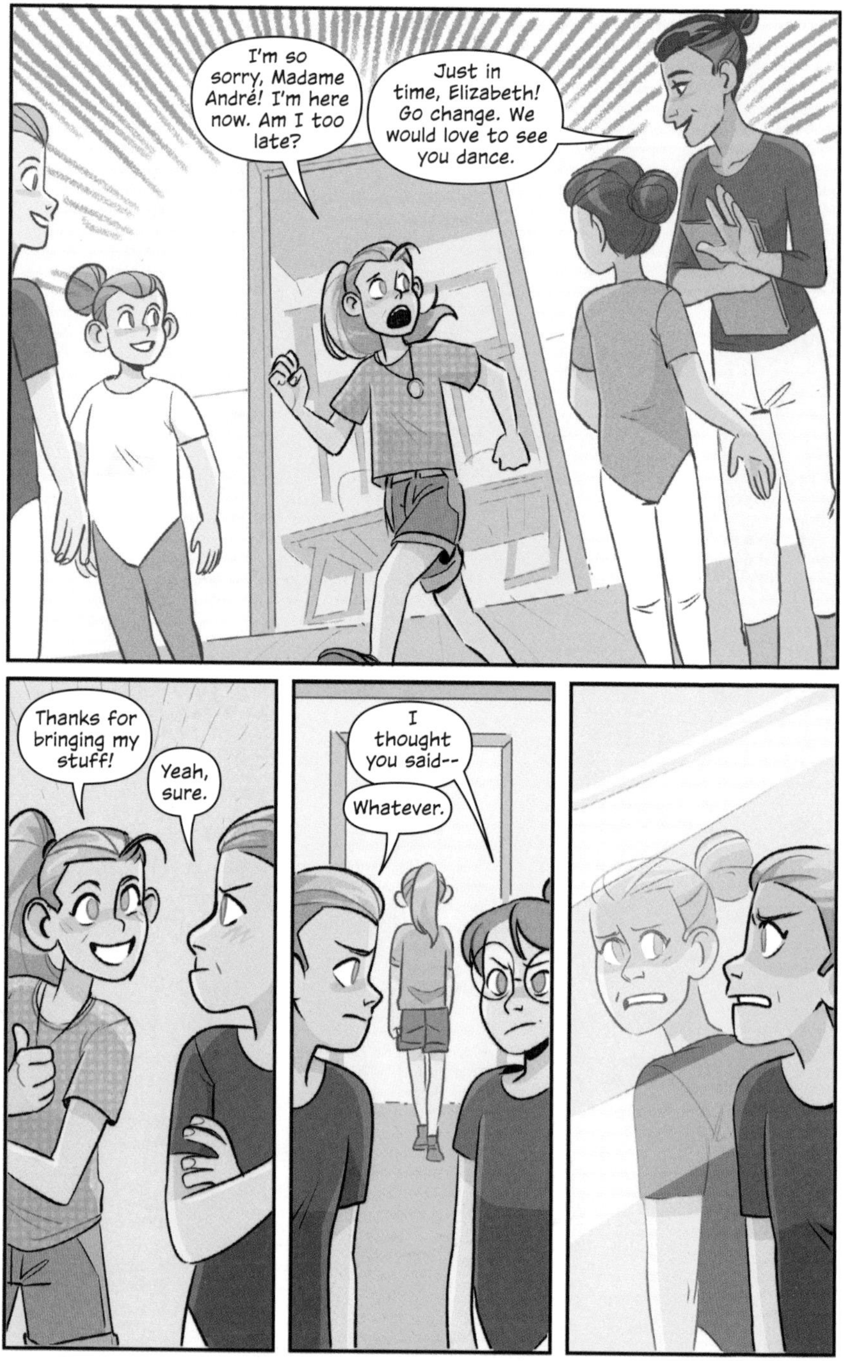
I'm so sorry, Madame André! I'm here now. Am I too late?
Just in time, Elizabeth! Go change. We would love to see you dance.
Thanks for bringing my stuff!
Yeah, sure.
I thought you said--
Whatever.

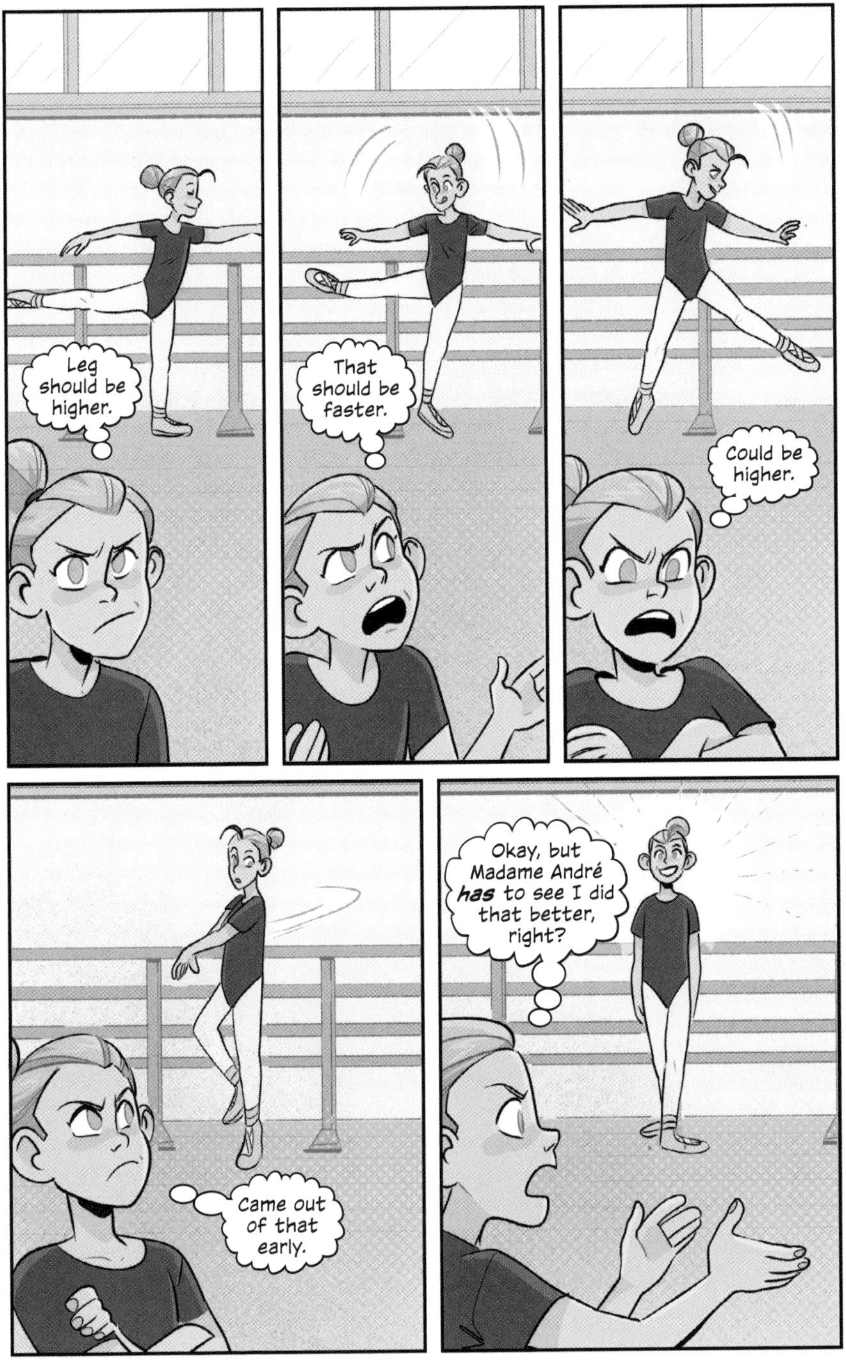
Leg should be higher.
That should be faster.
Could be higher.
Came out of that early.
Okay, but Madame André ***has*** to see I did that better, right?

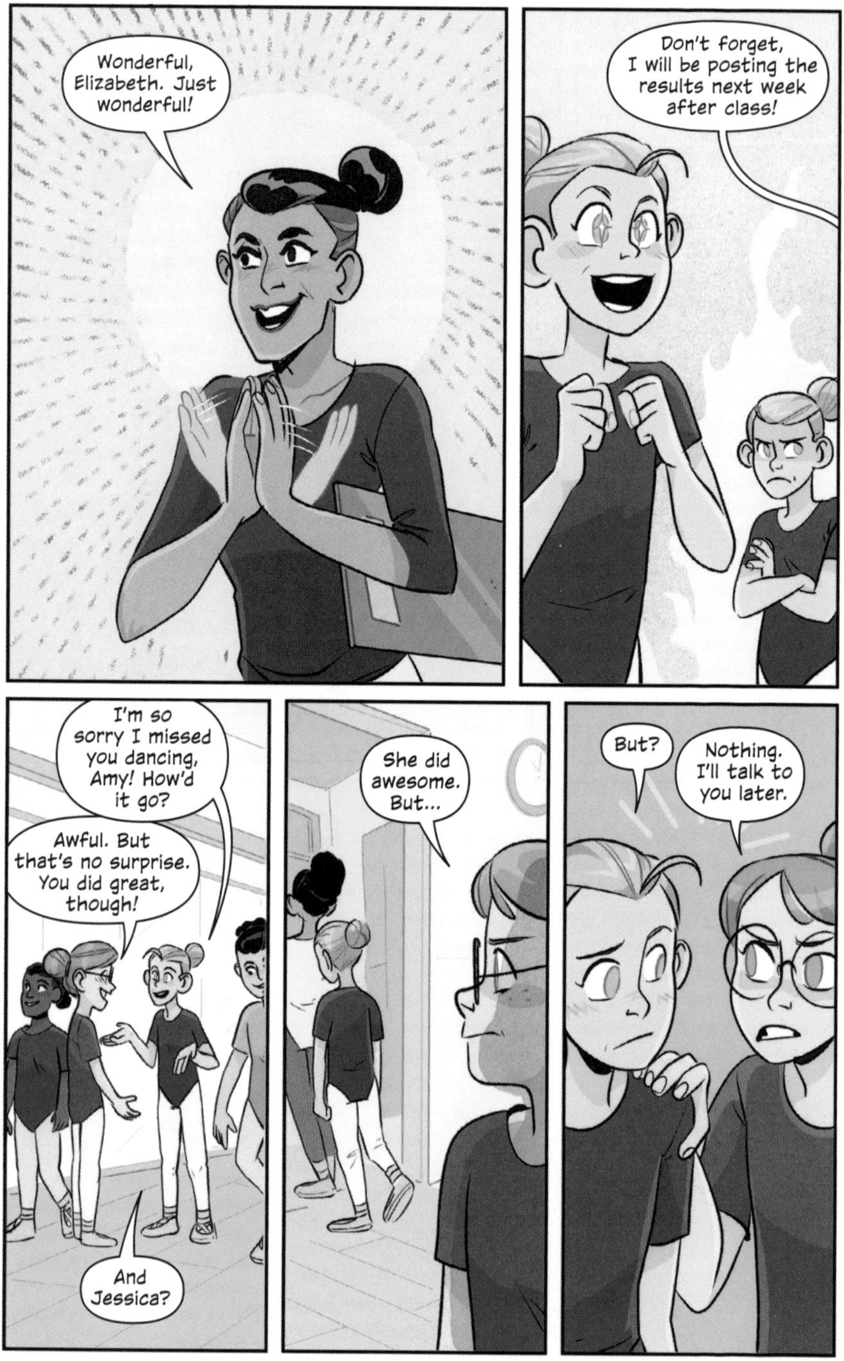
Wonderful, Elizabeth. Just wonderful!
Don't forget, I will be posting the results next week after class!
I'm so sorry I missed you dancing, Amy! How'd it go?
Awful. But that's no surprise. You did great, though!
And Jessica?
She did awesome. But...
But?
Nothing. I'll talk to you later.

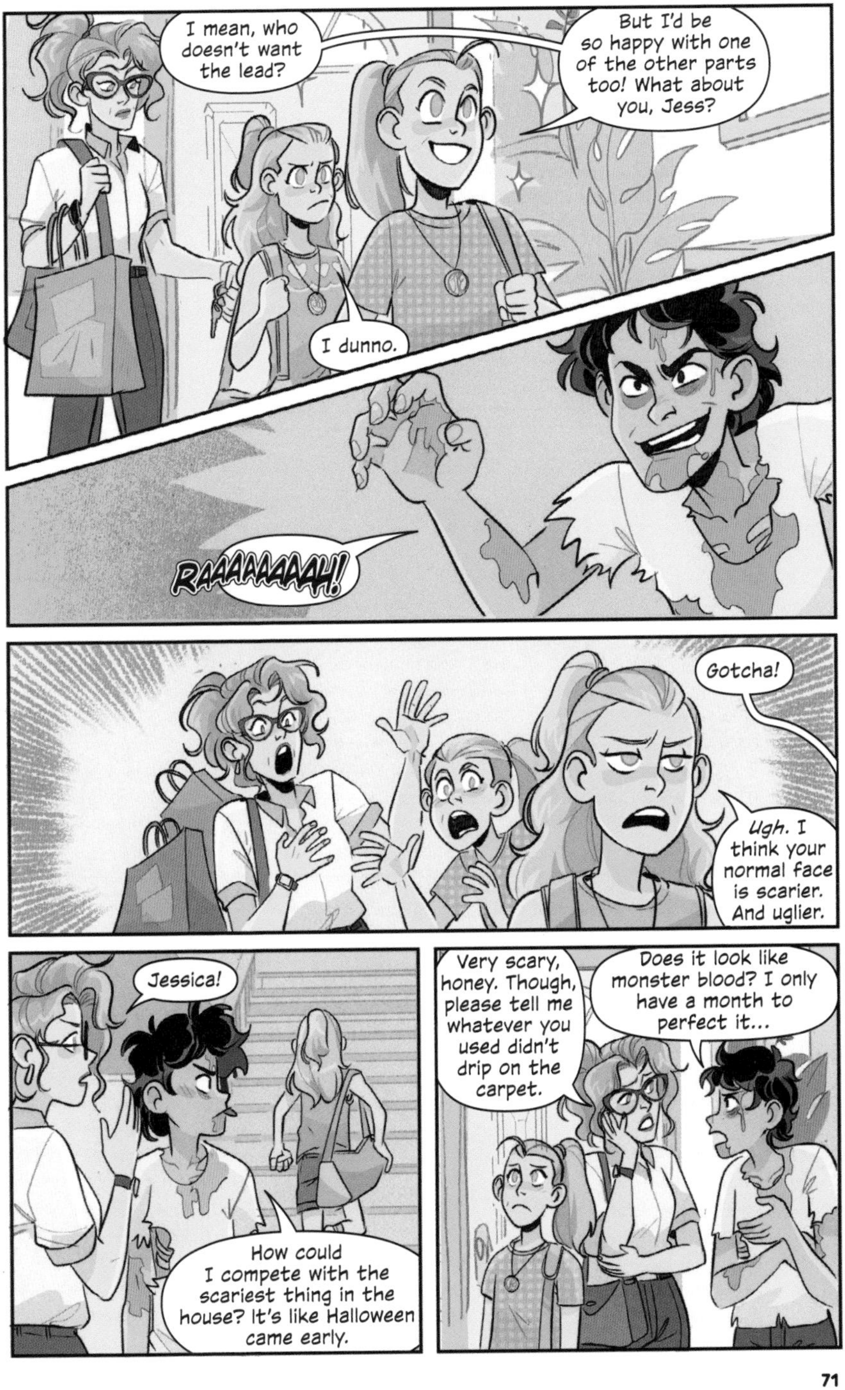
I mean, who doesn't want the lead?
But I'd be so happy with one of the other parts too! What about you, Jess?
I dunno.
RAAAAAAAAH!
Gotcha!
Ugh. I think your normal face is scarier. And uglier.
Jessica!
How could I compete with the scariest thing in the house? It's like Halloween came early.
Very scary, honey. Though, please tell me whatever you used didn't drip on the carpet.
Does it look like monster blood? I only have a month to perfect it...

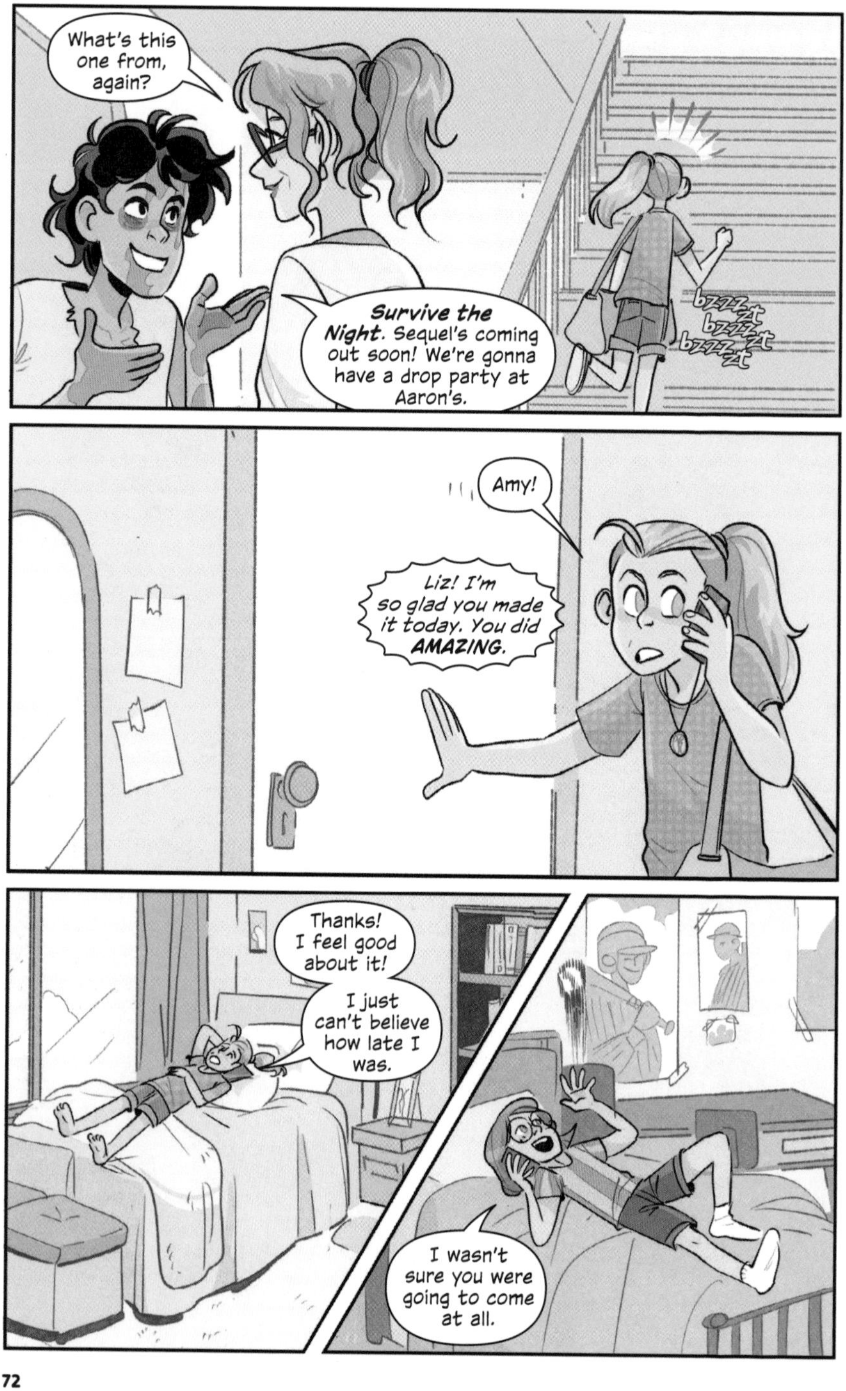
What's this one from, again?
Survive the Night. Sequel's coming out soon! We're gonna have a drop party at Aaron's.
bzzzzt bzzzzt bzzzzt
Amy!
Liz! I'm so glad you made it today. You did AMAZING.
Thanks! I feel good about it!
I just can't believe how late I was.
I wasn't sure you were going to come at all.

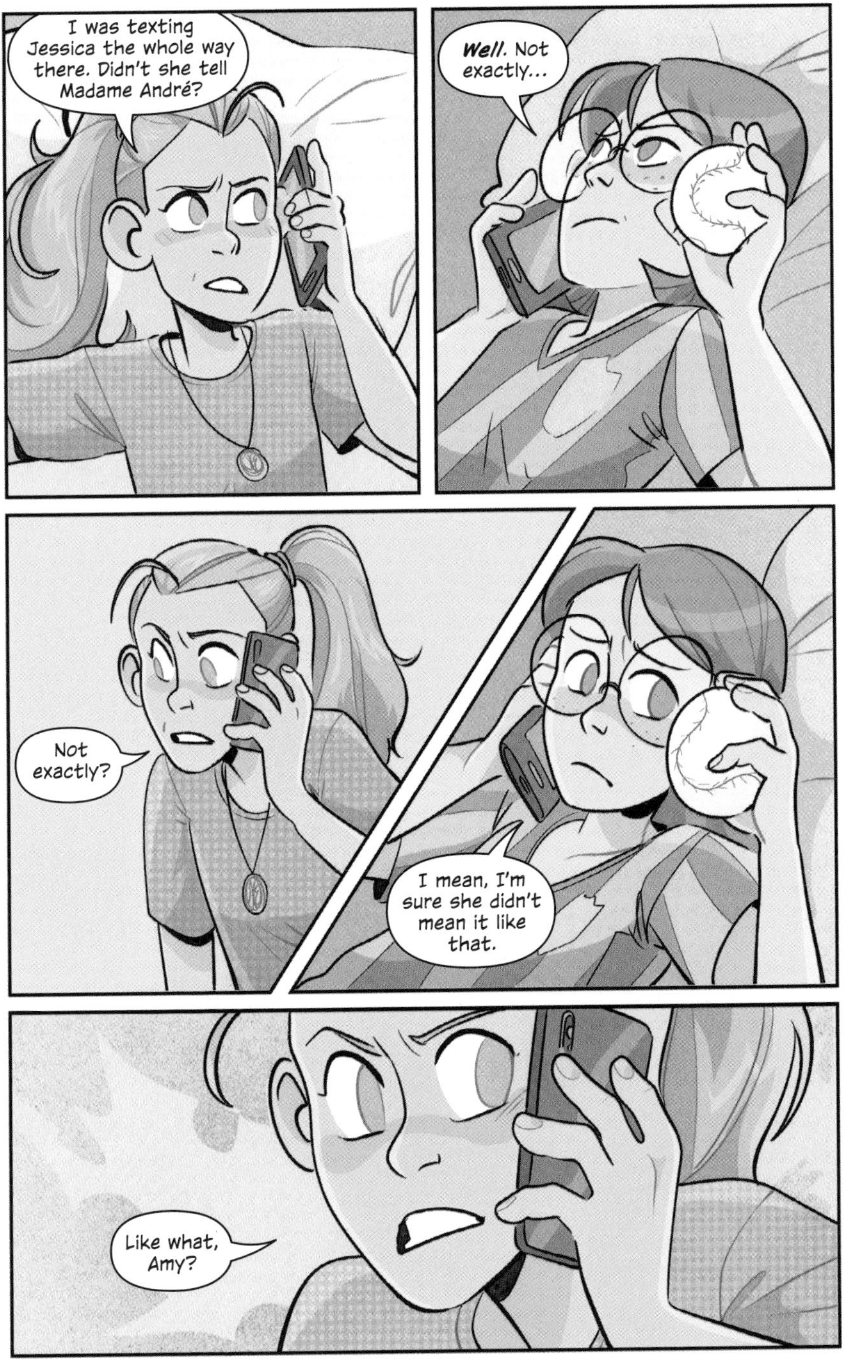
I was texting Jessica the whole way there. Didn't she tell Madame André?
Well. Not exactly...
Not exactly?
I mean, I'm sure she didn't mean it like that.
Like what, Amy?

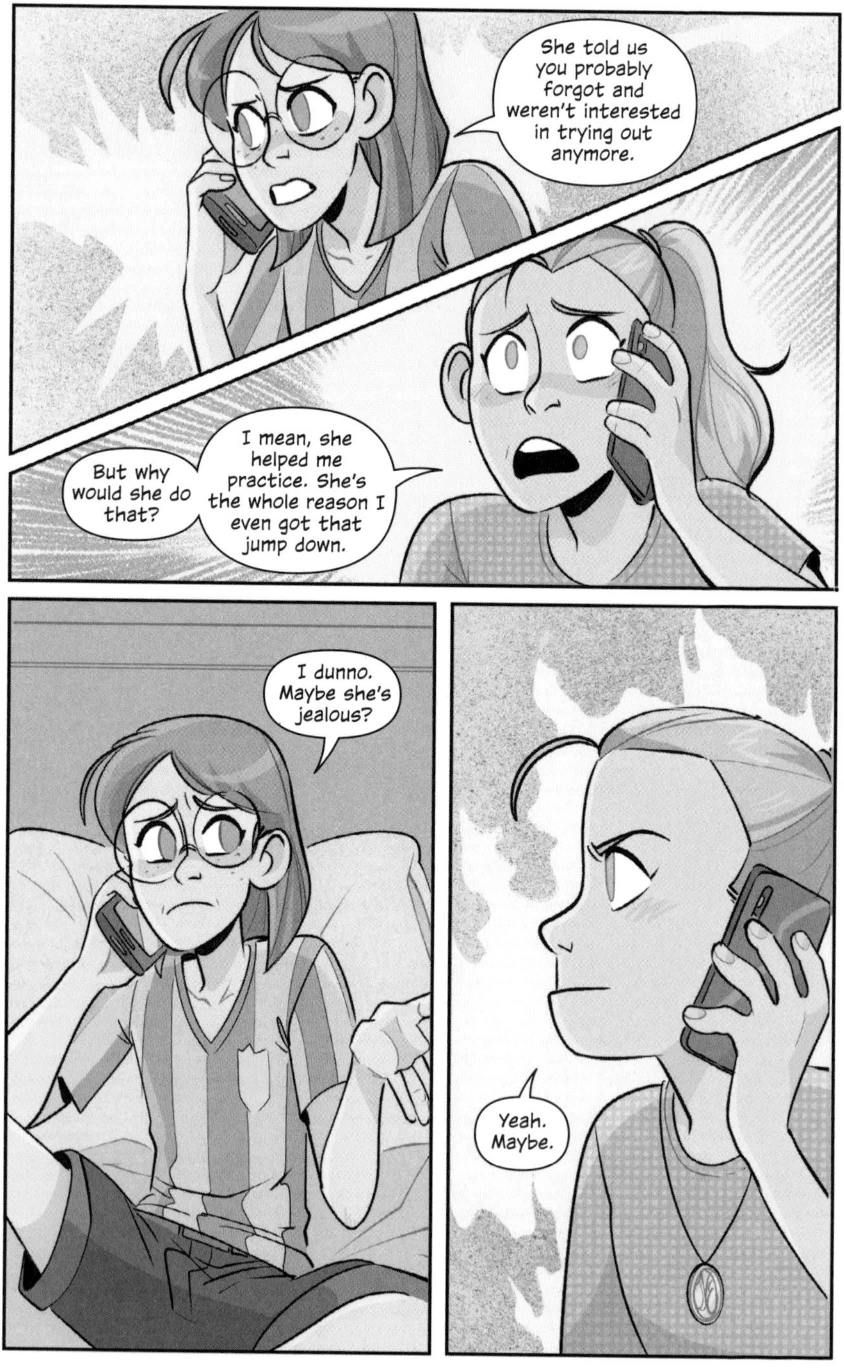
She told us you probably forgot and weren't interested in trying out anymore.
But why would she do that?
I mean, she helped me practice. She's the whole reason I even got that jump down.
I dunno. Maybe she's jealous?
Yeah. Maybe.

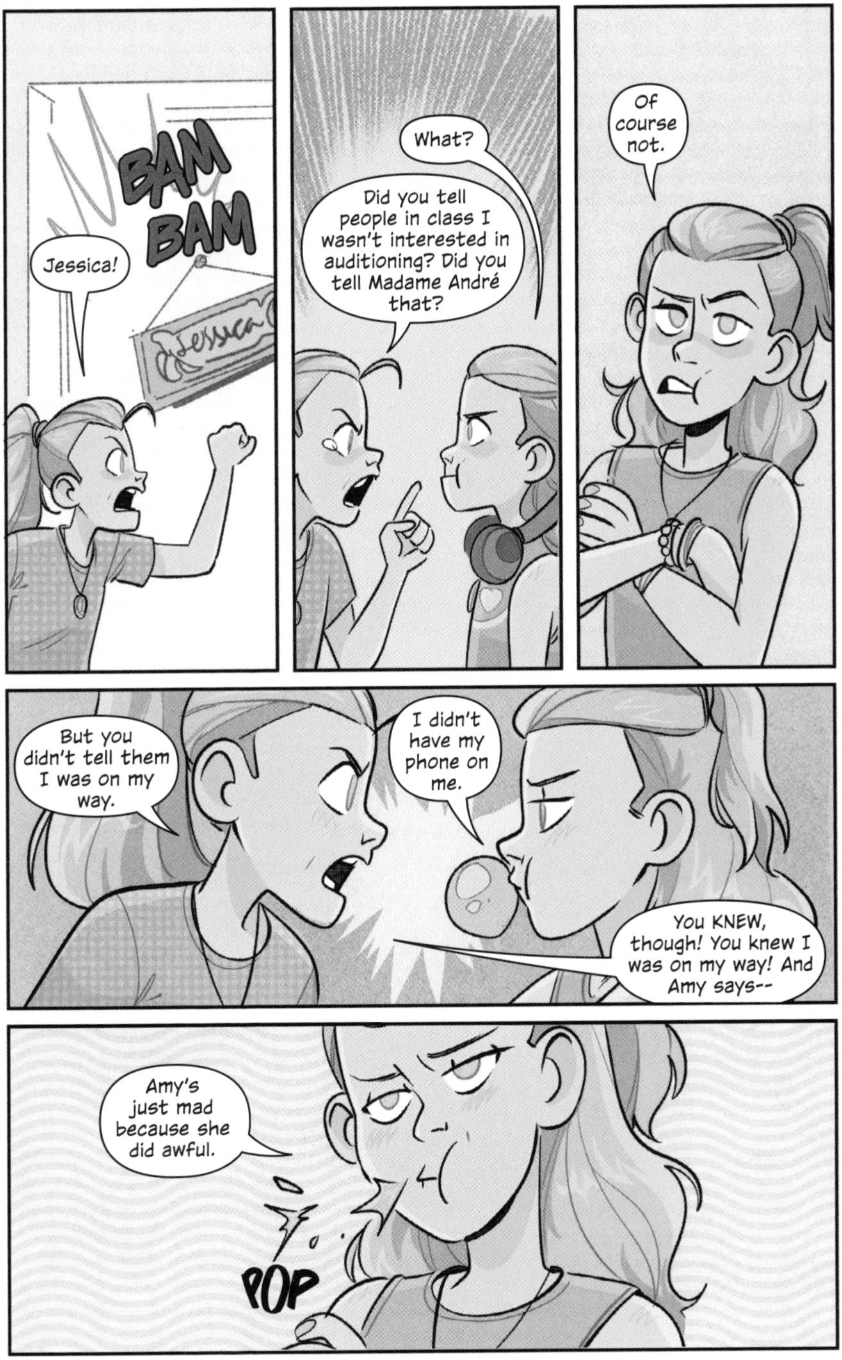
BAM
BAM
Jessica!
Jessica
Did you tell people in class I wasn't interested in auditioning? Did you tell Madame André that?
What?
Of course not.
But you didn't tell them I was on my way.
I didn't have my phone on me.
You KNEW, though! You knew I was on my way! And Amy says--
Amy's just mad because she did awful.
POP

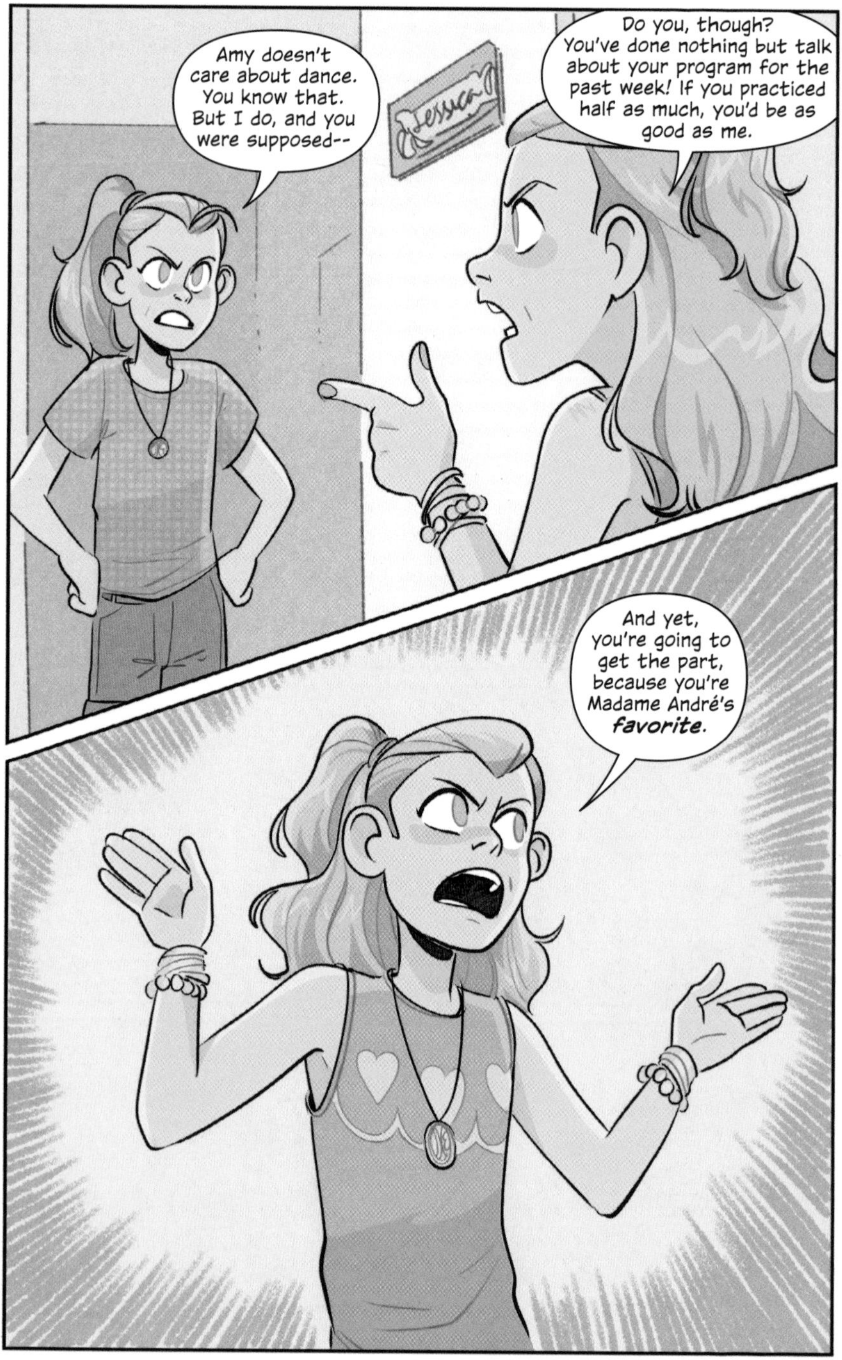
Amy doesn't care about dance. You know that. But I do, and you were supposed--
Do you, though? You've done nothing but talk about your program for the past week! If you practiced half as much, you'd be as good as me.
And yet, you're going to get the part, because you're Madame André's *favorite*.

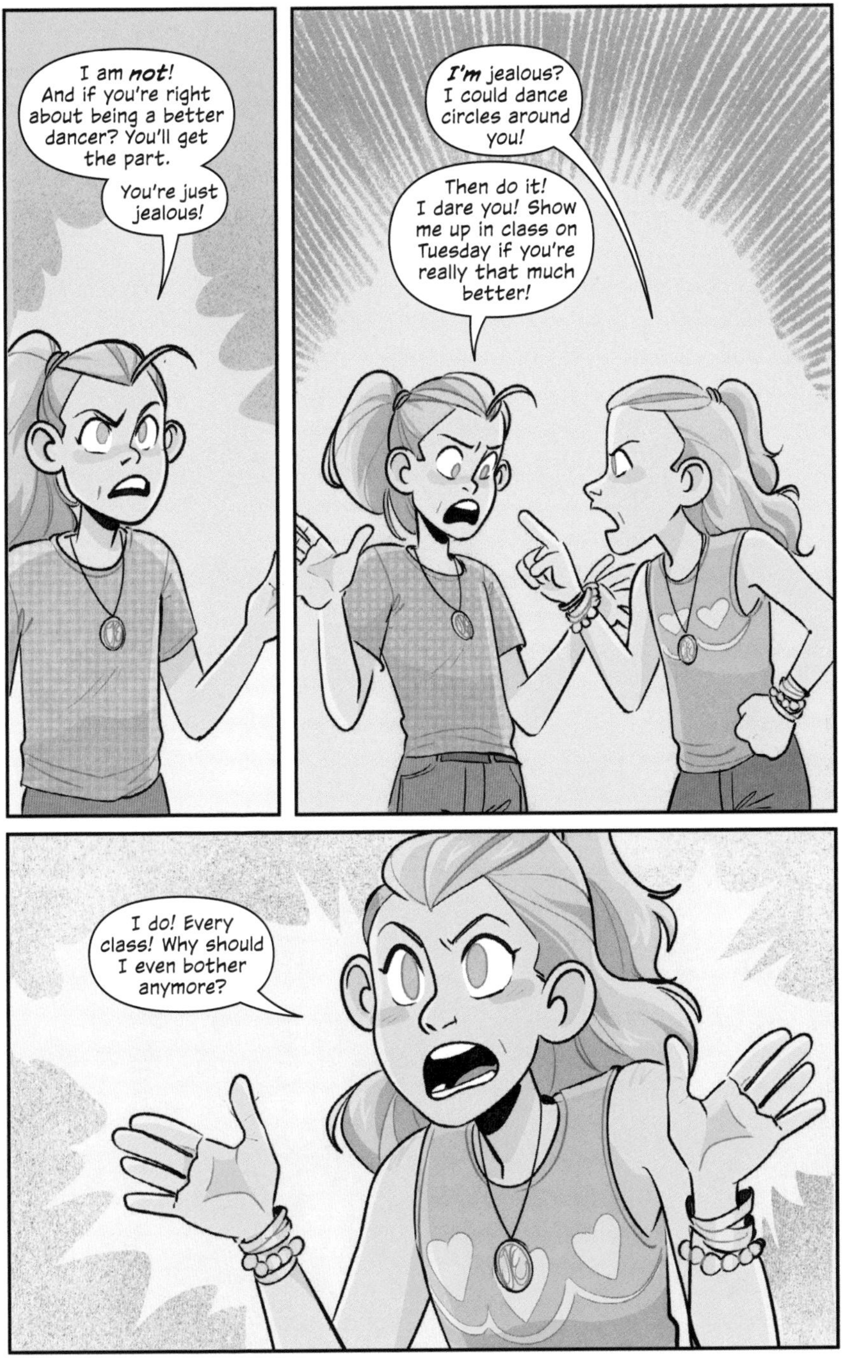
I am ***not***!
And if you're right about being a better dancer? You'll get the part.
You're just jealous!
I'm jealous? I could dance circles around you!
Then do it! I dare you! Show me up in class on Tuesday if you're really that much better!
I do! Every class! Why should I even bother anymore?

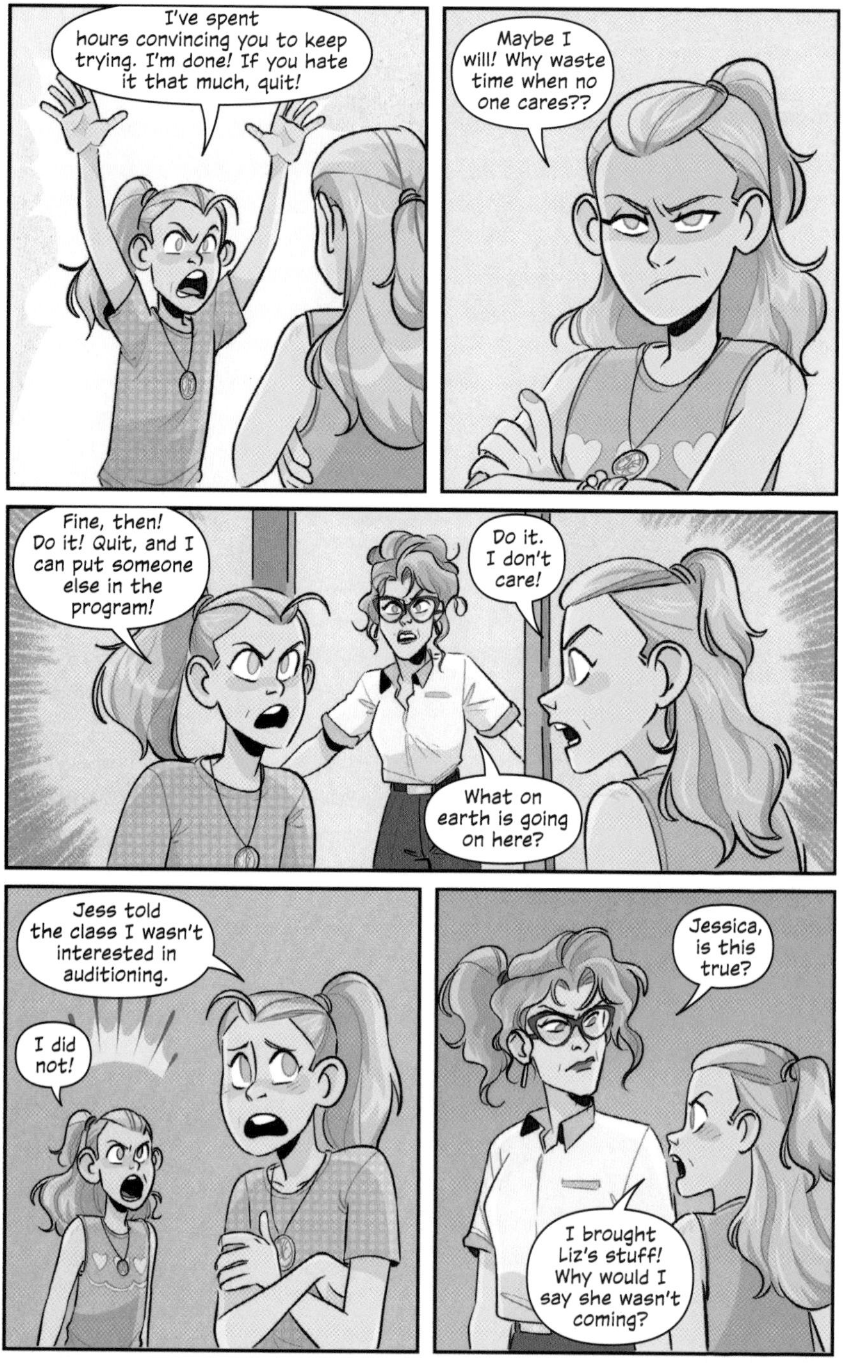
I've spent hours convincing you to keep trying. I'm done! If you hate it that much, quit!
Maybe I will! Why waste time when no one cares??
Fine, then! Do it! Quit, and I can put someone else in the program!
Do it. I don't care!
What on earth is going on here?
Jess told the class I wasn't interested in auditioning.
I did not!
Jessica, is this true?
I brought Liz's stuff! Why would I say she wasn't coming?

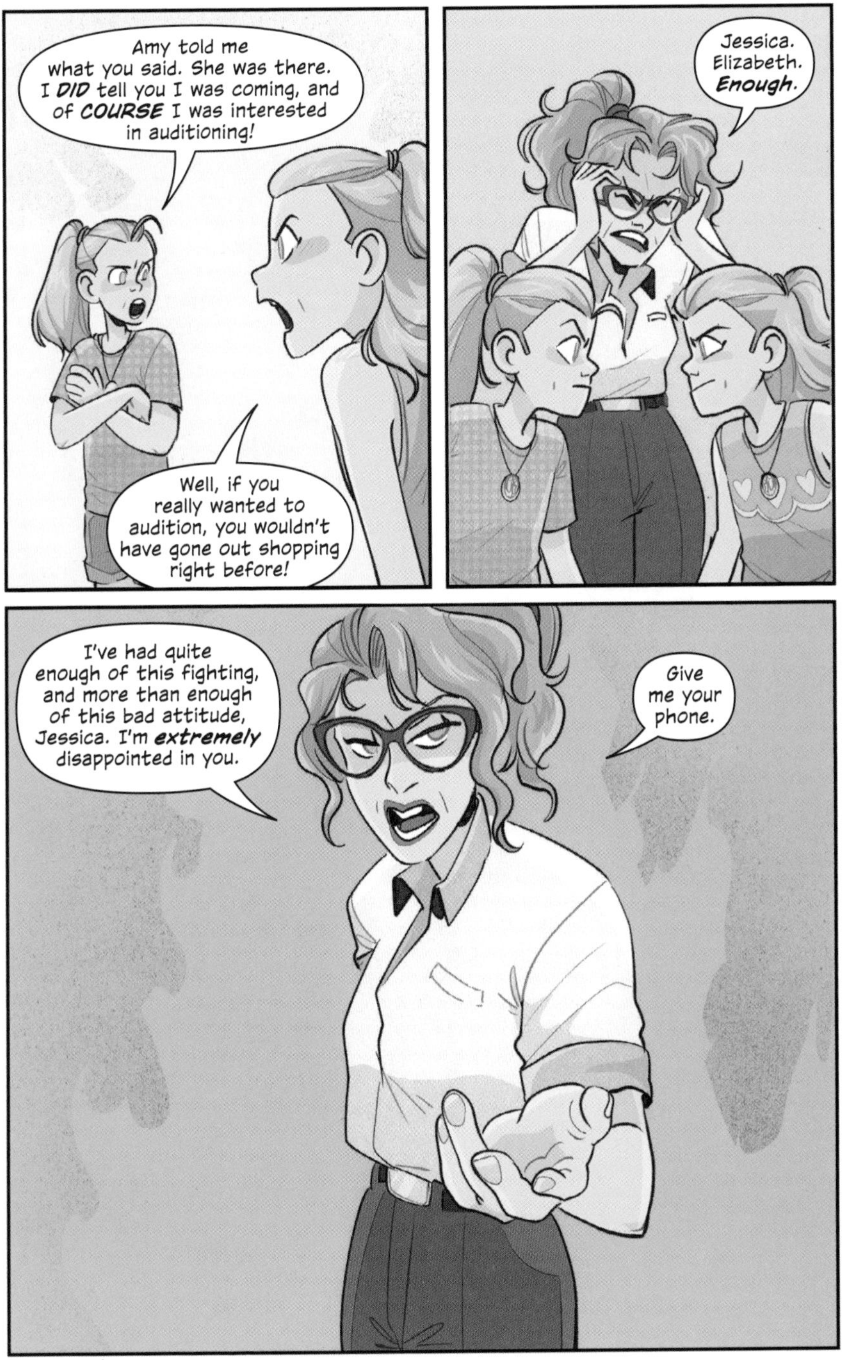
Amy told me what you said. She was there. I DID tell you I was coming, and of COURSE I was interested in auditioning!
Well, if you really wanted to audition, you wouldn't have gone out shopping right before!
Jessica. Elizabeth. Enough.
I've had quite enough of this fighting, and more than enough of this bad attitude, Jessica. I'm extremely disappointed in you.
Give me your phone.

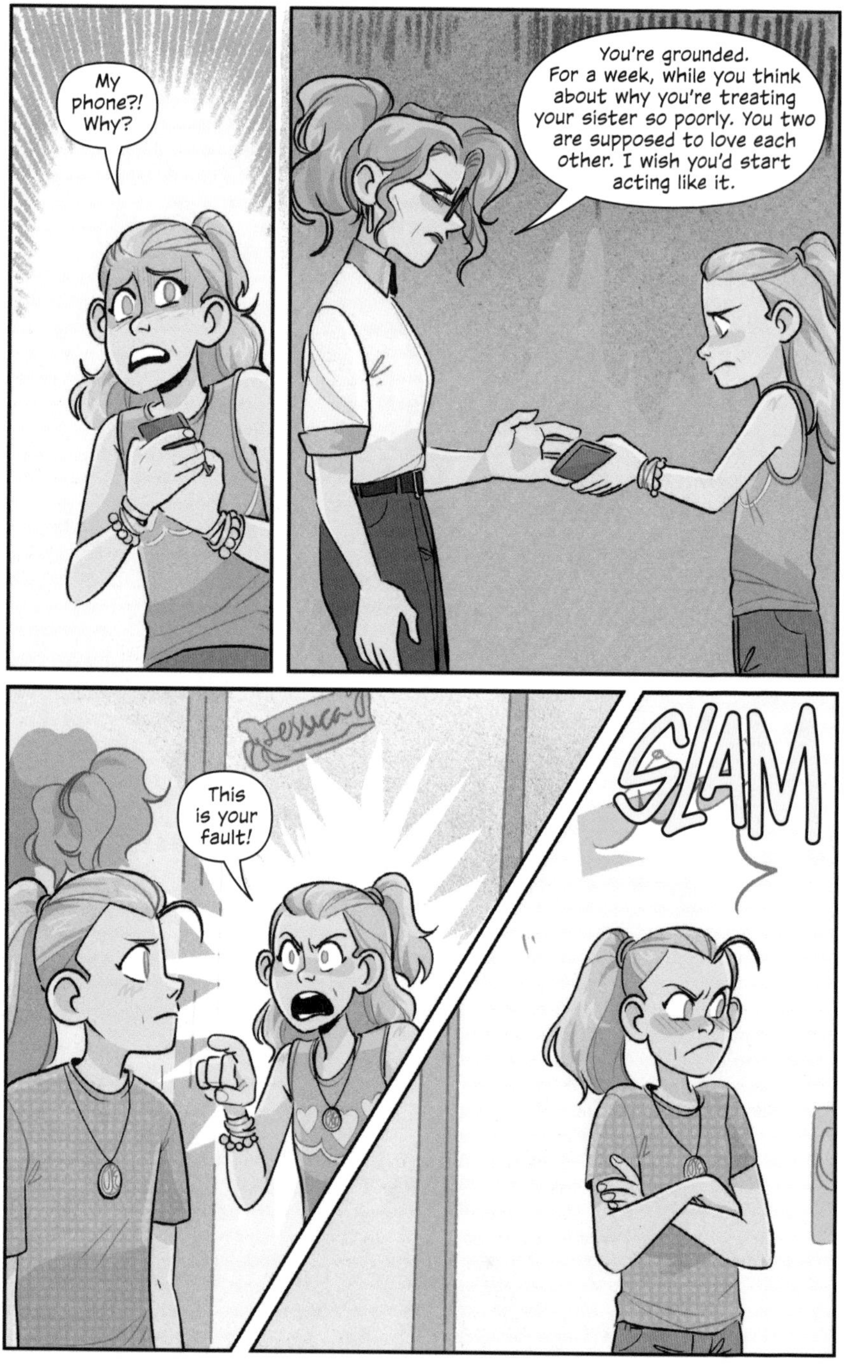
My phone?! Why?
You're grounded. For a week, while you think about why you're treating your sister so poorly. You two are supposed to love each other. I wish you'd start acting like it.
Jessica
This is your fault!
SLAM

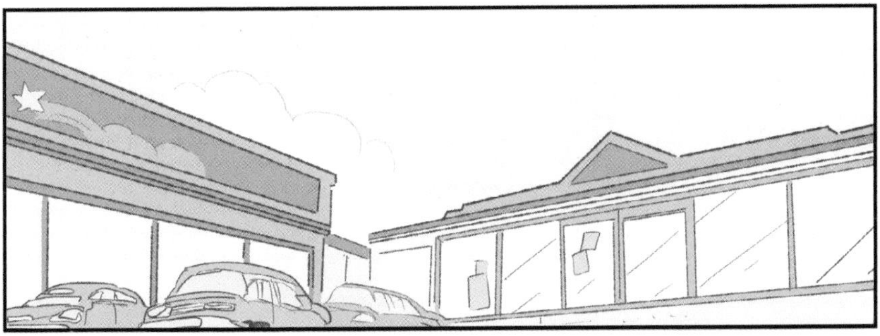

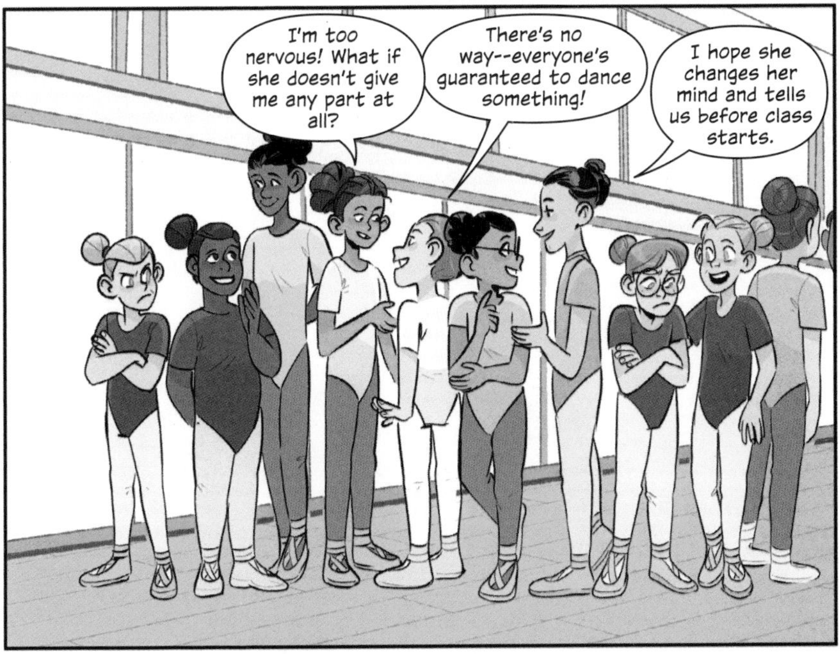

I'm too nervous! What if she doesn't give me any part at all?
There's no way--everyone's guaranteed to dance something!
I hope she changes her mind and tells us before class starts.

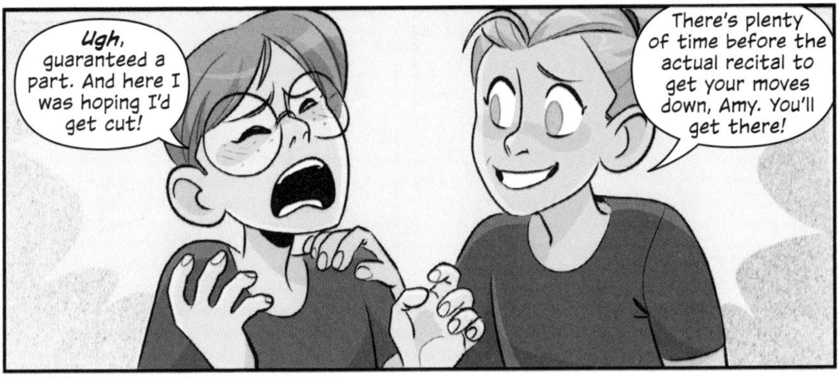

Ugh, guaranteed a part. And here I was hoping I'd get cut!
There's plenty of time before the actual recital to get your moves down, Amy. You'll get there!

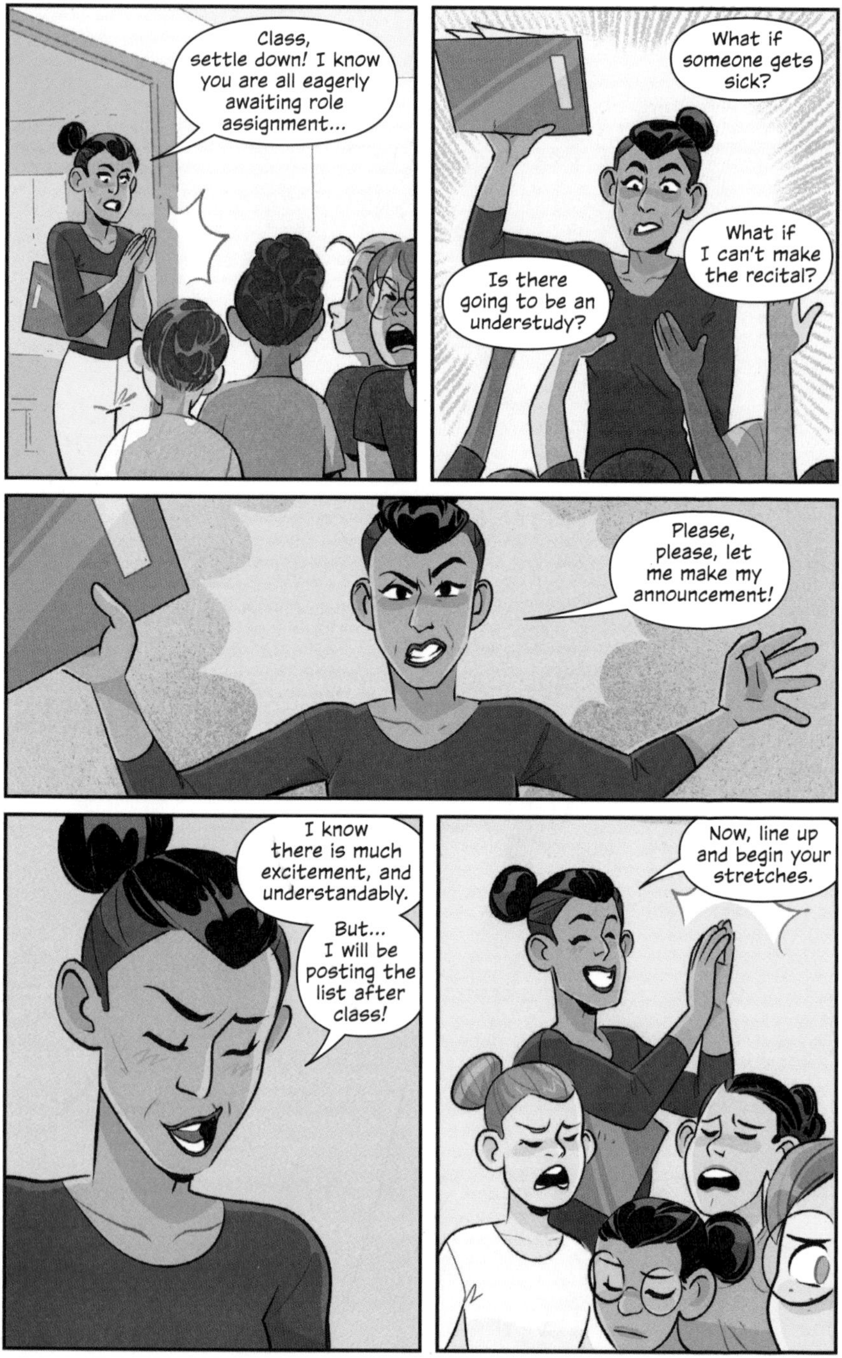
Class, settle down! I know you are all eagerly awaiting role assignment...
What if someone gets sick?
Is there going to be an understudy?
What if I can't make the recital?
Please, please, let me make my announcement!
I know there is much excitement, and understandably.
But... I will be posting the list after class!
Now, line up and begin your stretches.

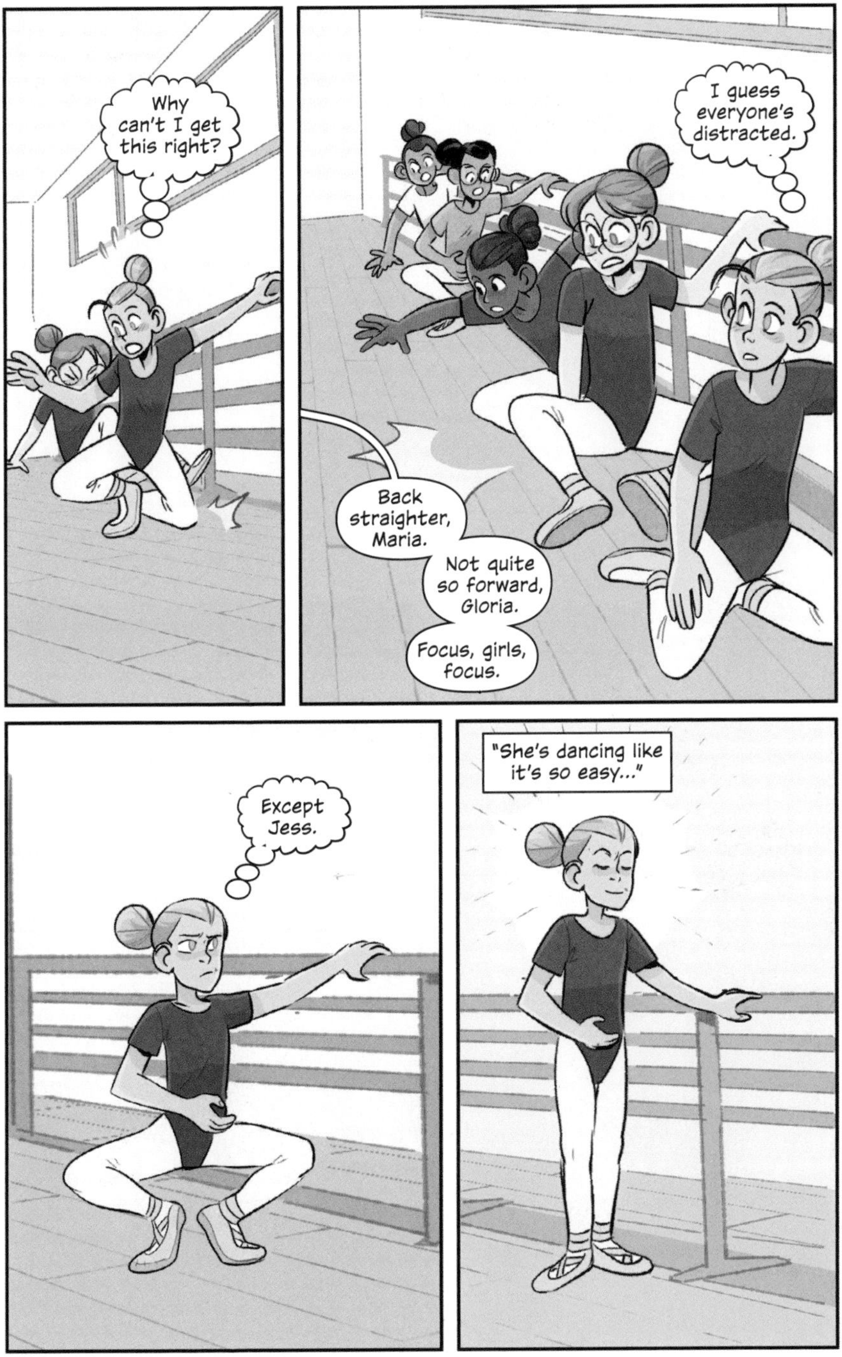
Why can't I get this right?
I guess everyone's distracted.
Back straighter, Maria.
Not quite so forward, Gloria.
Focus, girls, focus.
Except Jess.
"She's dancing like it's so easy..."

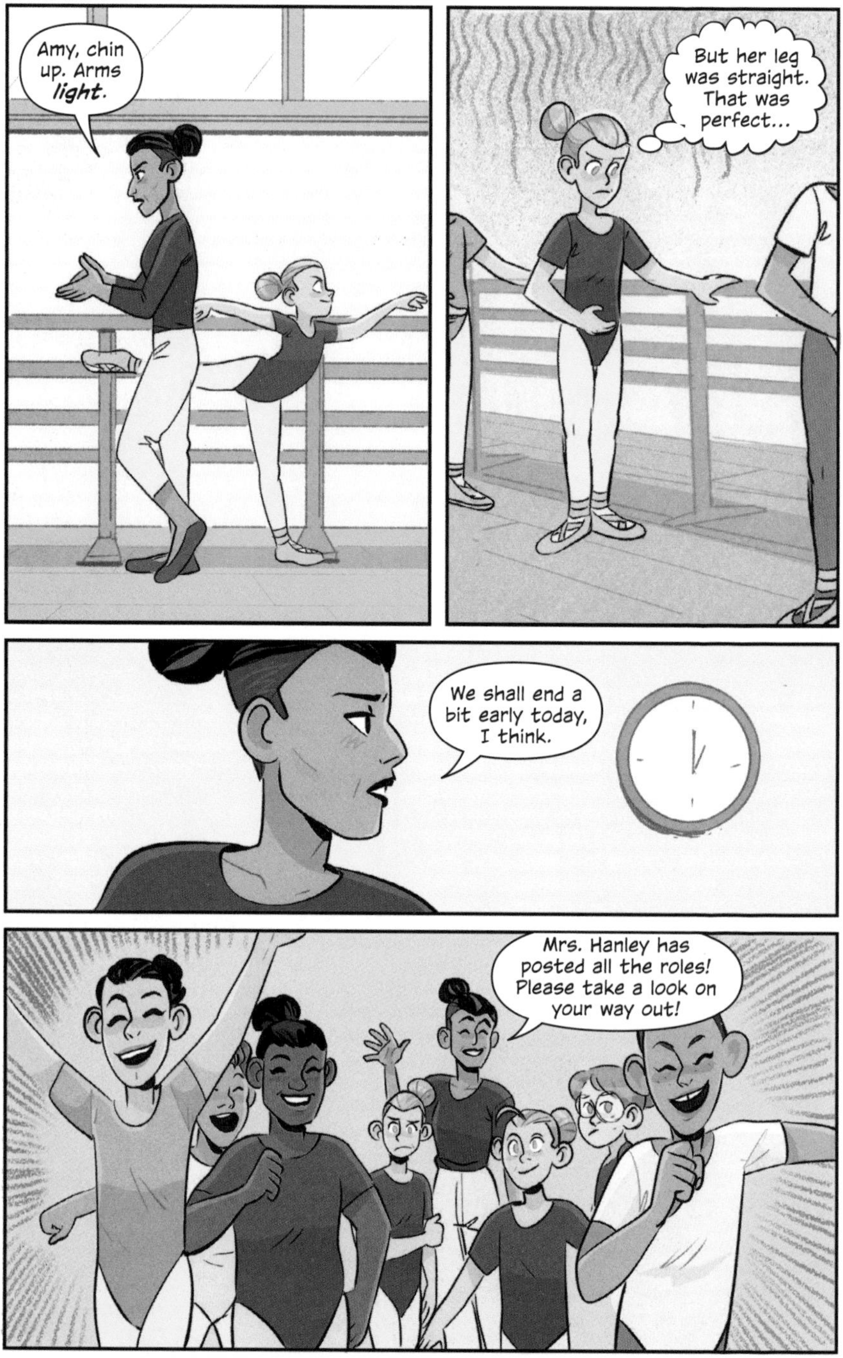
Amy, chin up. Arms *light*.
But her leg was straight. That was perfect...
We shall end a bit early today, I think.
Mrs. Hanley has posted all the roles! Please take a look on your way out!

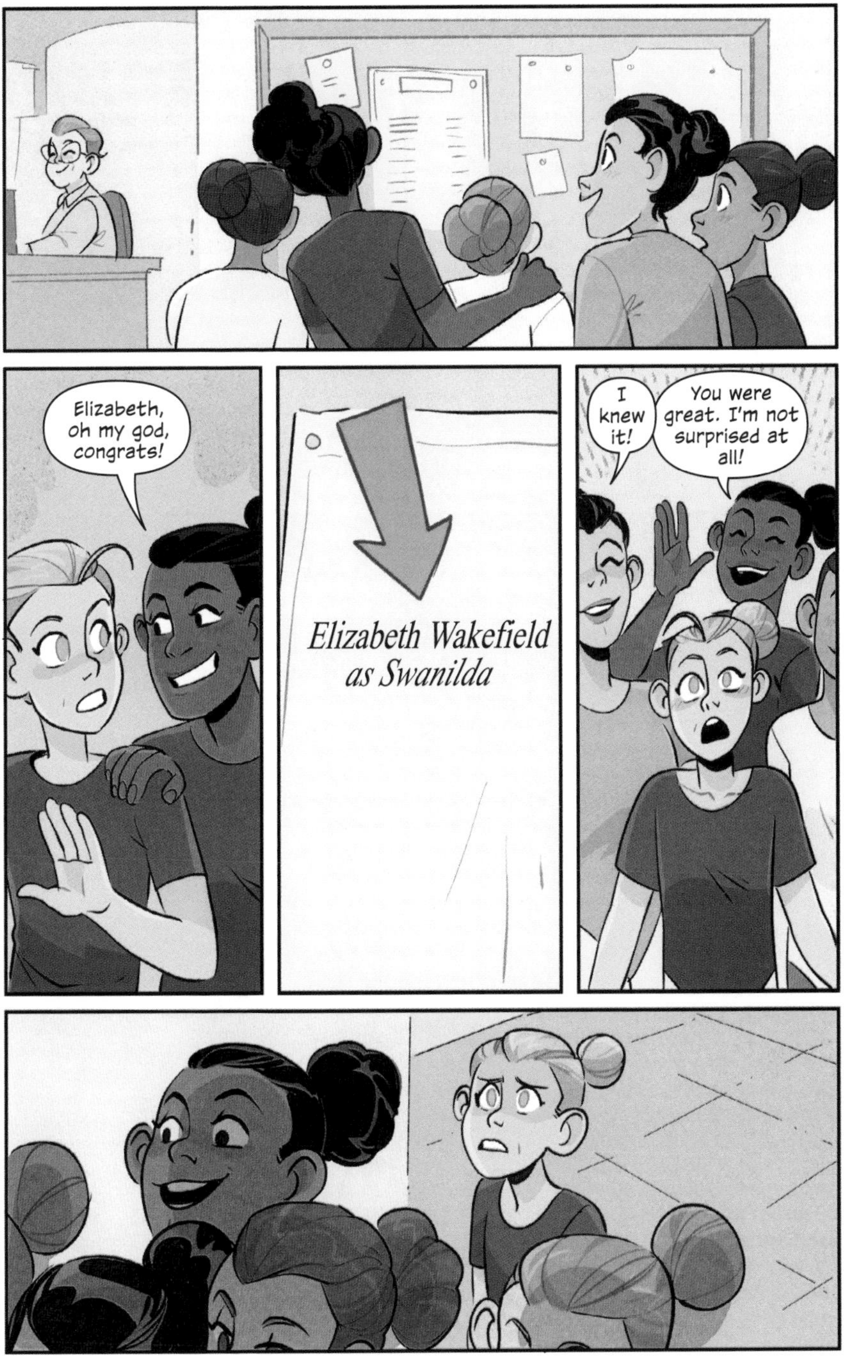
Elizabeth, oh my god, congrats!
Elizabeth Wakefield as Swanilda
I knew it!
You were great. I'm not surprised at all!

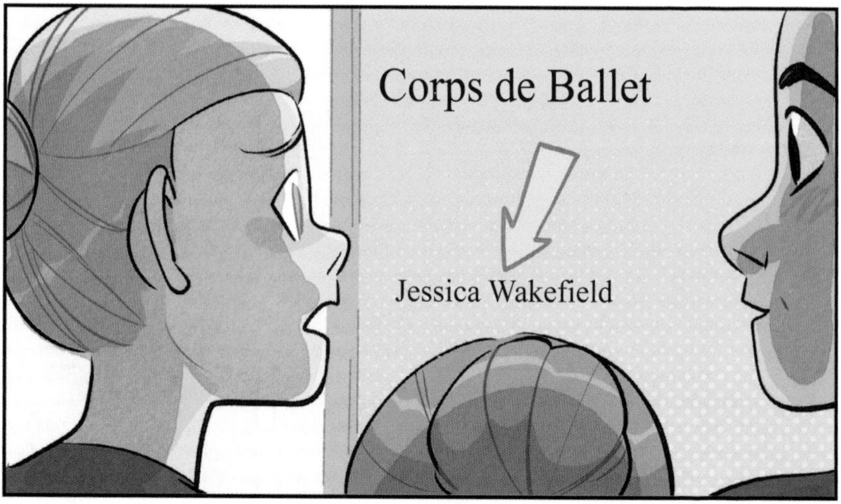
Corps de Ballet
Jessica Wakefield

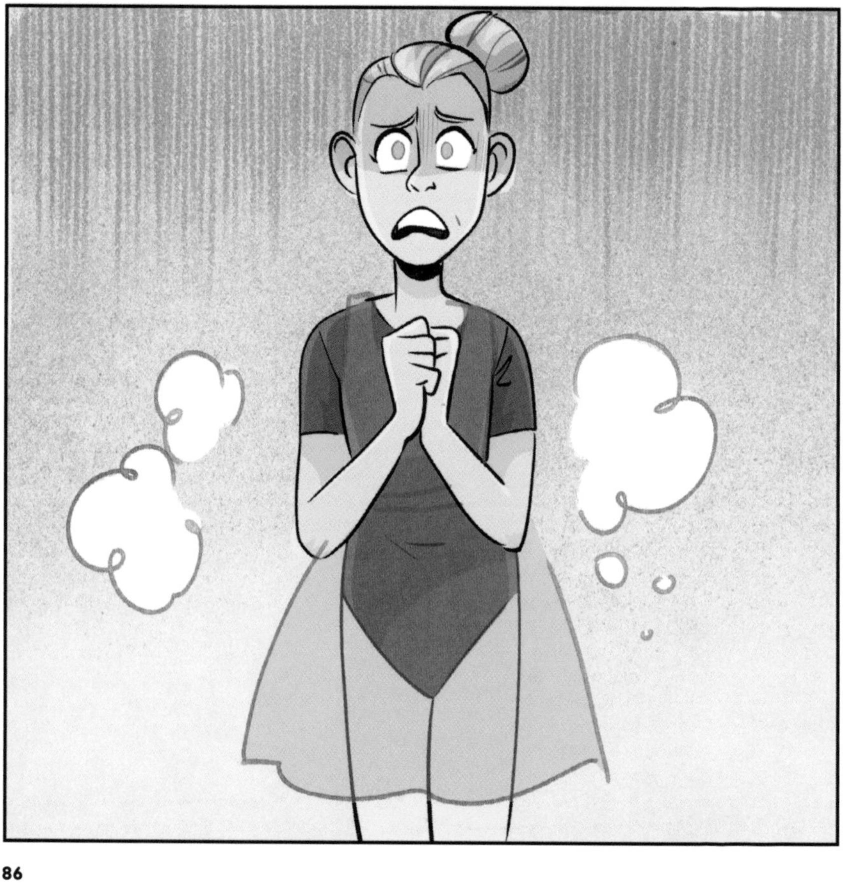

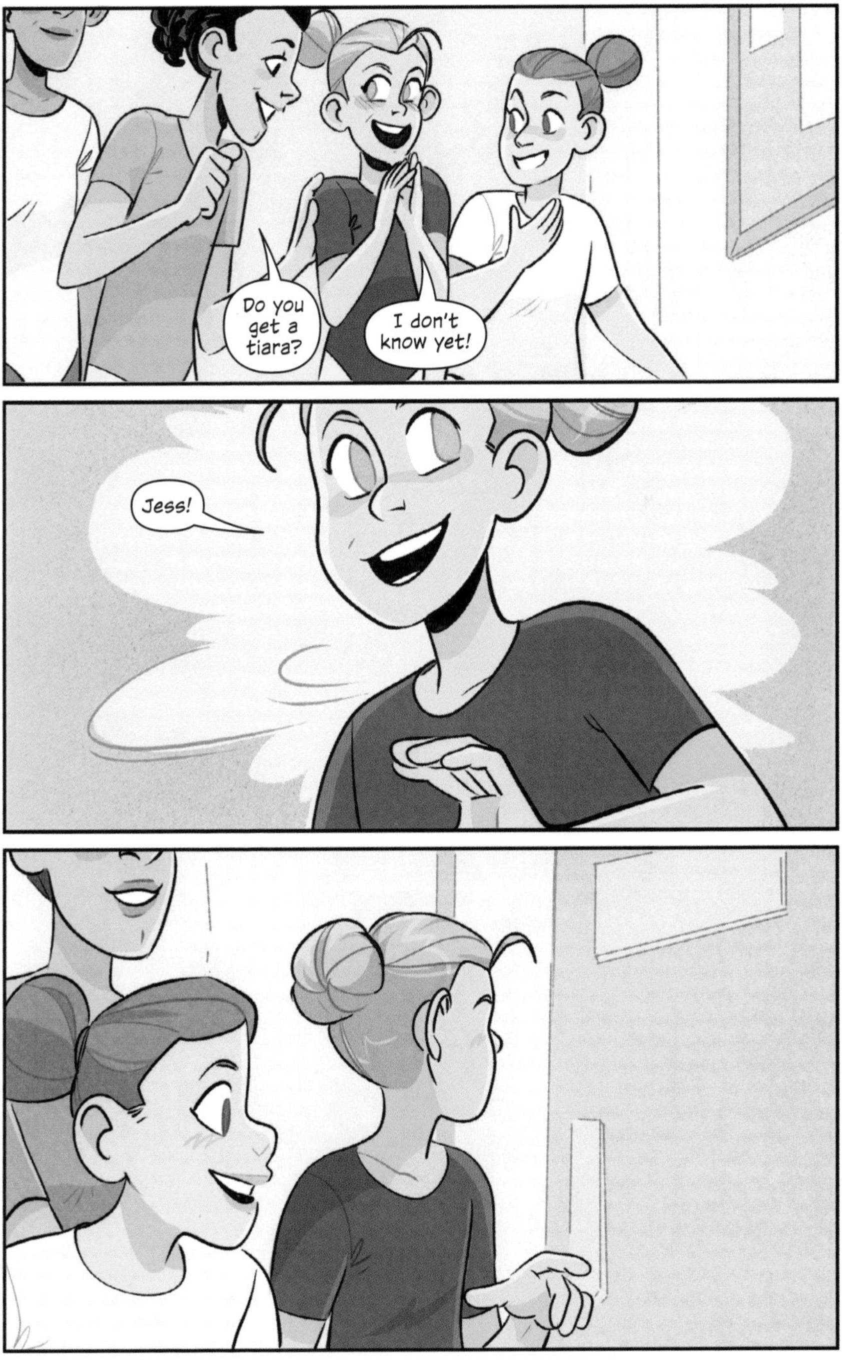
Do you get a tiara?
I don't know yet!
Jess!

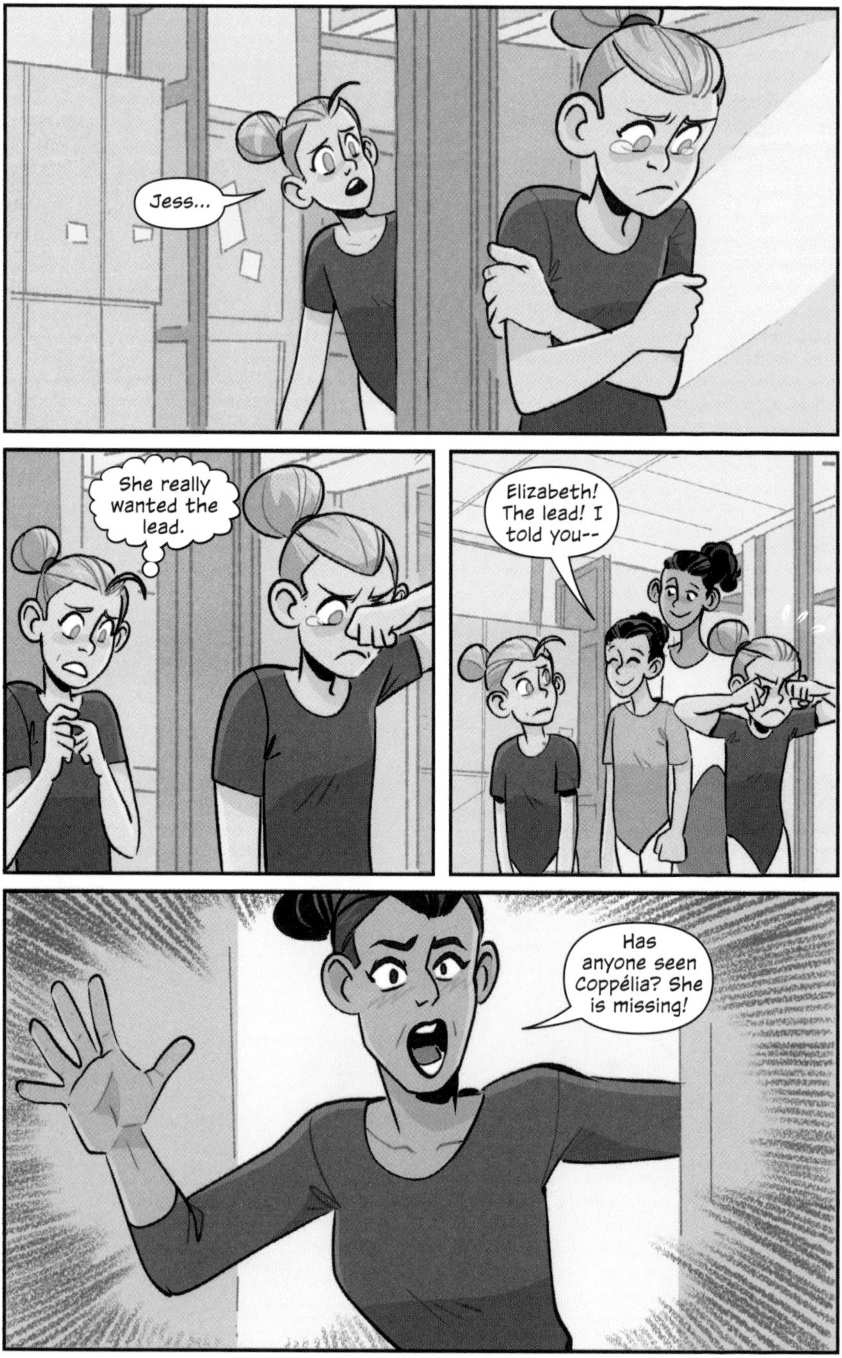
Jess...
She really wanted the lead.
Elizabeth! The lead! I told you--
Has anyone seen Coppélia? She is missing!

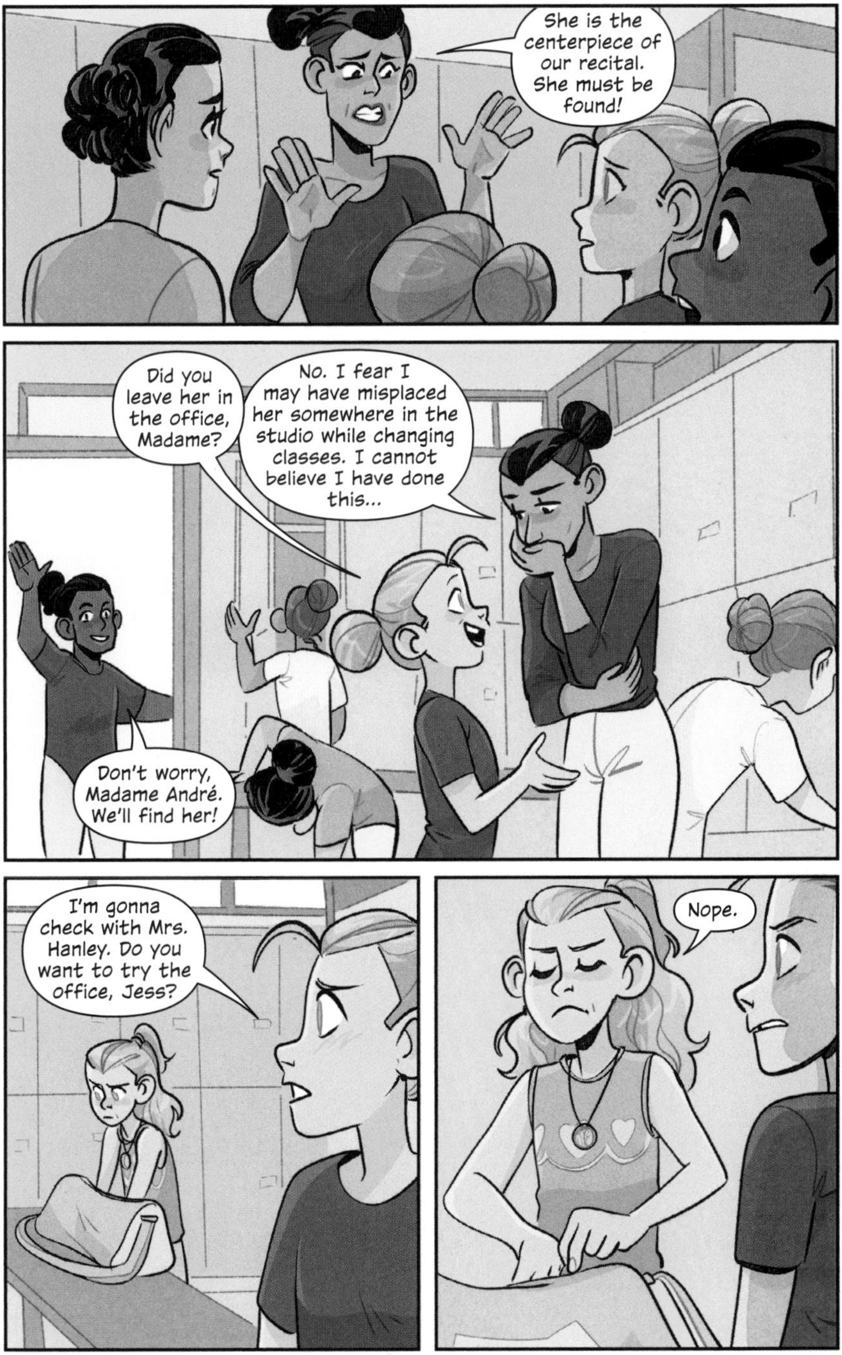
She is the centerpiece of our recital. She must be found!
Did you leave her in the office, Madame?
No. I fear I may have misplaced her somewhere in the studio while changing classes. I cannot believe I have done this...
Don't worry, Madame André. We'll find her!
I'm gonna check with Mrs. Hanley. Do you want to try the office, Jess?
Nope.

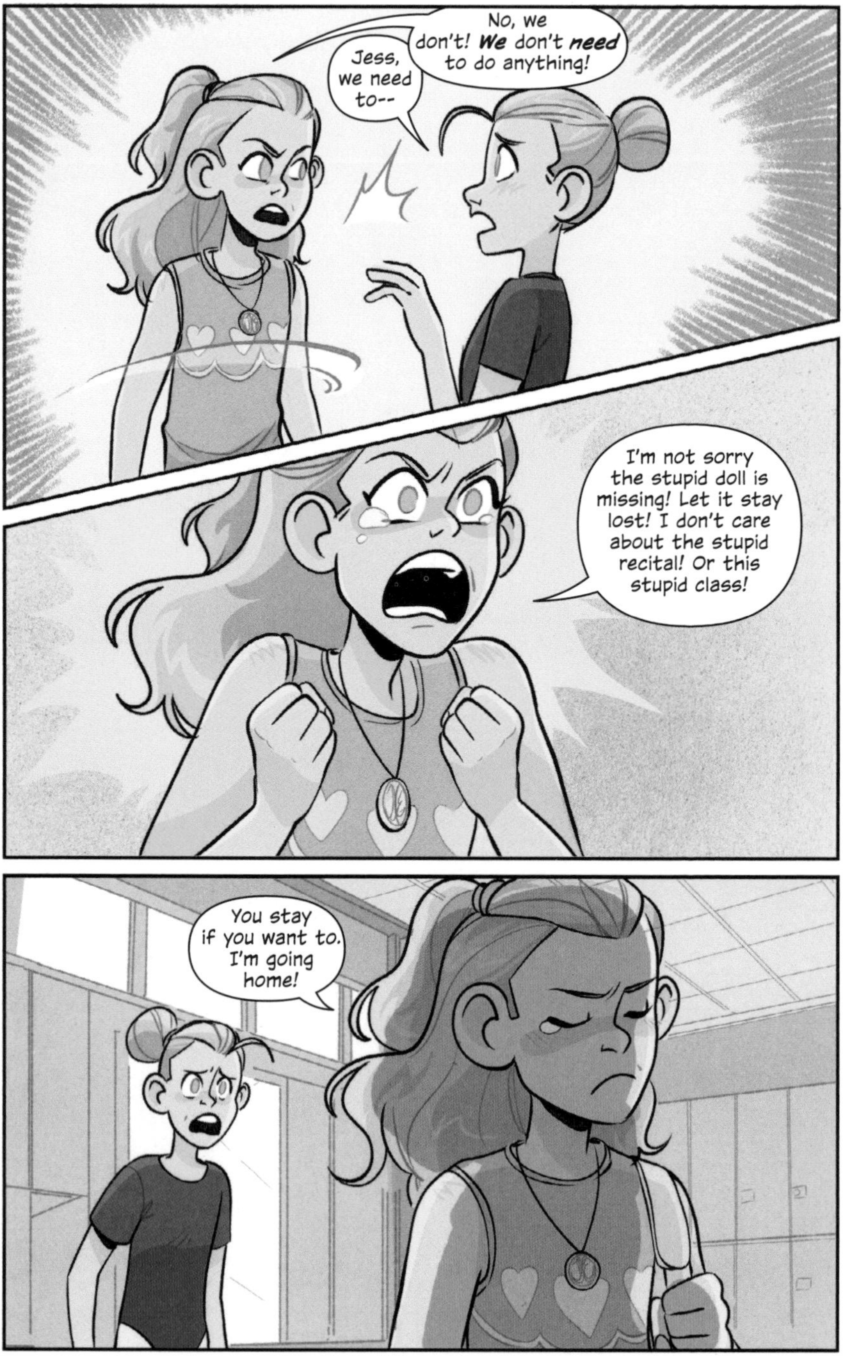
Jess, we need to--
No, we don't! **We** don't **need** to do anything!
I'm not sorry the stupid doll is missing! Let it stay lost! I don't care about the stupid recital! Or this stupid class!
You stay if you want to. I'm going home!

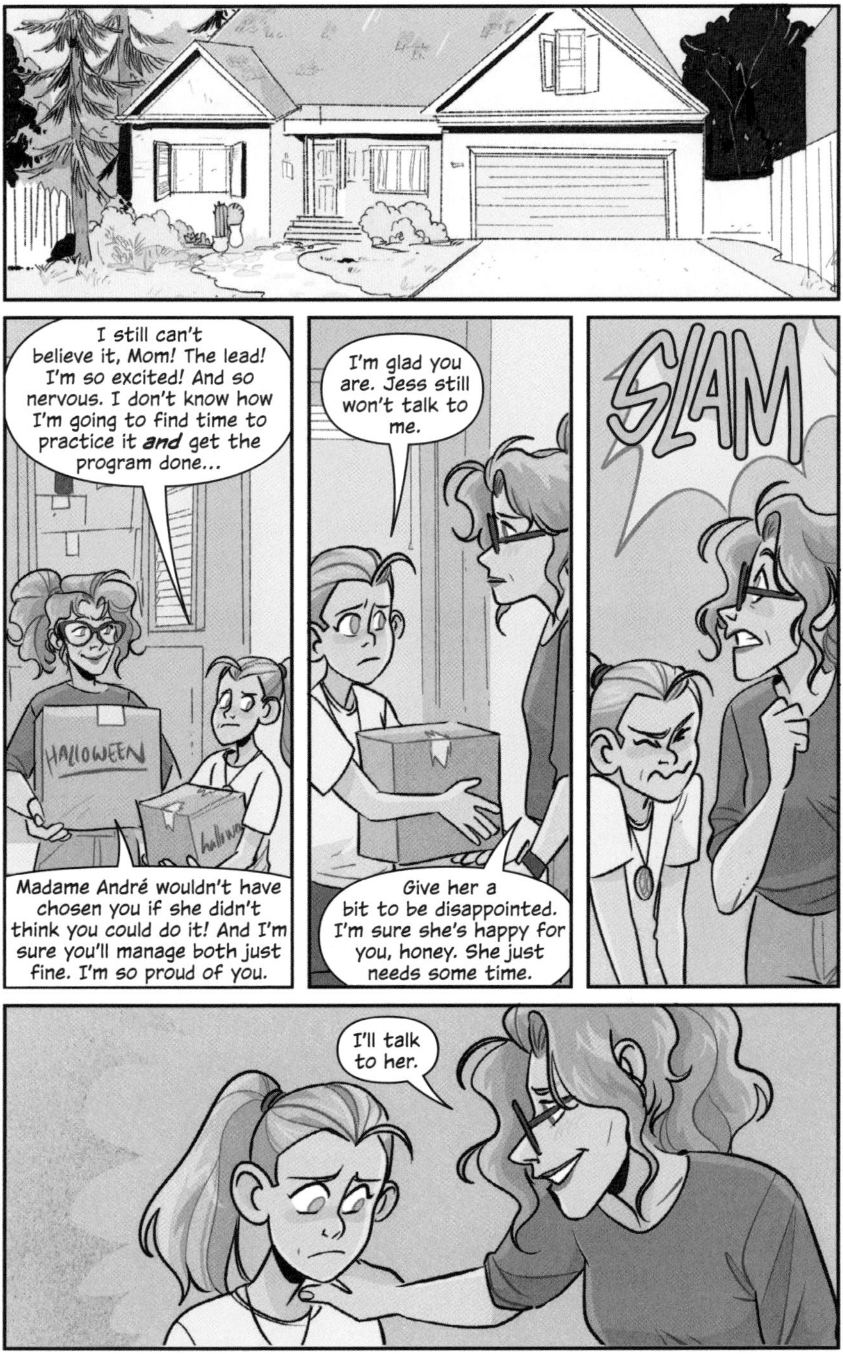
I still can't believe it, Mom! The lead! I'm so excited! And so nervous. I don't know how I'm going to find time to practice it *and* get the program done...
HALLOWEEN
Madame André wouldn't have chosen you if she didn't think you could do it! And I'm sure you'll manage both just fine. I'm so proud of you.
I'm glad you are. Jess still won't talk to me.
Give her a bit to be disappointed. I'm sure she's happy for you, honey. She just needs some time.
SLAM
I'll talk to her.

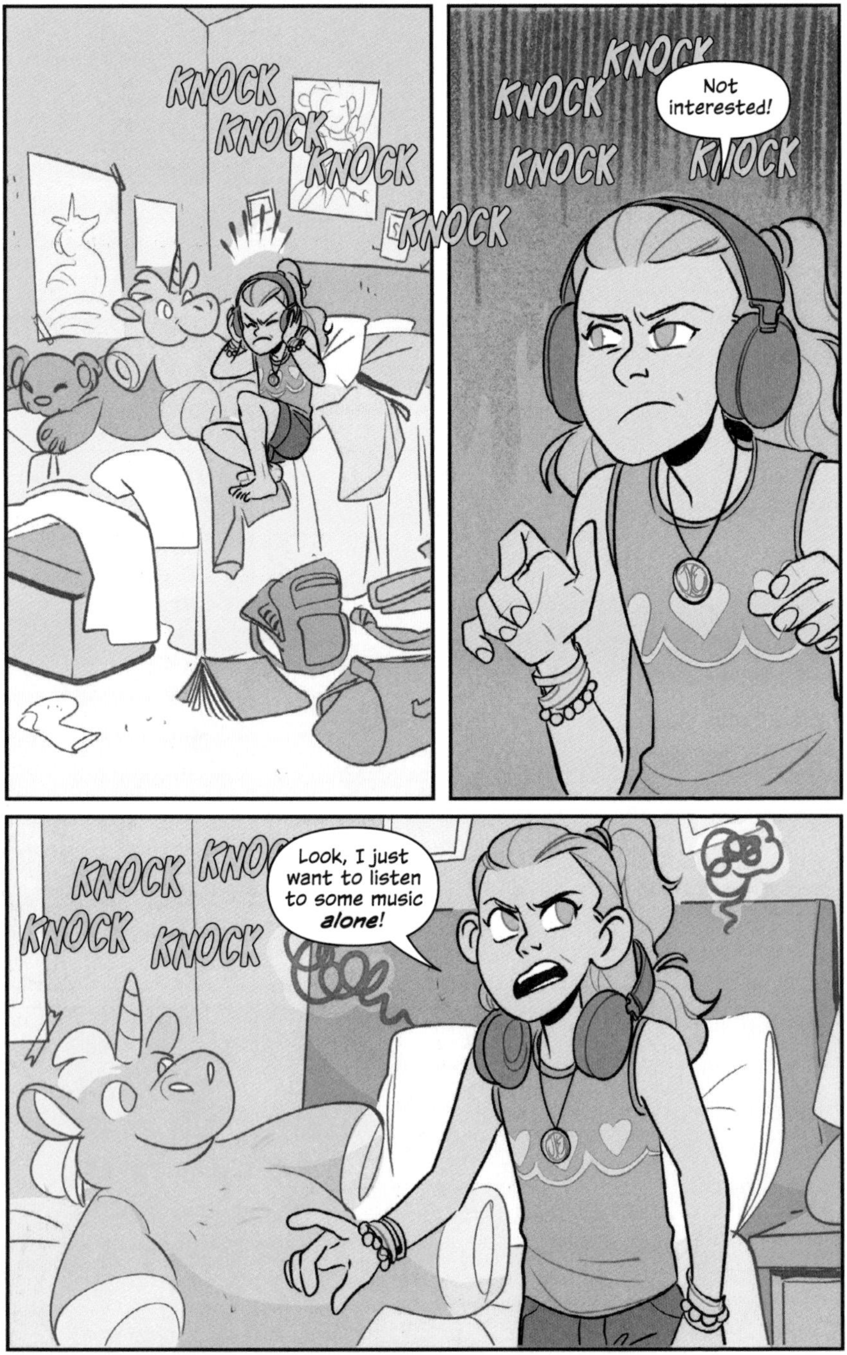
KNOCK
KNOCK
KNOCK
KNOCK
KNOCK
KNOCK
Not interested!
KNOCK
KNOCK
KNOCK
KNOCK
Look, I just want to listen to some music *alone*!
KNOCK
KNOCK

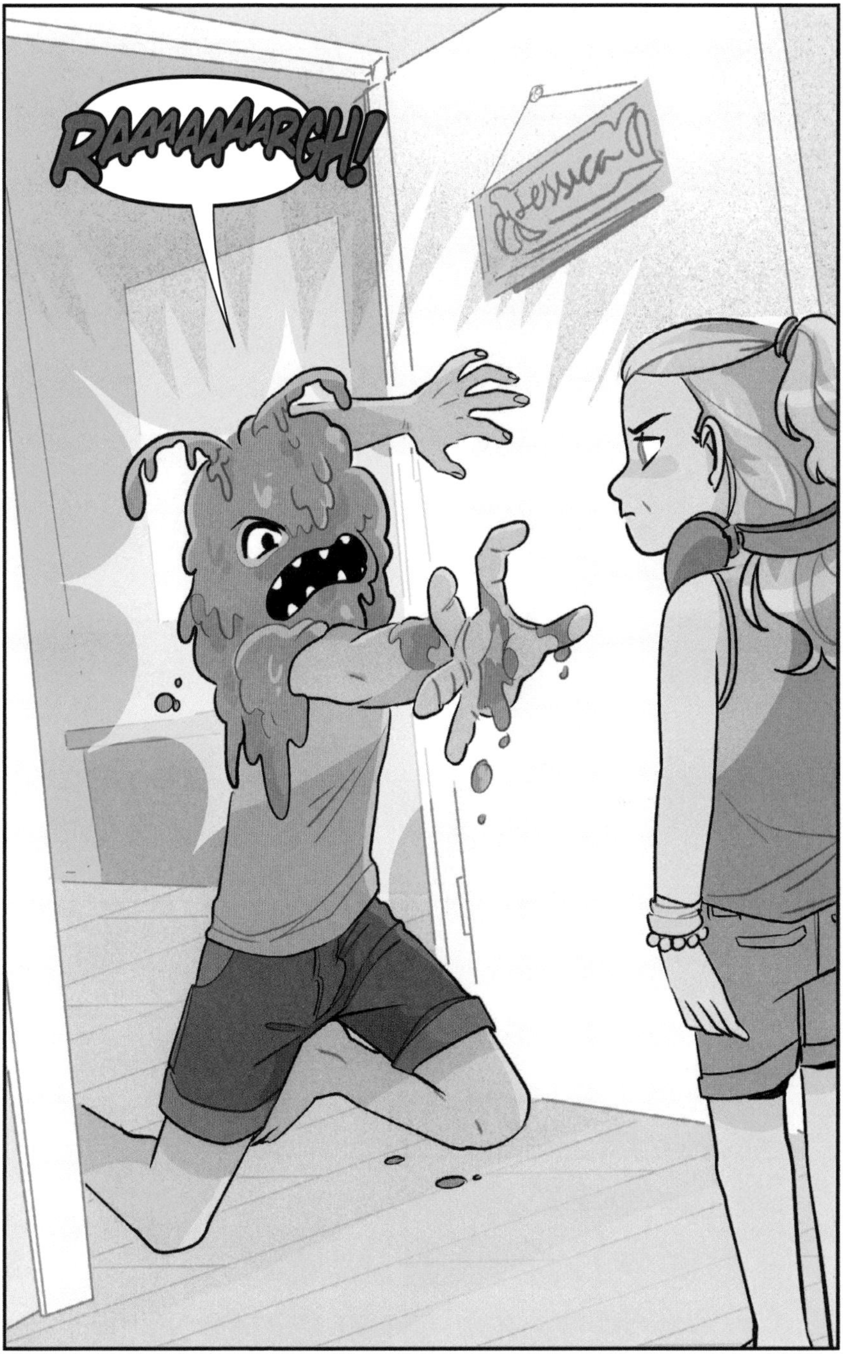
RAAAAAAARGH!
Jessica

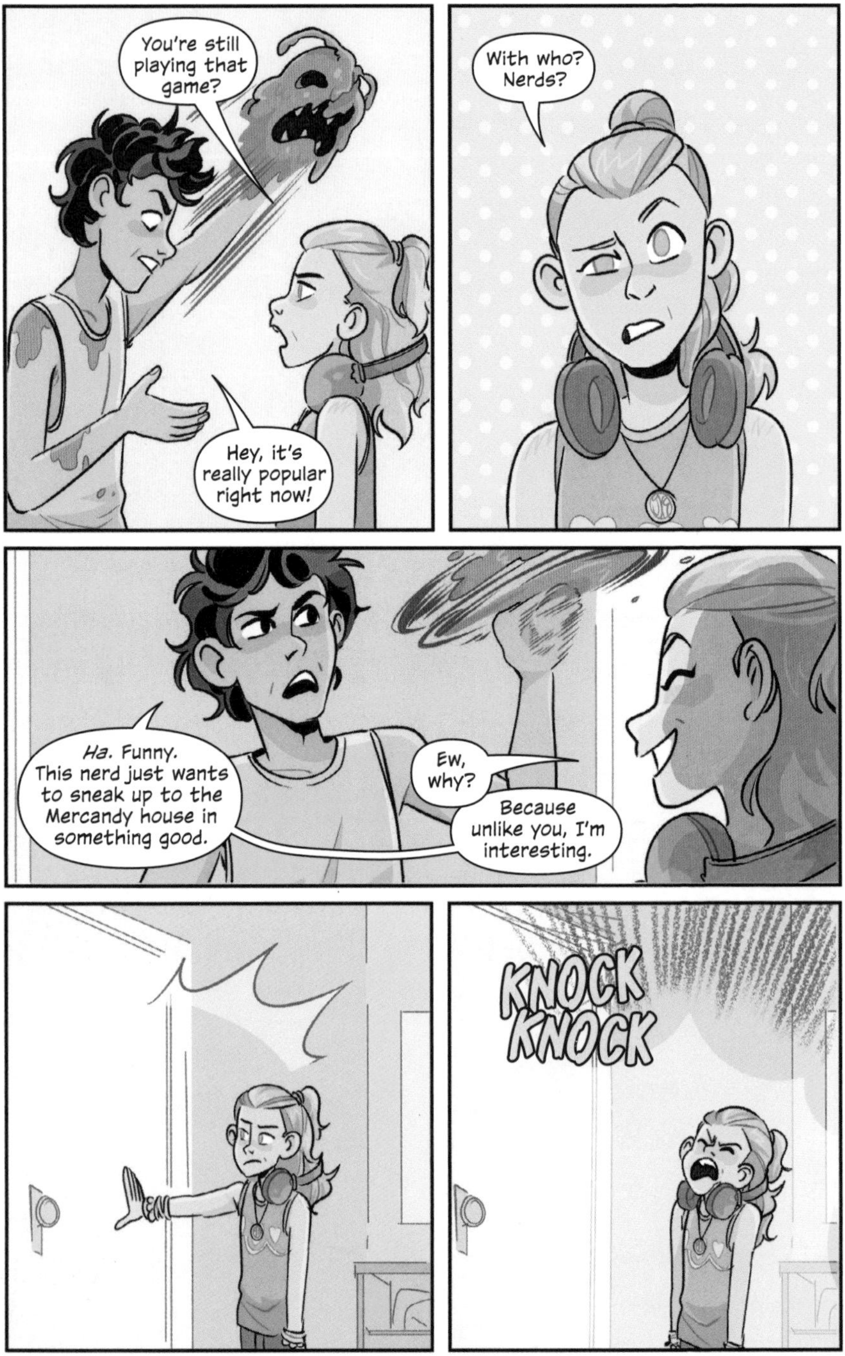
You're still playing that game?
Hey, it's really popular right now!
With who? Nerds?
Ha. Funny. This nerd just wants to sneak up to the Mercandy house in something good.
Ew, why?
Because unlike you, I'm interesting.
KNOCK KNOCK

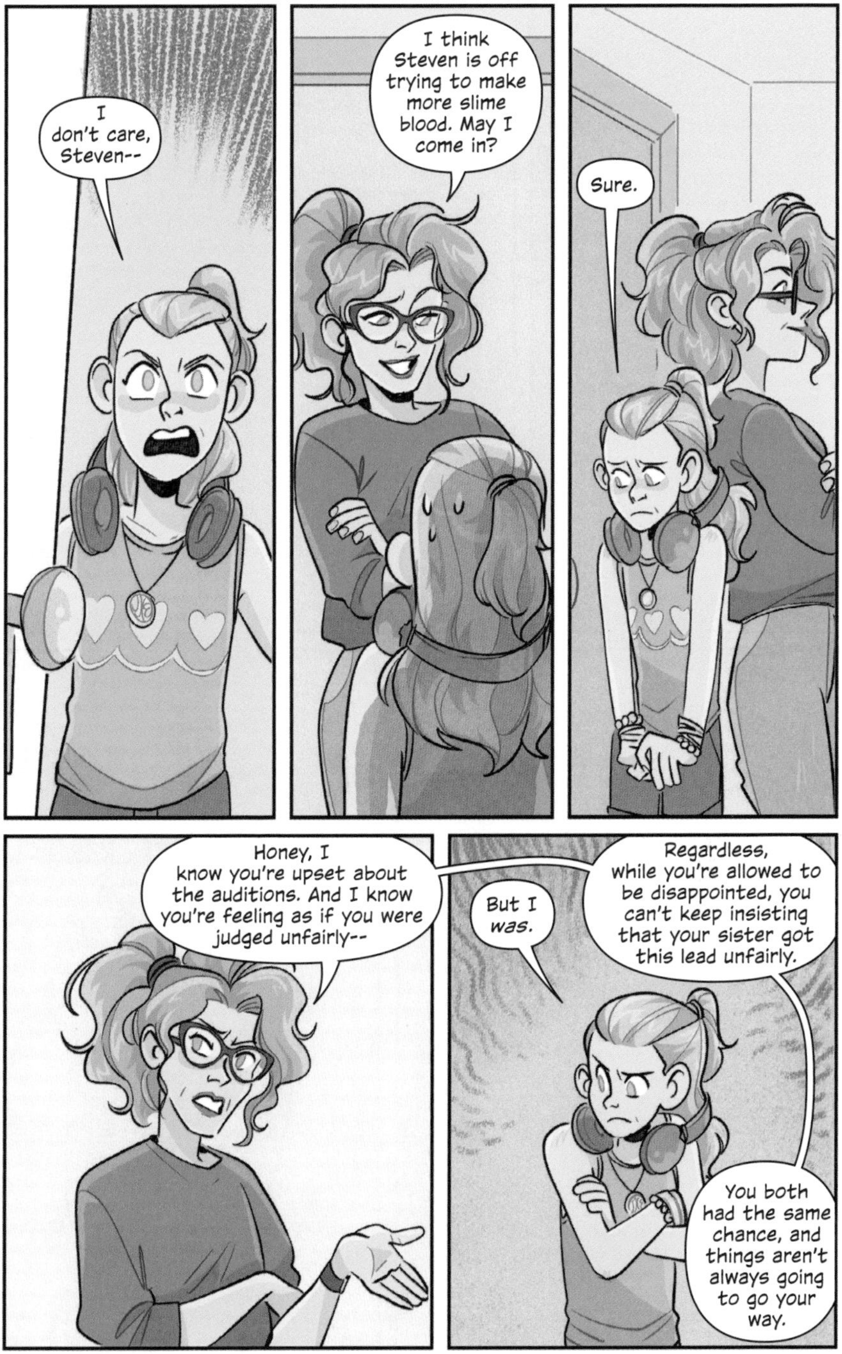
I don't care, Steven--
I think Steven is off trying to make more slime blood. May I come in?
Sure.
Honey, I know you're upset about the auditions. And I know you're feeling as if you were judged unfairly--
But I *was*.
Regardless, while you're allowed to be disappointed, you can't keep insisting that your sister got this lead unfairly.
You both had the same chance, and things aren't always going to go your way.

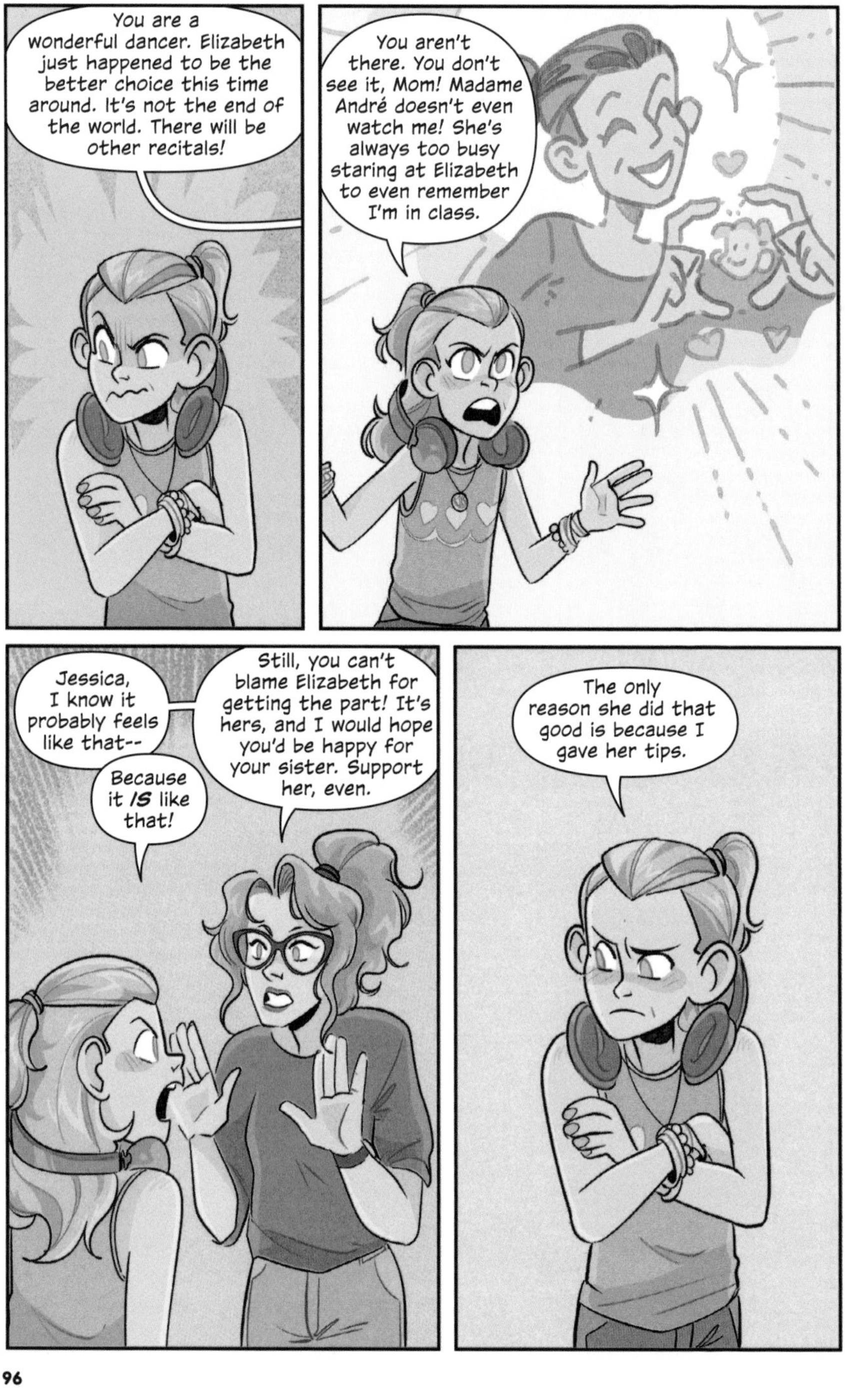
You are a wonderful dancer. Elizabeth just happened to be the better choice this time around. It's not the end of the world. There will be other recitals!
You aren't there. You don't see it, Mom! Madame André doesn't even watch me! She's always too busy staring at Elizabeth to even remember I'm in class.
Jessica, I know it probably feels like that--
Because it *IS* like that!
Still, you can't blame Elizabeth for getting the part! It's hers, and I would hope you'd be happy for your sister. Support her, even.
The only reason she did that good is because I gave her tips.

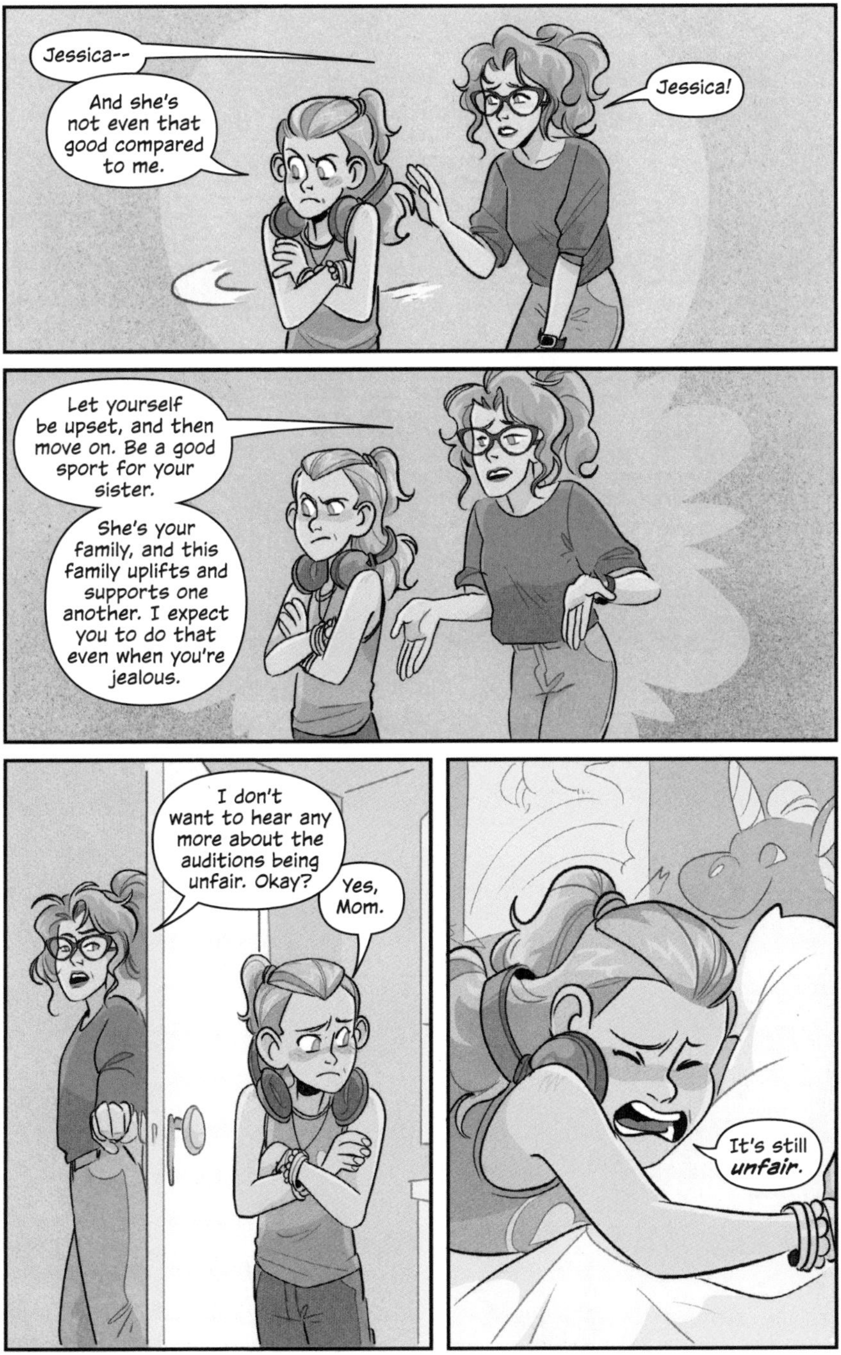

Jessica--
And she's not even that good compared to me.
Jessica!
Let yourself be upset, and then move on. Be a good sport for your sister.
She's your family, and this family uplifts and supports one another. I expect you to do that even when you're jealous.
I don't want to hear any more about the auditions being unfair. Okay?
Yes, Mom.
It's still *unfair*.

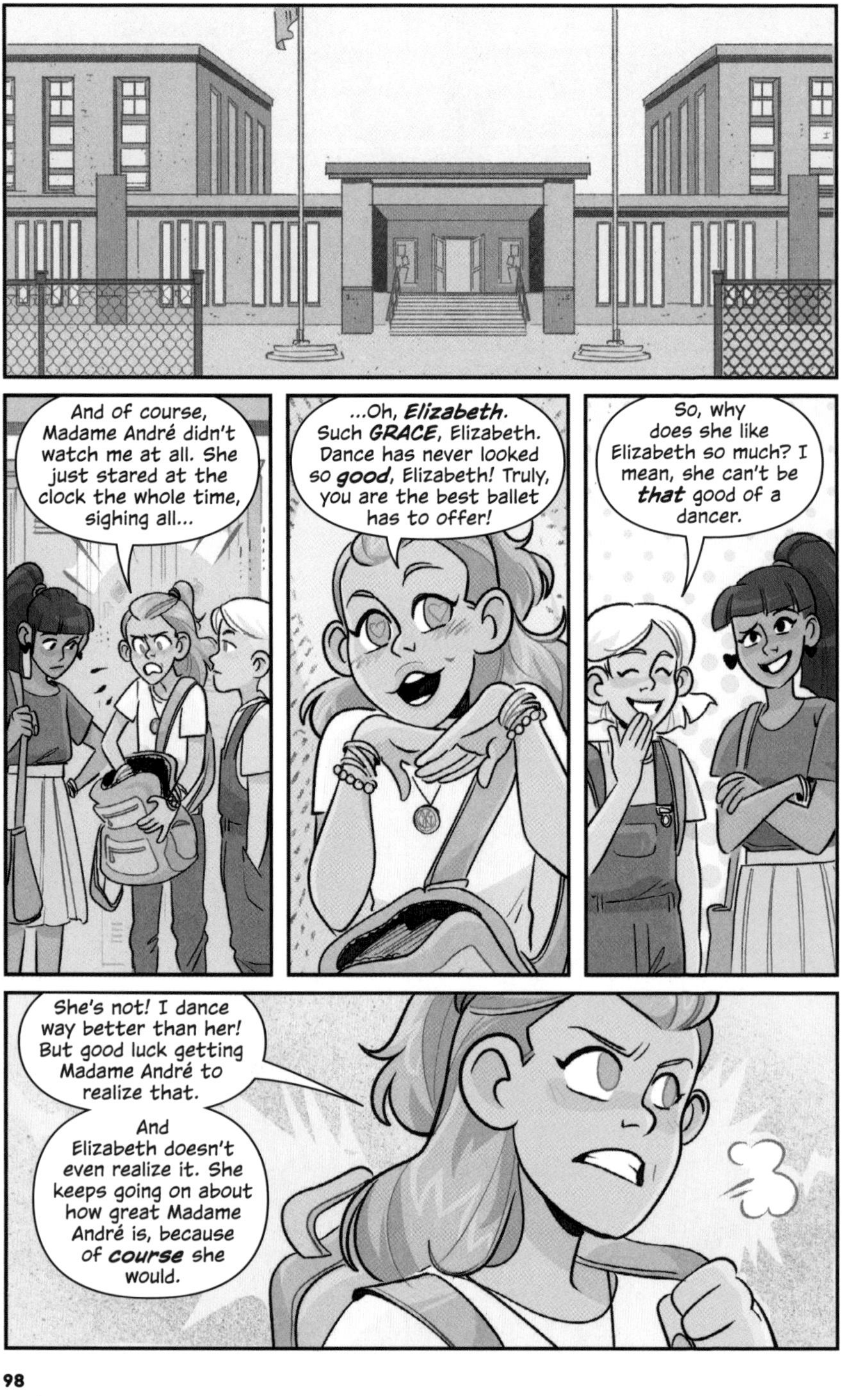
And of course, Madame André didn't watch me at all. She just stared at the clock the whole time, sighing all...
...Oh, Elizabeth. Such GRACE, Elizabeth. Dance has never looked so good, Elizabeth! Truly, you are the best ballet has to offer!
So, why does she like Elizabeth so much? I mean, she can't be that good of a dancer.
She's not! I dance way better than her! But good luck getting Madame André to realize that.
And Elizabeth doesn't even realize it. She keeps going on about how great Madame André is, because of course she would.

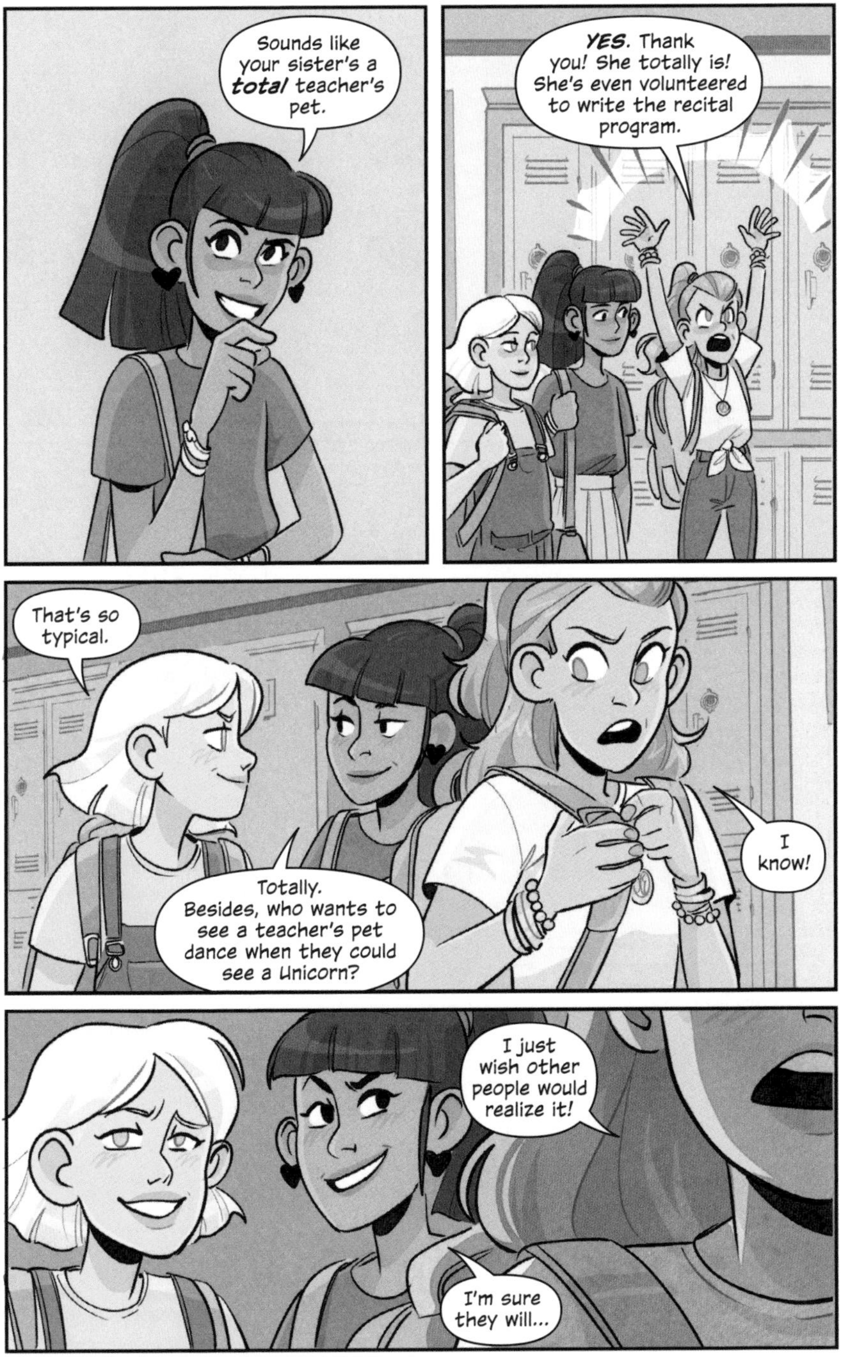
Sounds like your sister's a **total** teacher's pet.
YES. Thank you! She totally is! She's even volunteered to write the recital program.
That's so typical.
Totally. Besides, who wants to see a teacher's pet dance when they could see a Unicorn?
I know!
I just wish other people would realize it!
I'm sure they will...

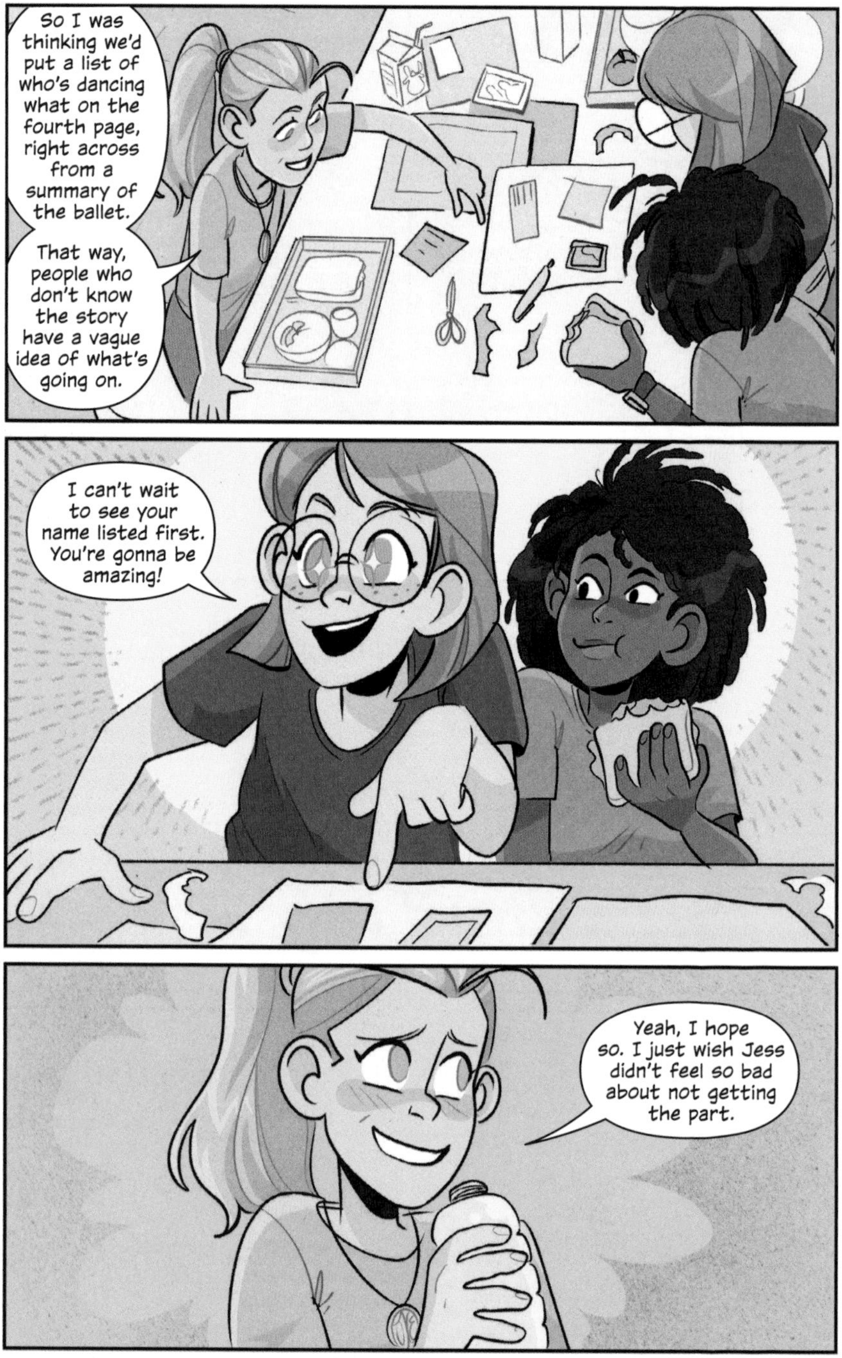
So I was thinking we'd put a list of who's dancing what on the fourth page, right across from a summary of the ballet.
That way, people who don't know the story have a vague idea of what's going on.
I can't wait to see your name listed first. You're gonna be amazing!
Yeah, I hope so. I just wish Jess didn't feel so bad about not getting the part.

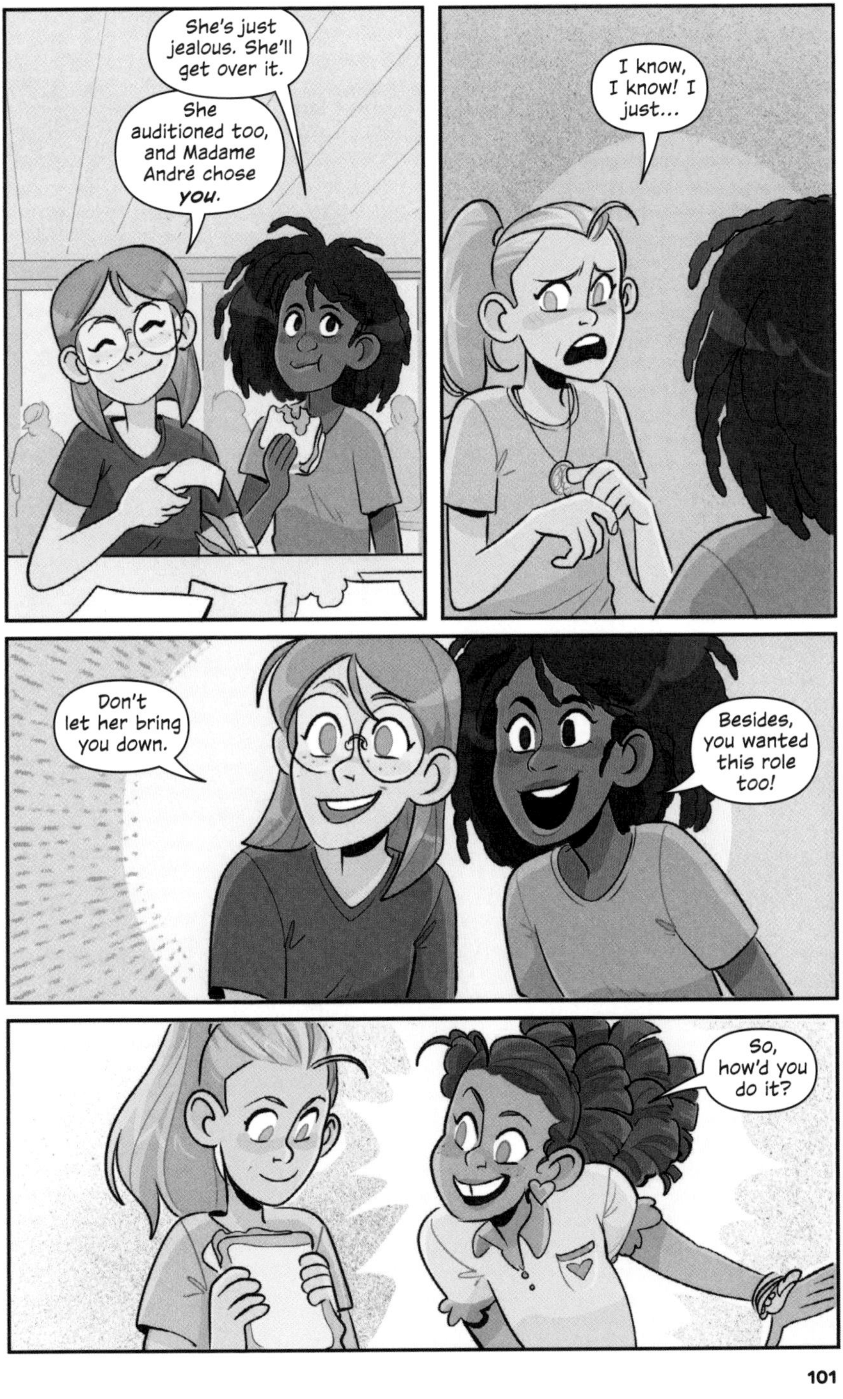
She's just jealous. She'll get over it.
She auditioned too, and Madame André chose *you*.
I know, I know! I just...
Don't let her bring you down.
Besides, you wanted this role too!
So, how'd you do it?

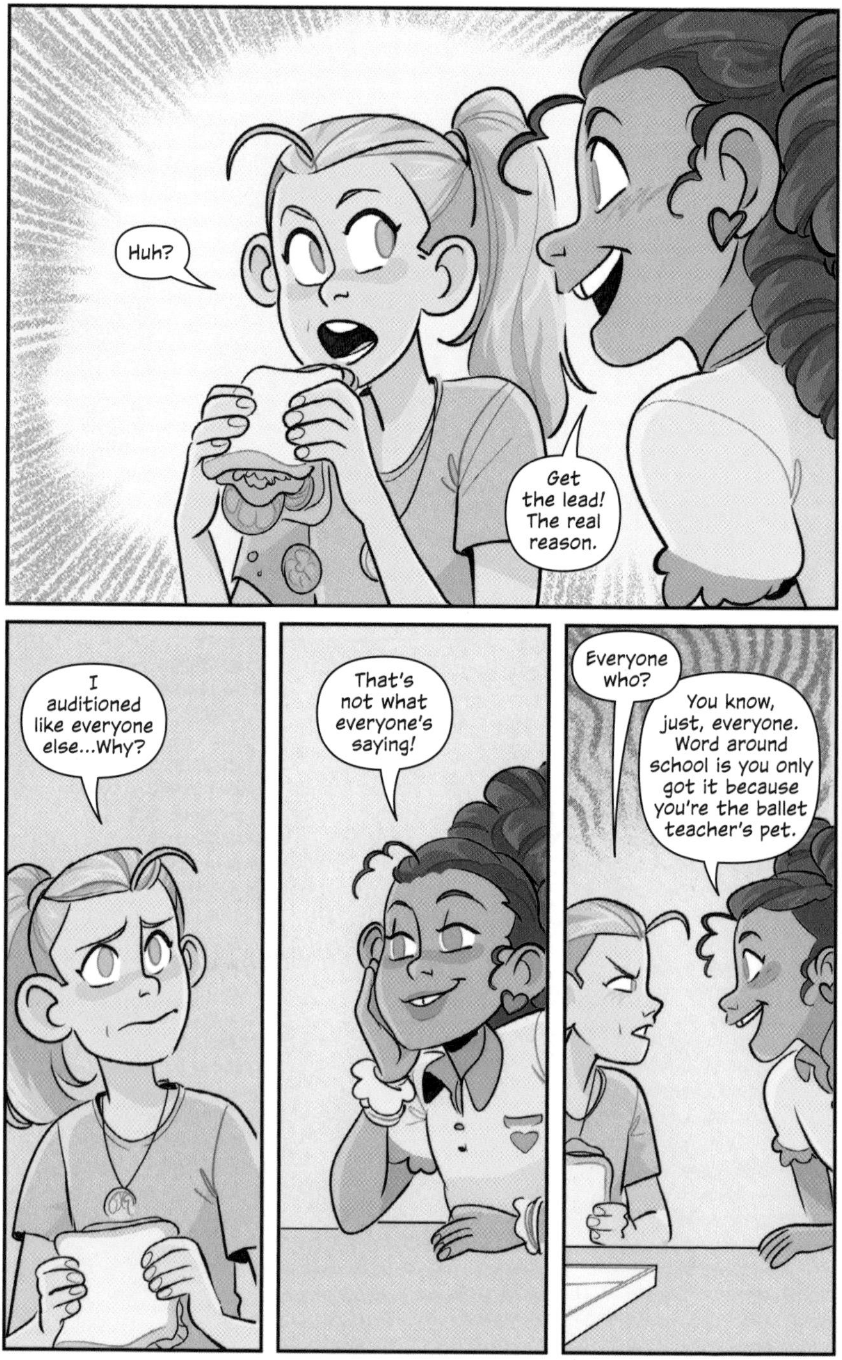
Huh?
Get the lead! The real reason.
I auditioned like everyone else...Why?
That's not what everyone's saying!
Everyone who?
You know, just, everyone. Word around school is you only got it because you're the ballet teacher's pet.

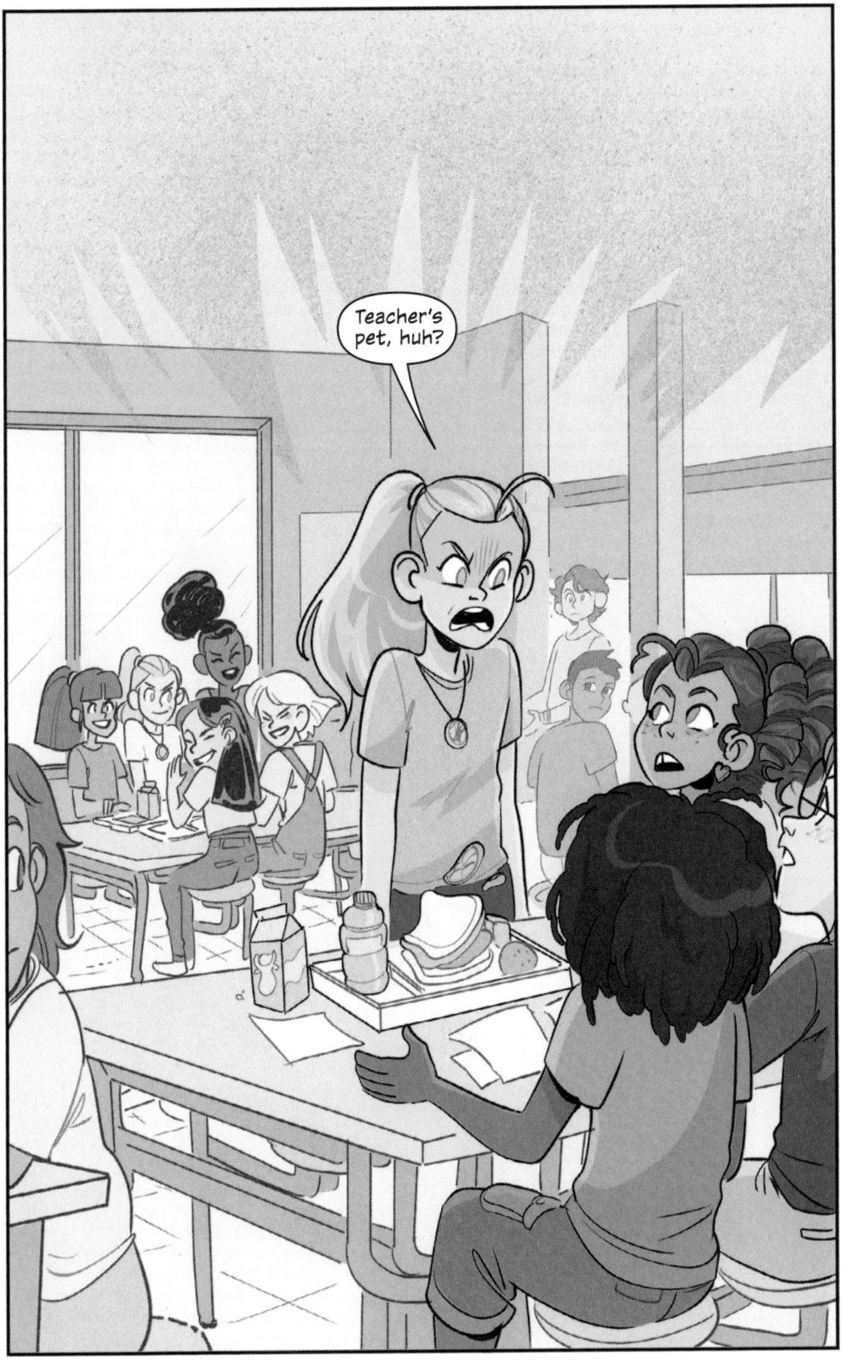
Teacher's
pet, huh?

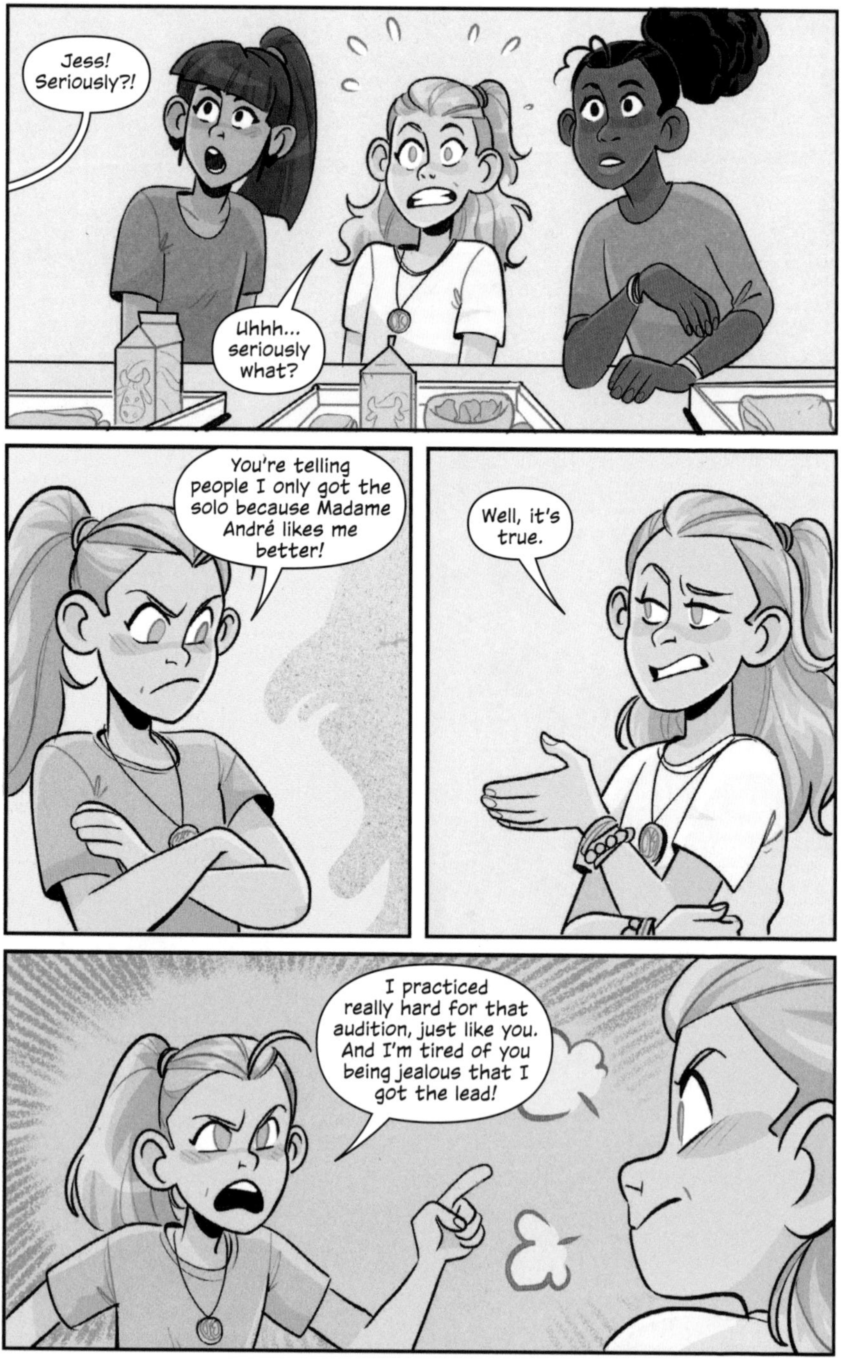
Jess! Seriously?!
Uhhh... seriously what?
You're telling people I only got the solo because Madame André likes me better!
Well, it's true.
I practiced really hard for that audition, just like you. And I'm tired of you being jealous that I got the lead!

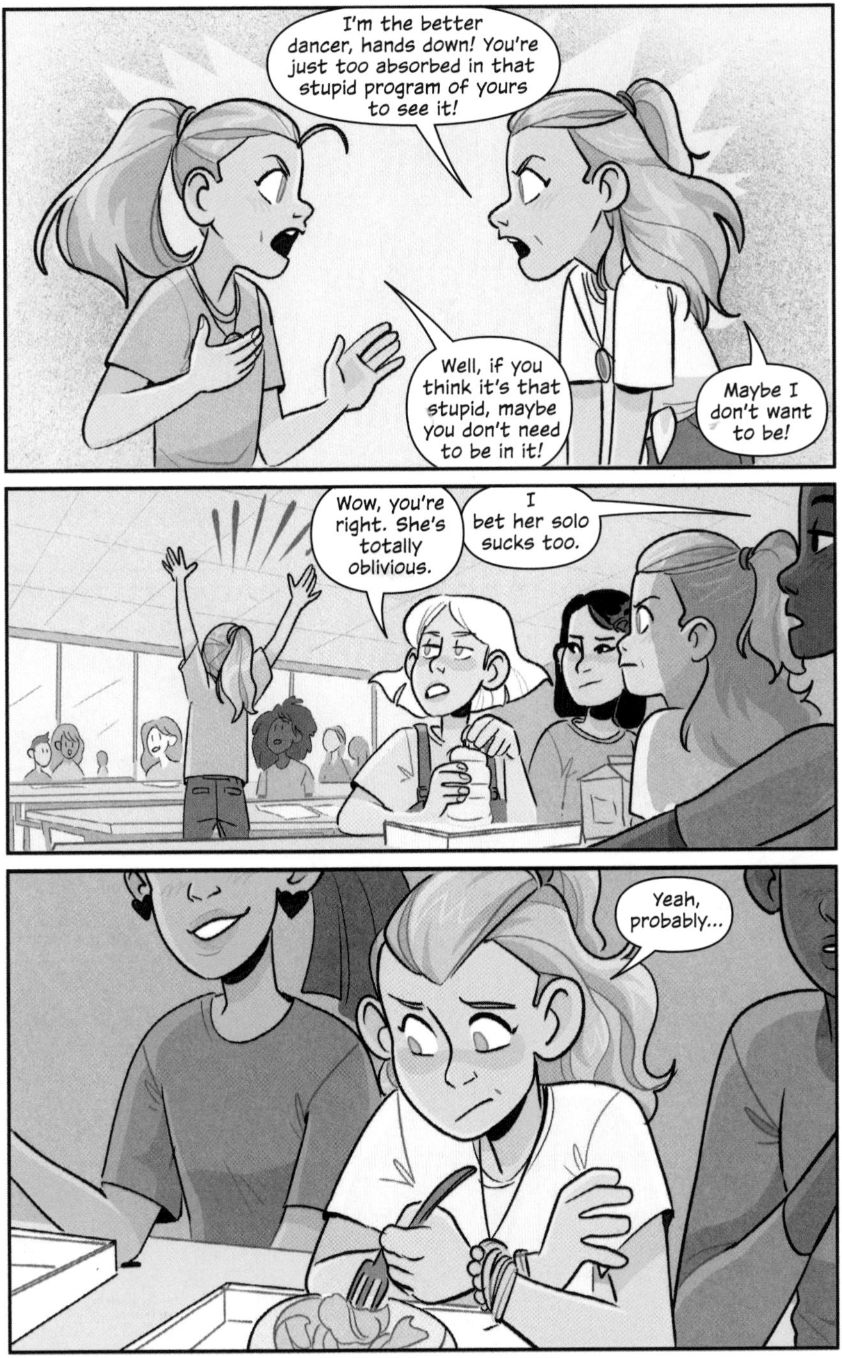
I'm the better dancer, hands down! You're just too absorbed in that stupid program of yours to see it!
Well, if you think it's that stupid, maybe you don't need to be in it!
Maybe I don't want to be!
Wow, you're right. She's totally oblivious.
I bet her solo sucks too.
Yeah, probably...

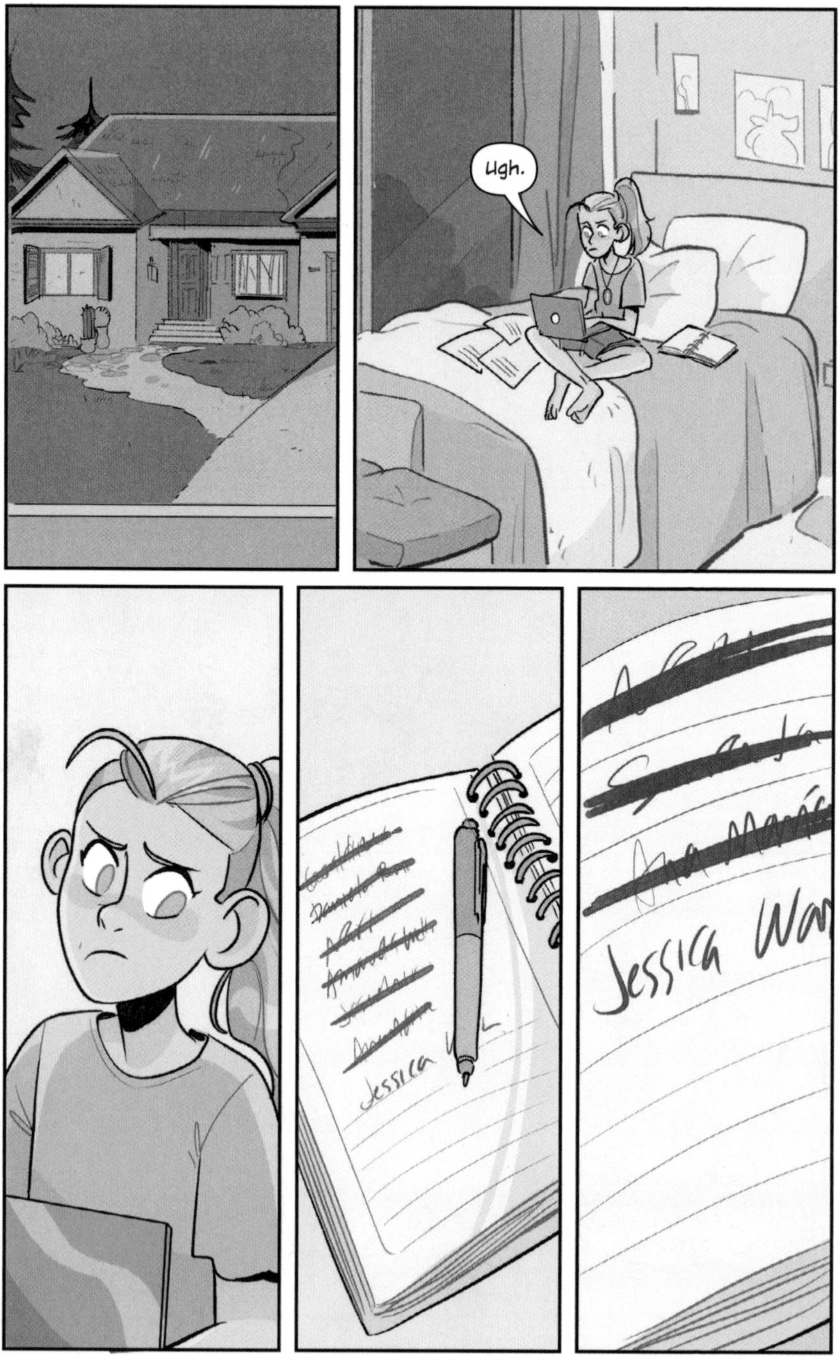
Ugh.
Jessica

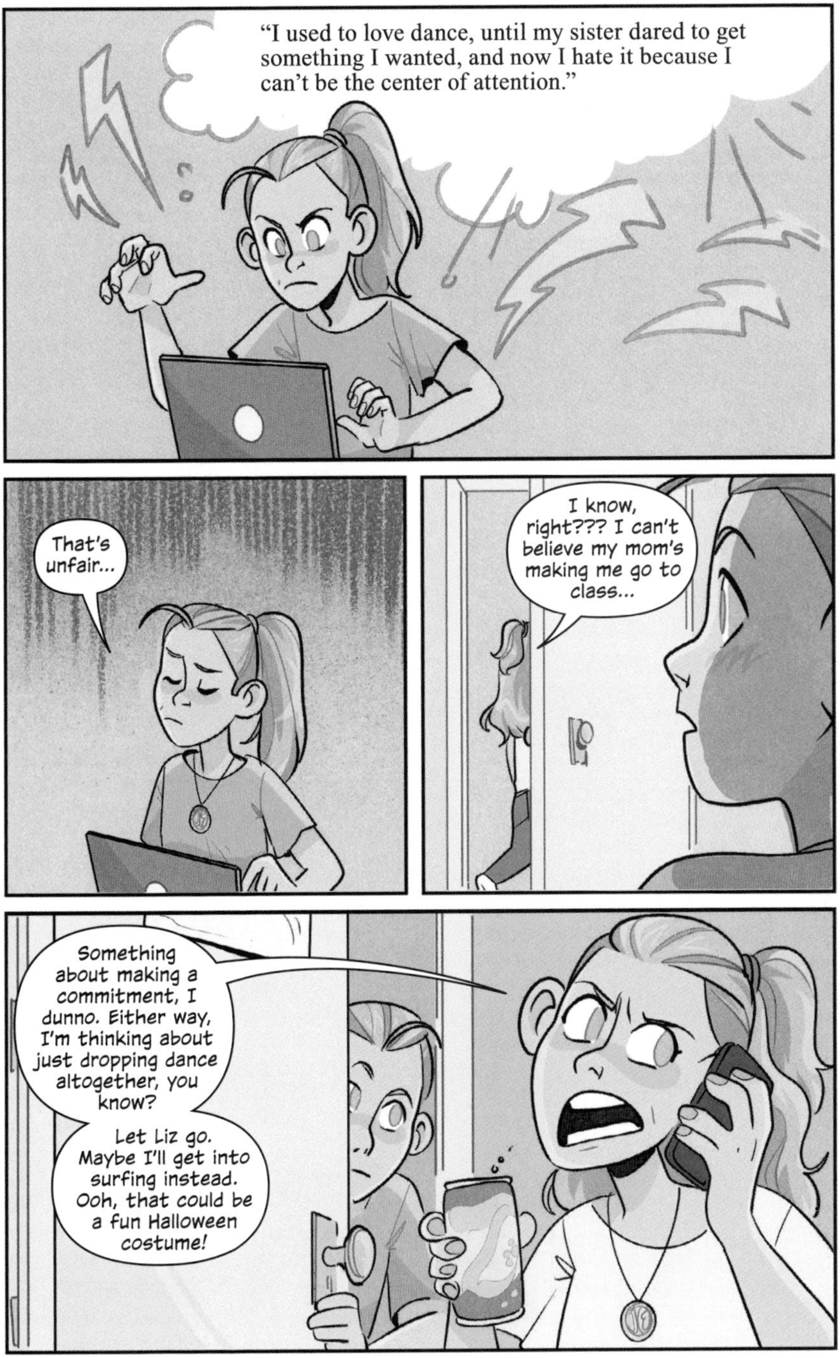
"I used to love dance, until my sister dared to get something I wanted, and now I hate it because I can't be the center of attention."
That's unfair...
I know, right??? I can't believe my mom's making me go to class...
Something about making a commitment, I dunno. Either way, I'm thinking about just dropping dance altogether, you know?
Let Liz go. Maybe I'll get into surfing instead. Ooh, that could be a fun Halloween costume!

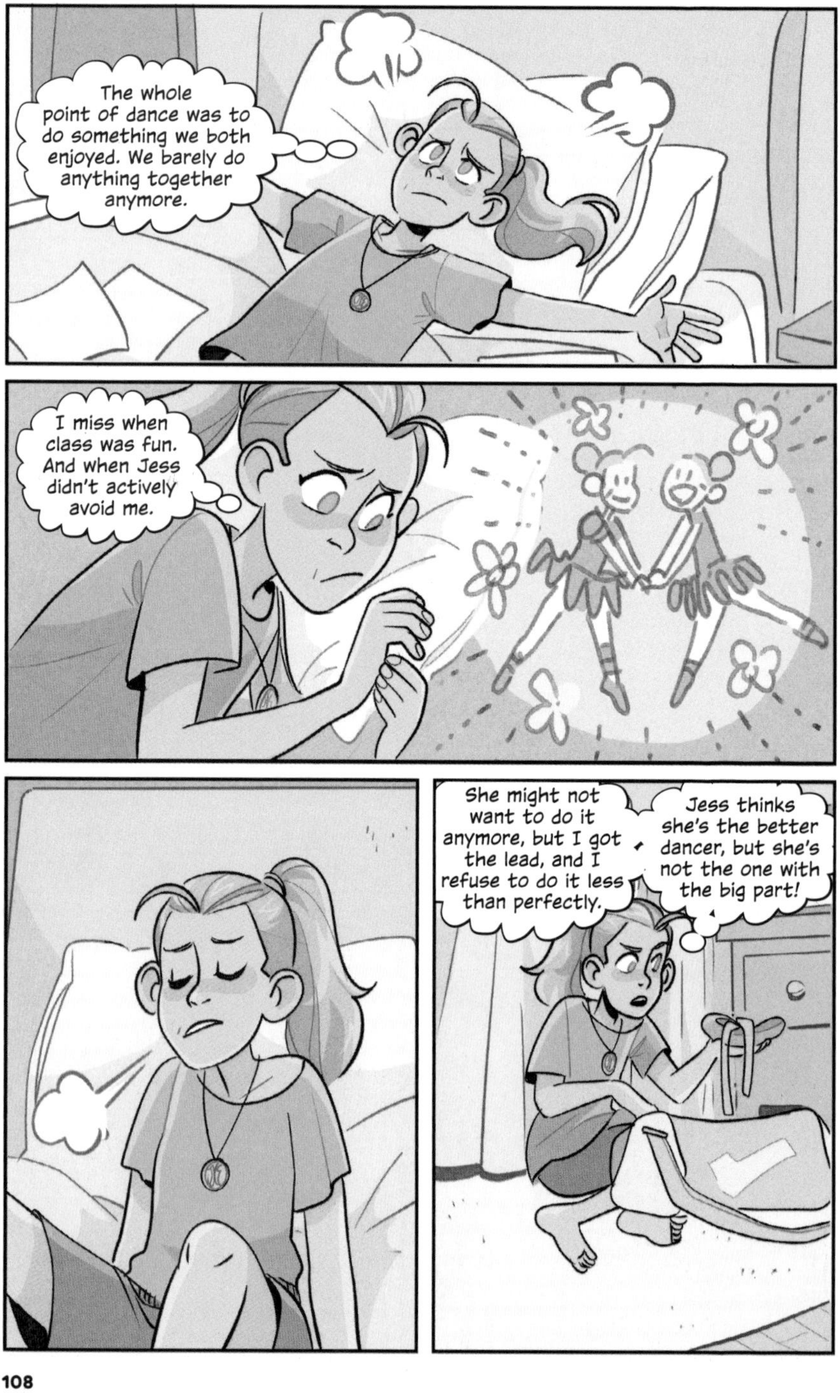
The whole point of dance was to do something we both enjoyed. We barely do anything together anymore.
I miss when class was fun. And when Jess didn't actively avoid me.
She might not want to do it anymore, but I got the lead, and I refuse to do it less than perfectly.
Jess thinks she's the better dancer, but she's not the one with the big part!

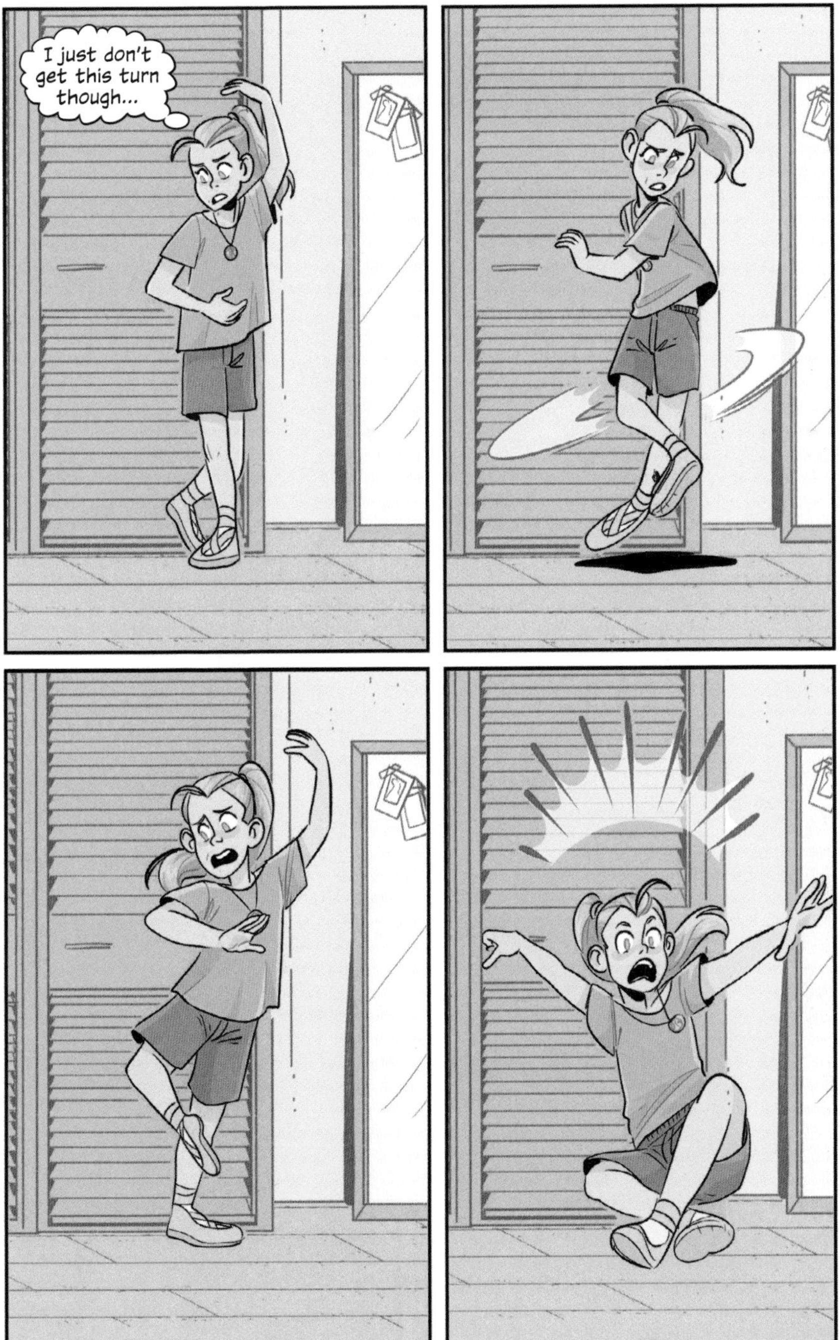
I just don't get this turn though...

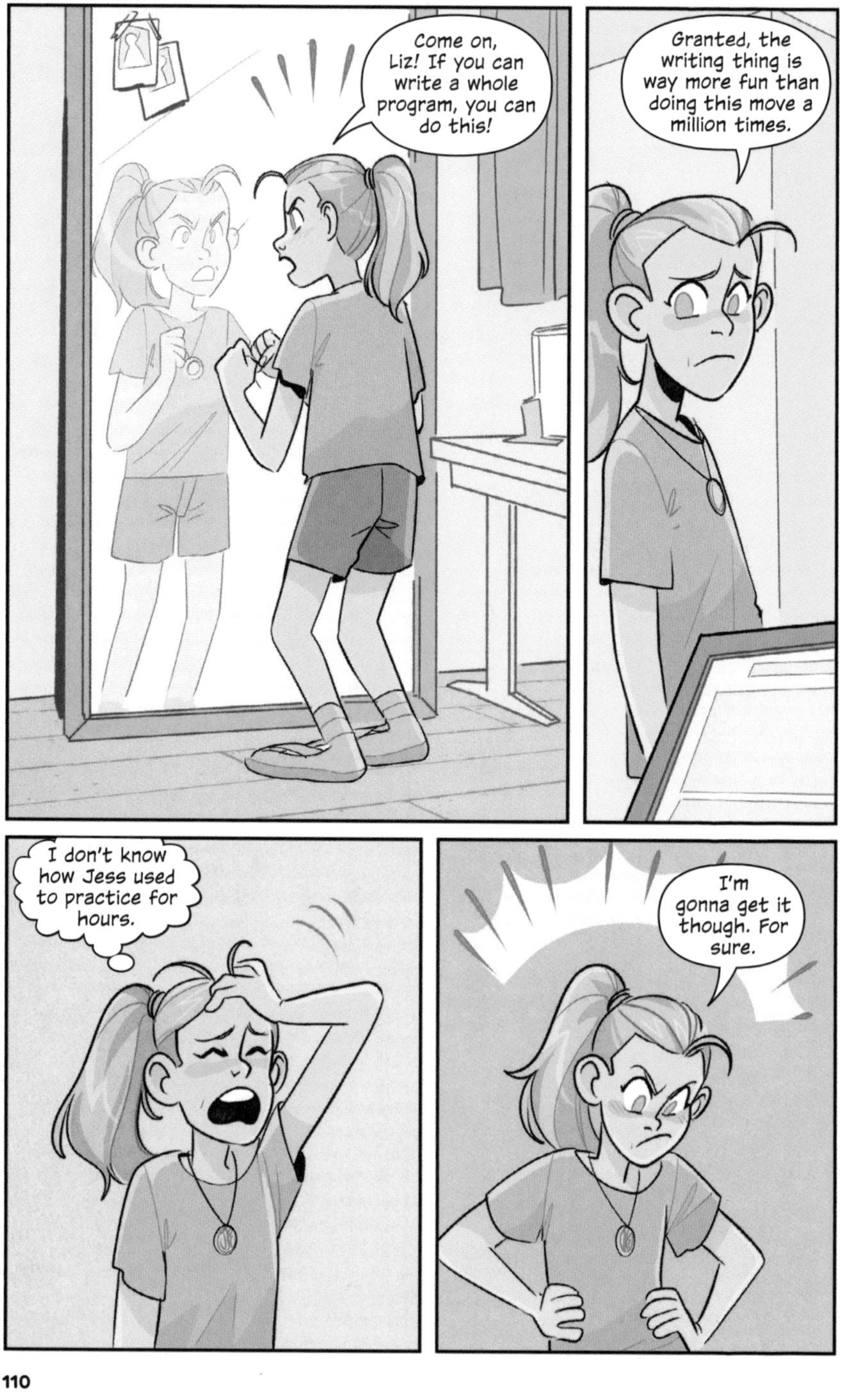
Come on, Liz! If you can write a whole program, you can do this!
Granted, the writing thing is way more fun than doing this move a million times.
I don't know how Jess used to practice for hours.
I'm gonna get it though. For sure.

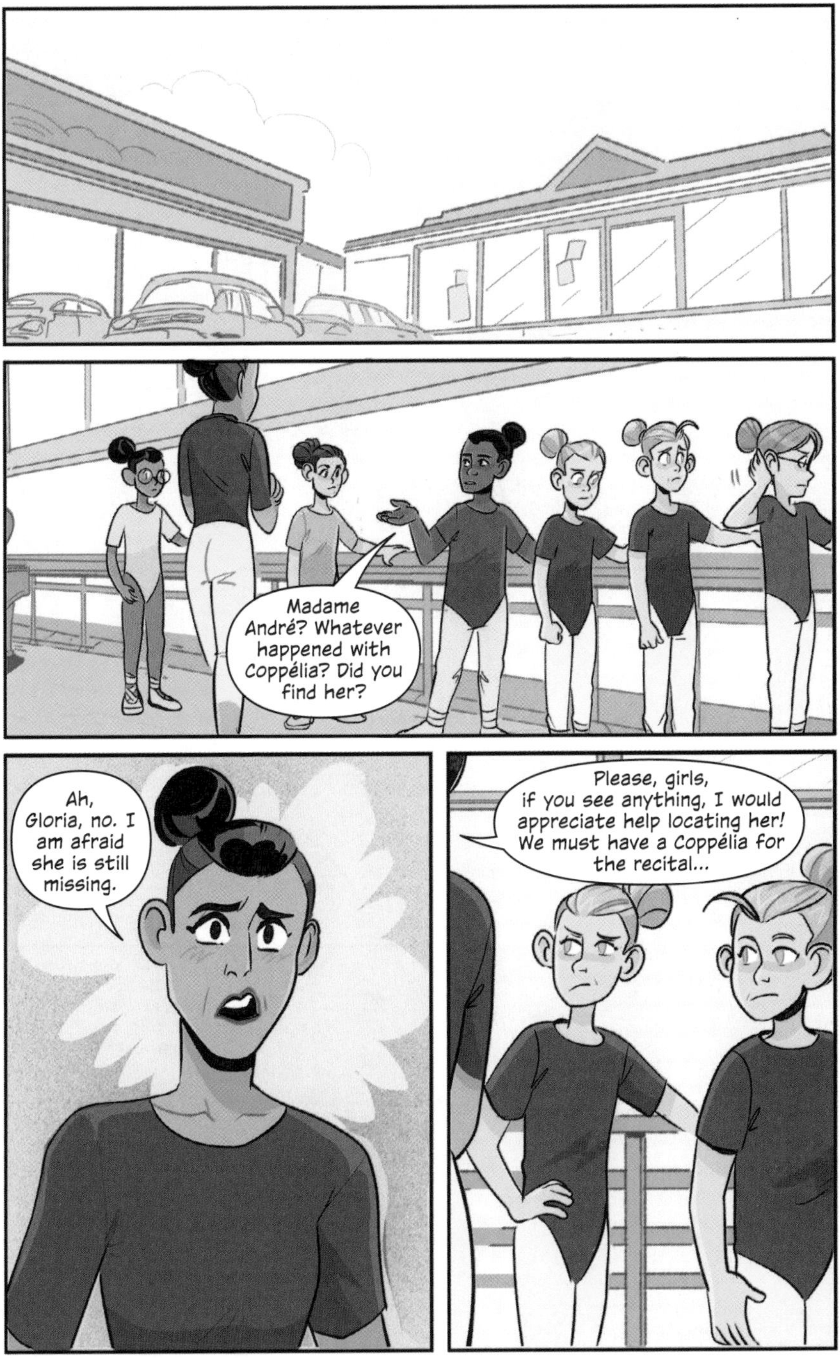
Madame André? Whatever happened with Coppélia? Did you find her?
Ah, Gloria, no. I am afraid she is still missing.
Please, girls, if you see anything, I would appreciate help locating her! We must have a Coppélia for the recital...

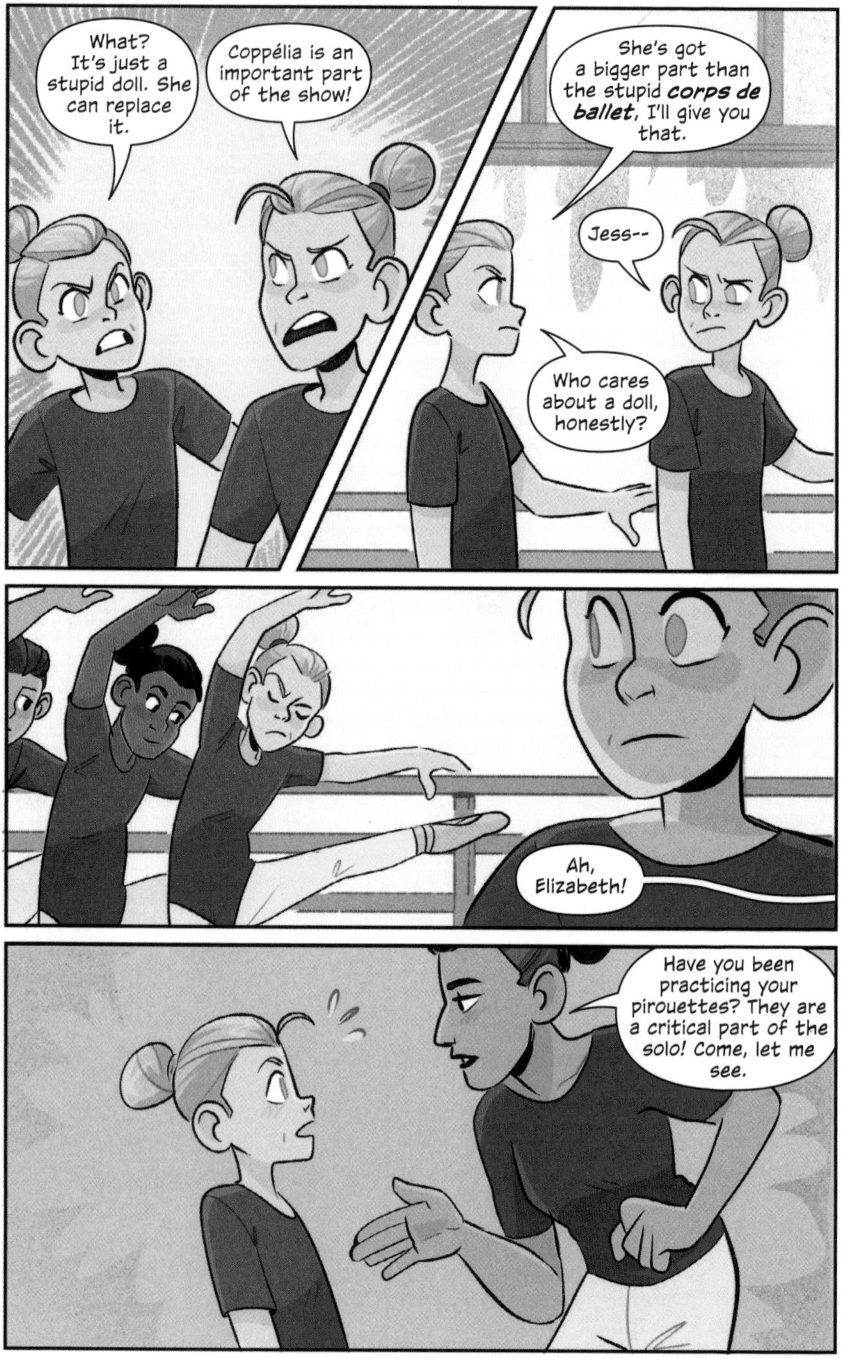
What? It's just a stupid doll. She can replace it.
Coppélia is an important part of the show!
She's got a bigger part than the stupid ***corps de ballet***, I'll give you that.
Jess--
Who cares about a doll, honestly?
Ah, Elizabeth!
Have you been practicing your pirouettes? They are a critical part of the solo! Come, let me see.

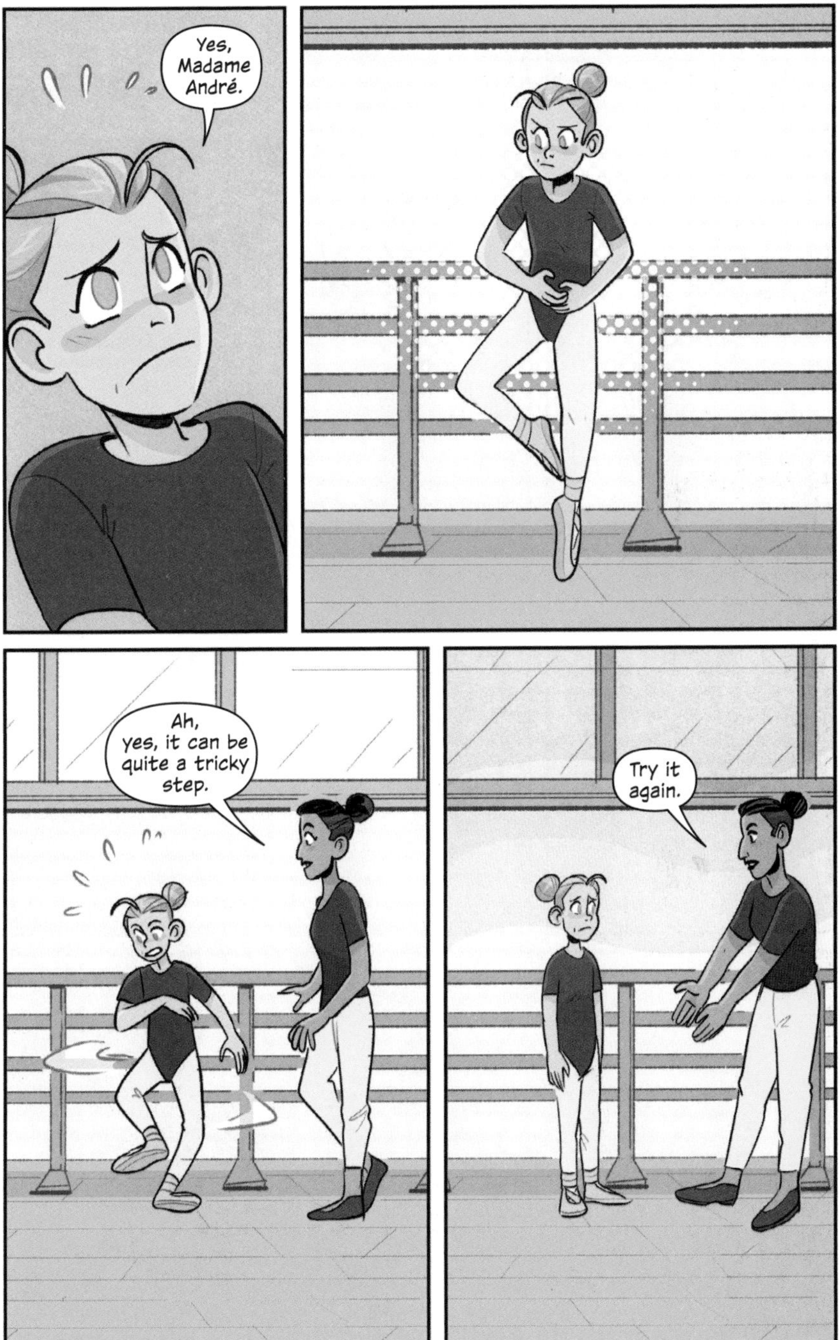
Yes, Madame André.
Ah, yes, it can be quite a tricky step.
Try it again.

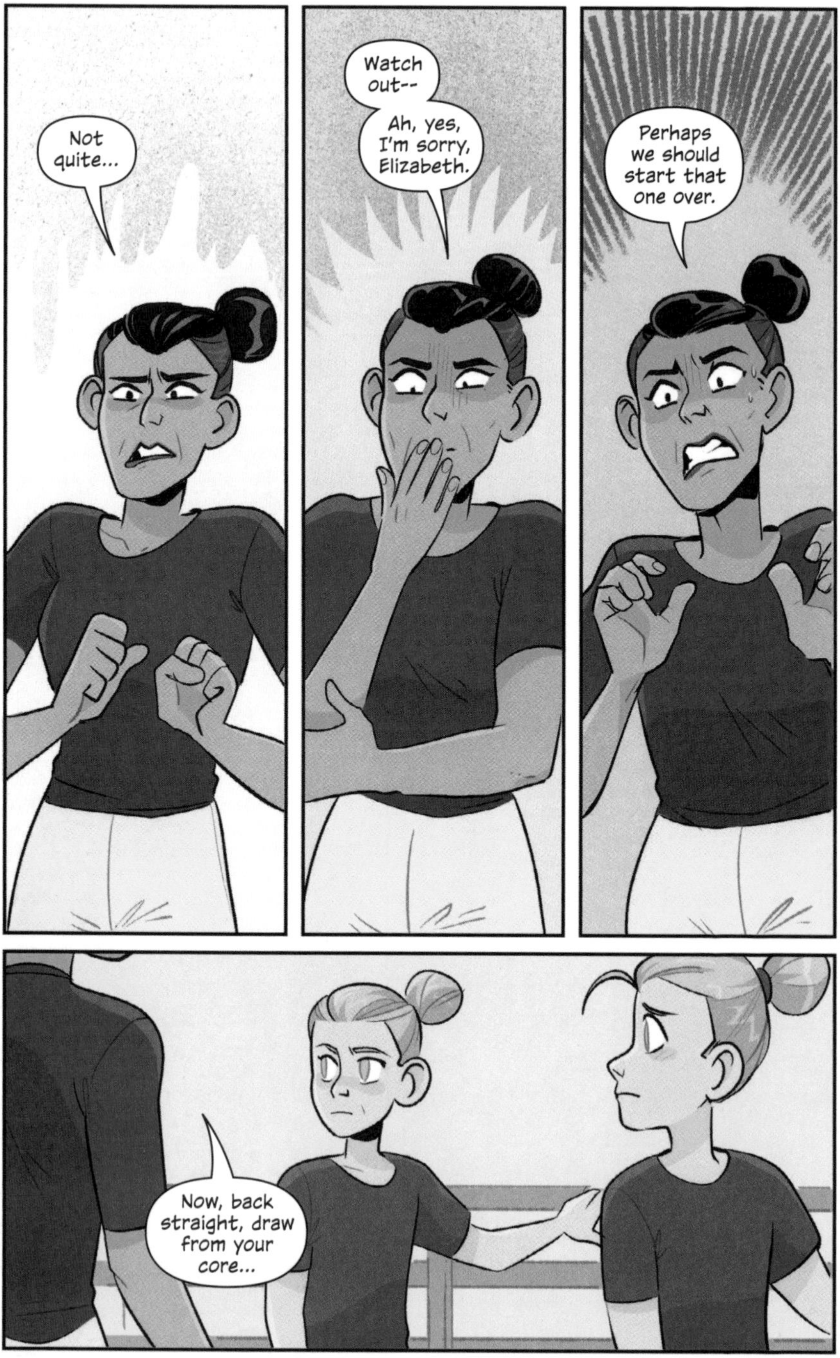
Not quite...
Watch out--
Ah, yes, I'm sorry, Elizabeth.
Perhaps we should start that one over.
Now, back straight, draw from your core...

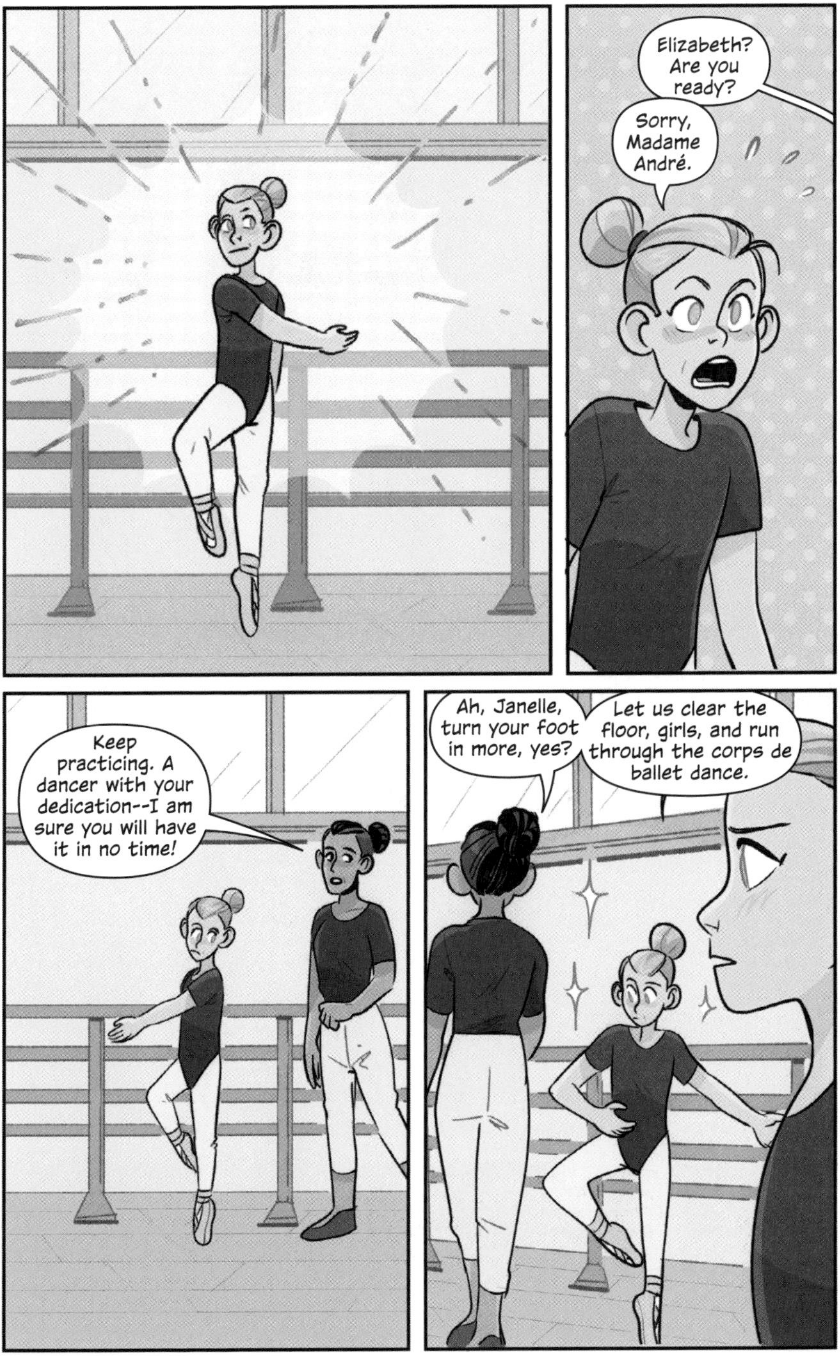
Elizabeth? Are you ready?
Sorry, Madame André.
Keep practicing. A dancer with your dedication--I am sure you will have it in no time!
Ah, Janelle, turn your foot in more, yes?
Let us clear the floor, girls, and run through the corps de ballet dance.

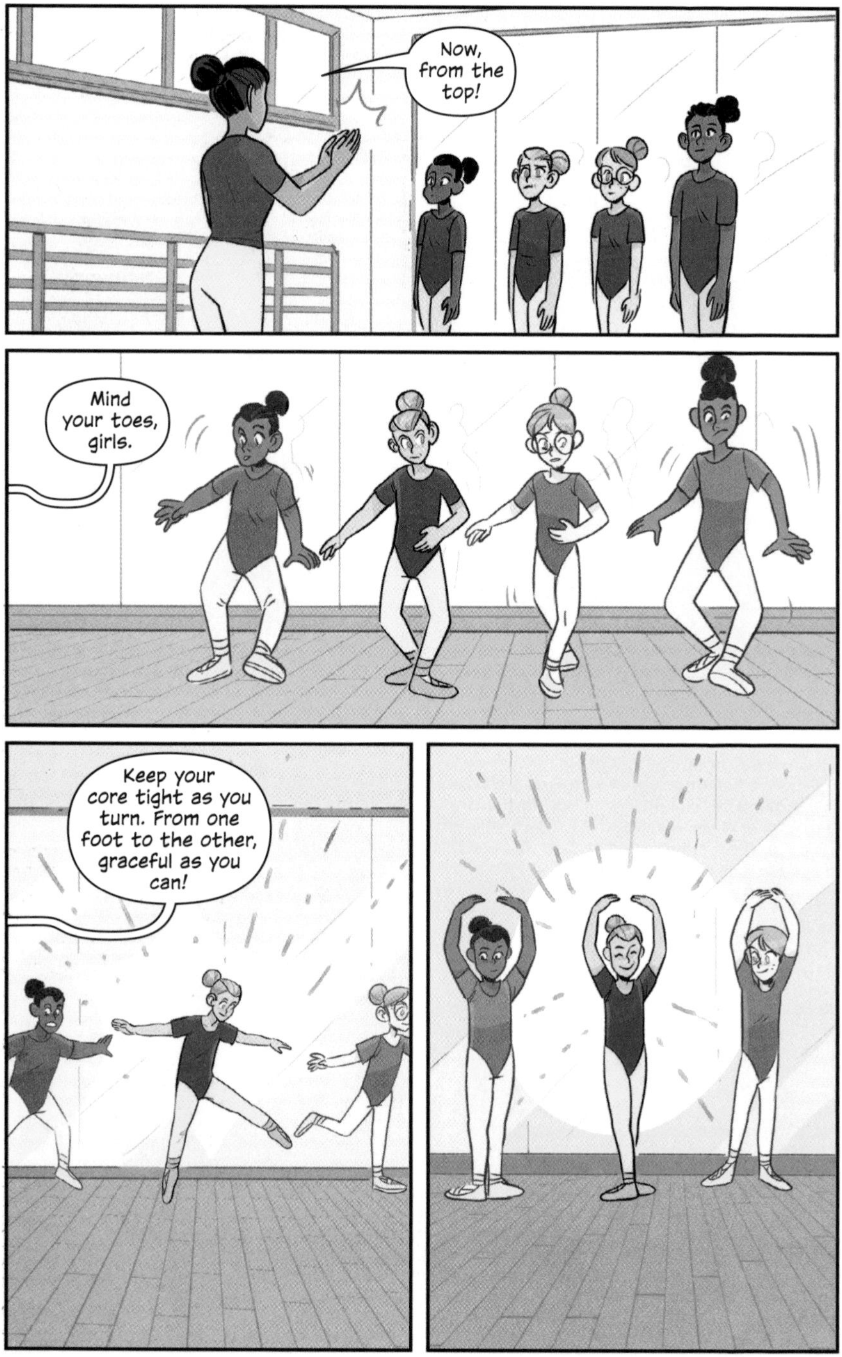
Now, from the top!
Mind your toes, girls.
Keep your core tight as you turn. From one foot to the other, graceful as you can!

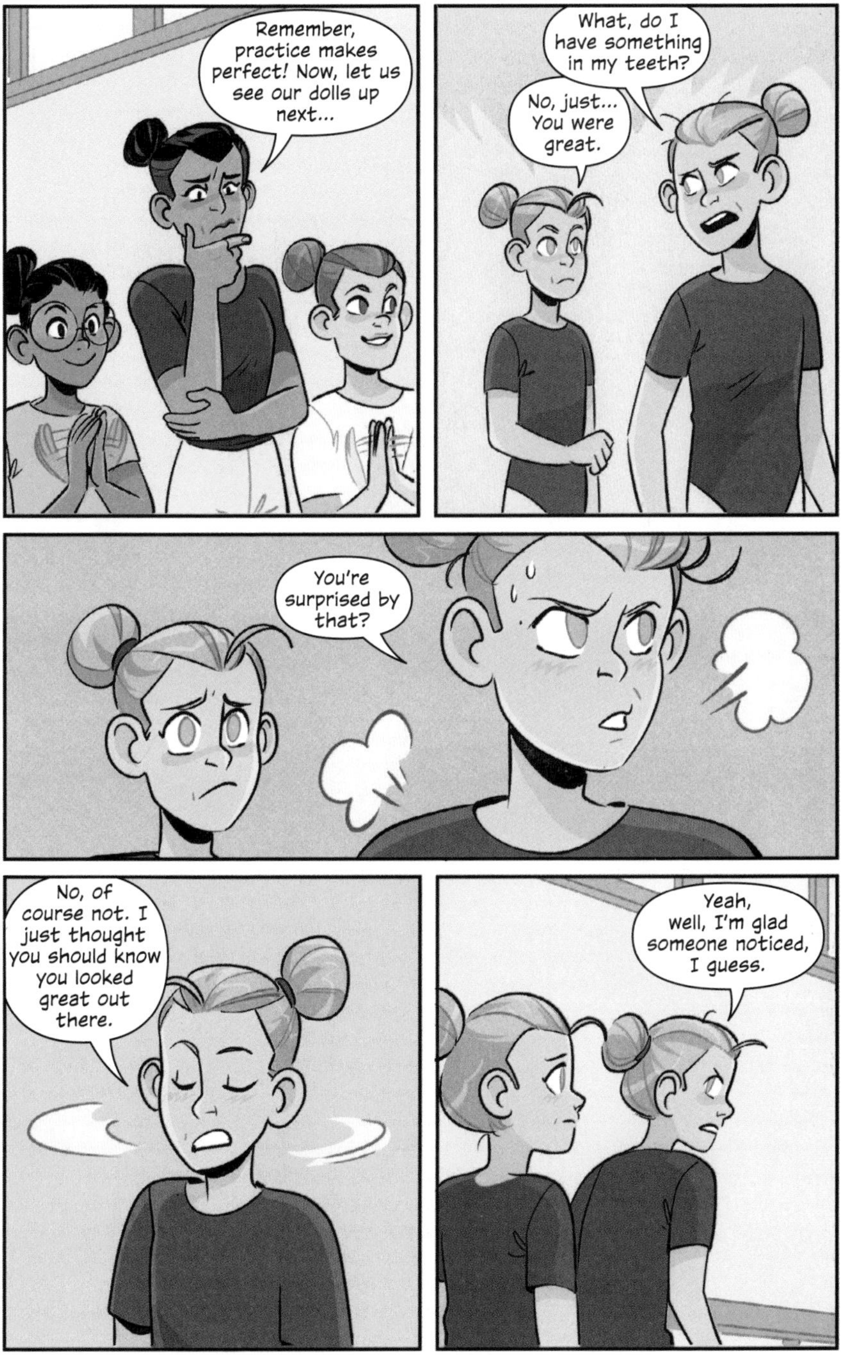
Remember, practice makes perfect! Now, let us see our dolls up next...
What, do I have something in my teeth?
No, just... You were great.
You're surprised by that?
No, of course not. I just thought you should know you looked great out there.
Yeah, well, I'm glad someone noticed, I guess.

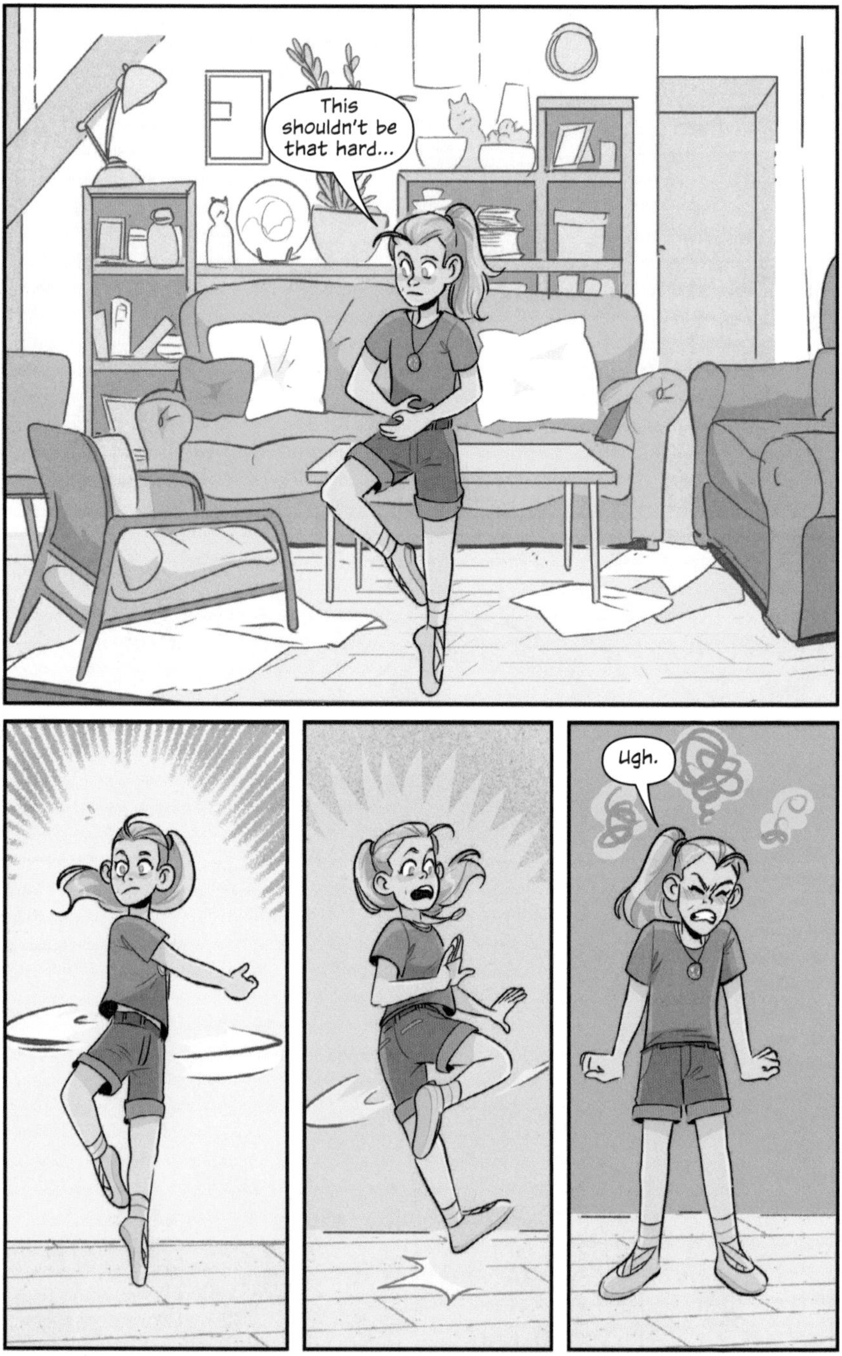
This shouldn't be that hard...
Ugh.

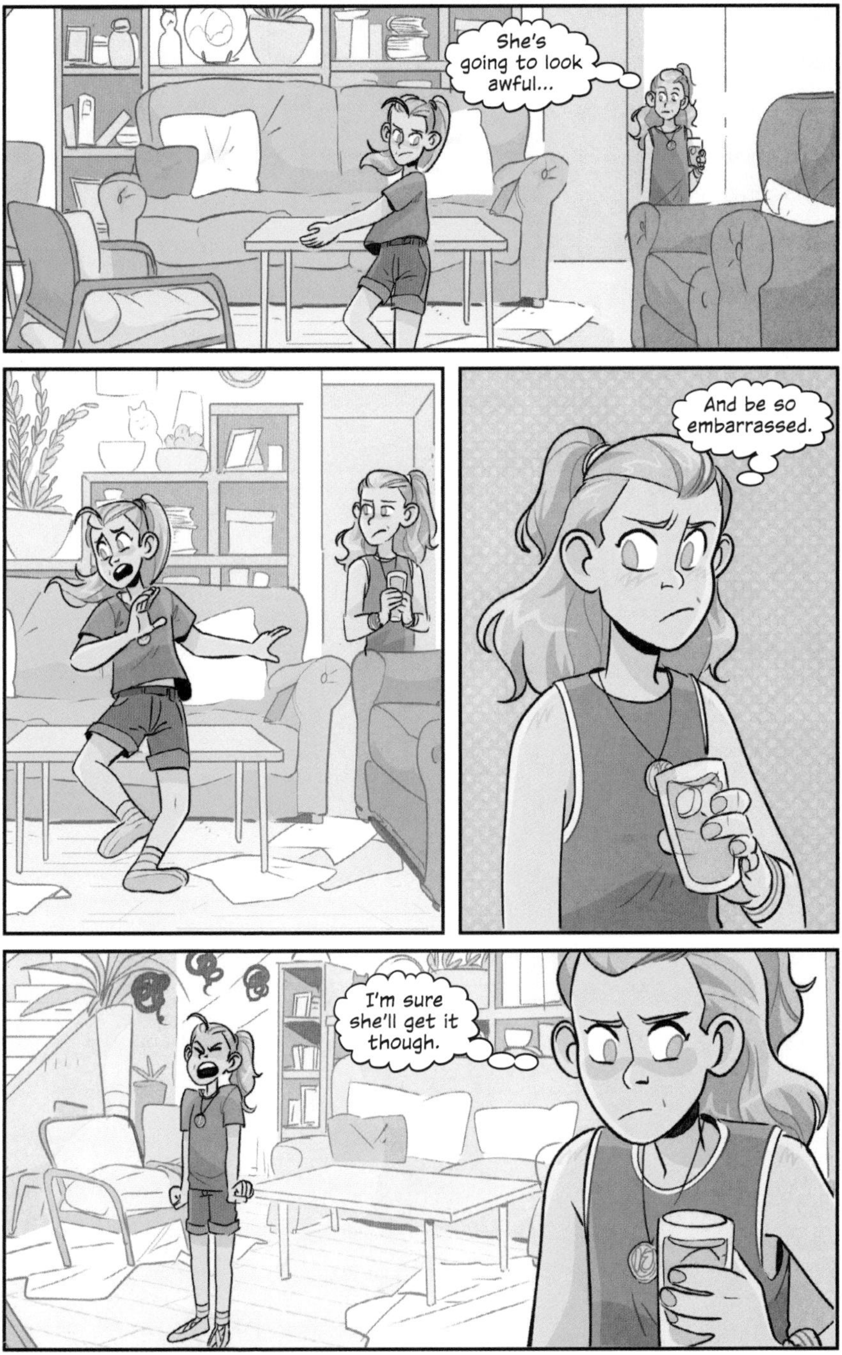
She's going to look awful...
And be so embarrassed.
I'm sure she'll get it though.

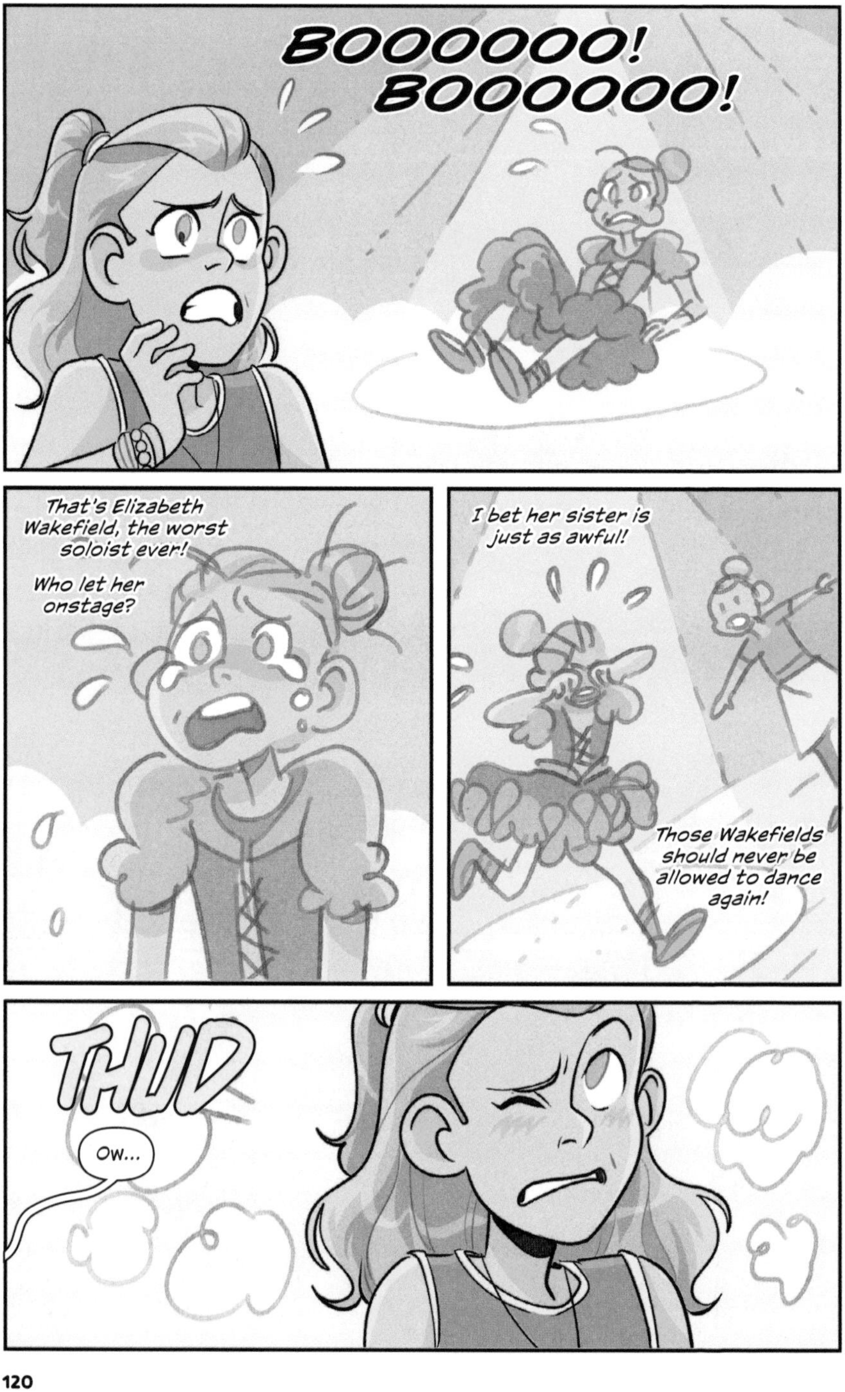
BOOOOOO!
BOOOOOO!
That's Elizabeth Wakefield, the worst soloist ever!
Who let her onstage?
I bet her sister is just as awful!
Those Wakefields should never be allowed to dance again!
THUD
Ow...

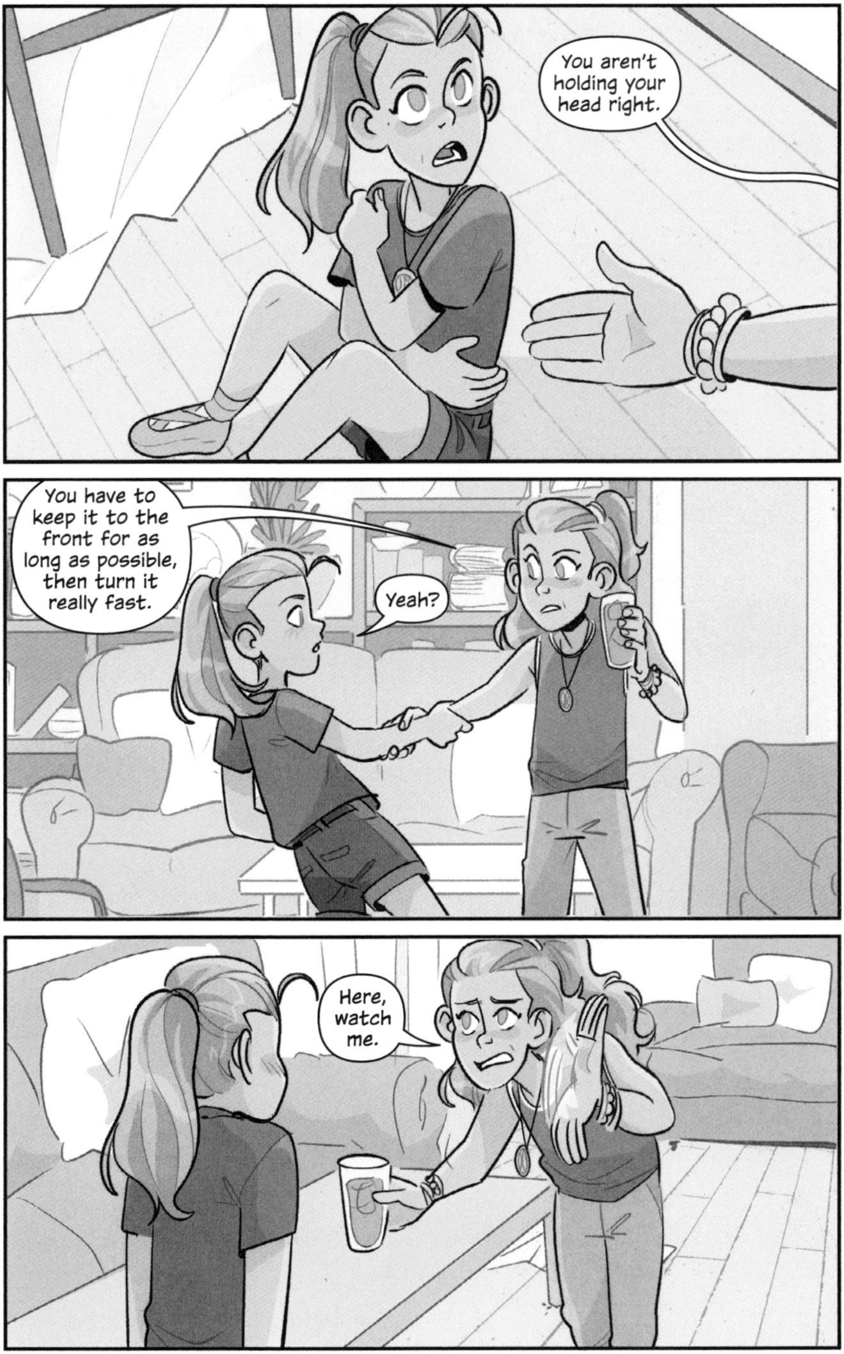
You aren't holding your head right.
You have to keep it to the front for as long as possible, then turn it really fast.
Yeah?
Here, watch me.

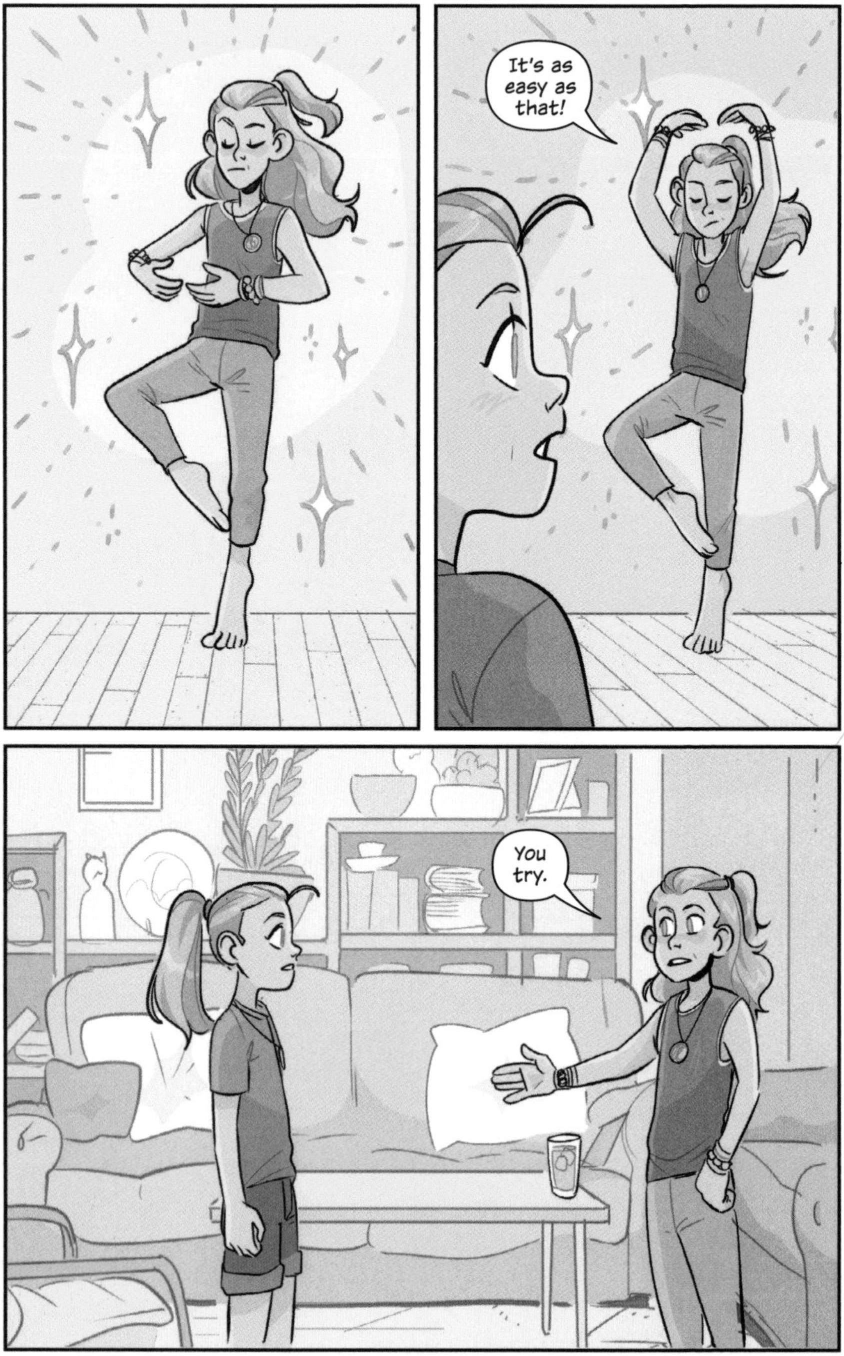
It's as easy as that!
You try.

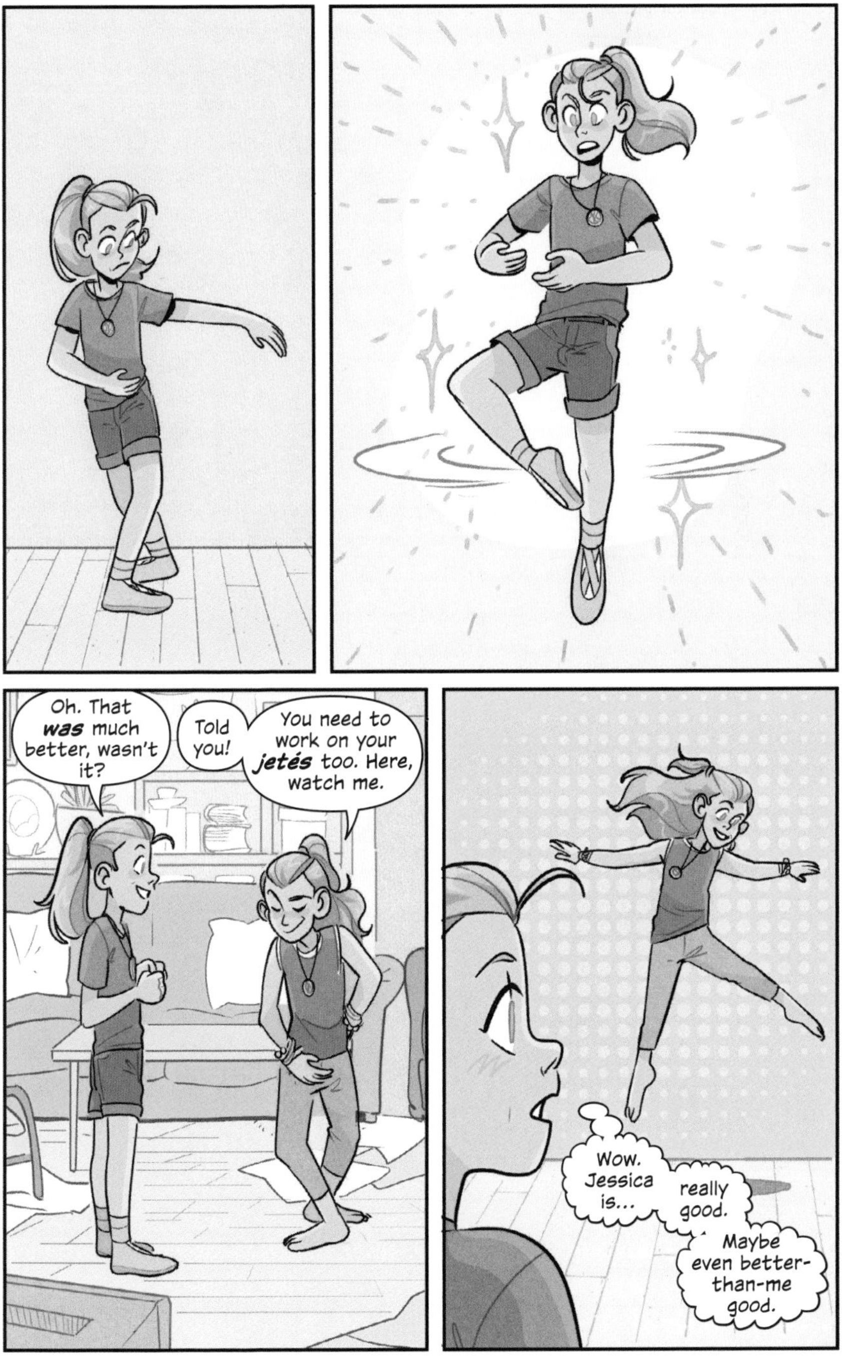
Oh. That **was** much better, wasn't it?
Told you!
You need to work on your ***jetés*** too. Here, watch me.
Wow. Jessica is...
really good.
Maybe even better-than-me good.

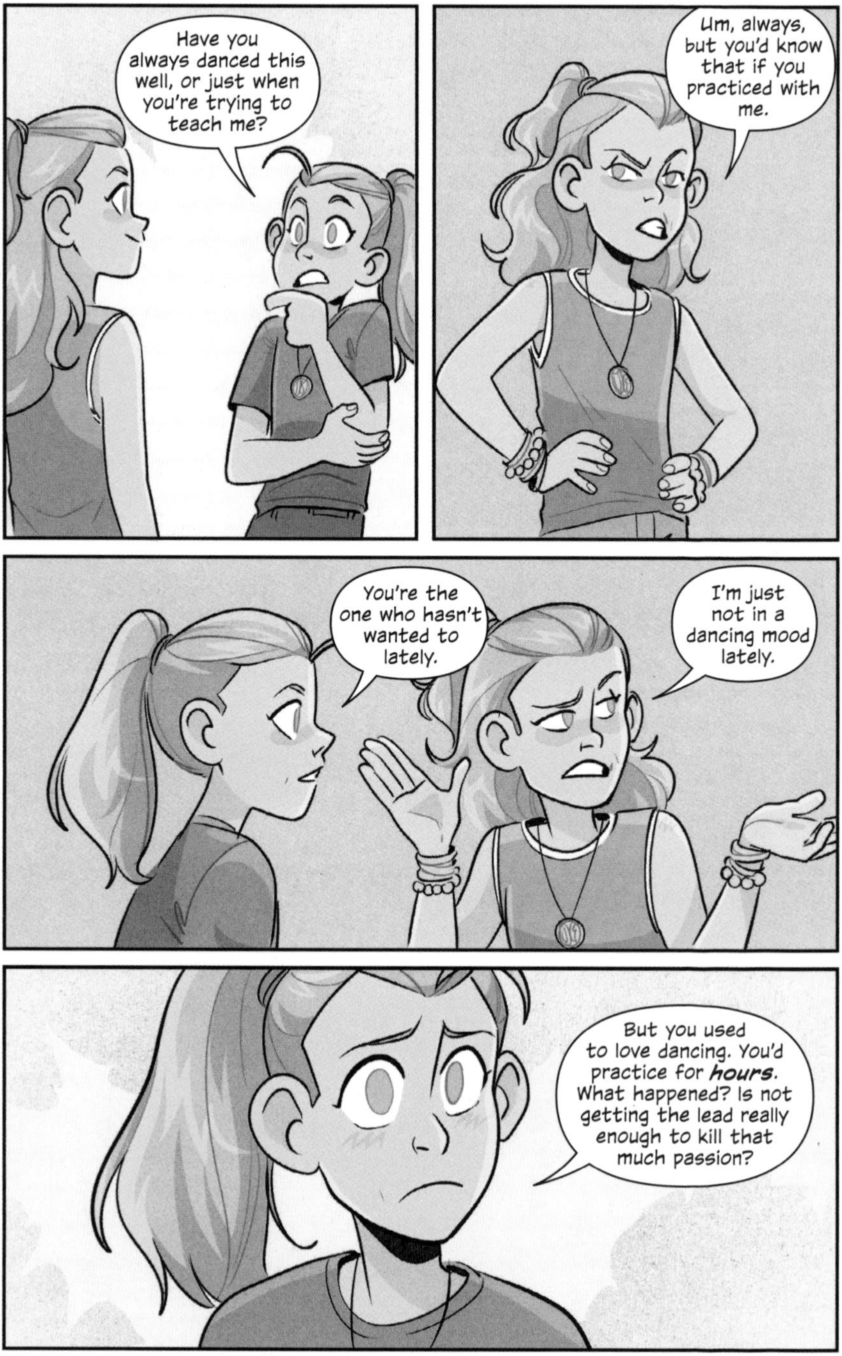
Have you always danced this well, or just when you're trying to teach me?
Um, always, but you'd know that if you practiced with me.
You're the one who hasn't wanted to lately.
I'm just not in a dancing mood lately.
But you used to love dancing. You'd practice for ***hours***. What happened? Is not getting the lead really enough to kill that much passion?

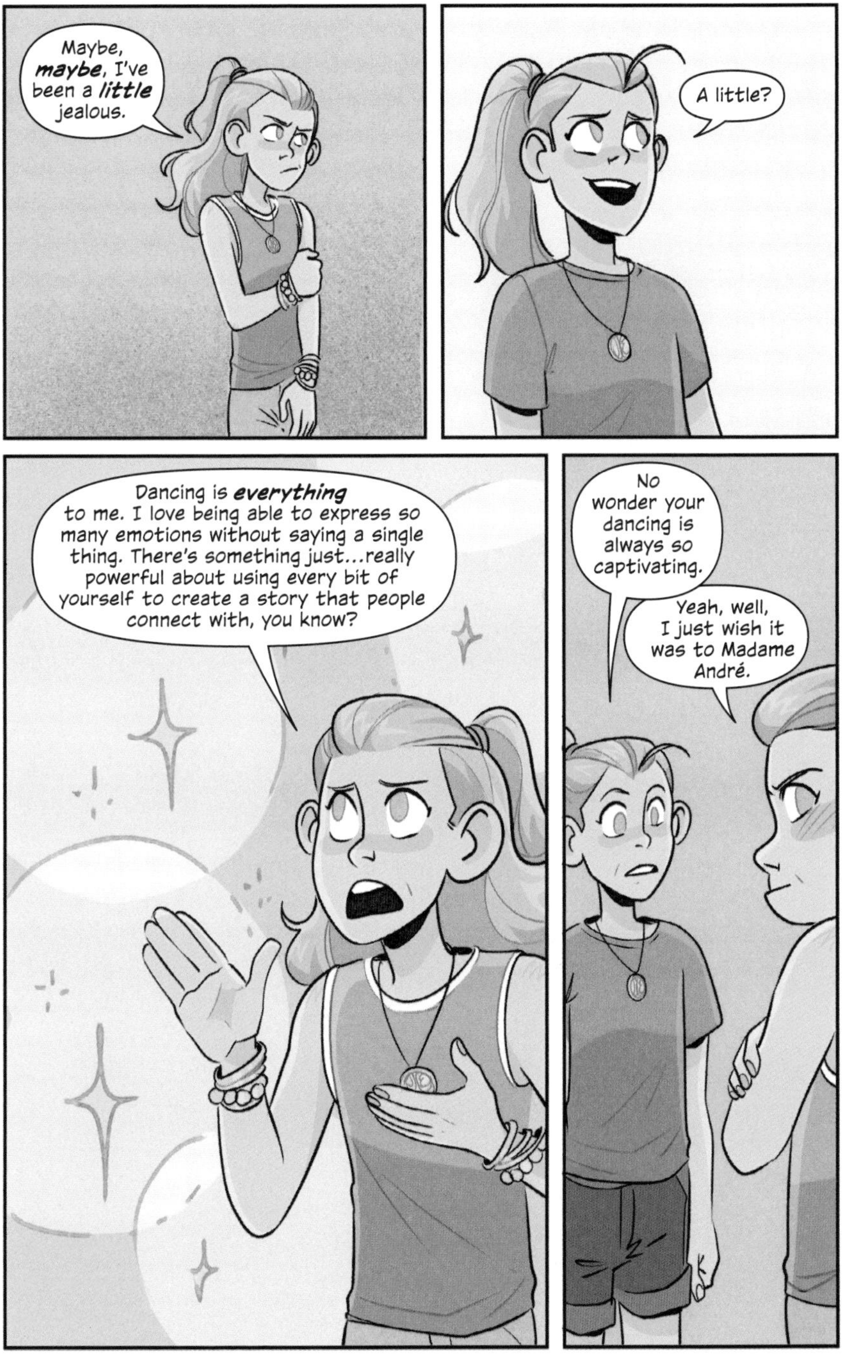

Maybe, **maybe**, I've been a ***little*** jealous.
A little?
Dancing is ***everything*** to me. I love being able to express so many emotions without saying a single thing. There's something just...really powerful about using every bit of yourself to create a story that people connect with, you know?
No wonder your dancing is always so captivating.
Yeah, well, I just wish it was to Madame André.

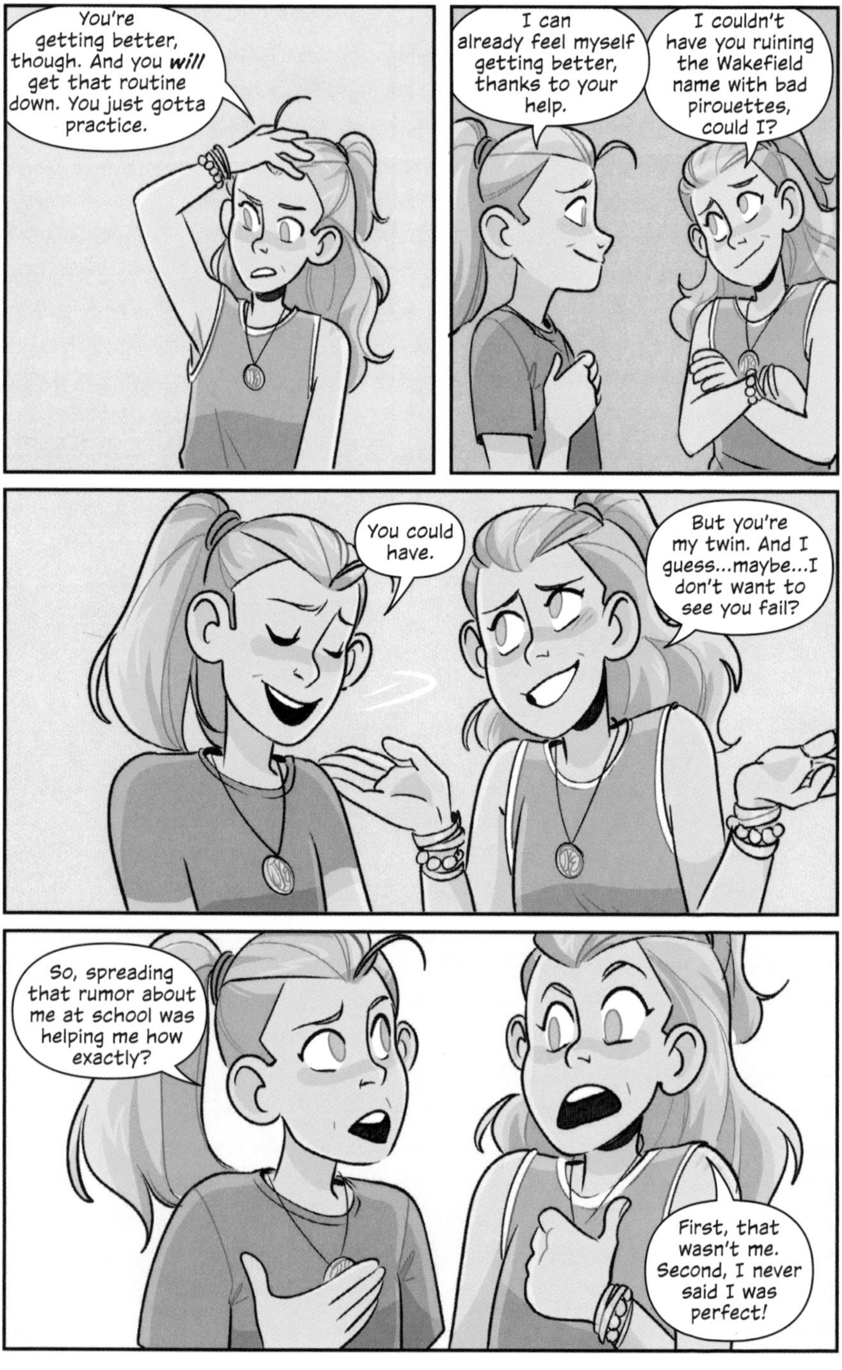
You're getting better, though. And you *will* get that routine down. You just gotta practice.
I can already feel myself getting better, thanks to your help.
I couldn't have you ruining the Wakefield name with bad pirouettes, could I?
You could have.
But you're my twin. And I guess...maybe...I don't want to see you fail?
So, spreading that rumor about me at school was helping me how exactly?
First, that wasn't me. Second, I never said I was perfect!

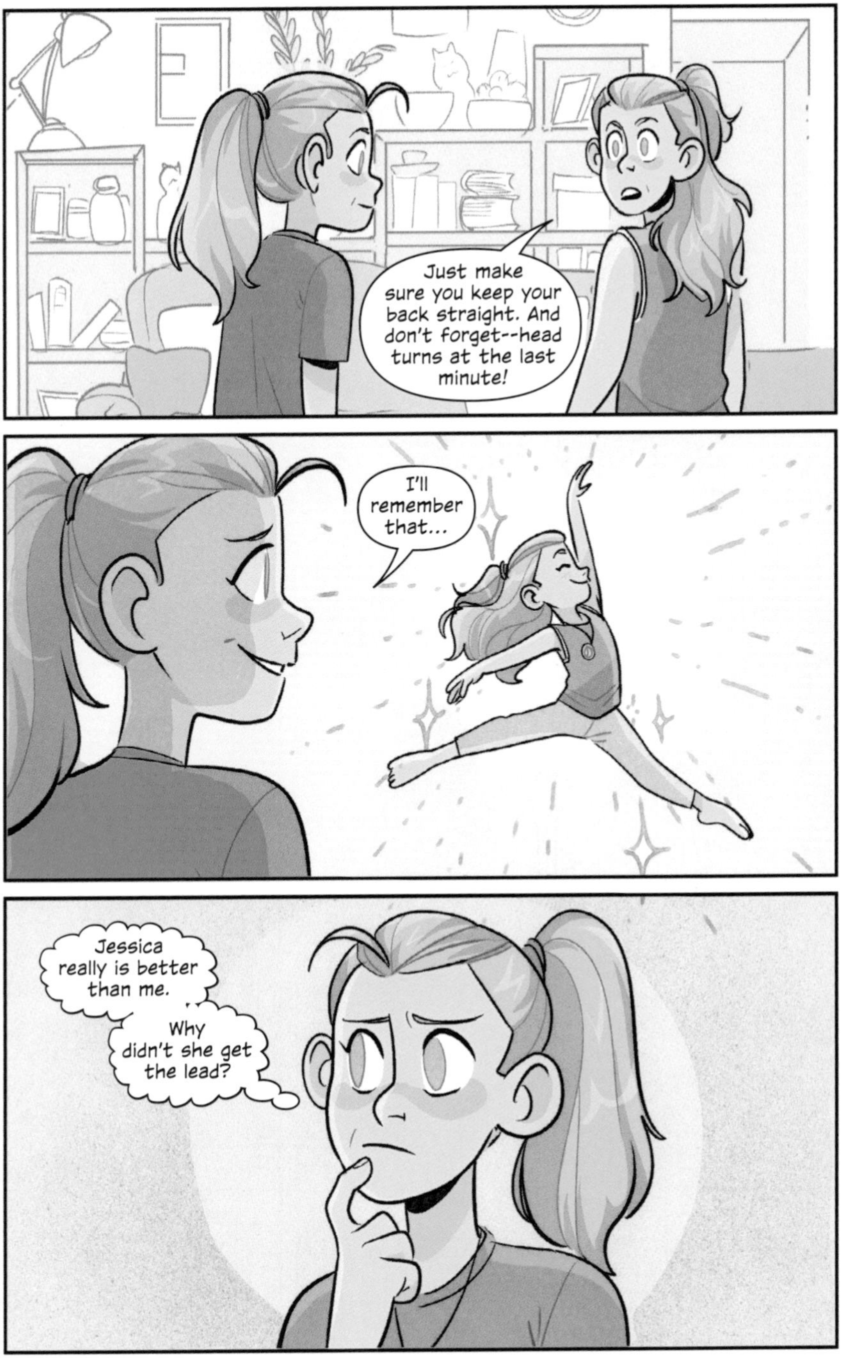
Just make sure you keep your back straight. And don't forget--head turns at the last minute!
I'll remember that...
Jessica really is better than me.
Why didn't she get the lead?

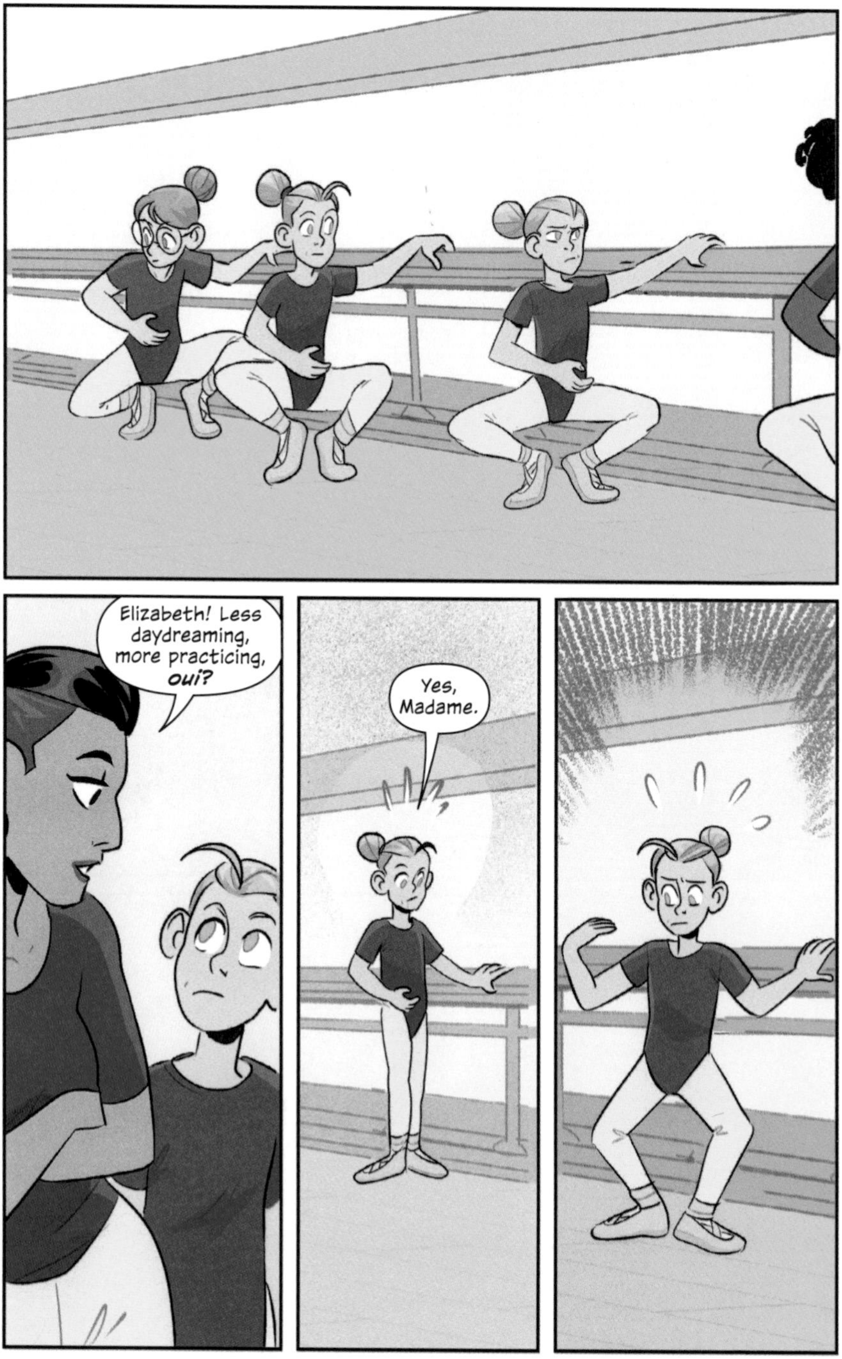
Elizabeth! Less daydreaming, more practicing, oui?
Yes, Madame.

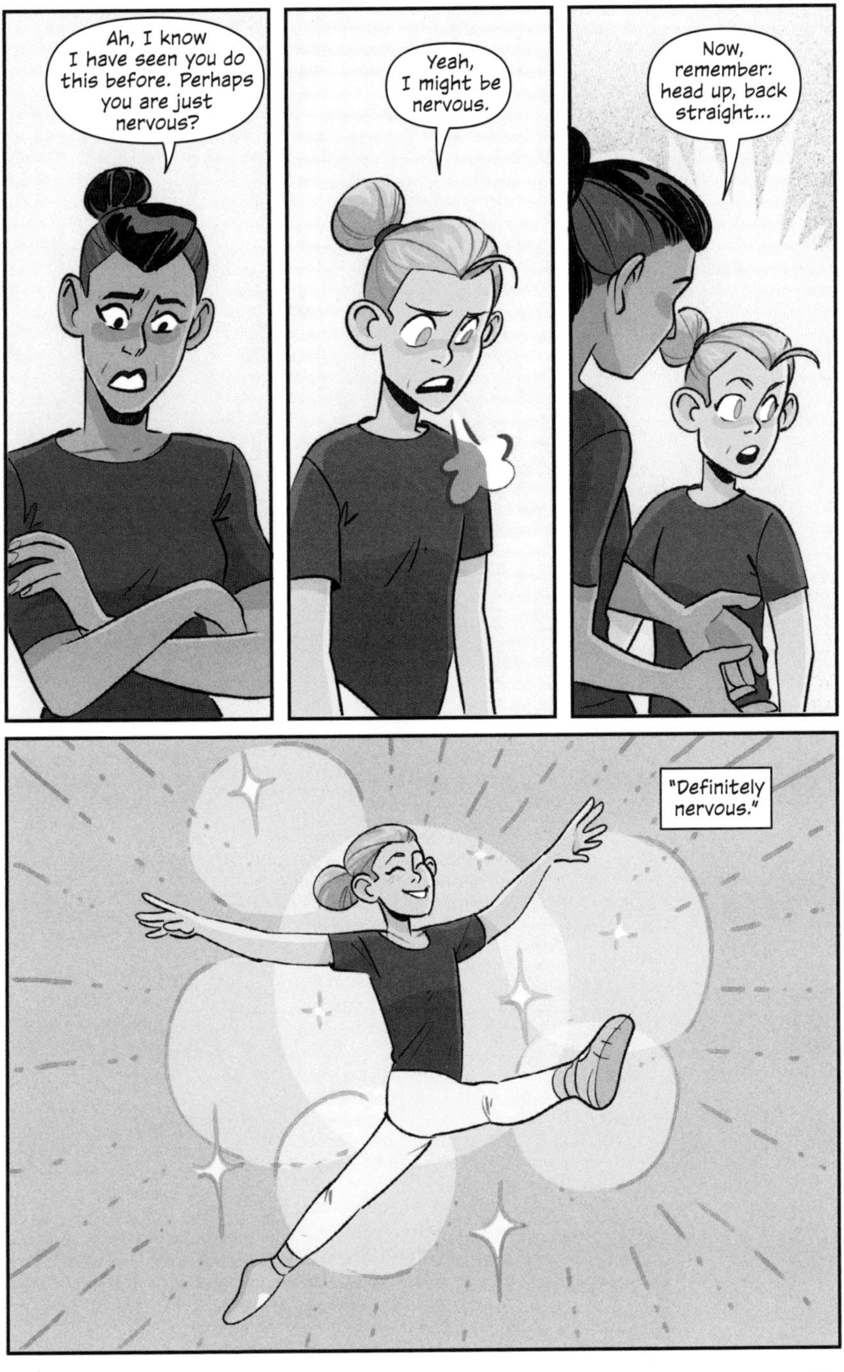
Ah, I know I have seen you do this before. Perhaps you are just nervous?
Yeah, I might be nervous.
Now, remember: head up, back straight...
"Definitely nervous."

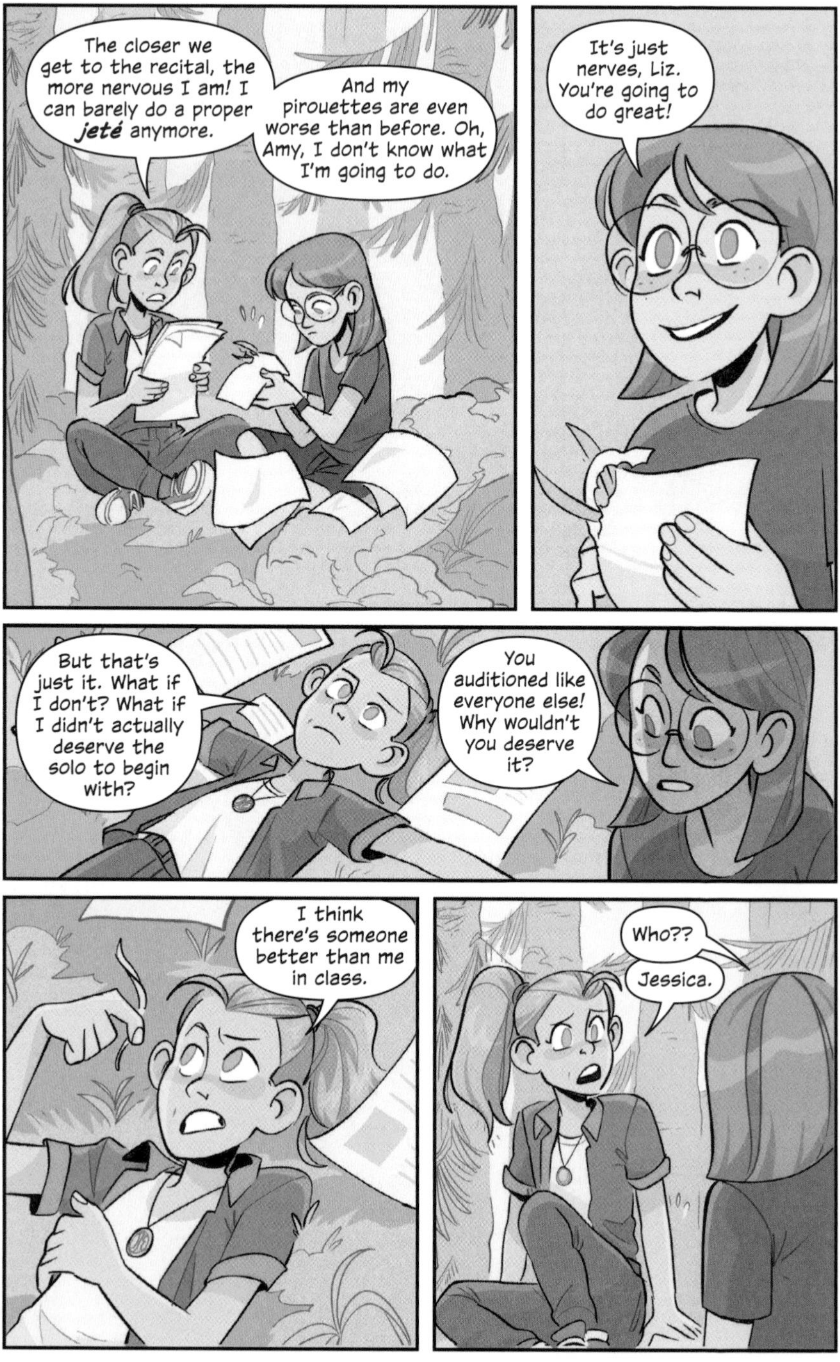
The closer we get to the recital, the more nervous I am! I can barely do a proper **jeté** anymore.
And my pirouettes are even worse than before. Oh, Amy, I don't know what I'm going to do.
It's just nerves, Liz. You're going to do great!
But that's just it. What if I don't? What if I didn't actually deserve the solo to begin with?
You auditioned like everyone else! Why wouldn't you deserve it?
I think there's someone better than me in class.
Who??
Jessica.

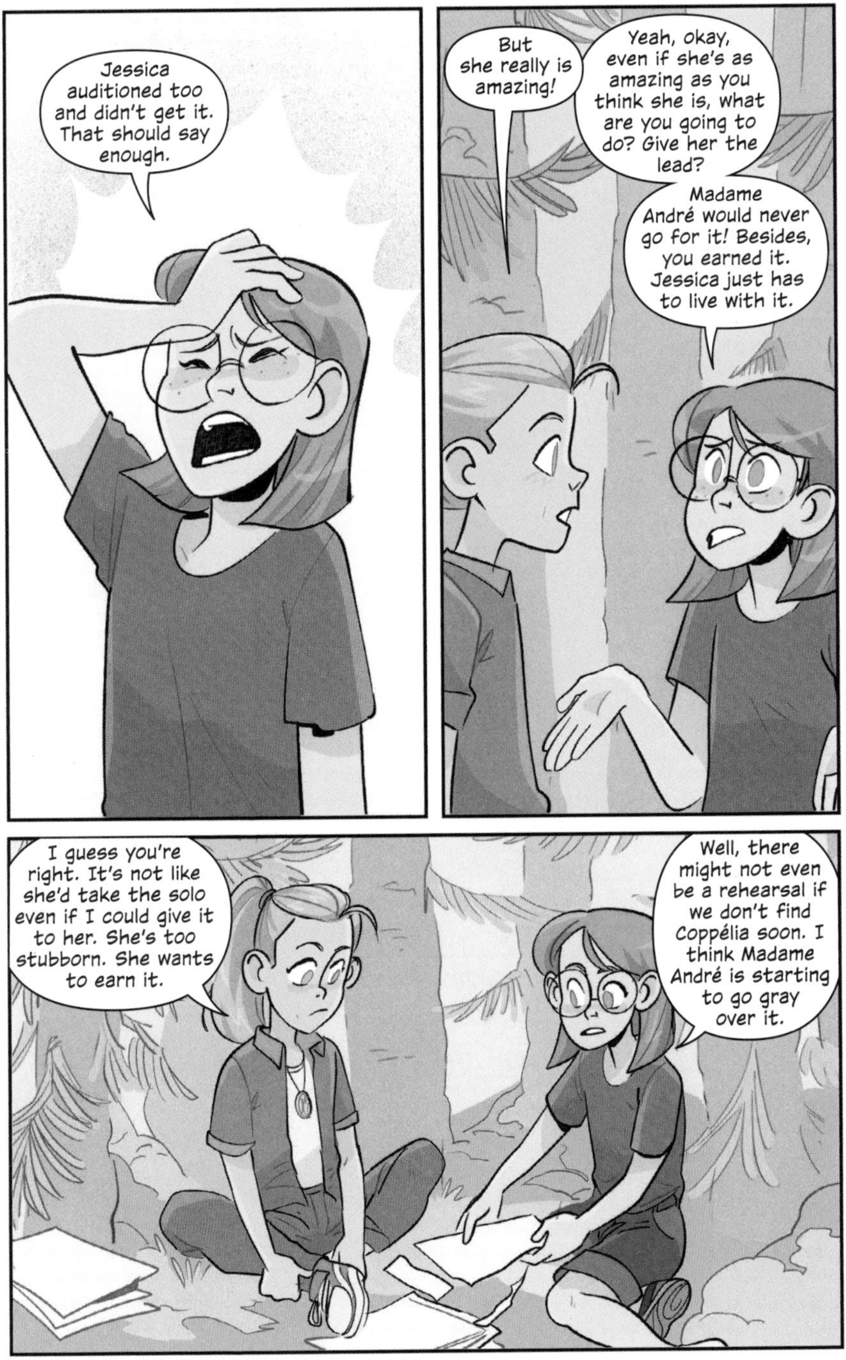

Jessica auditioned too and didn't get it. That should say enough.
But she really is amazing!
Yeah, okay, even if she's as amazing as you think she is, what are you going to do? Give her the lead?
Madame André would never go for it! Besides, you earned it. Jessica just has to live with it.
I guess you're right. It's not like she'd take the solo even if I could give it to her. She's too stubborn. She wants to earn it.
Well, there might not even be a rehearsal if we don't find Coppélia soon. I think Madame André is starting to go gray over it.

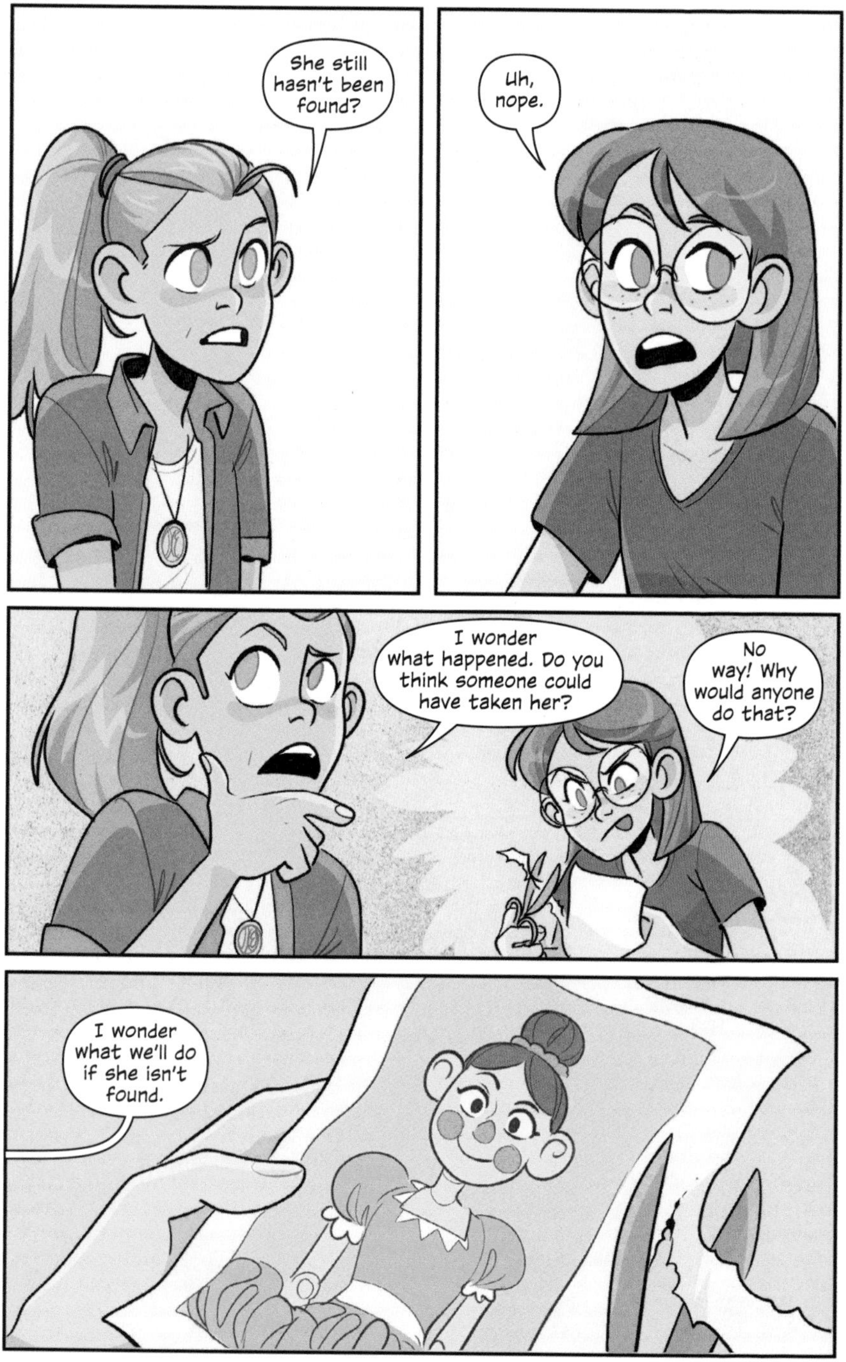
She still hasn't been found?
Uh, nope.
I wonder what happened. Do you think someone could have taken her?
No way! Why would anyone do that?
I wonder what we'll do if she isn't found.

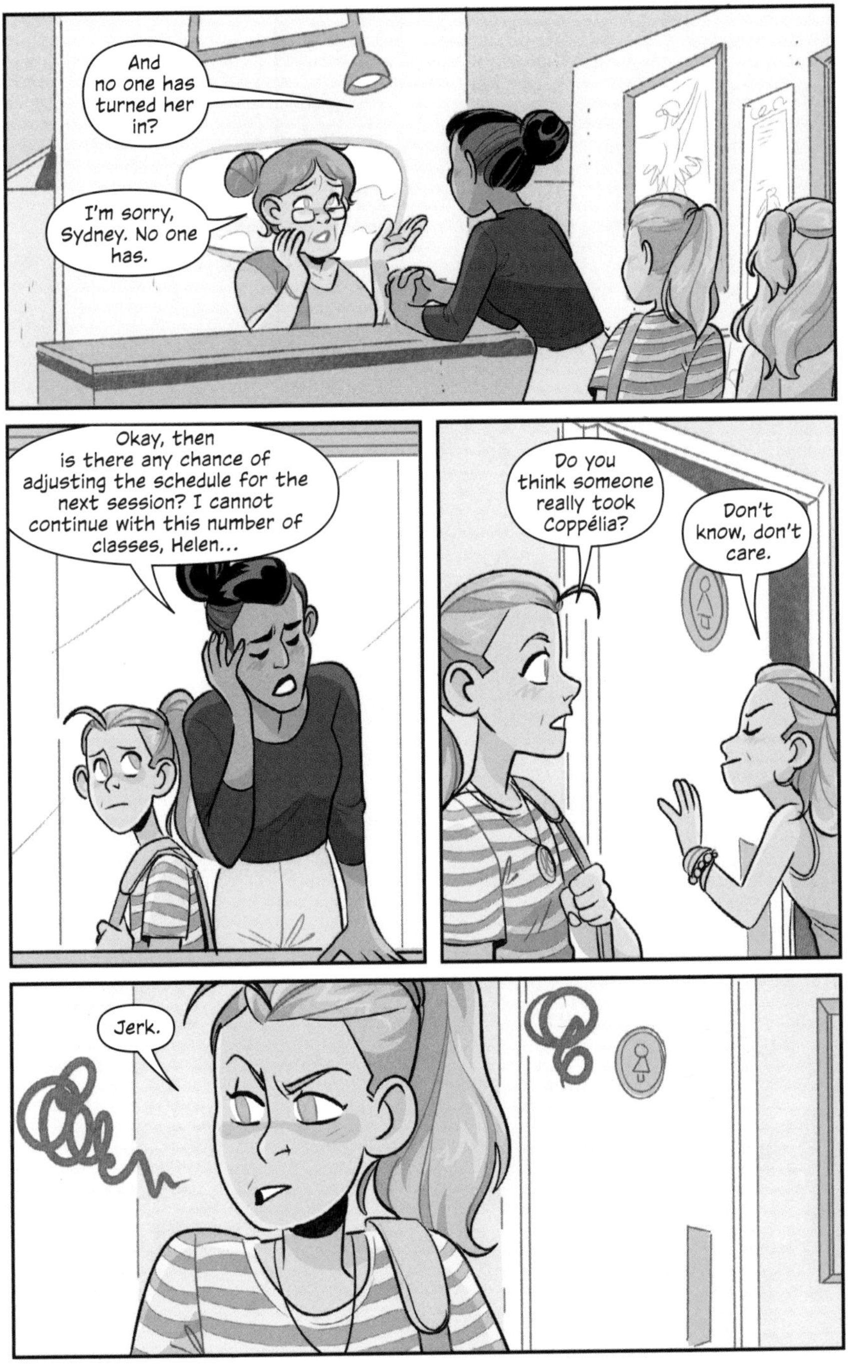

And no one has turned her in?
I'm sorry, Sydney. No one has.
Okay, then is there any chance of adjusting the schedule for the next session? I cannot continue with this number of classes, Helen...
Do you think someone really took Coppélia?
Don't know, don't care.
Jerk.

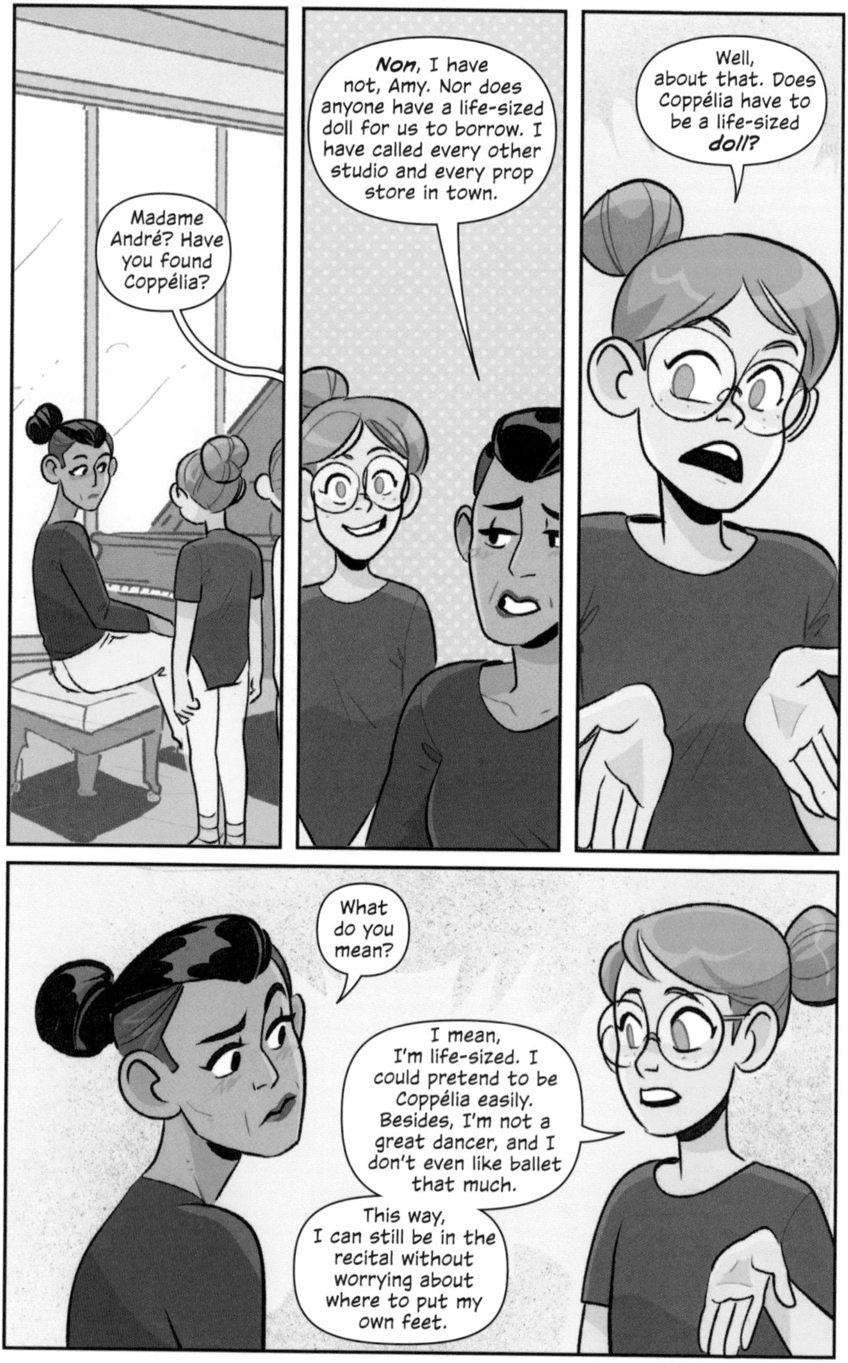
Madame André? Have you found Coppélia?
Non, I have not, Amy. Nor does anyone have a life-sized doll for us to borrow. I have called every other studio and every prop store in town.
Well, about that. Does Coppélia have to be a life-sized doll?
What do you mean?
I mean, I'm life-sized. I could pretend to be Coppélia easily. Besides, I'm not a great dancer, and I don't even like ballet that much.
This way, I can still be in the recital without worrying about where to put my own feet.

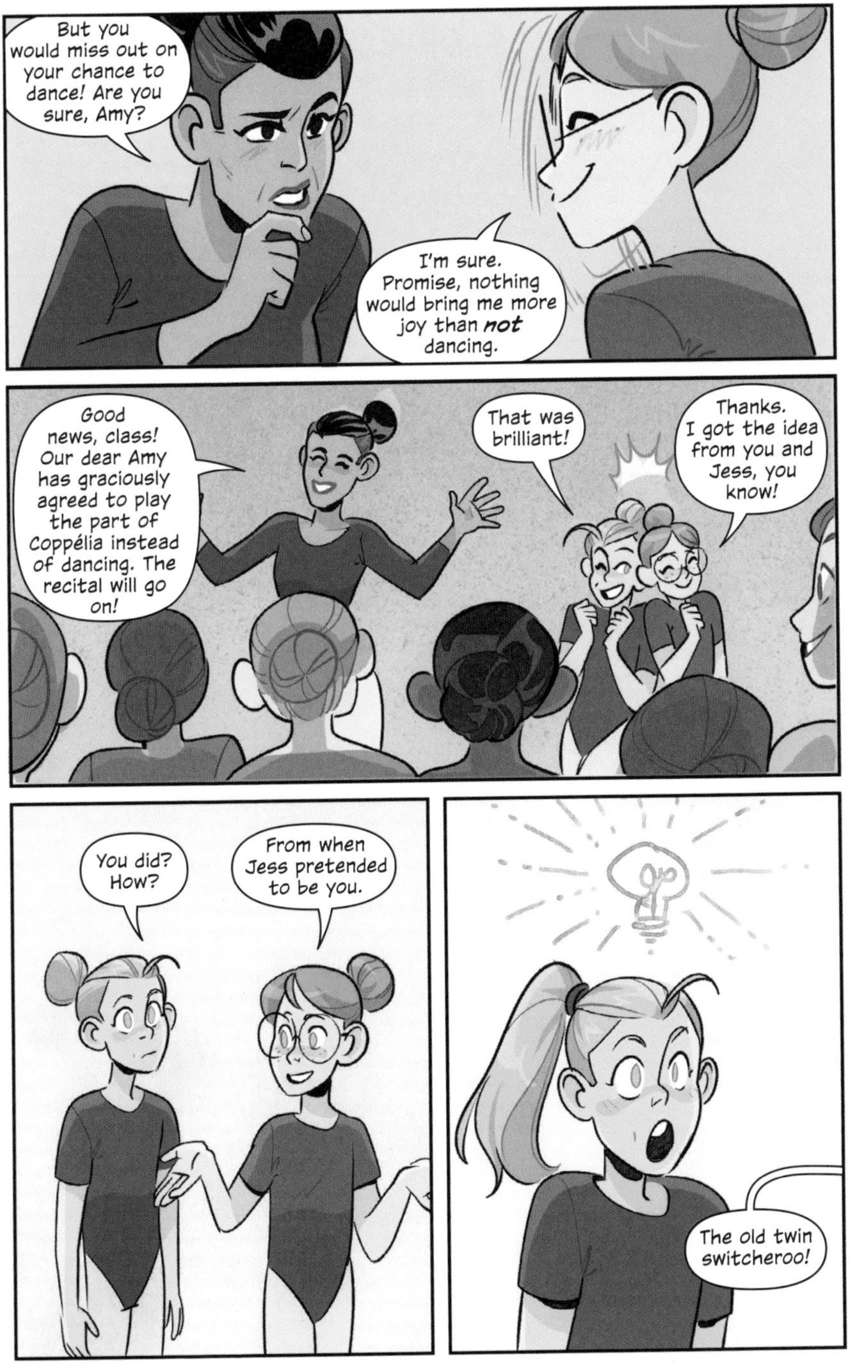
But you would miss out on your chance to dance! Are you sure, Amy?
I'm sure. Promise, nothing would bring me more joy than ***not*** dancing.
Good news, class! Our dear Amy has graciously agreed to play the part of Coppélia instead of dancing. The recital will go on!
That was brilliant!
Thanks. I got the idea from you and Jess, you know!
You did? How?
From when Jess pretended to be you.
The old twin switcheroo!

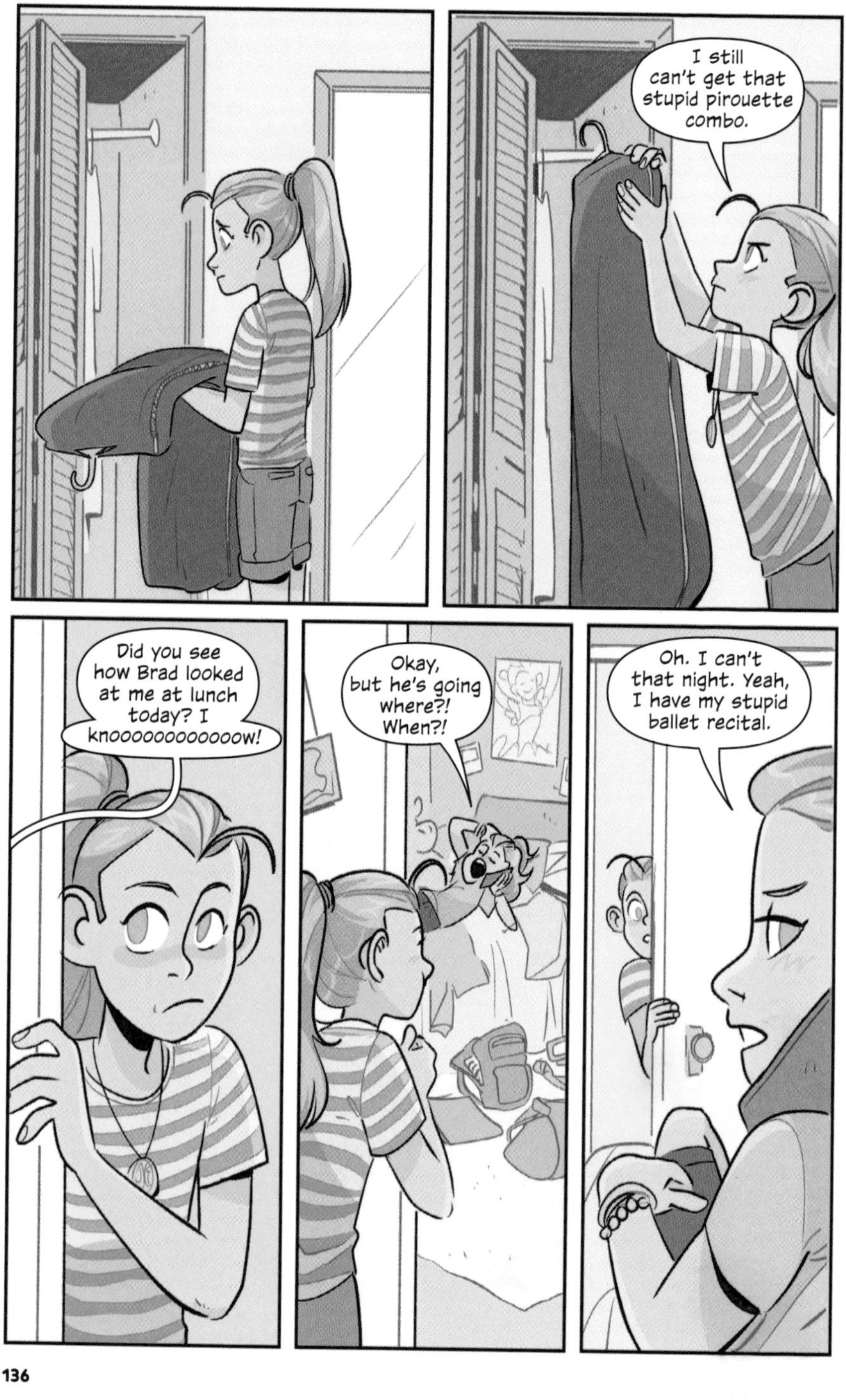
I still can't get that stupid pirouette combo.
Did you see how Brad looked at me at lunch today? I knoooooooooooow!
Okay, but he's going where?! When?!
Oh. I can't that night. Yeah, I have my stupid ballet recital.

Yeah. I was looking forward to it, but...

Tell me about the party though. What are you going to wear?

The old twin switcheroo!

She'd never go for it. She barely even wants to dance! How do I convince her?

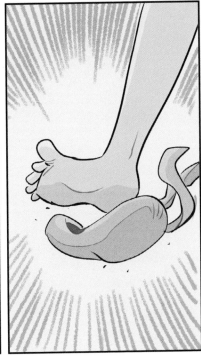

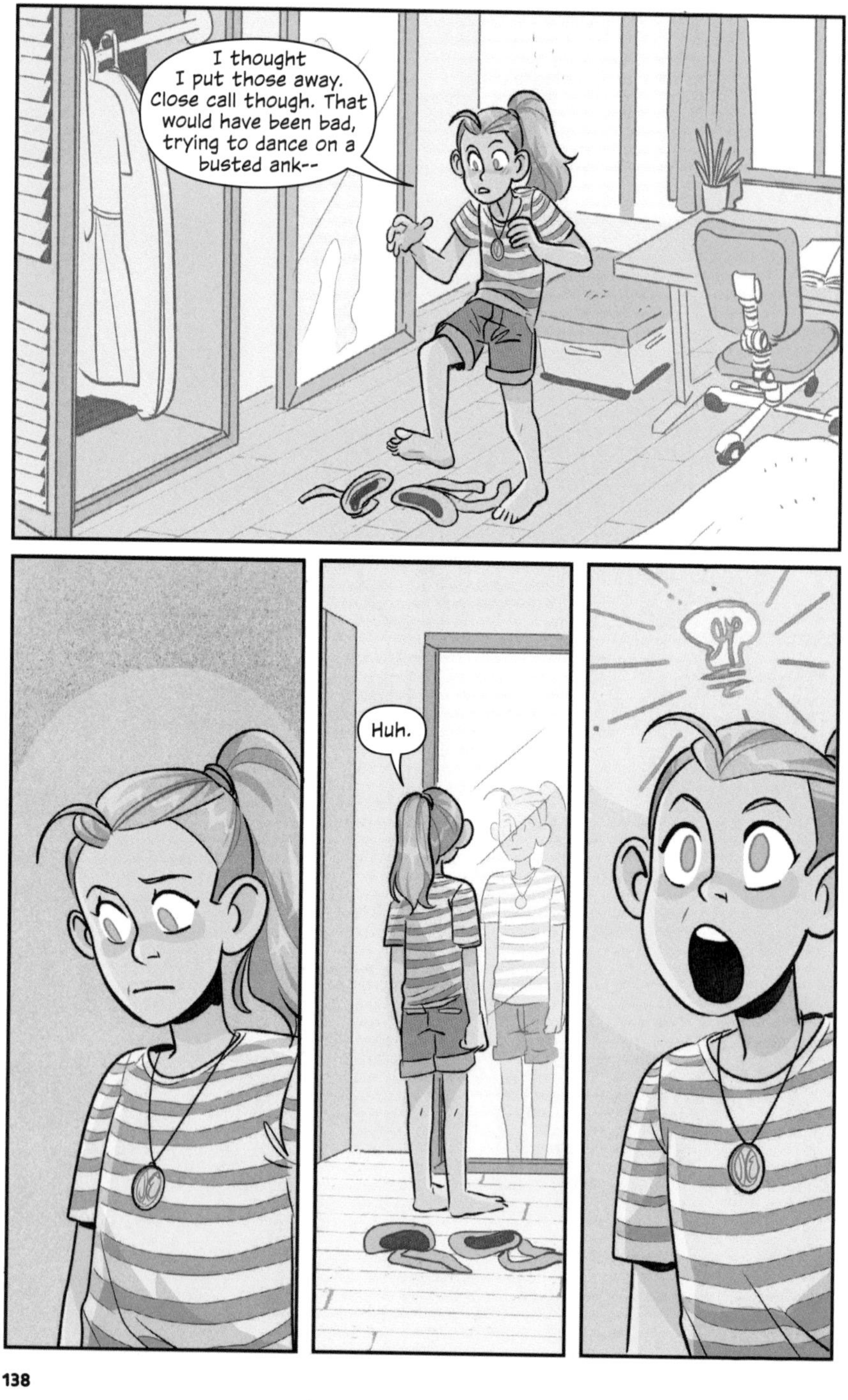
I thought I put those away. Close call though. That would have been bad, trying to dance on a busted ank--
Huh.

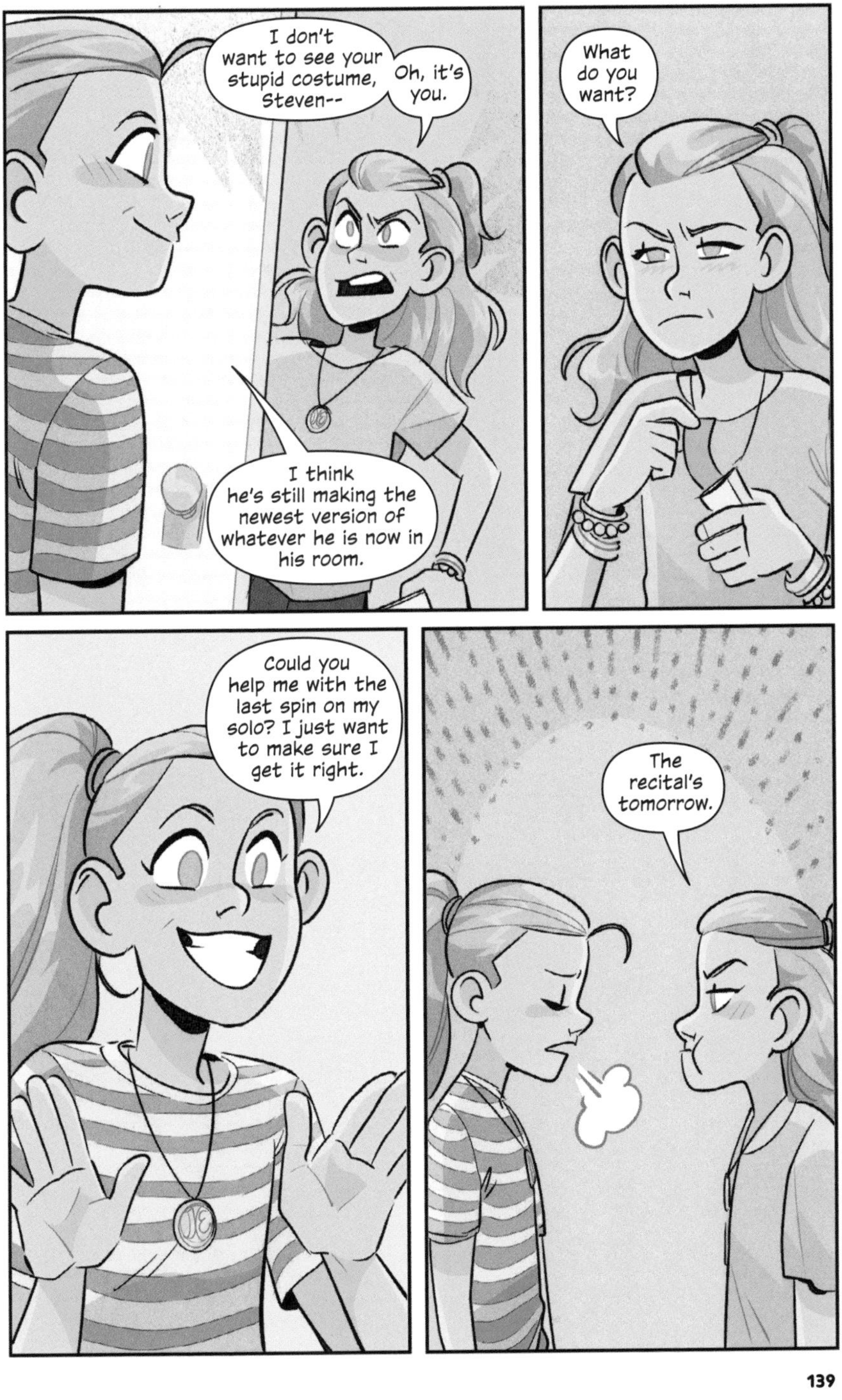
I don't want to see your stupid costume, Steven--
Oh, it's you.
I think he's still making the newest version of whatever he is now in his room.
What do you want?
Could you help me with the last spin on my solo? I just want to make sure I get it right.
The recital's tomorrow.

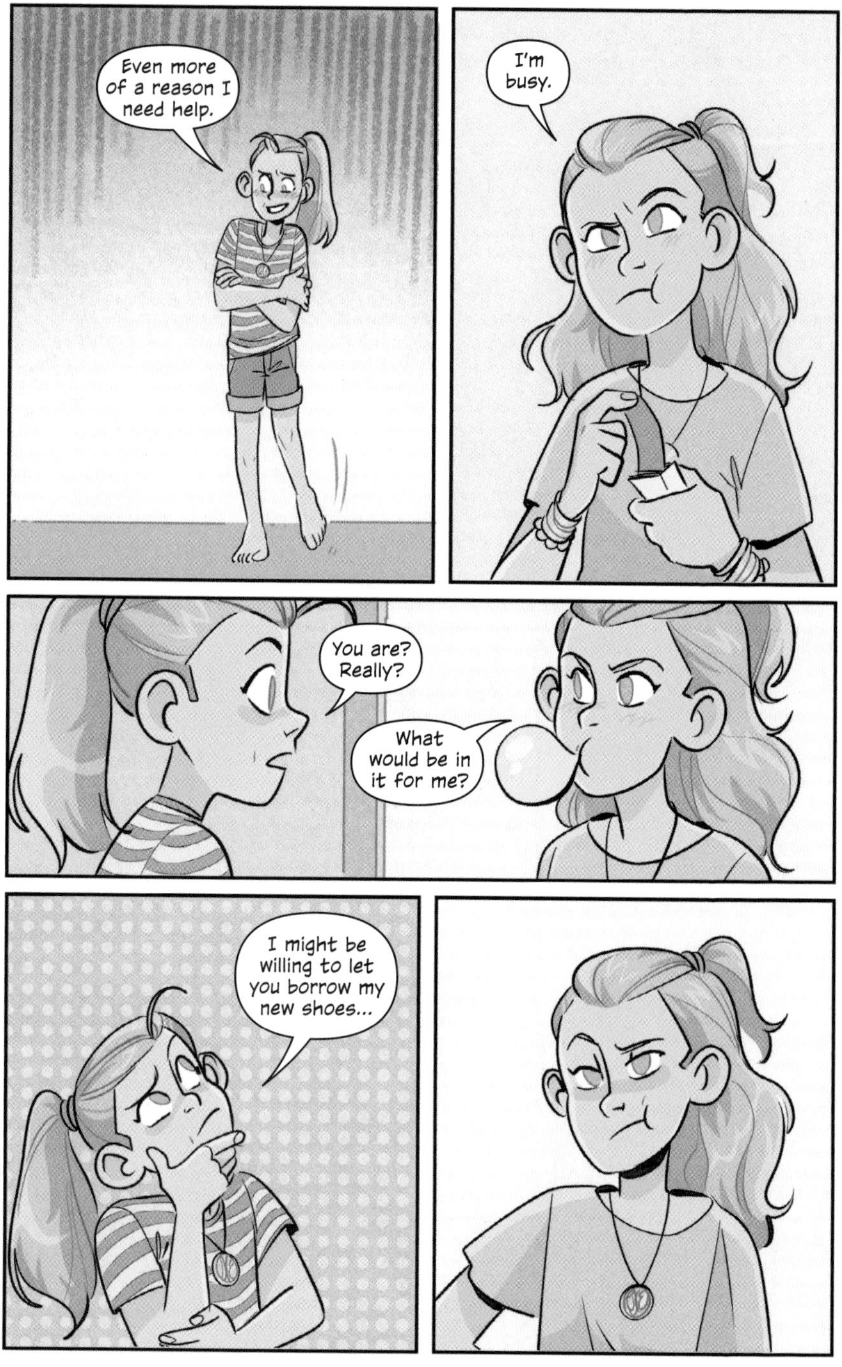
Even more of a reason I need help.
I'm busy.
You are? Really?
What would be in it for me?
I might be willing to let you borrow my new shoes...

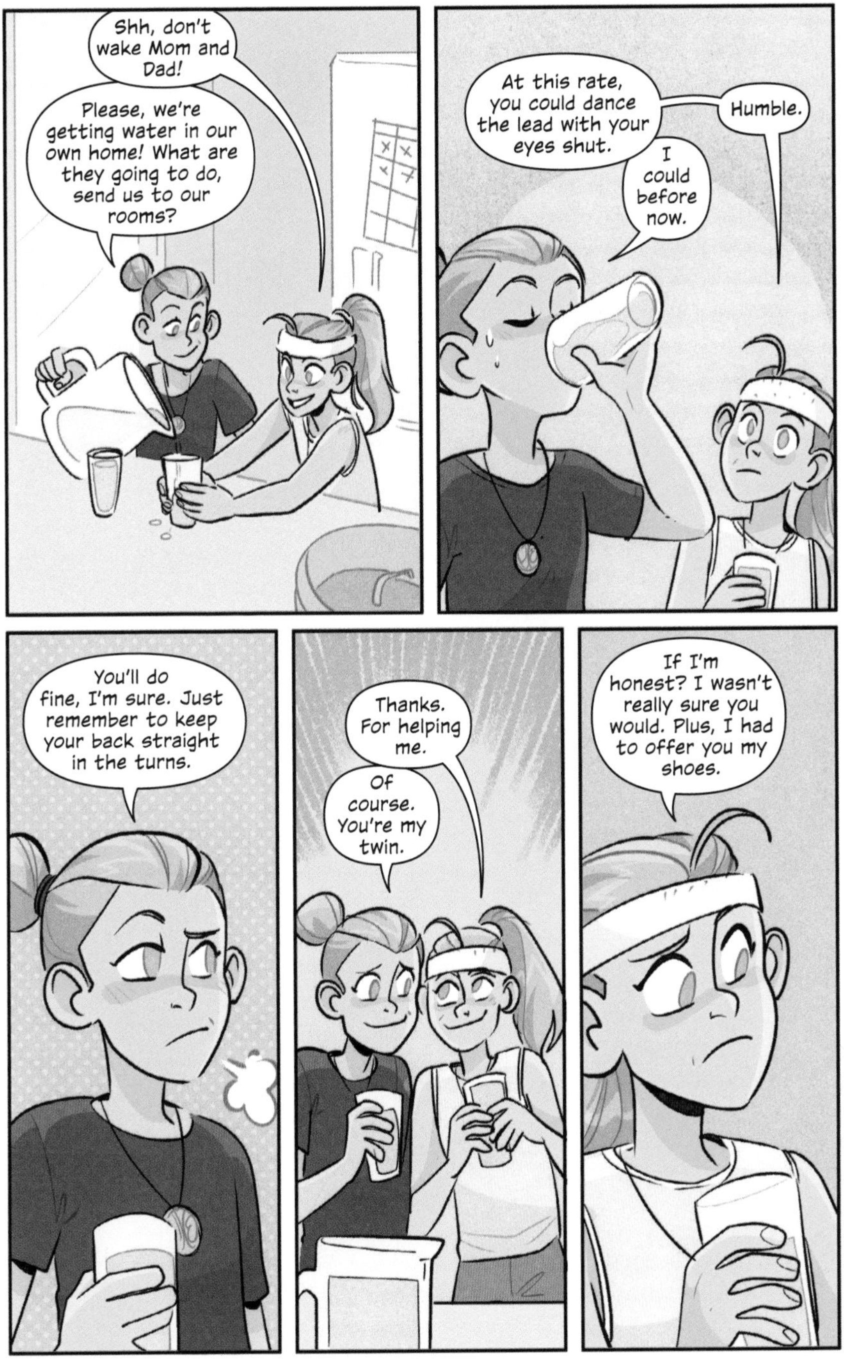
Shh, don't wake Mom and Dad!
Please, we're getting water in our own home! What are they going to do, send us to our rooms?
At this rate, you could dance the lead with your eyes shut.
Humble.
I could before now.
You'll do fine, I'm sure. Just remember to keep your back straight in the turns.
Thanks. For helping me.
Of course. You're my twin.
If I'm honest? I wasn't really sure you would. Plus, I had to offer you my shoes.

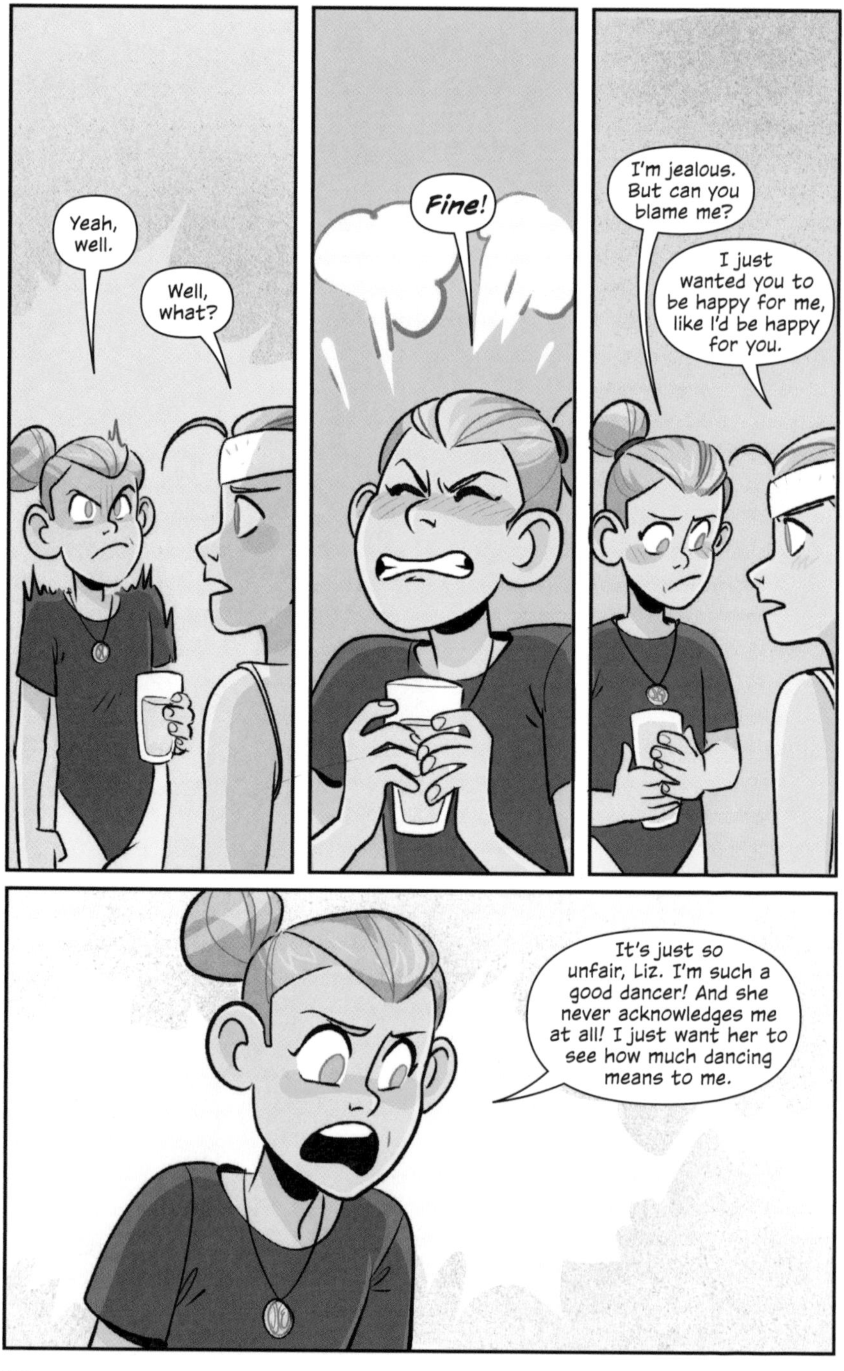
Yeah, well.
Well, what?
Fine!
I'm jealous. But can you blame me?
I just wanted you to be happy for me, like I'd be happy for you.
It's just so unfair, Liz. I'm such a good dancer! And she never acknowledges me at all! I just want her to see how much dancing means to me.

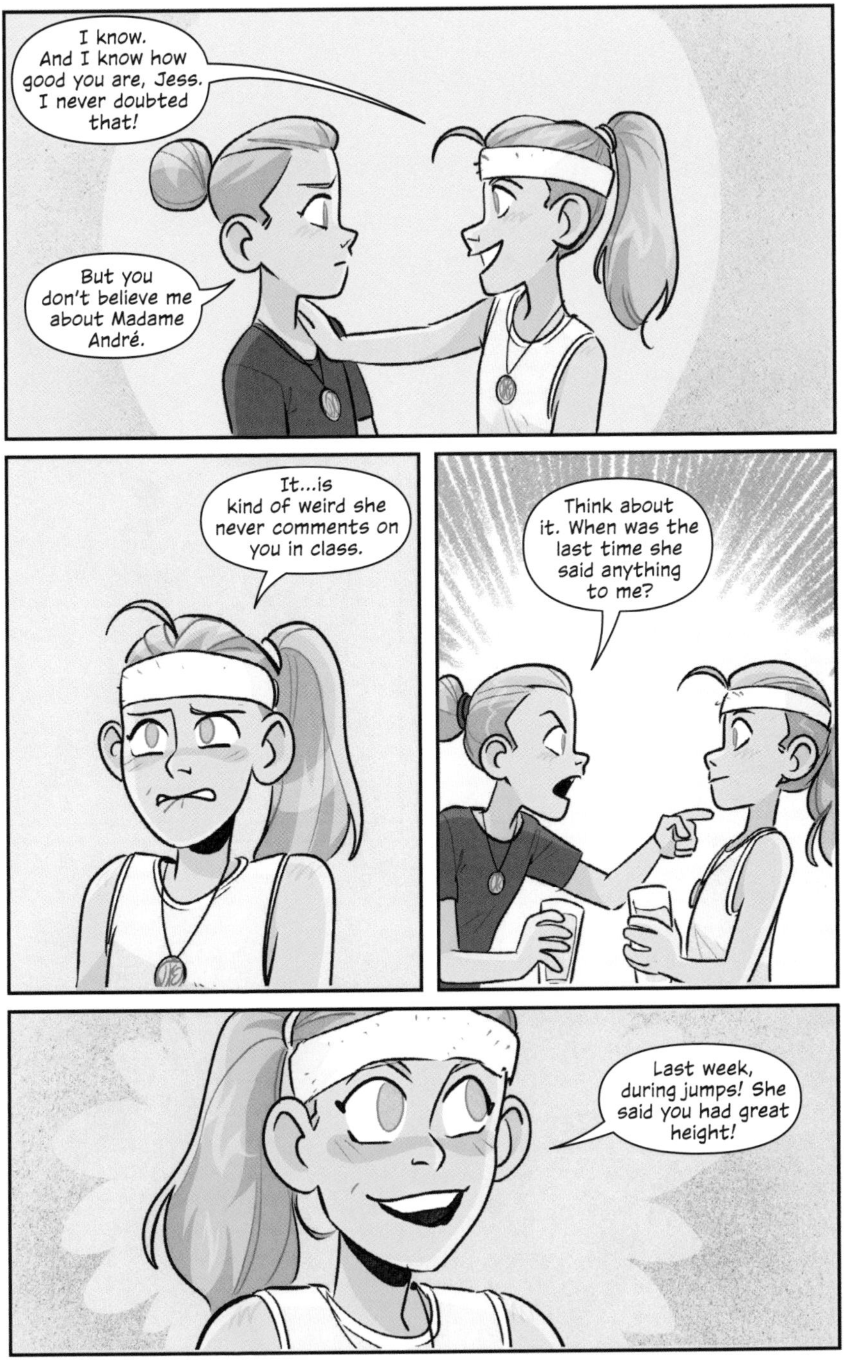
I know. And I know how good you are, Jess. I never doubted that!
But you don't believe me about Madame André.
It...is kind of weird she never comments on you in class.
Think about it. When was the last time she said anything to me?
Last week, during jumps! She said you had great height!

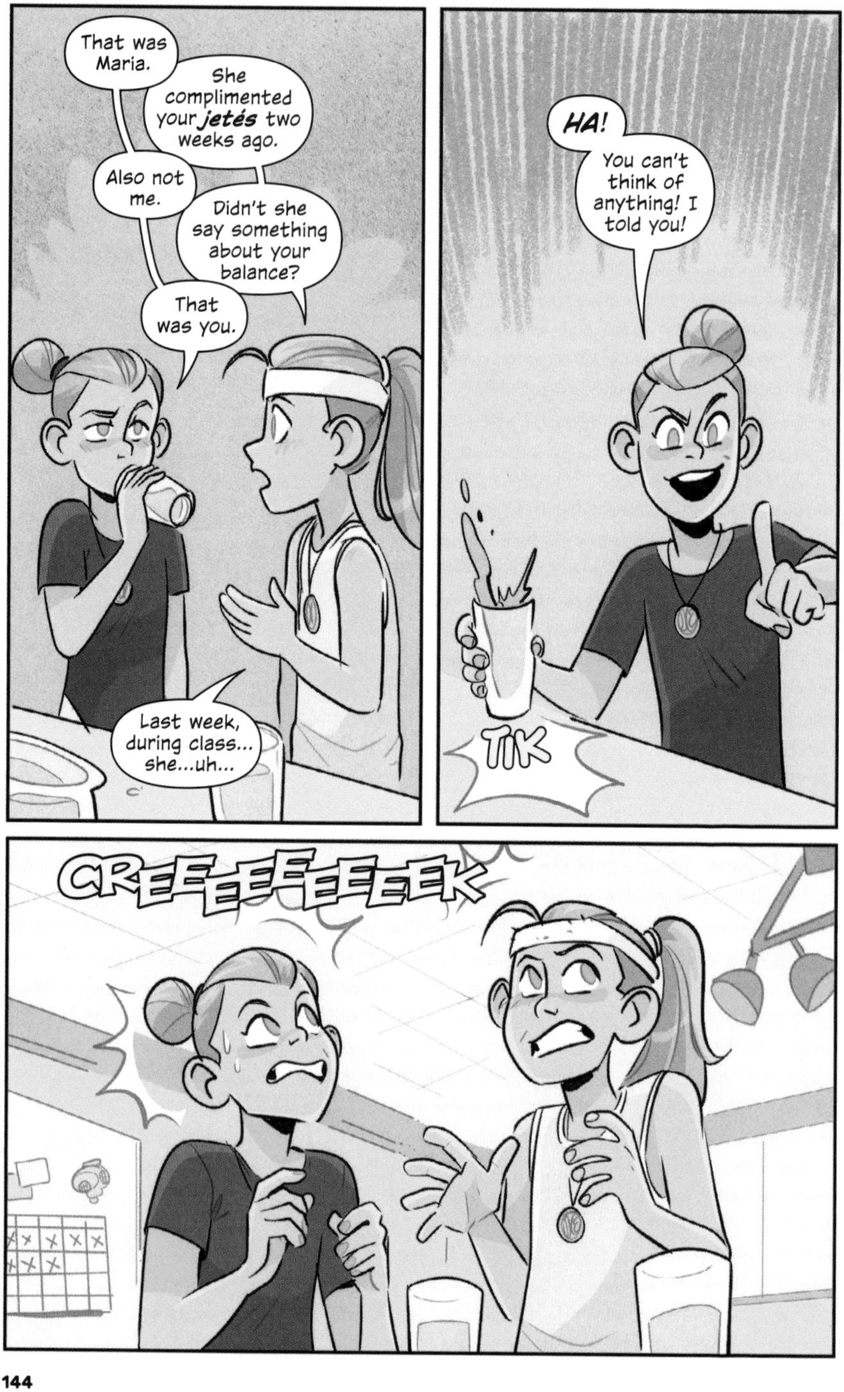

That was Maria.
She complimented your *jetés* two weeks ago.
Also not me.
Didn't she say something about your balance?
That was you.
Last week, during class... she...uh...
HA!
You can't think of anything! I told you!
TIK
CREEEEEEEEEEK

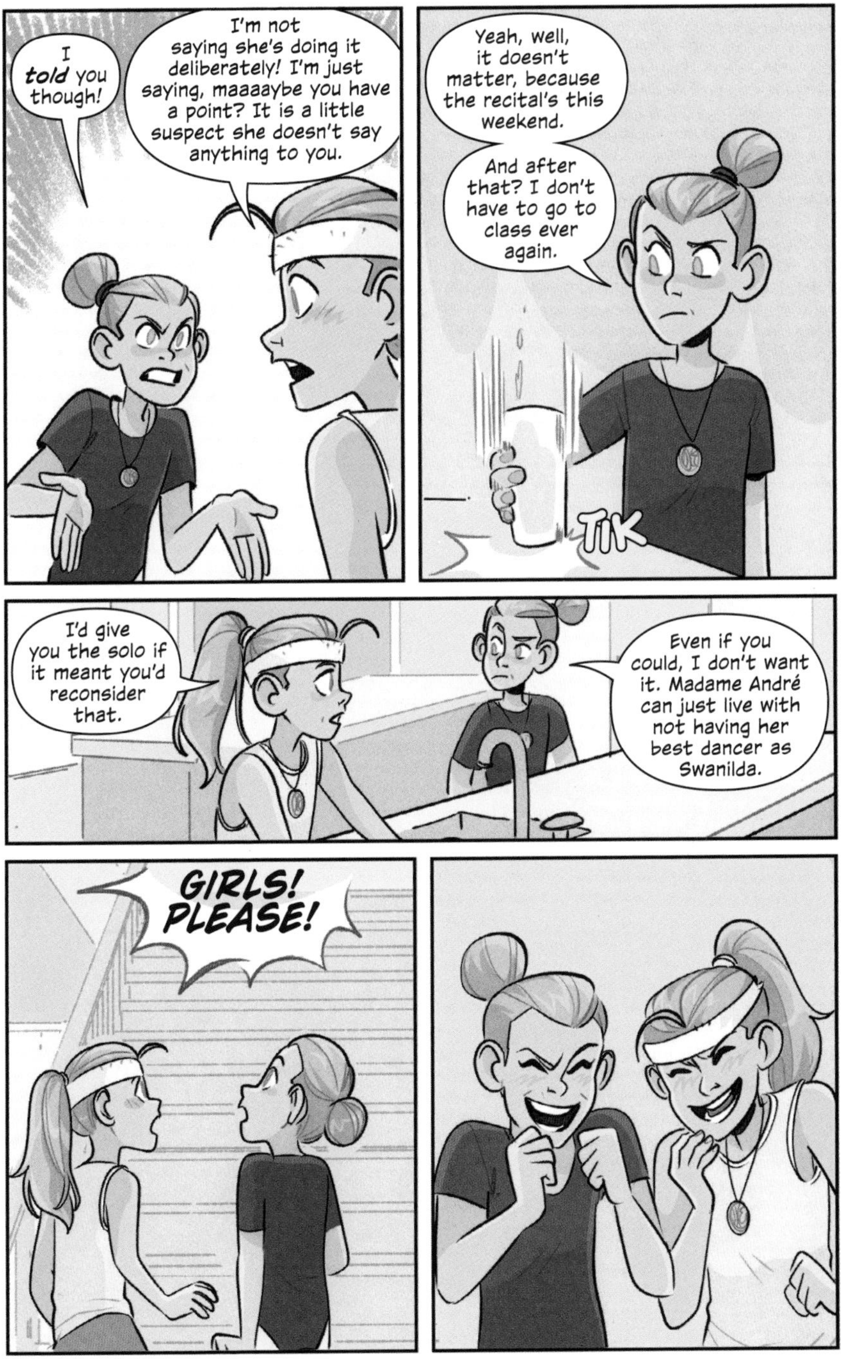

I *told* you though!
I'm not saying she's doing it deliberately! I'm just saying, maaaaybe you have a point? It is a little suspect she doesn't say anything to you.
Yeah, well, it doesn't matter, because the recital's this weekend.
And after that? I don't have to go to class ever again.
TIK
I'd give you the solo if it meant you'd reconsider that.
Even if you could, I don't want it. Madame André can just live with not having her best dancer as Swanilda.
GIRLS! PLEASE!

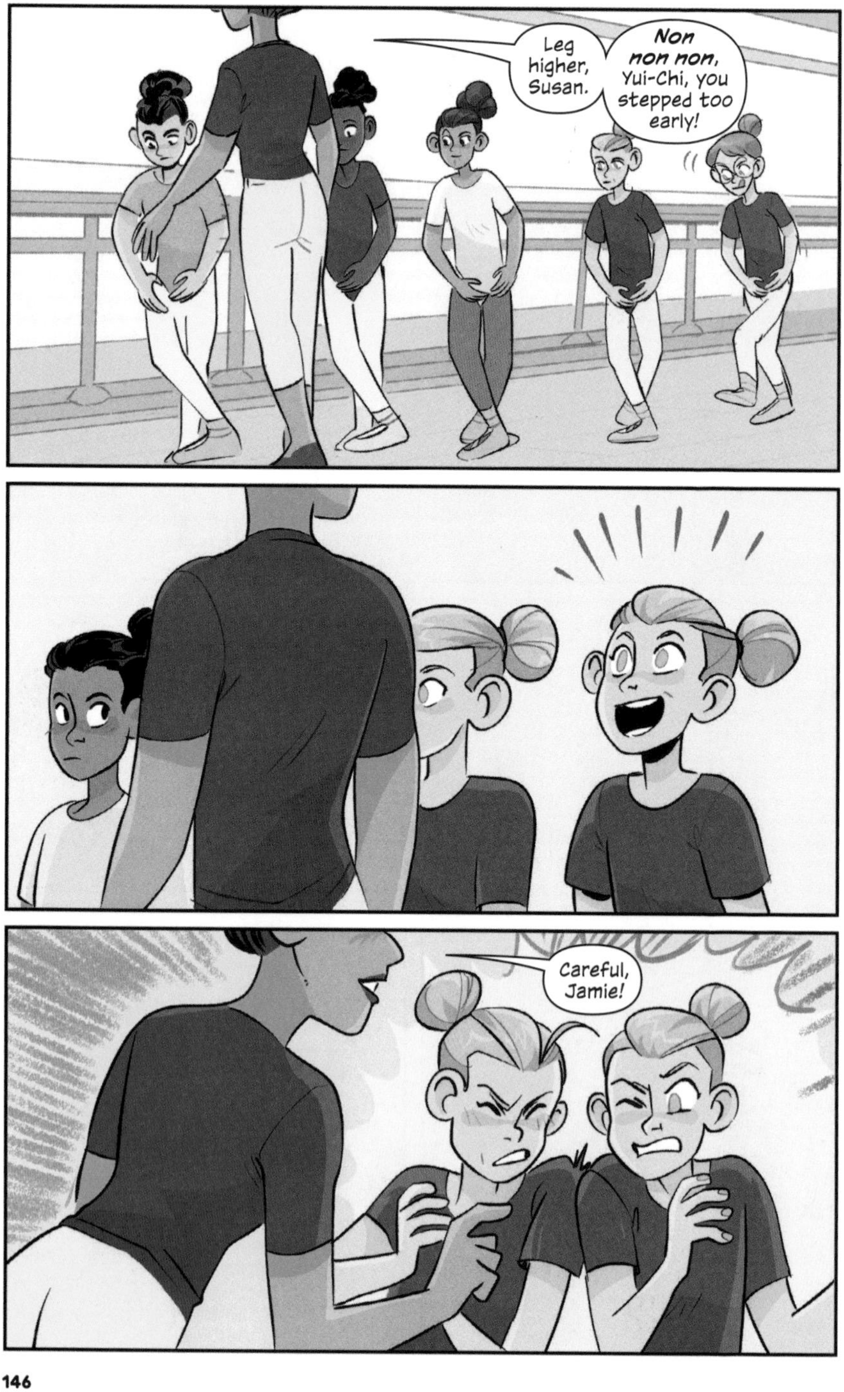
Leg higher, Susan.
Non non non, Yui-Chi, you stepped too early!
Careful, Jamie!

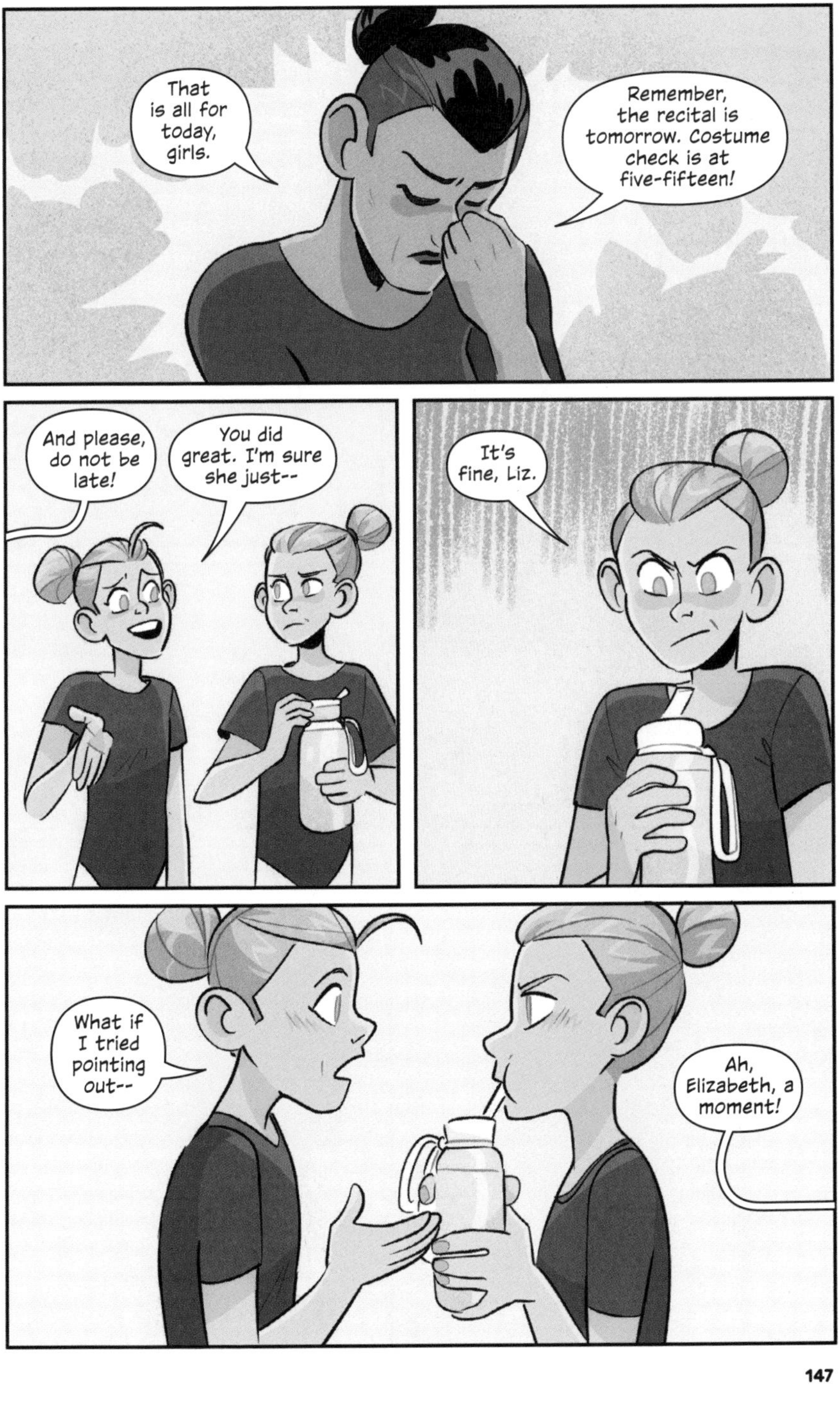
That is all for today, girls.
Remember, the recital is tomorrow. Costume check is at five-fifteen!
And please, do not be late!
You did great. I'm sure she just--
It's fine, Liz.
What if I tried pointing out--
Ah, Elizabeth, a moment!

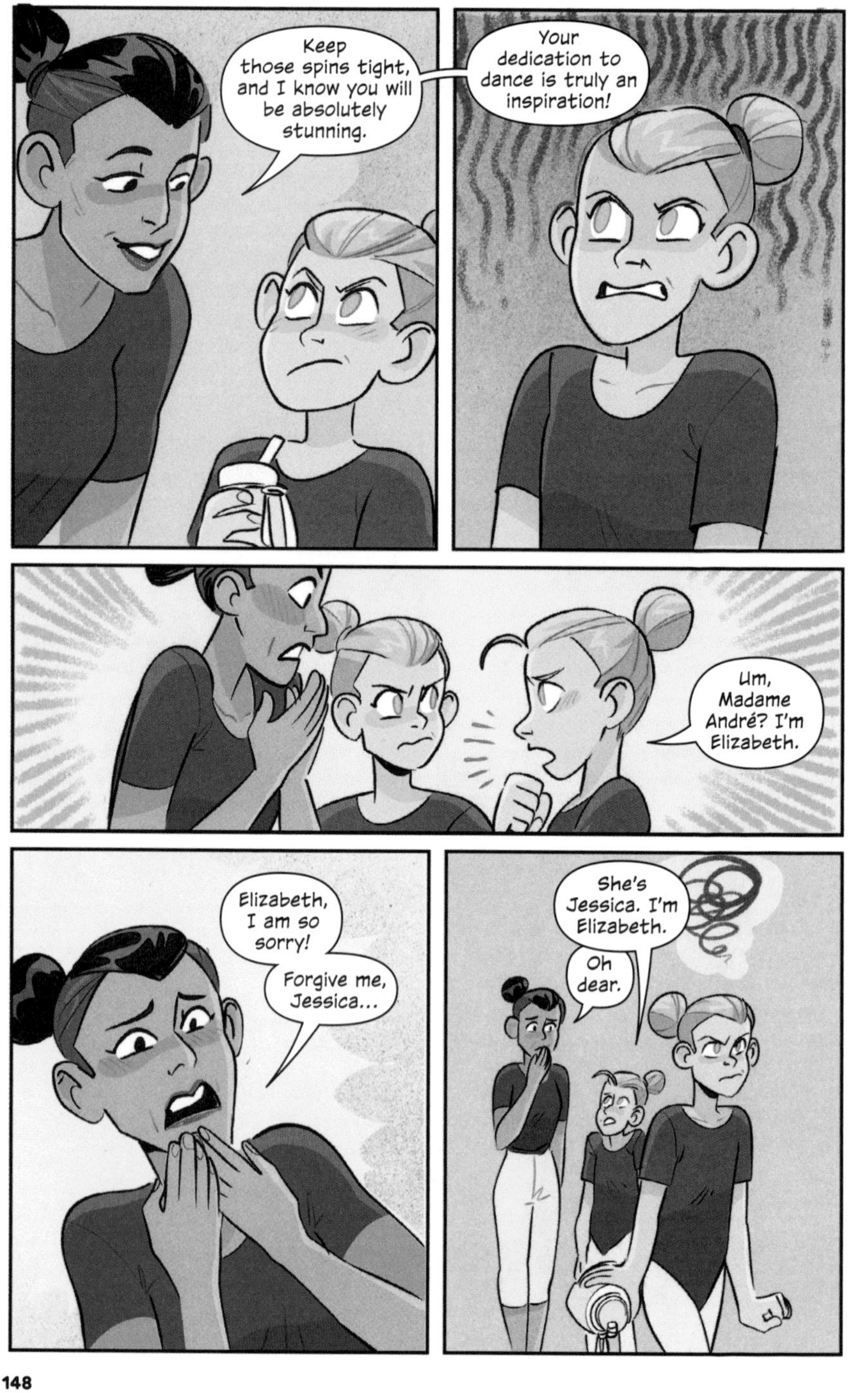
Keep those spins tight, and I know you will be absolutely stunning.
Your dedication to dance is truly an inspiration!
Um, Madame André? I'm Elizabeth.
Elizabeth, I am so sorry!
Forgive me, Jessica...
She's Jessica. I'm Elizabeth.
Oh dear.

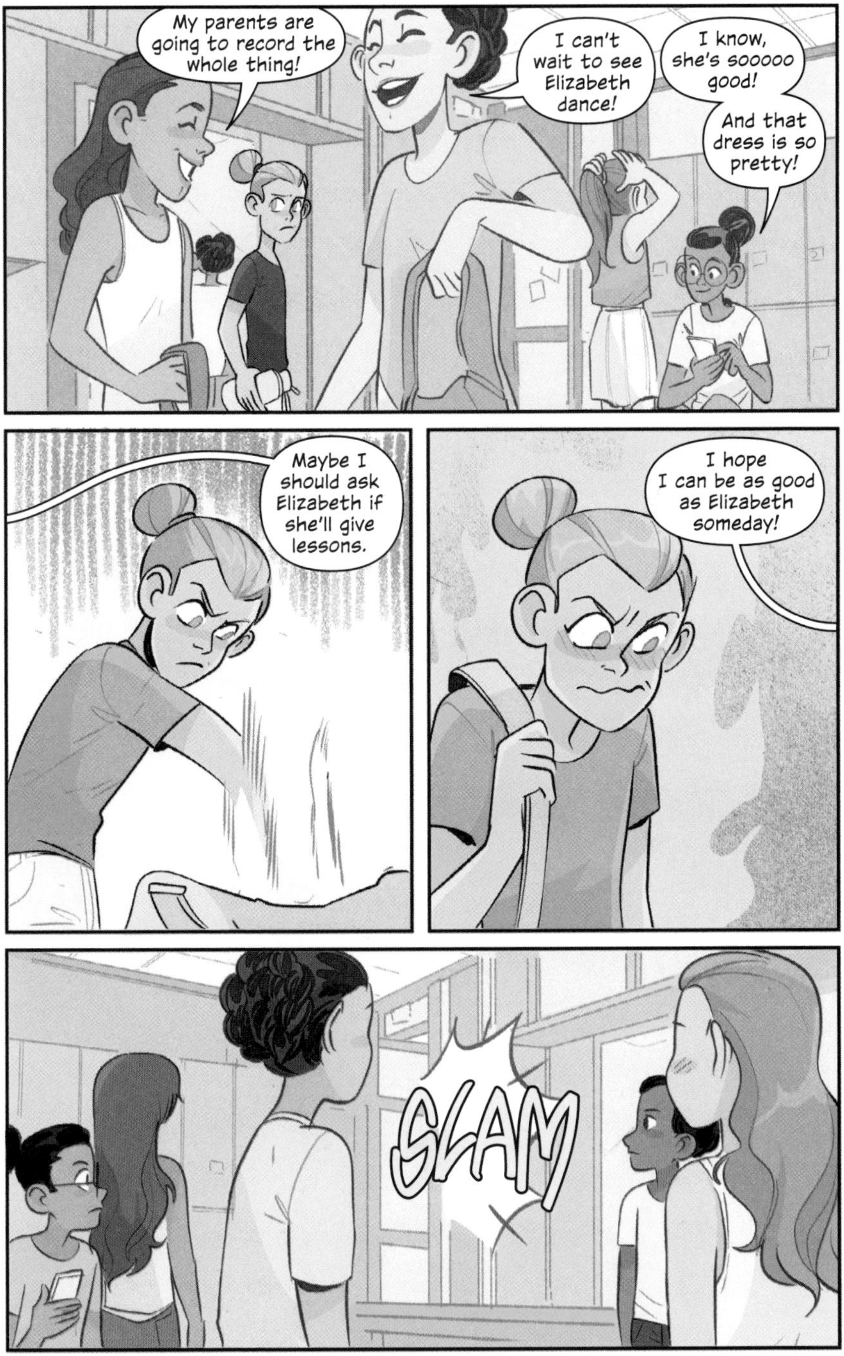
My parents are going to record the whole thing!
I can't wait to see Elizabeth dance!
I know, she's sooooo good!
And that dress is so pretty!
Maybe I should ask Elizabeth if she'll give lessons.
I hope I can be as good as Elizabeth someday!
SLAM

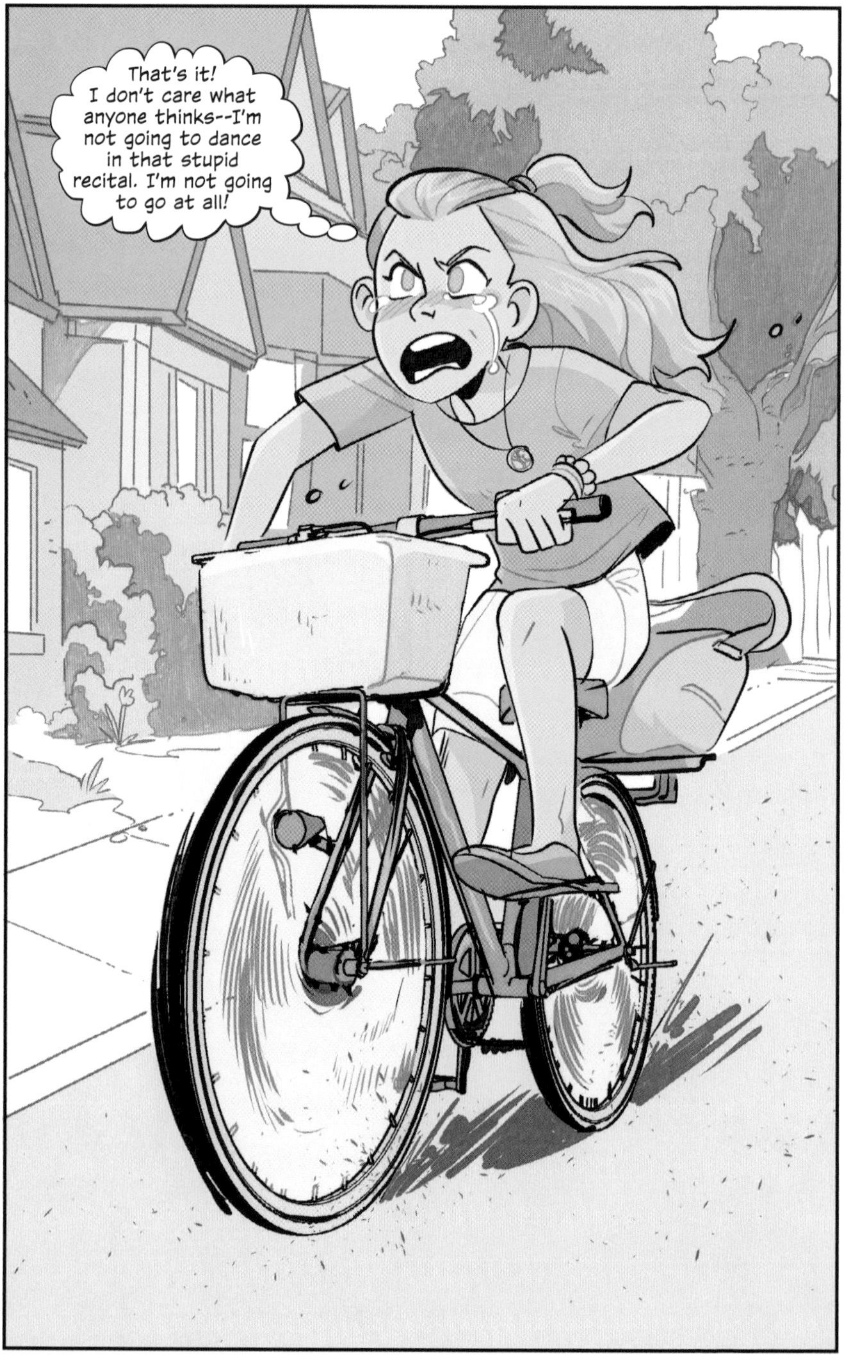
That's it! I don't care what anyone thinks--I'm not going to dance in that stupid recital. I'm not going to go at all!

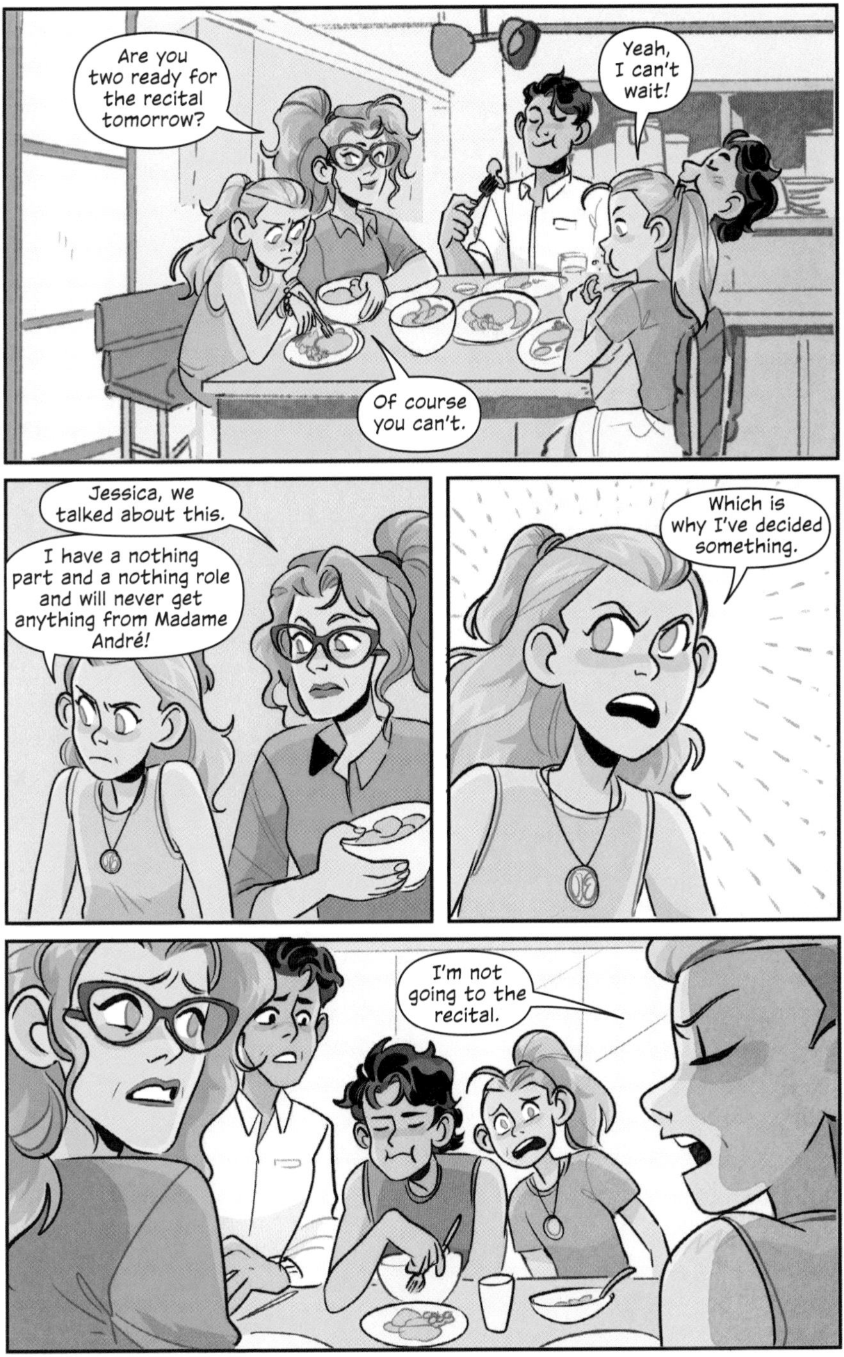
Are you two ready for the recital tomorrow?
Yeah, I can't wait!
Of course you can't.
Jessica, we talked about this.
I have a nothing part and a nothing role and will never get anything from Madame André!
Which is why I've decided something.
I'm not going to the recital.

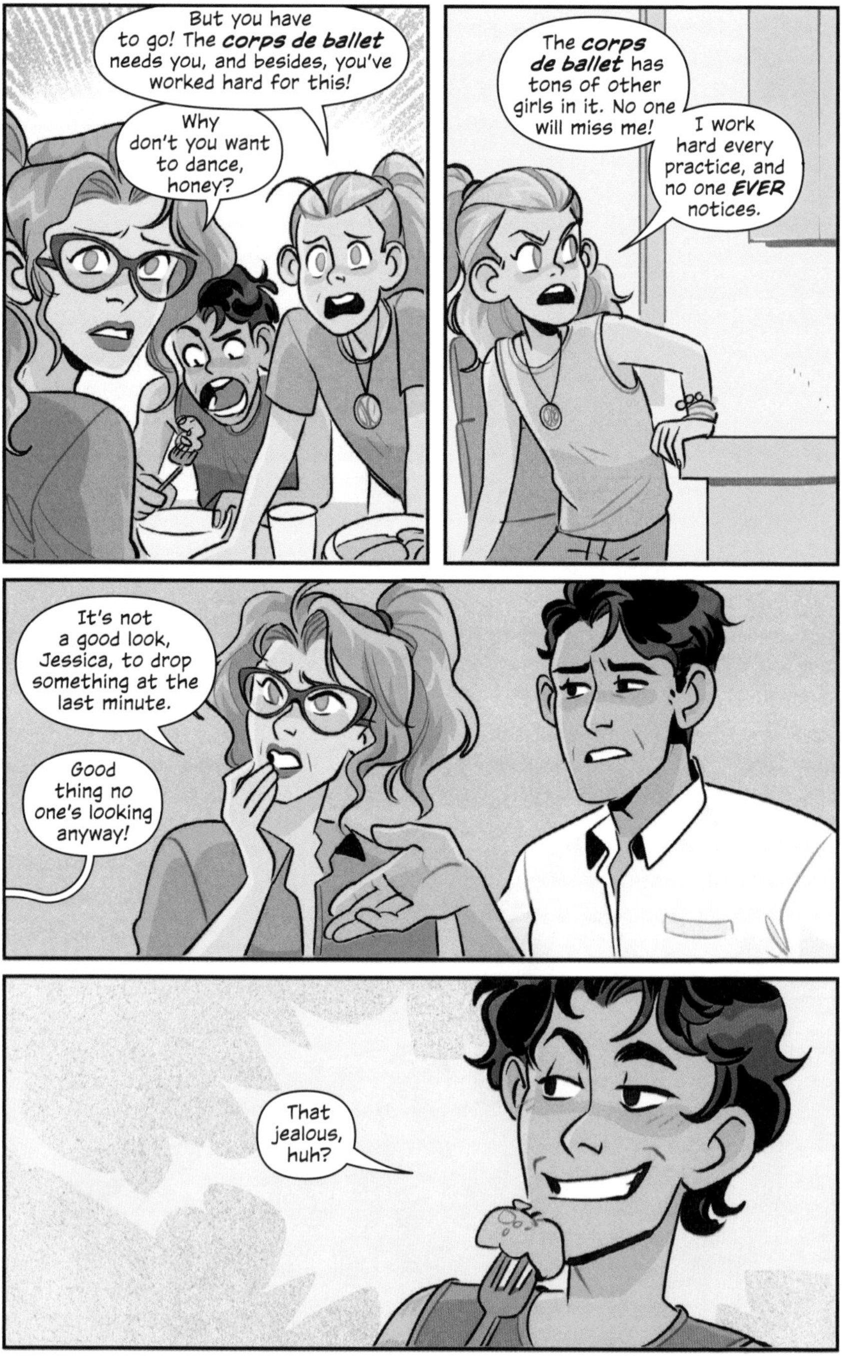
But you have to go! The ***corps de ballet*** needs you, and besides, you've worked hard for this!
Why don't you want to dance, honey?
The ***corps de ballet*** has tons of other girls in it. No one will miss me!
I work hard every practice, and no one ***EVER*** notices.
It's not a good look, Jessica, to drop something at the last minute.
Good thing no one's looking anyway!
That jealous, huh?

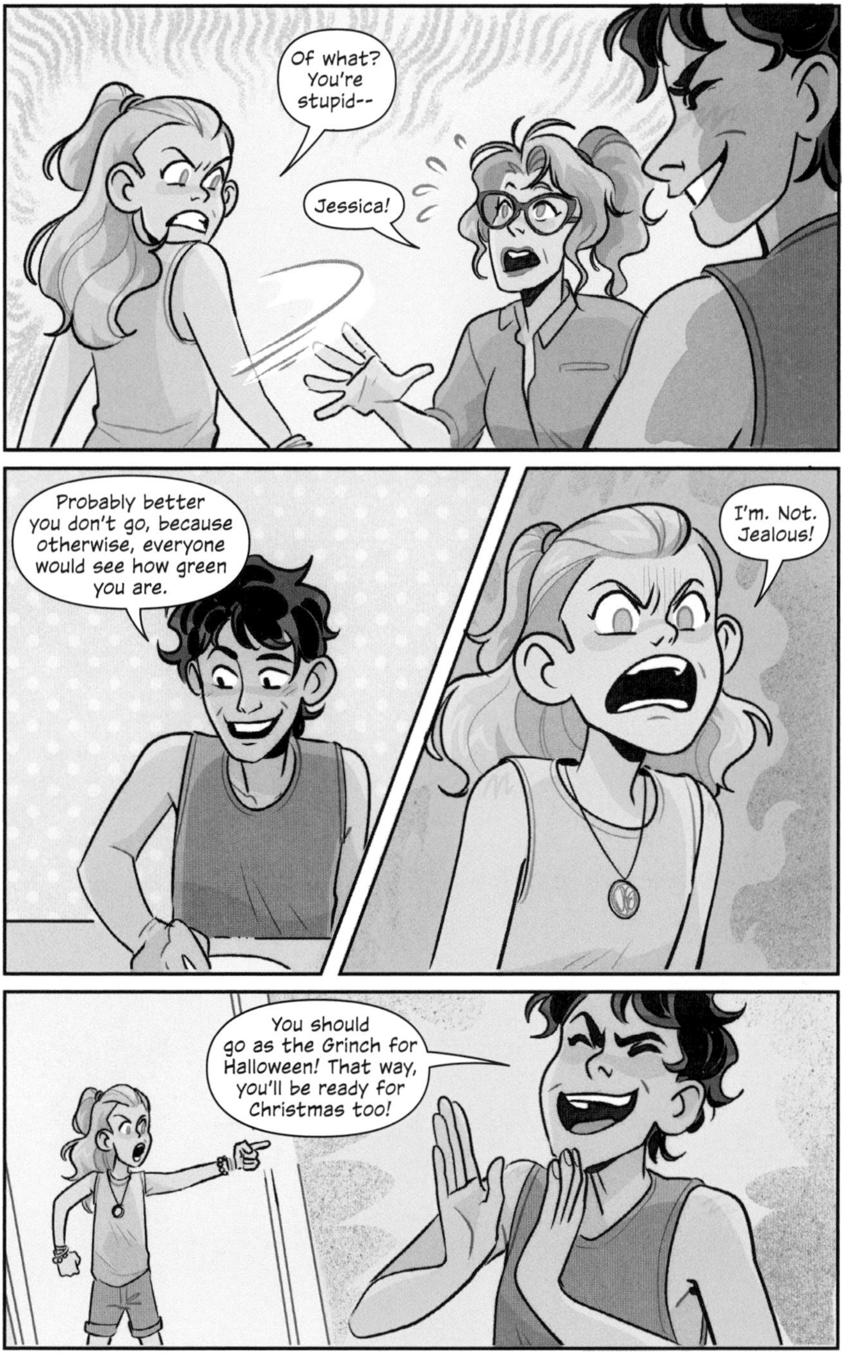
Of what? You're stupid--
Jessica!
Probably better you don't go, because otherwise, everyone would see how green you are.
I'm. Not. Jealous!
You should go as the Grinch for Halloween! That way, you'll be ready for Christmas too!

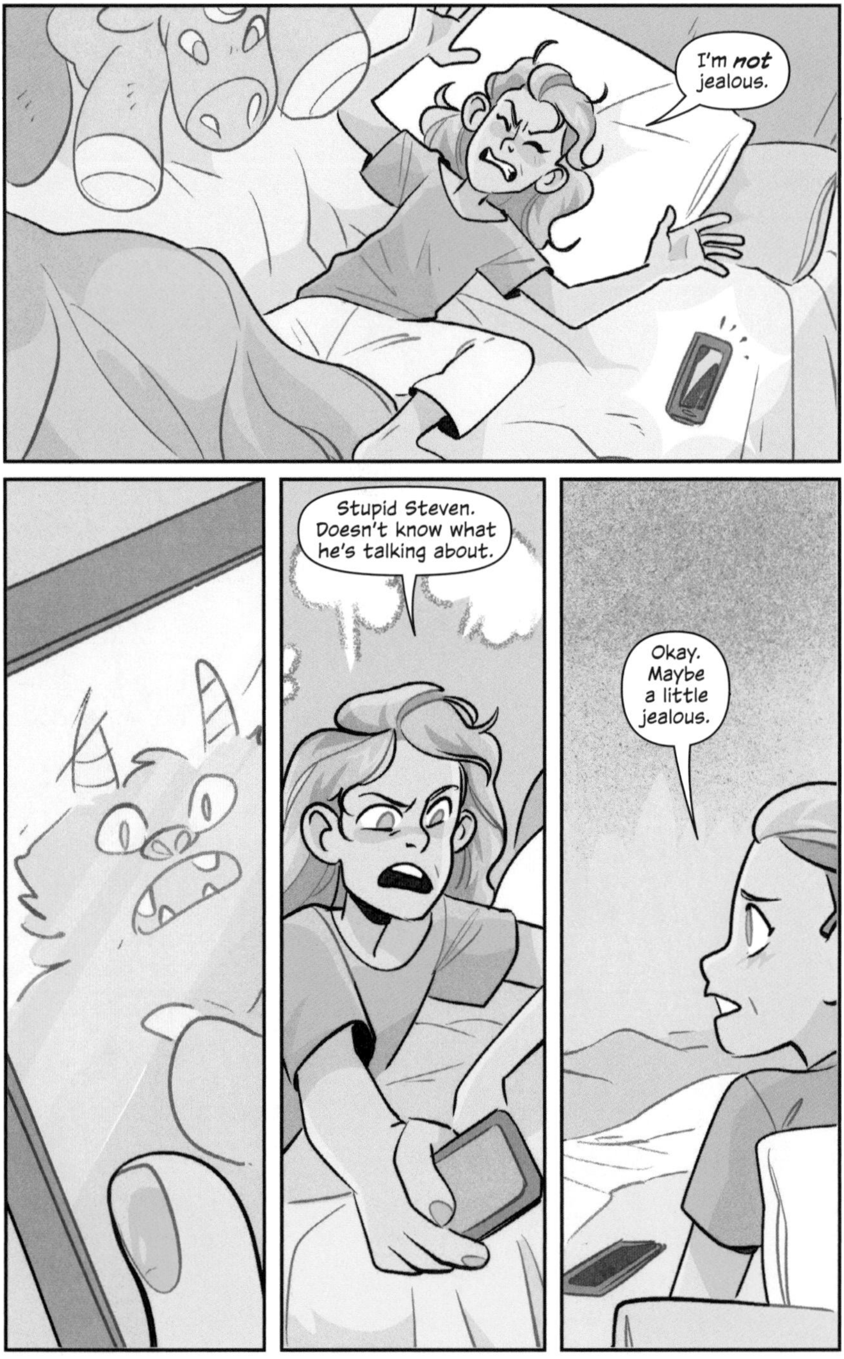
I'm **not** jealous.
Stupid Steven. Doesn't know what he's talking about.
Okay. Maybe a little jealous.

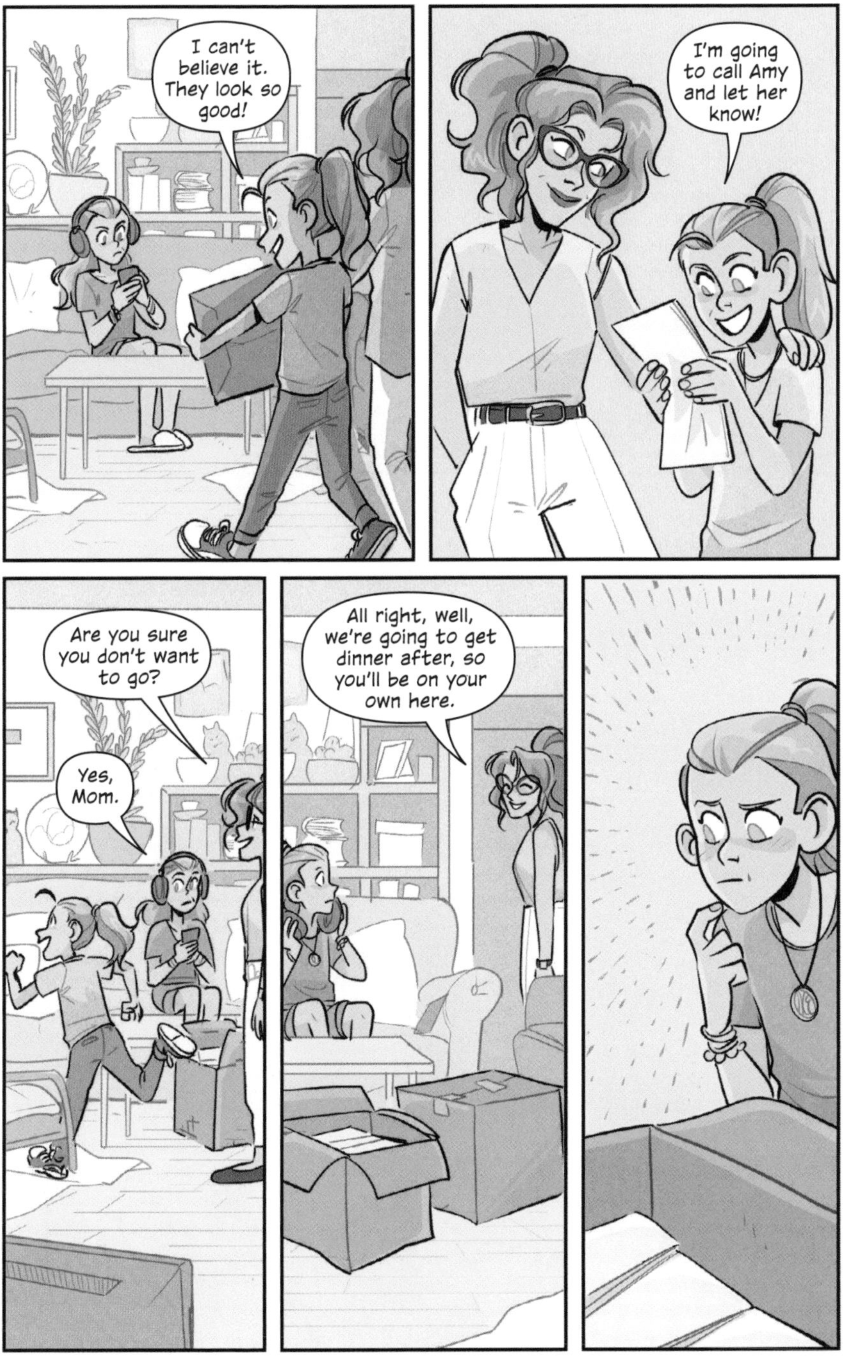
I can't believe it. They look so good!
I'm going to call Amy and let her know!
Are you sure you don't want to go?
Yes, Mom.
All right, well, we're going to get dinner after, so you'll be on your own here.

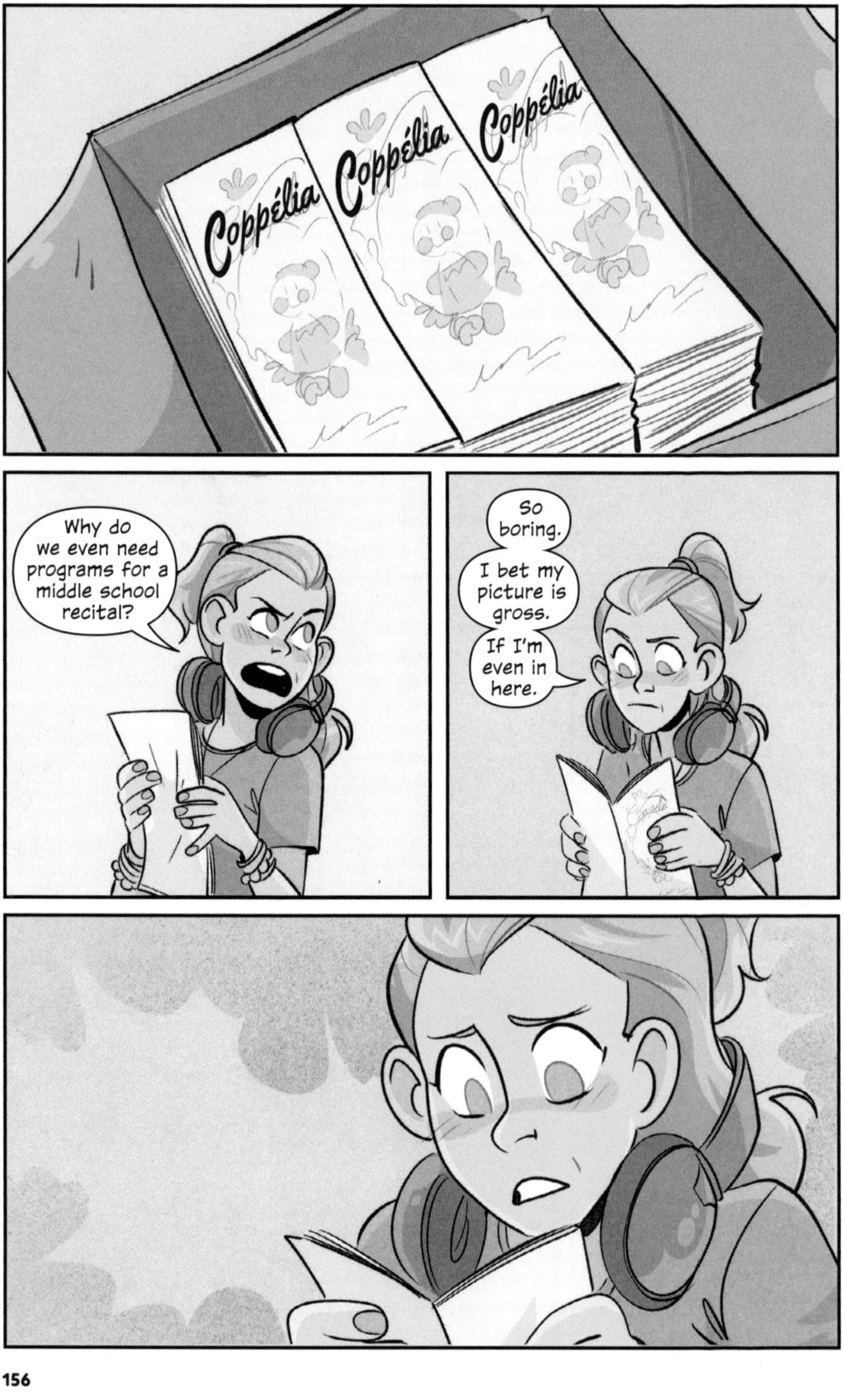
Coppélia
Coppélia
Coppélia
Why do we even need programs for a middle school recital?
So boring.
I bet my picture is gross.
If I'm even in here.

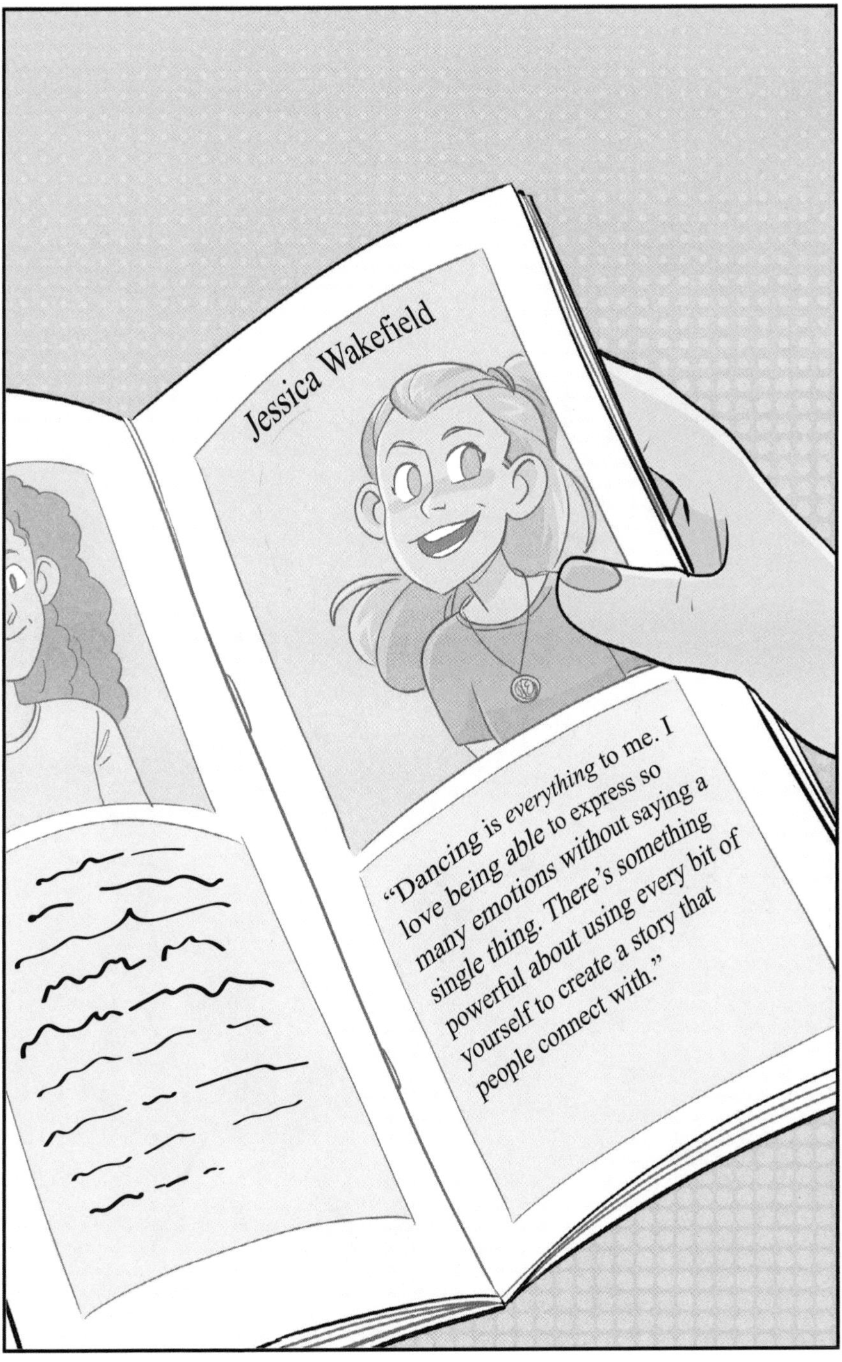
Jessica Wakefield
"Dancing is *everything* to me. I love being *able* to express so many emotions *without* saying a single thing. There's something powerful about using every bit of yourself to create a story that people connect with."

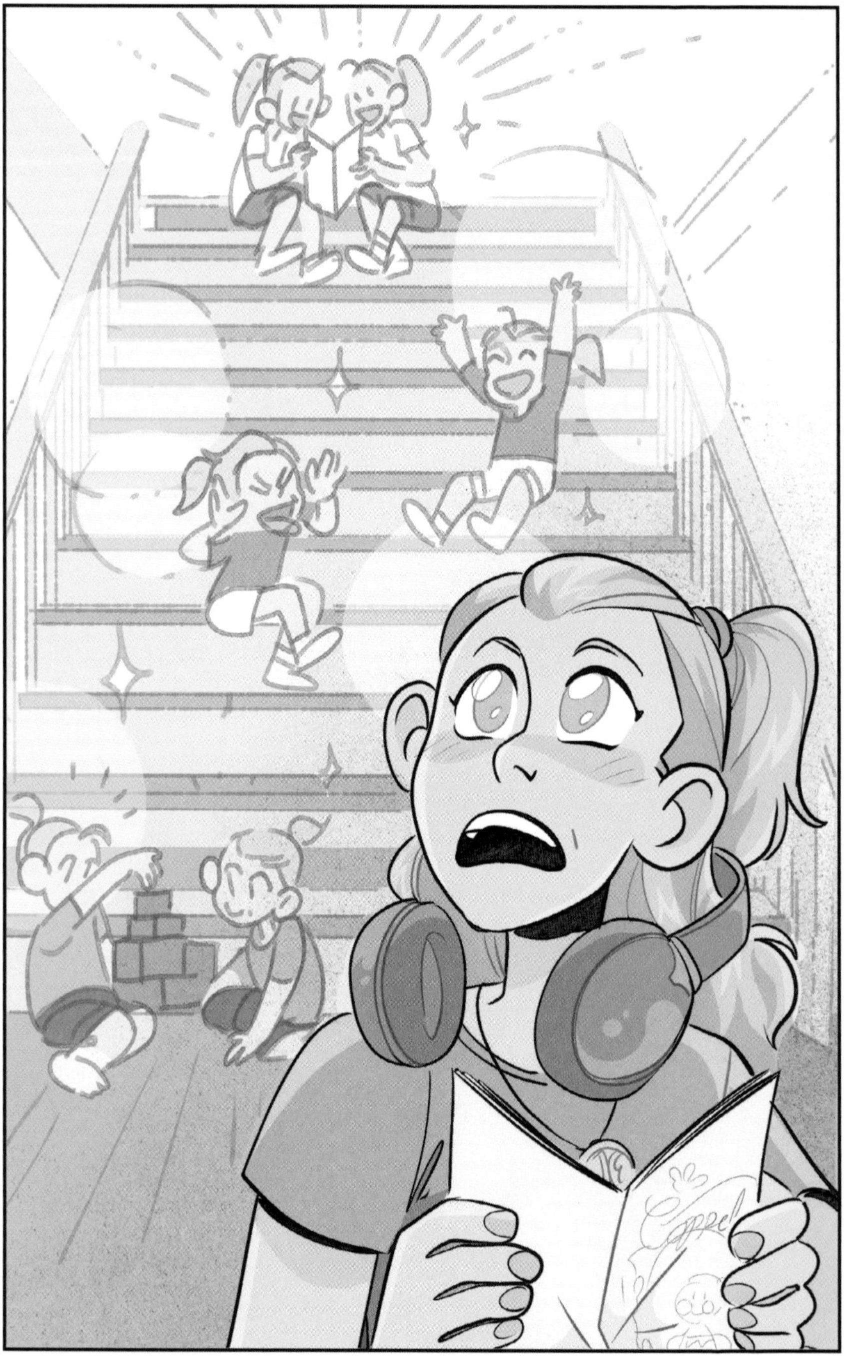

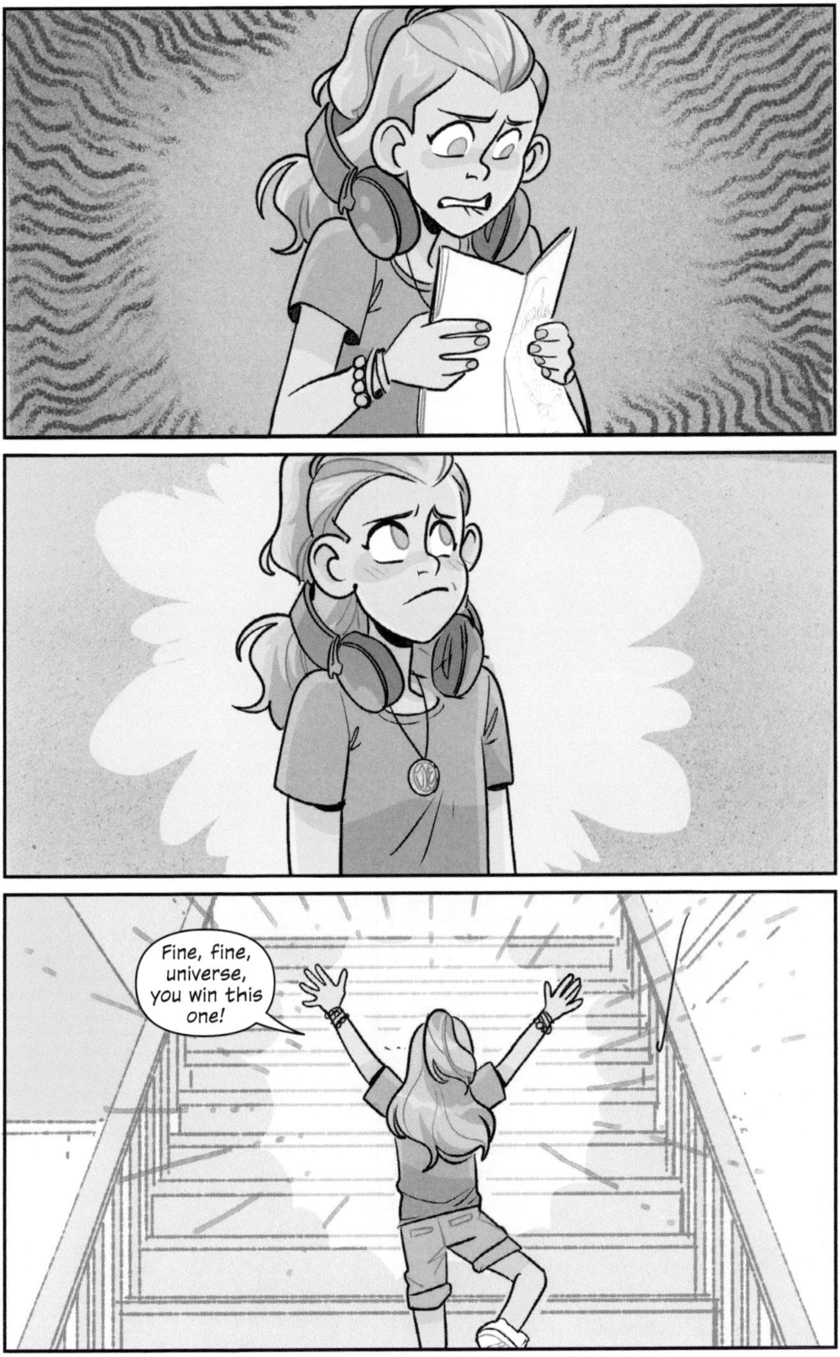
Fine, fine, universe, you win this one!

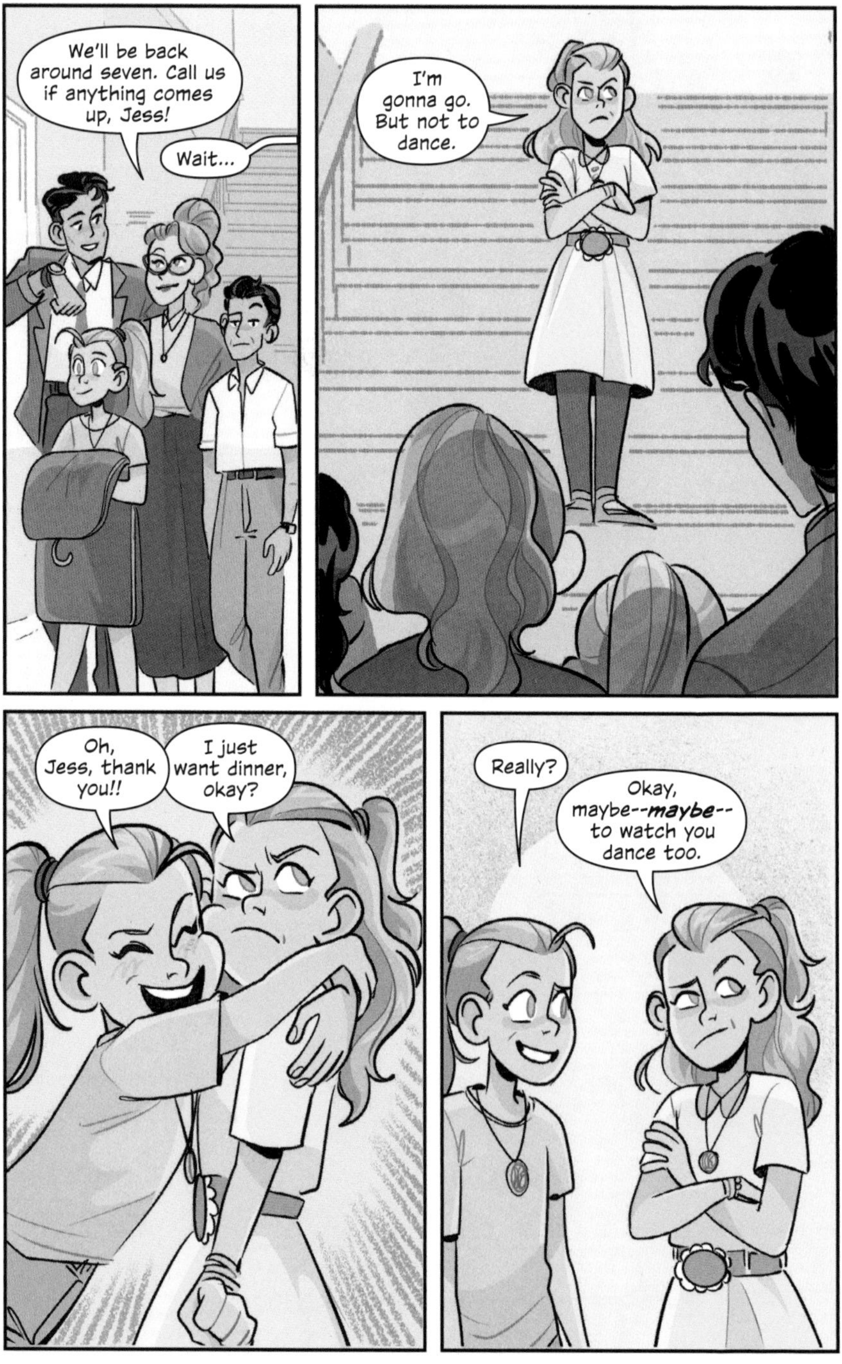
We'll be back around seven. Call us if anything comes up, Jess!
Wait...
I'm gonna go. But not to dance.
Oh, Jess, thank you!!
I just want dinner, okay?
Really?
Okay, maybe--**maybe**--to watch you dance too.

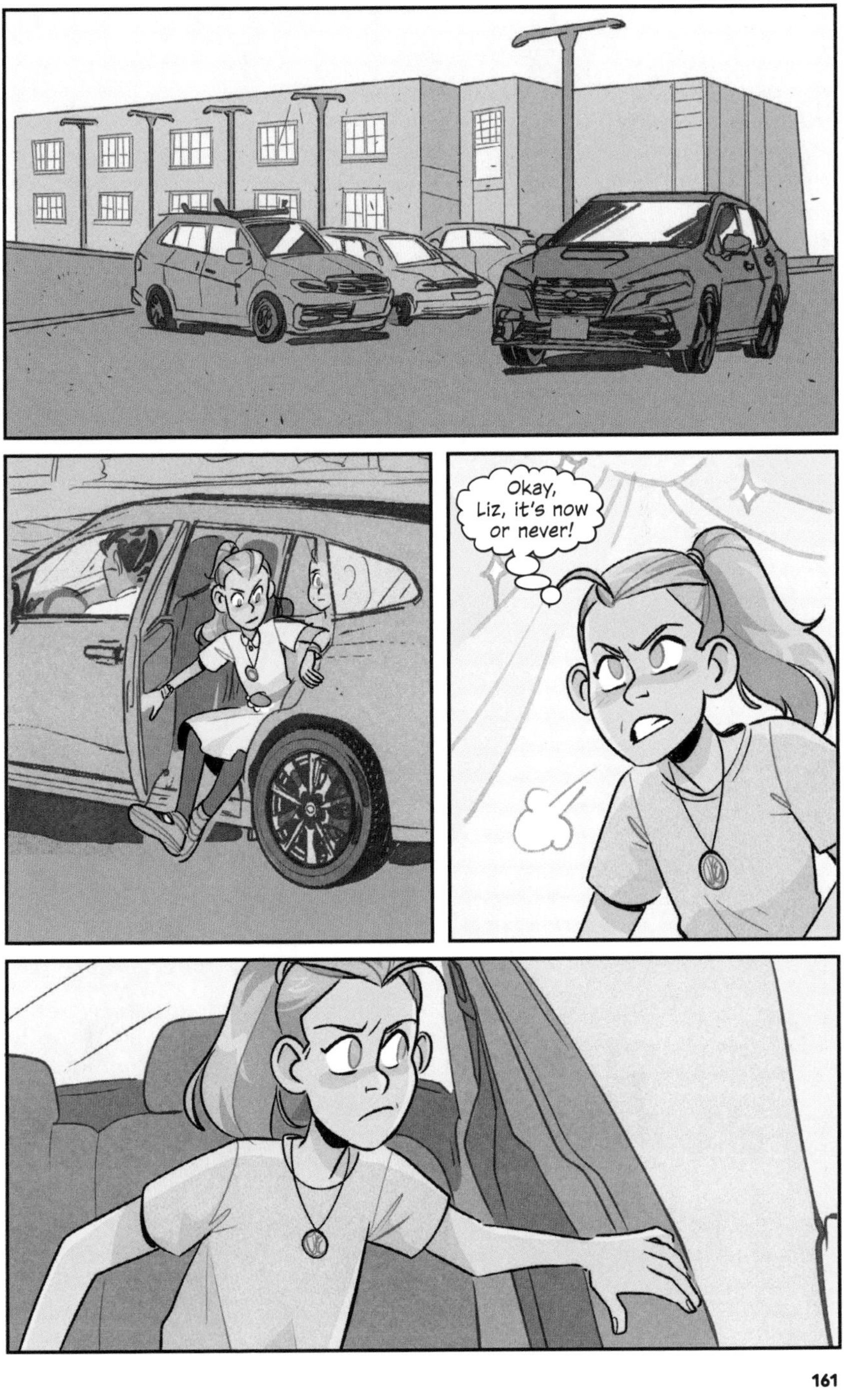
Okay, Liz, it's now or never!

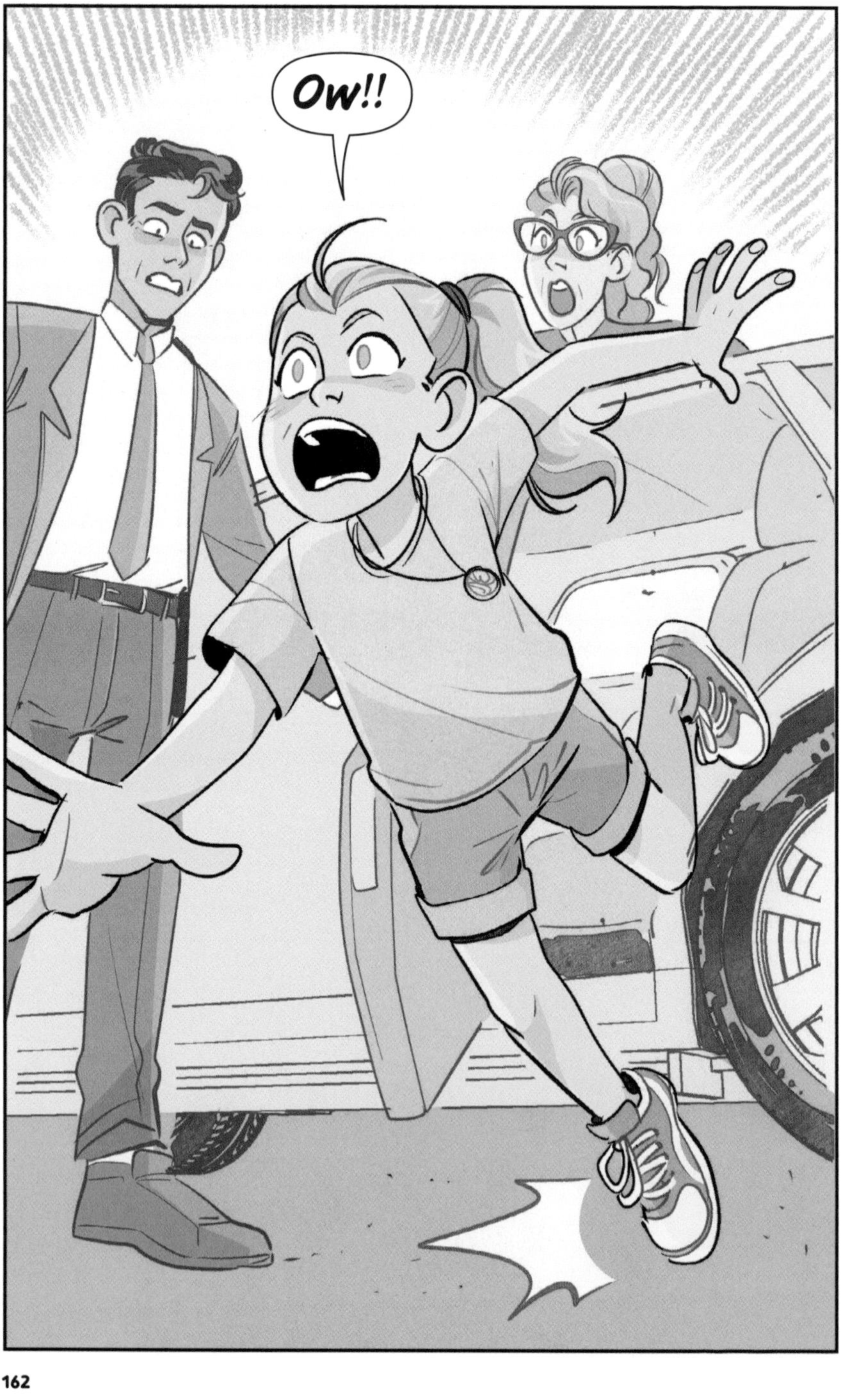
Ow!!

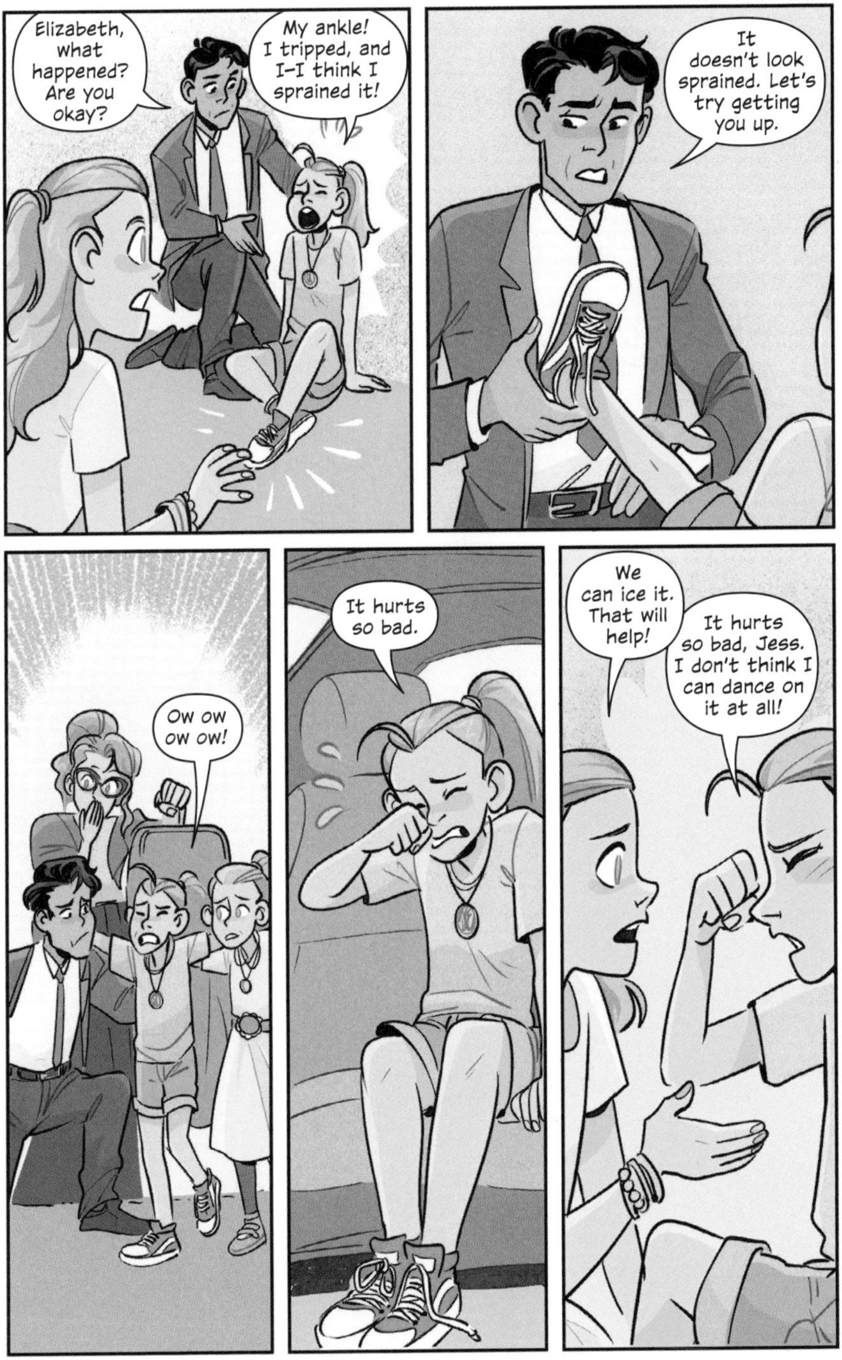
Elizabeth, what happened? Are you okay?
My ankle! I tripped, and I—I think I sprained it!
It doesn't look sprained. Let's try getting you up.
Ow ow ow ow!
It hurts so bad.
We can ice it. That will help!
It hurts so bad, Jess. I don't think I can dance on it at all!

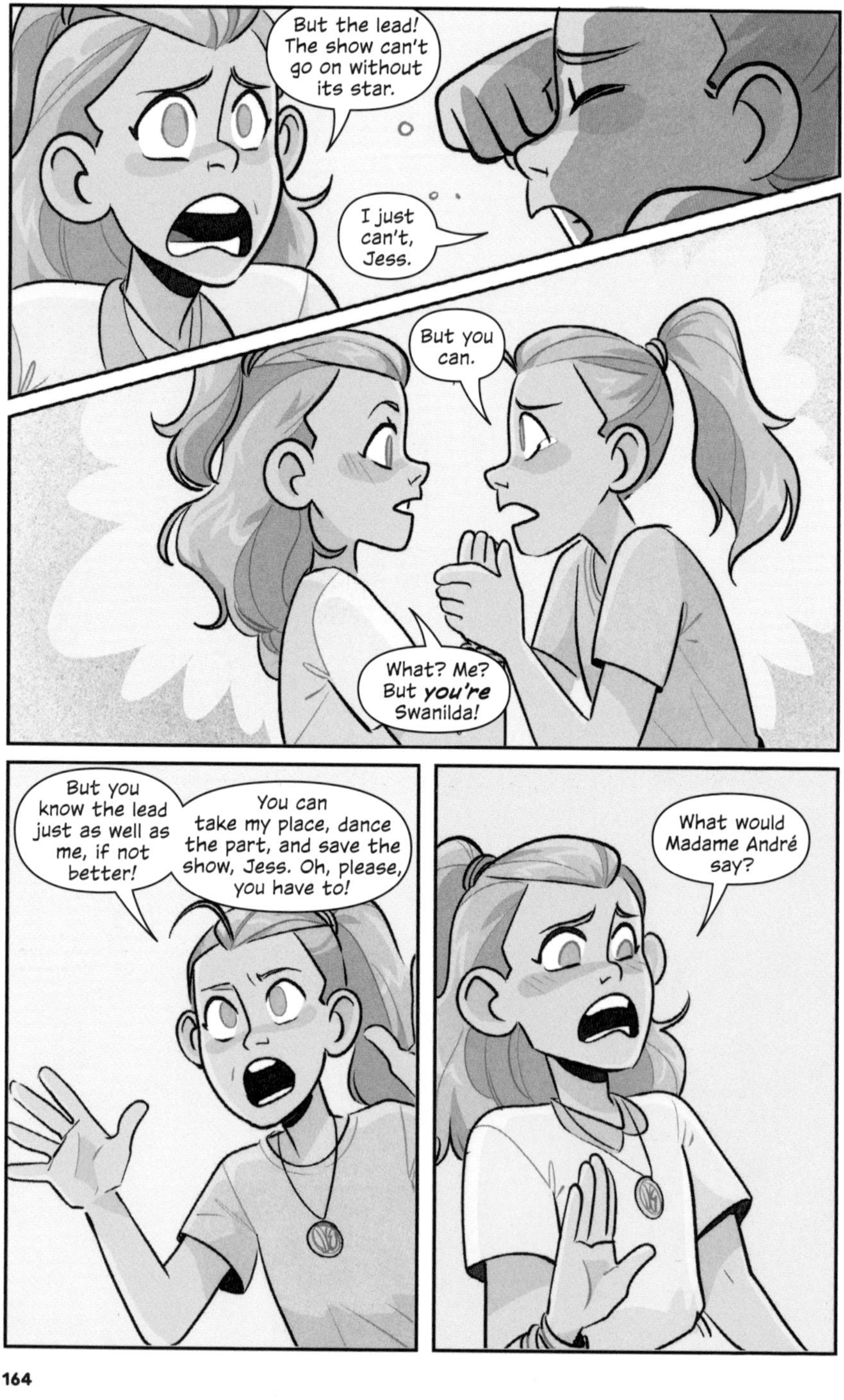

But the lead! The show can't go on without its star.
I just can't, Jess.
But you can.
What? Me? But *you're* Swanilda!
But you know the lead just as well as me, if not better!
You can take my place, dance the part, and save the show, Jess. Oh, please, you have to!
What would Madame André say?

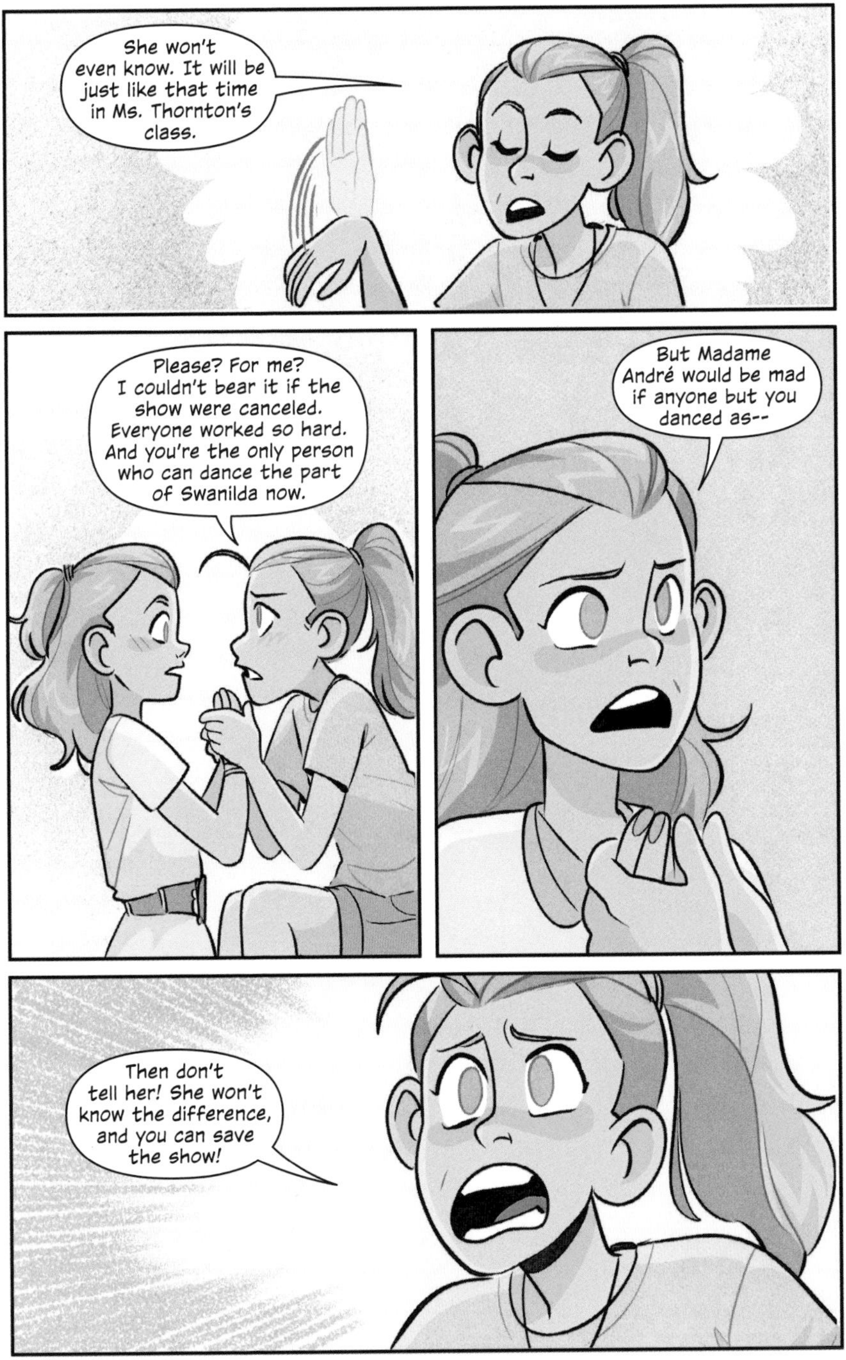
She won't even know. It will be just like that time in Ms. Thornton's class.
Please? For me? I couldn't bear it if the show were canceled. Everyone worked so hard. And you're the only person who can dance the part of Swanilda now.
But Madame André would be mad if anyone but you danced as--
Then don't tell her! She won't know the difference, and you can save the show!

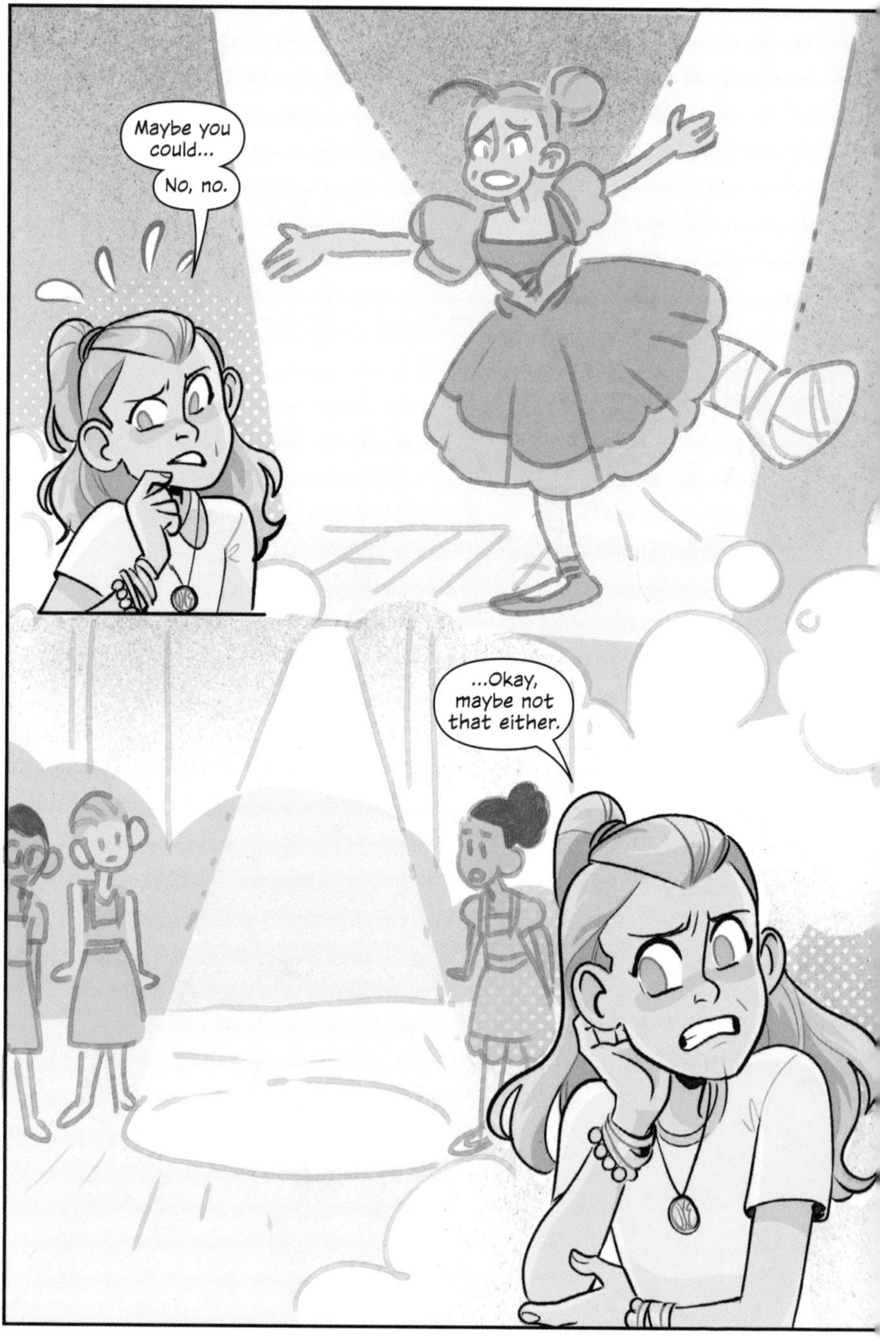
Maybe you could...
No, no.
...Okay, maybe not that either.

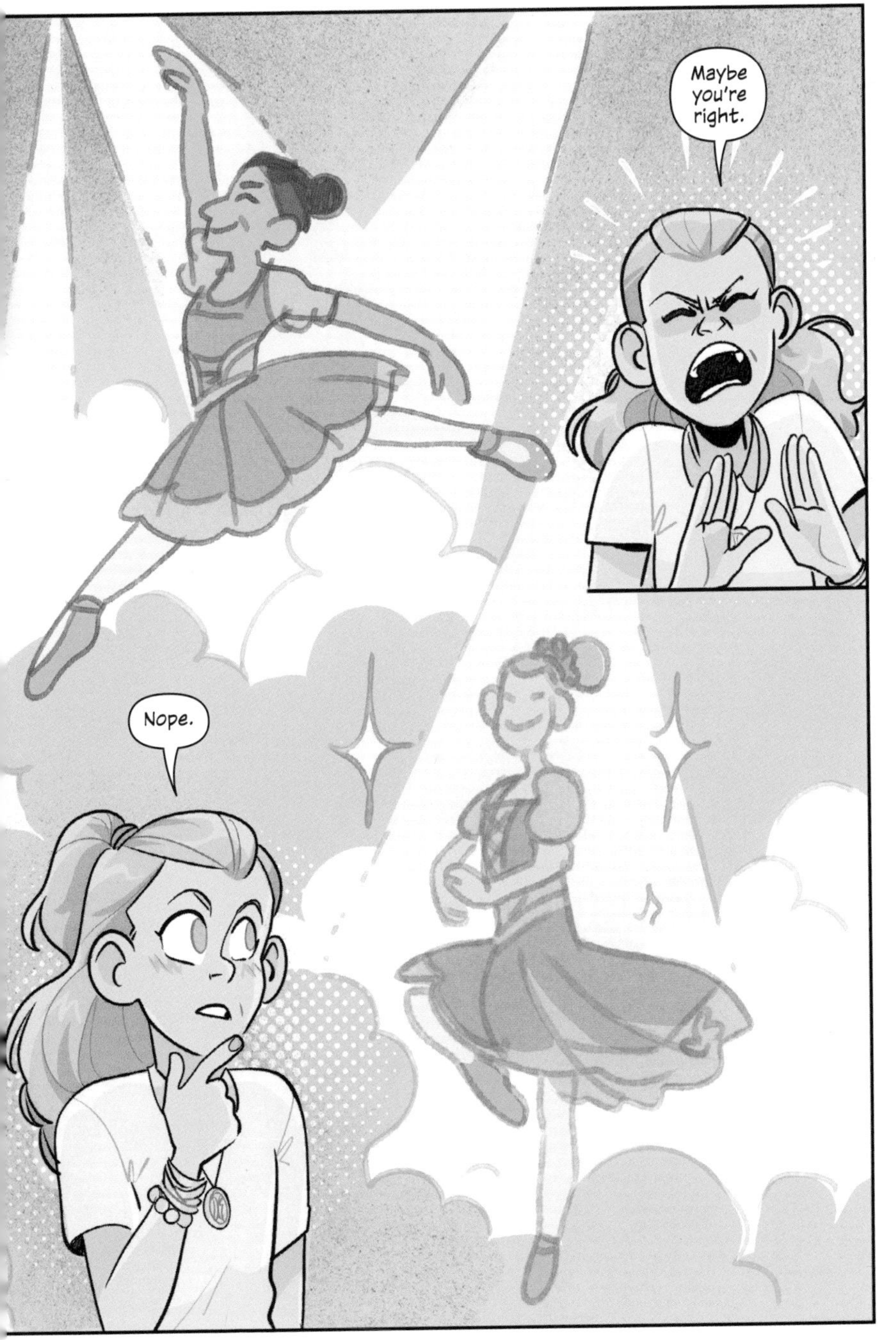
Maybe you're right.
Nope.

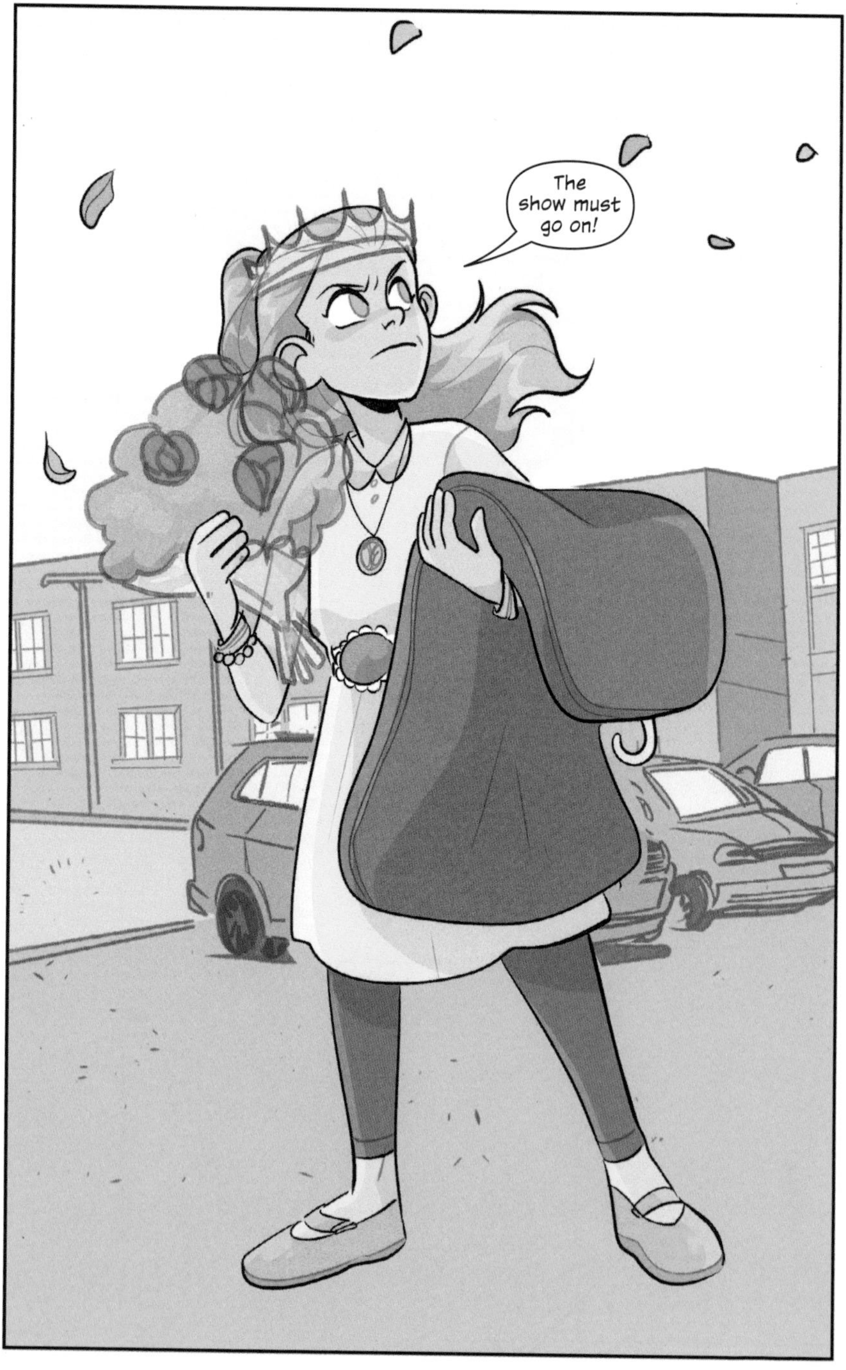
The show must go on!

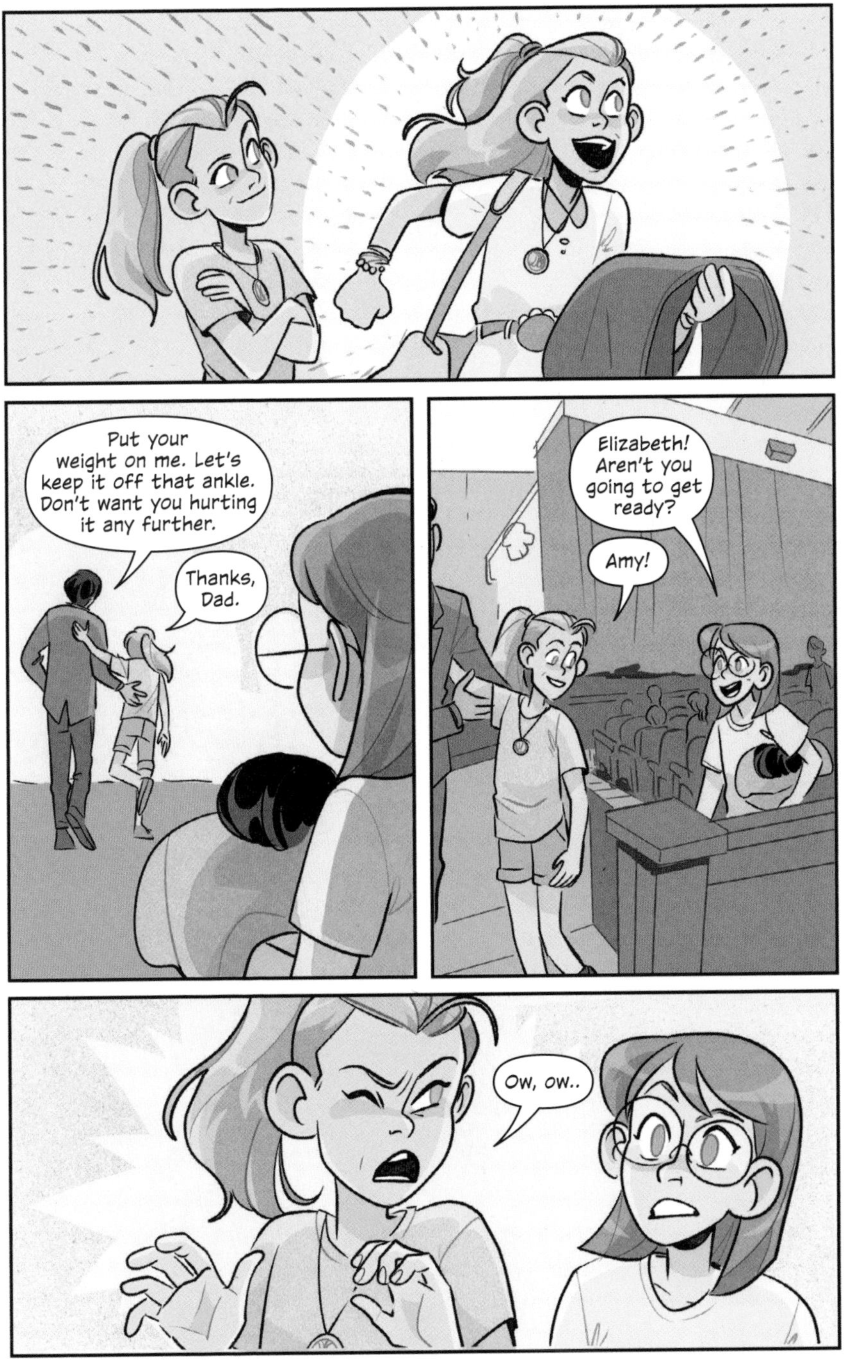
Put your weight on me. Let's keep it off that ankle. Don't want you hurting it any further.
Thanks, Dad.
Elizabeth! Aren't you going to get ready?
Amy!
Ow, ow..

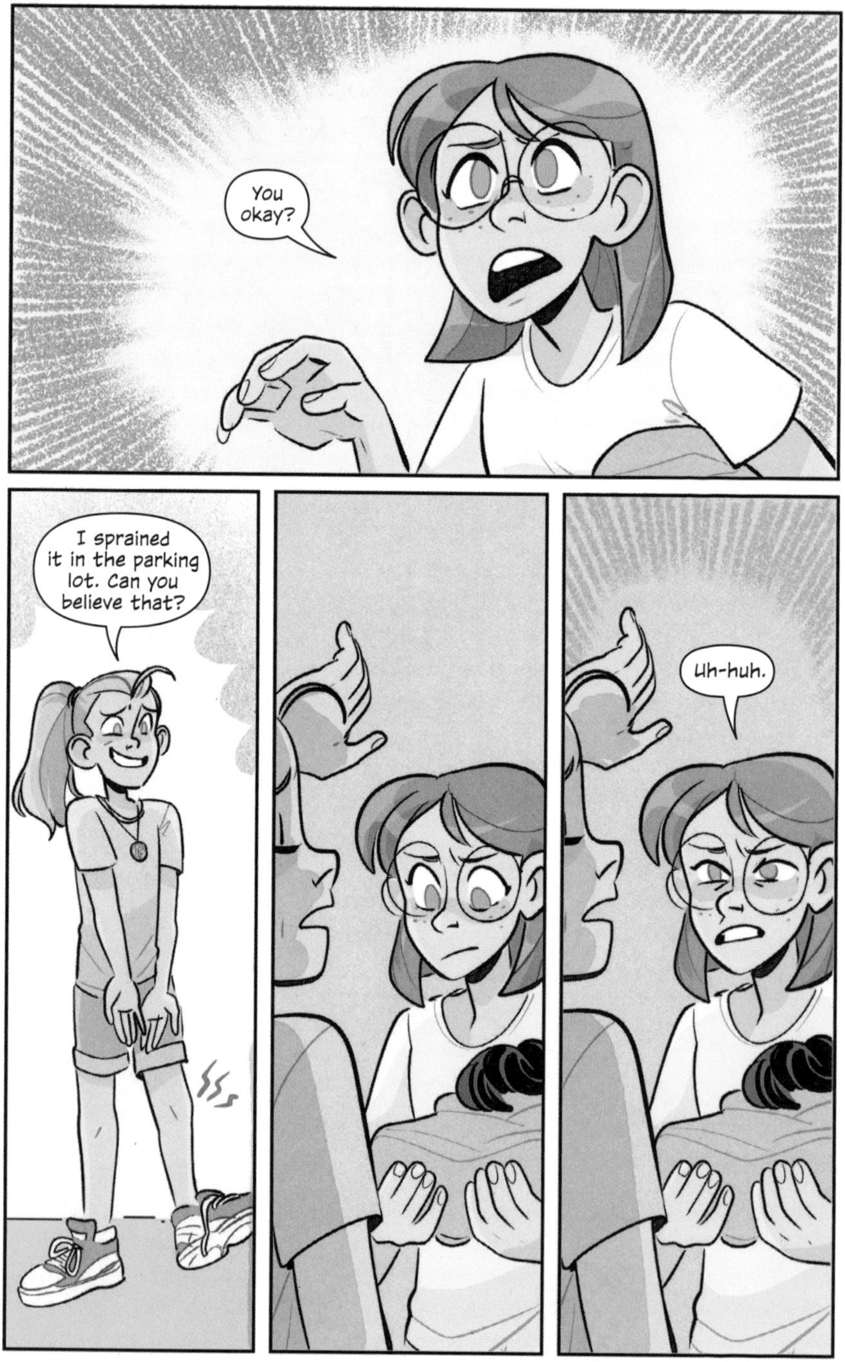
You okay?
I sprained it in the parking lot. Can you believe that?
Uh-huh.

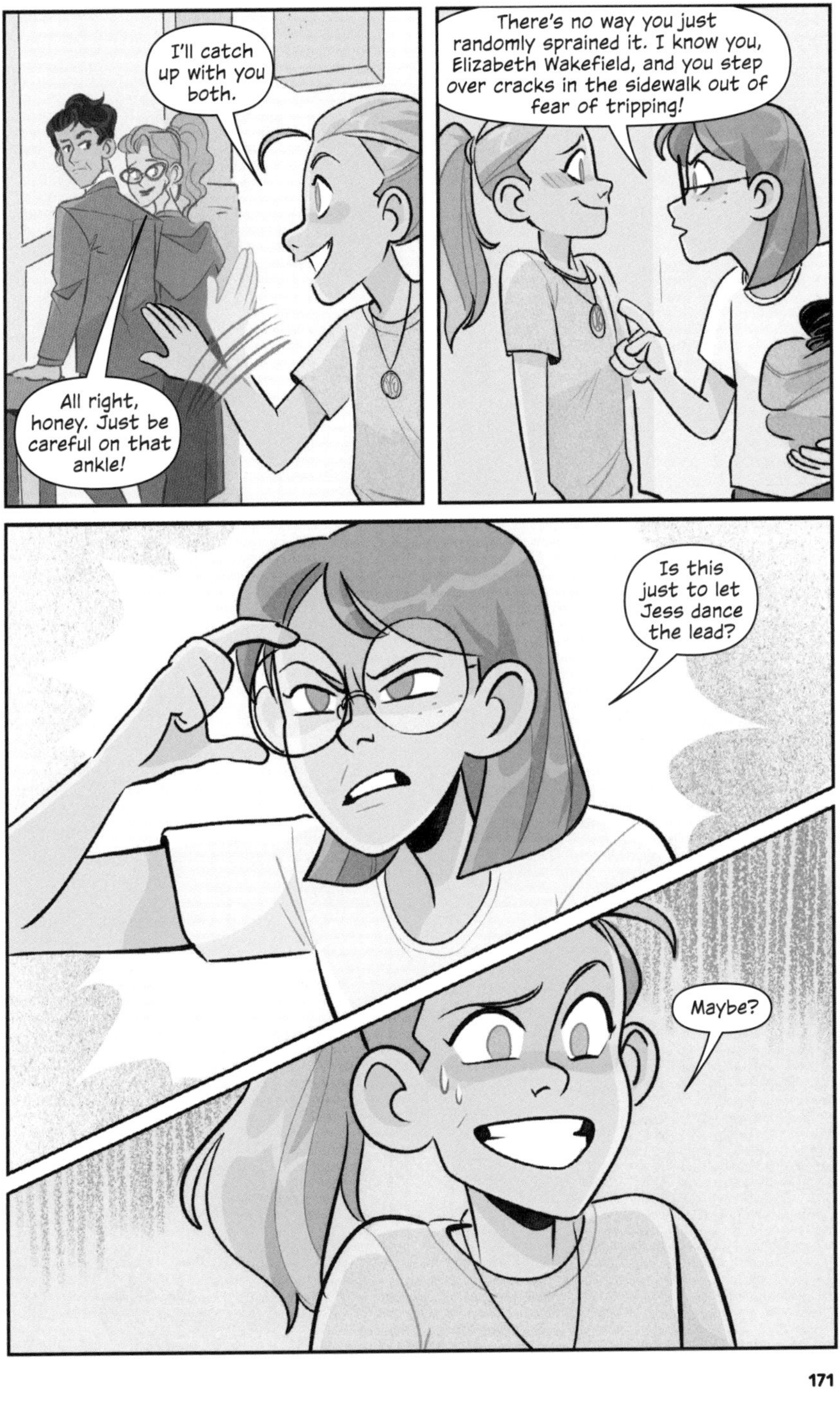
I'll catch up with you both.
All right, honey. Just be careful on that ankle!
There's no way you just randomly sprained it. I know you, Elizabeth Wakefield, and you step over cracks in the sidewalk out of fear of tripping!
Is this just to let Jess dance the lead?
Maybe?

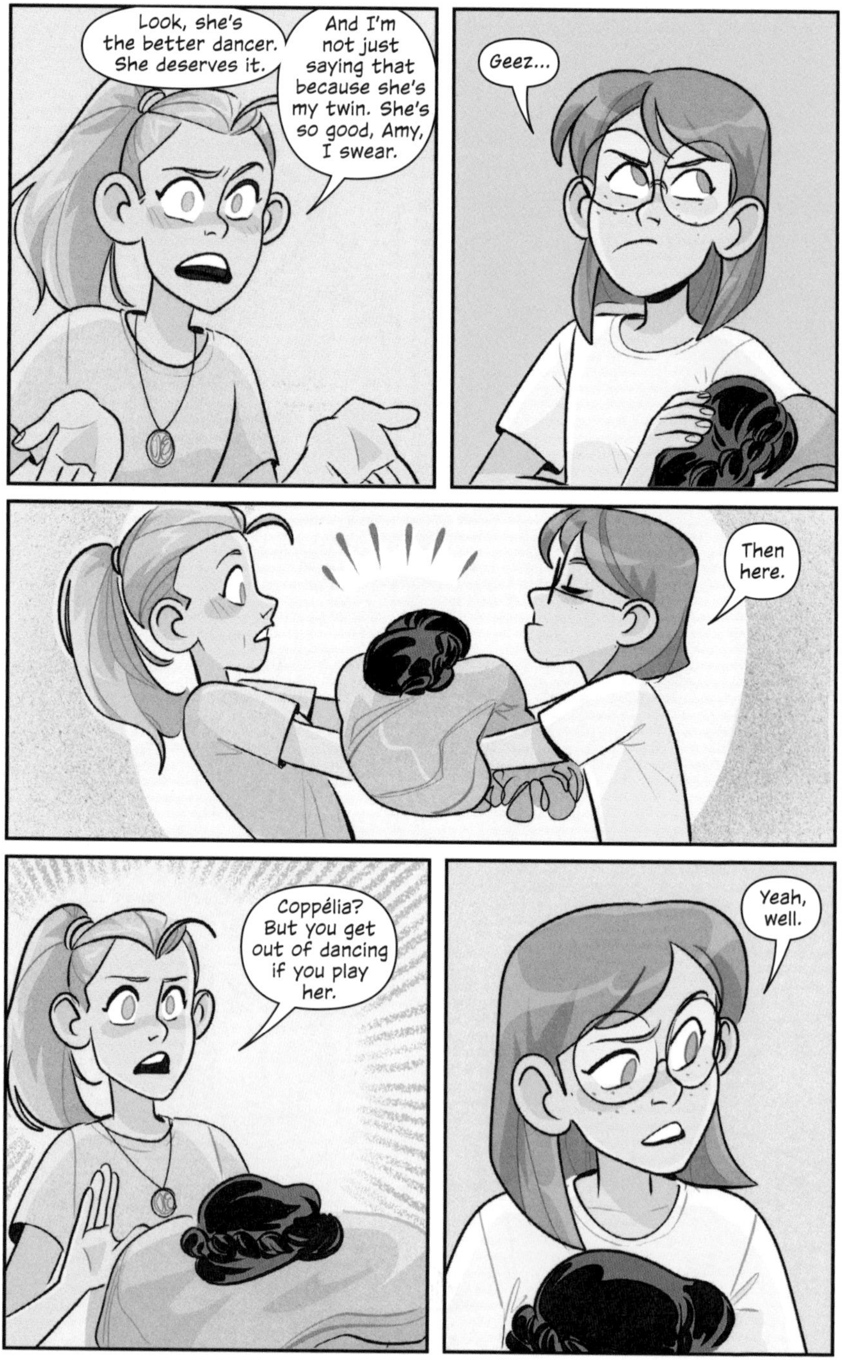
Look, she's the better dancer. She deserves it.
And I'm not just saying that because she's my twin. She's so good, Amy, I swear.
Geez...
Then here.
Coppélia? But you get out of dancing if you play her.
Yeah, well.

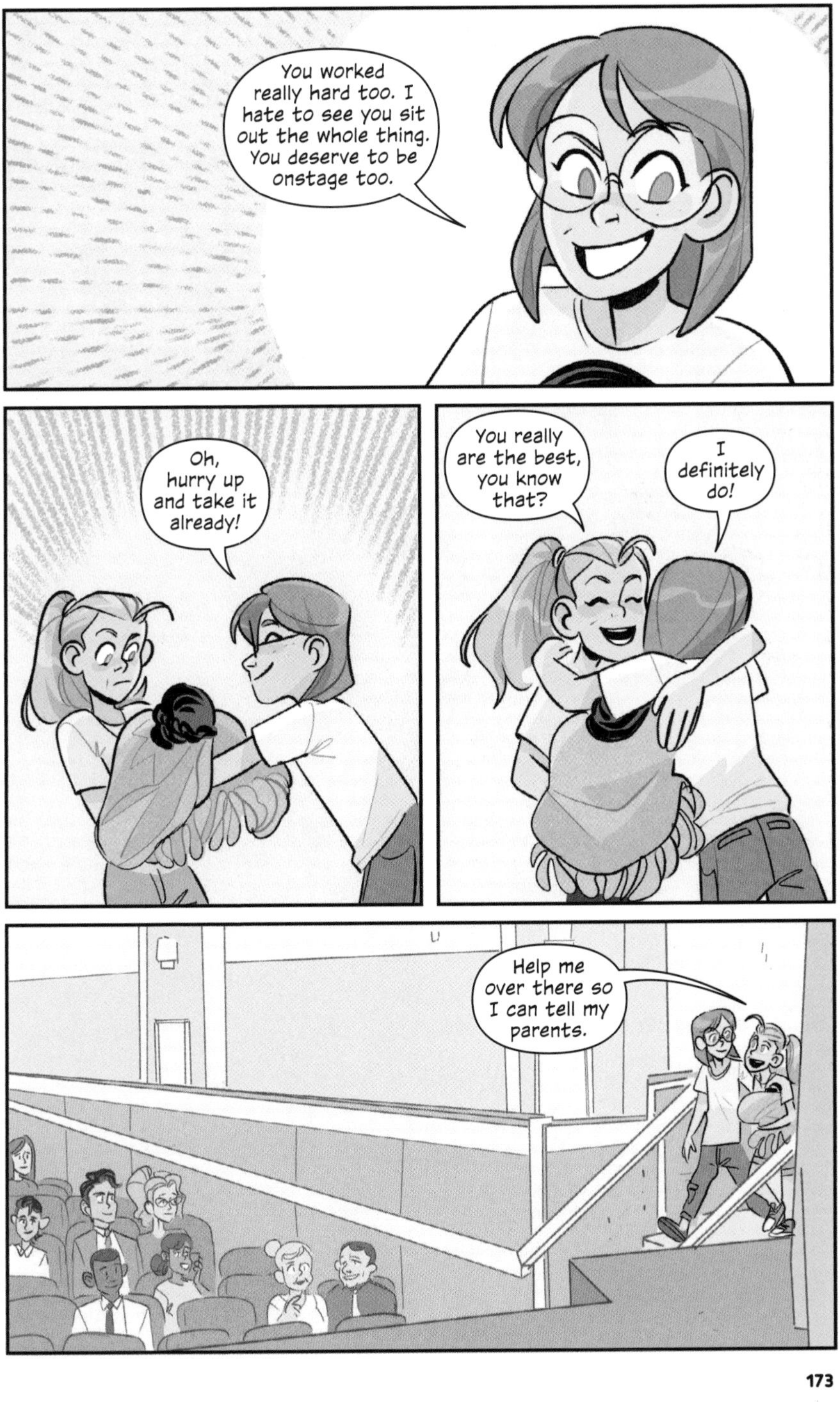
You worked really hard too. I hate to see you sit out the whole thing. You deserve to be onstage too.
Oh, hurry up and take it already!
You really are the best, you know that?
I definitely do!
Help me over there so I can tell my parents.

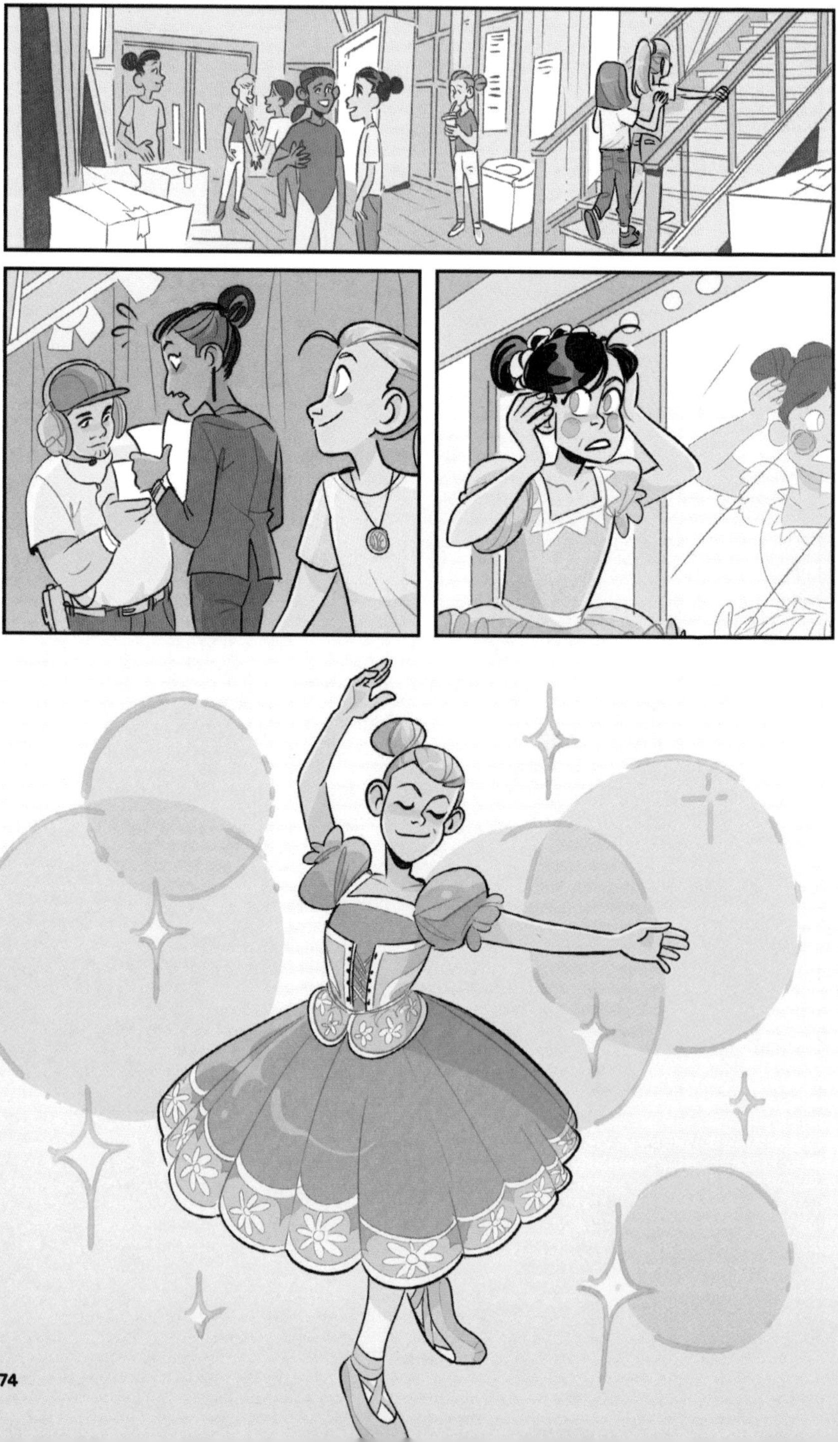

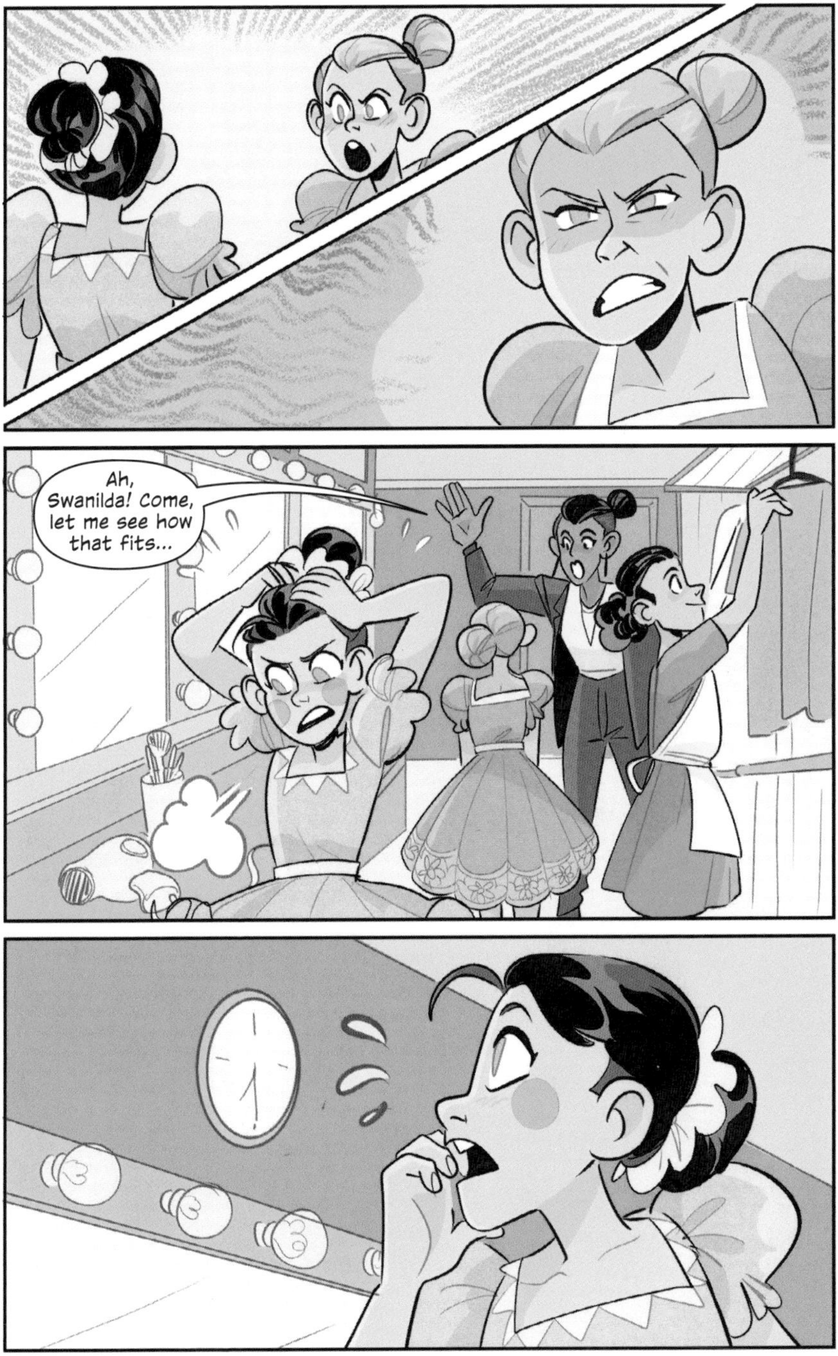

Ah, Swanilda! Come, let me see how that fits...

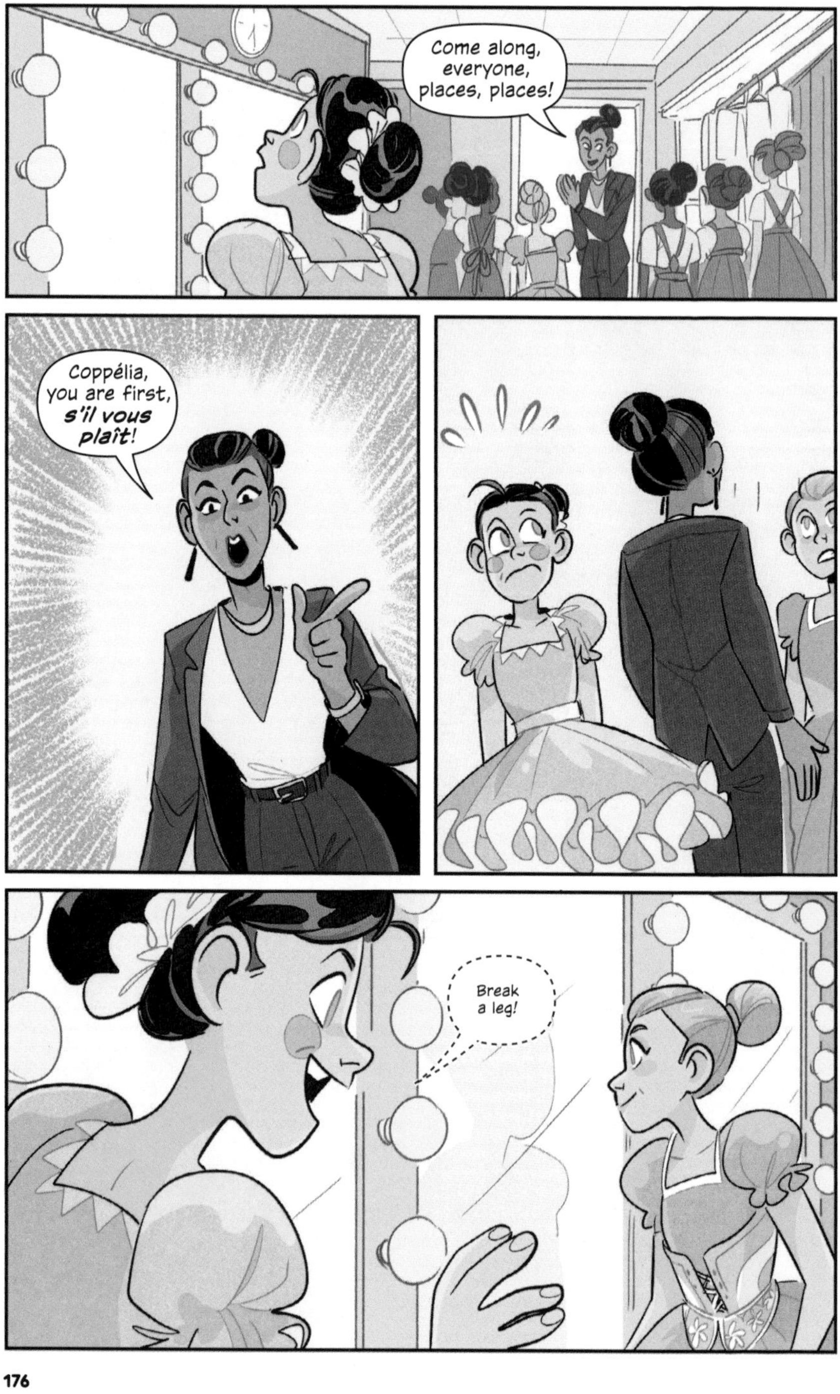
Come along, everyone, places, places!
Coppélia, you are first, ***s'il vous plaît***!
Break a leg!

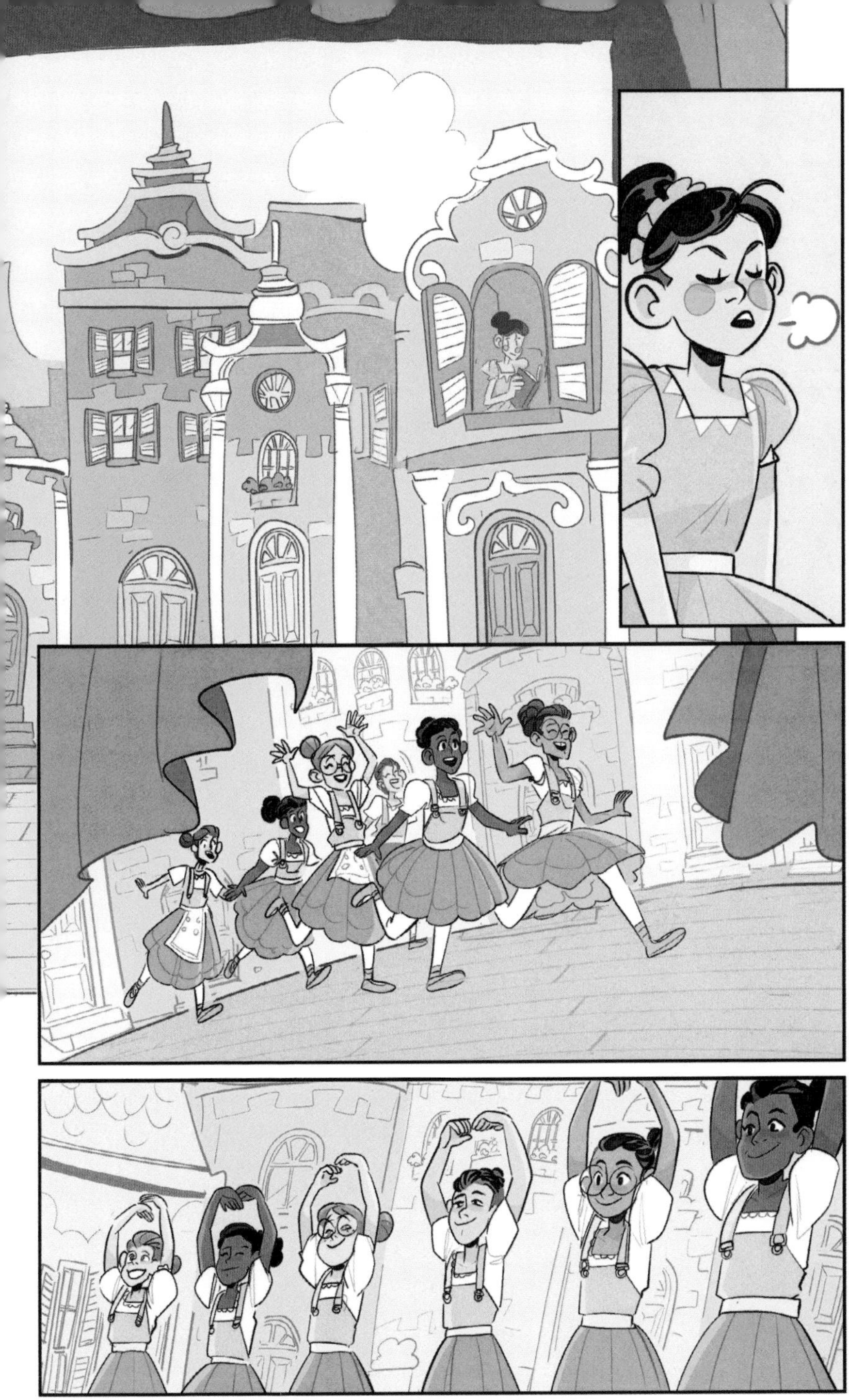

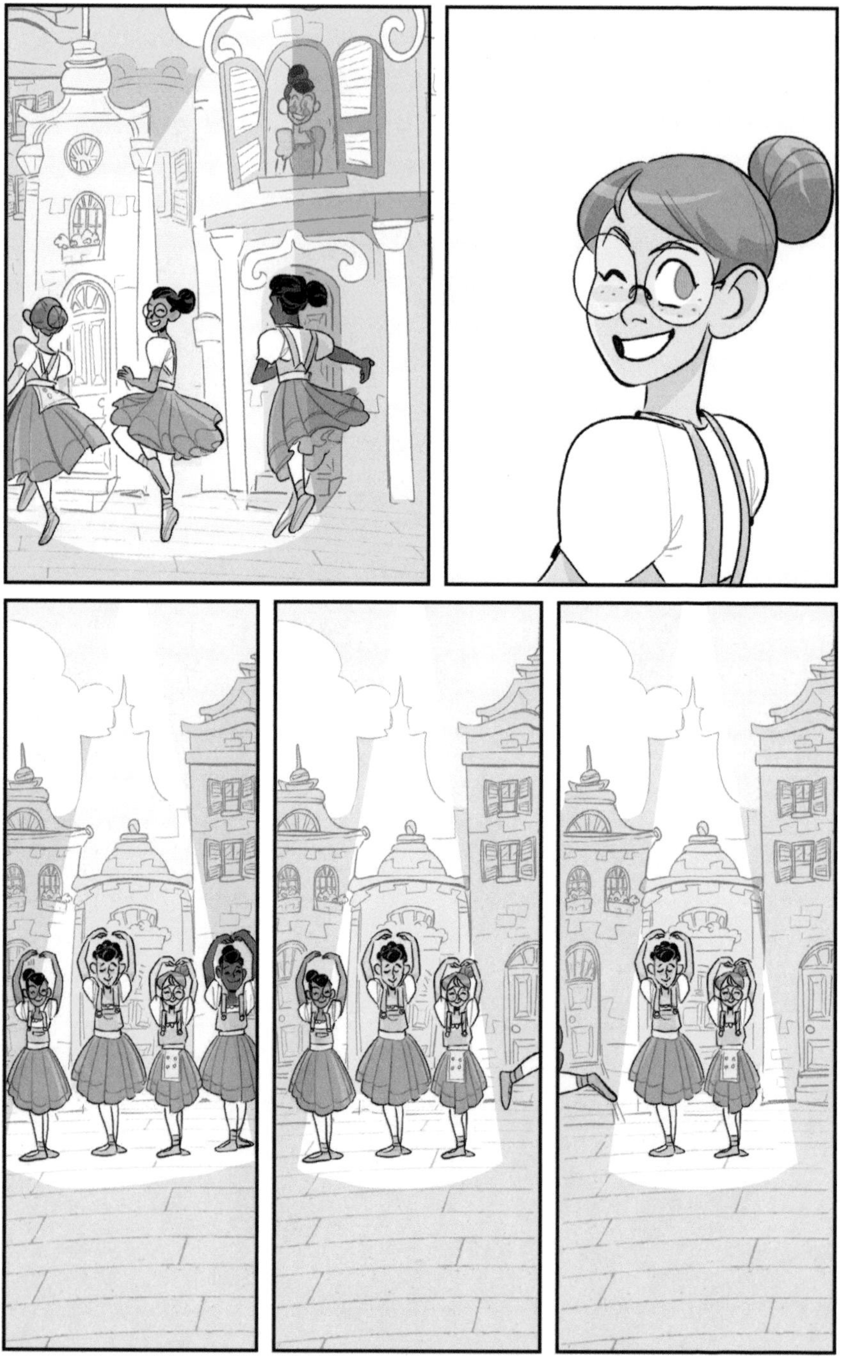

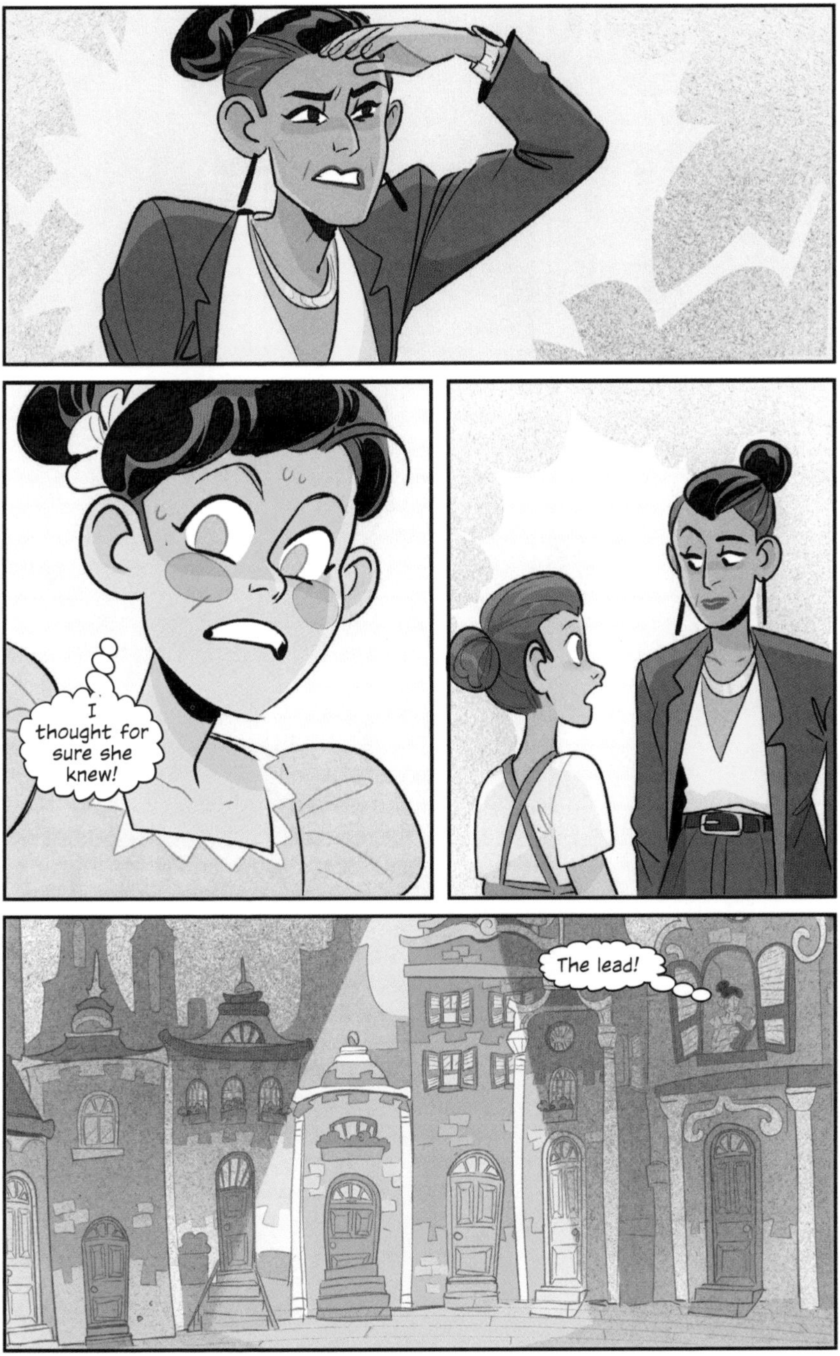
I thought for sure she knew!
The lead!

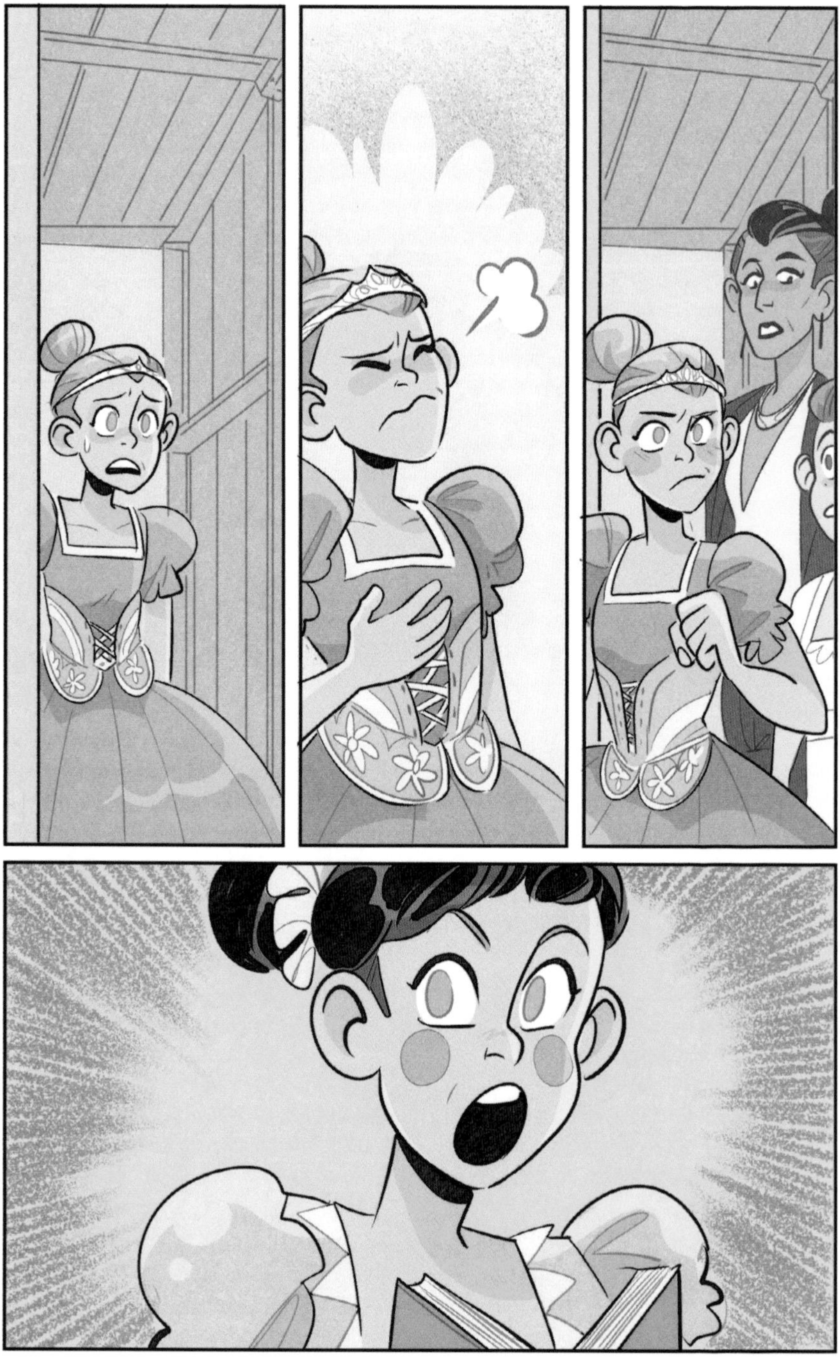

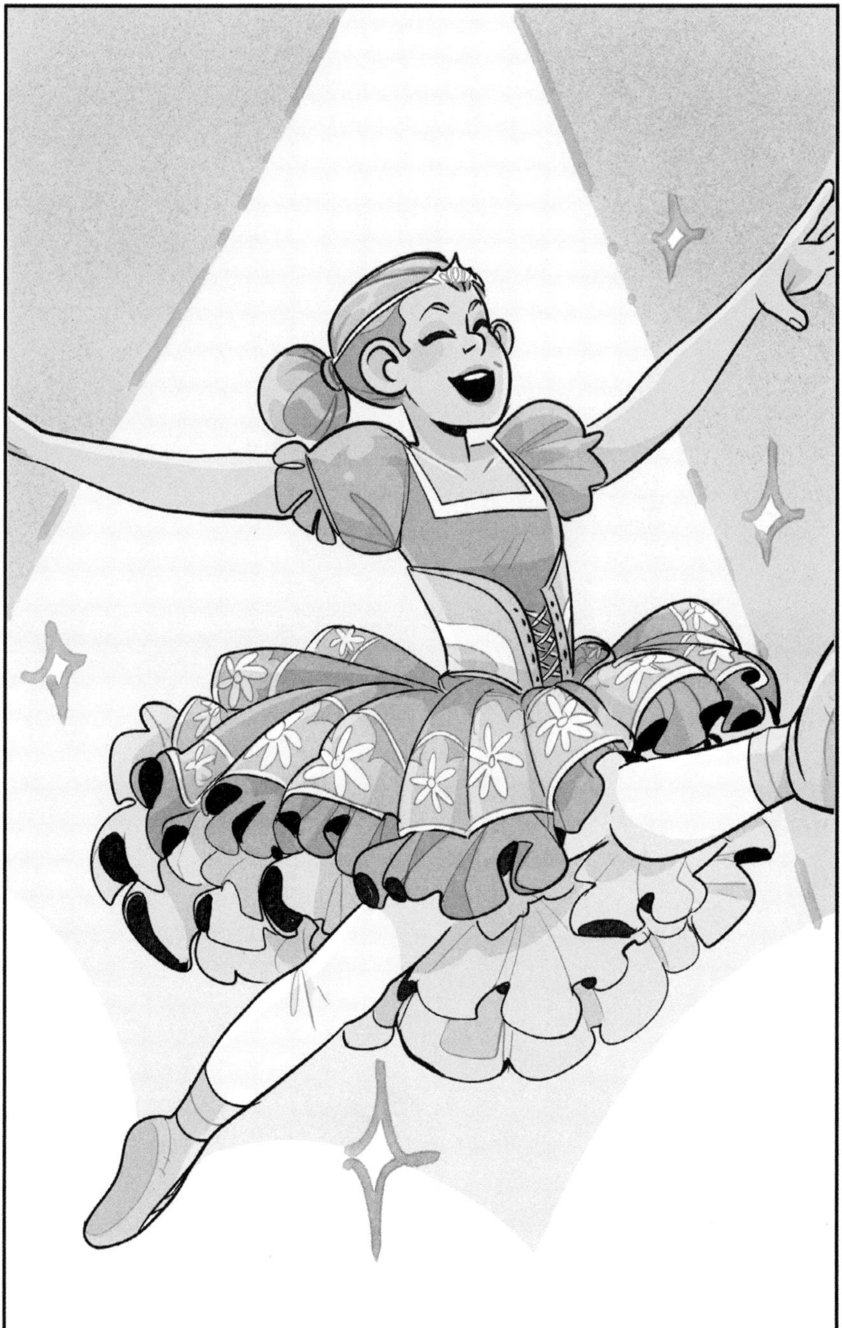

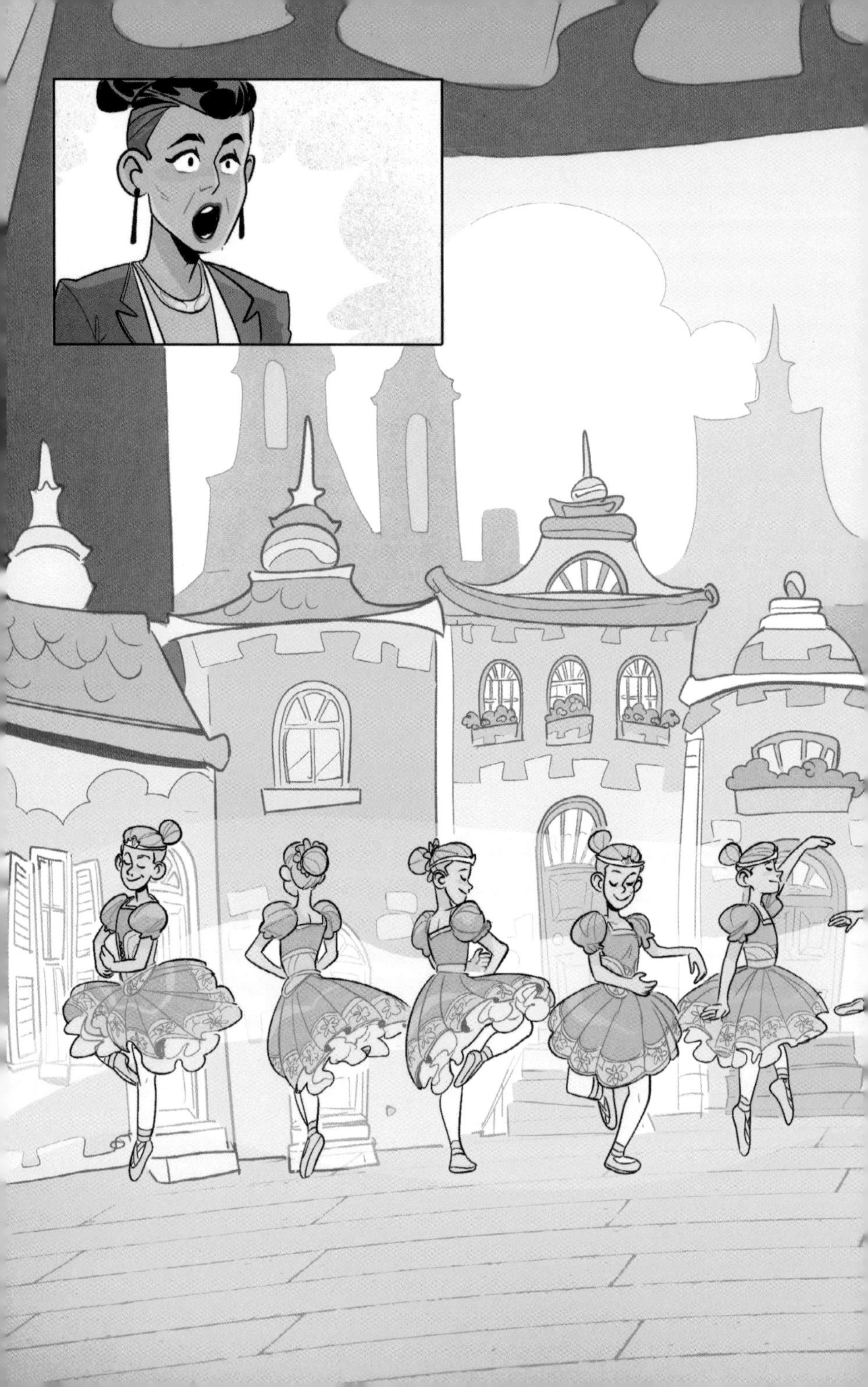

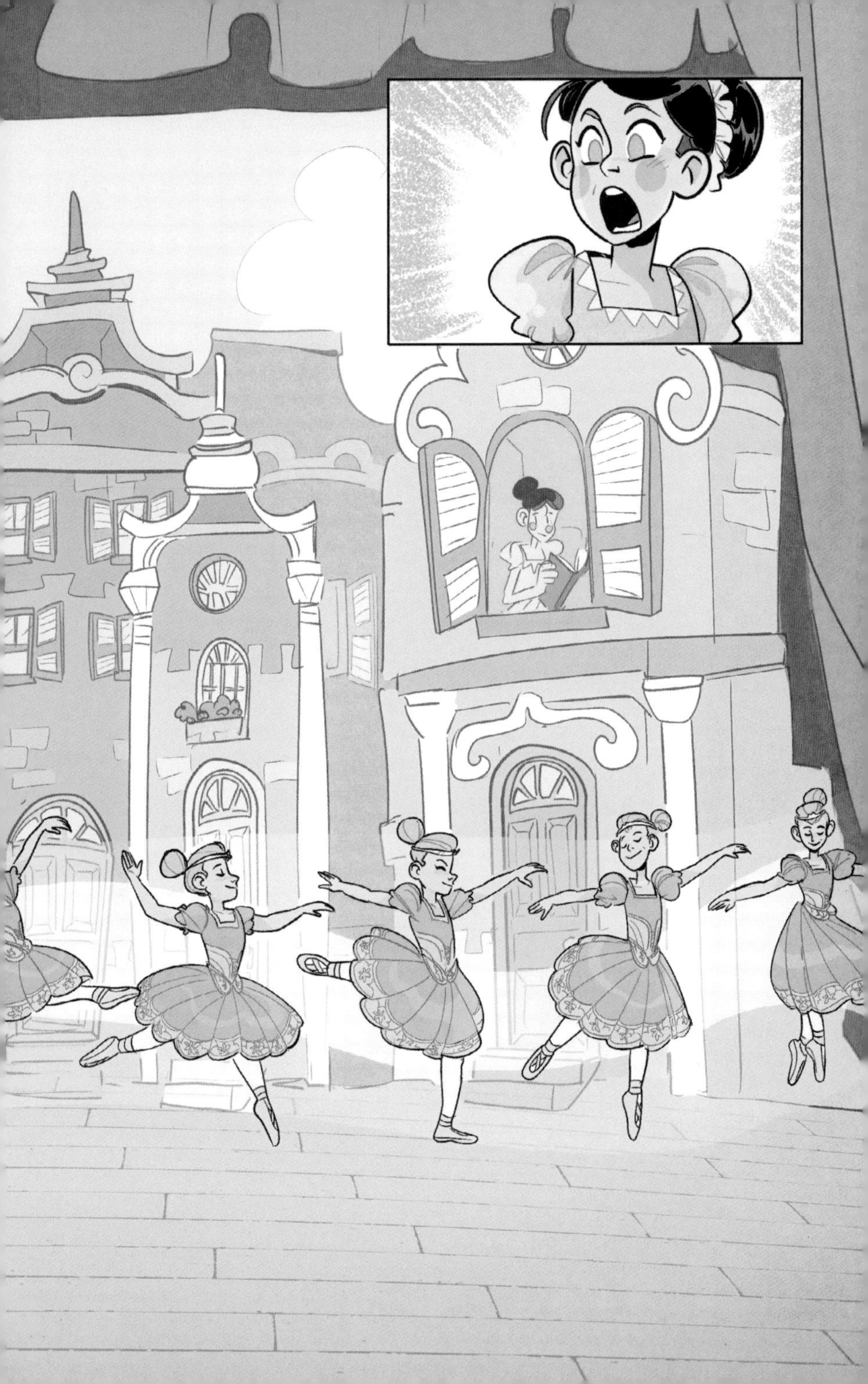

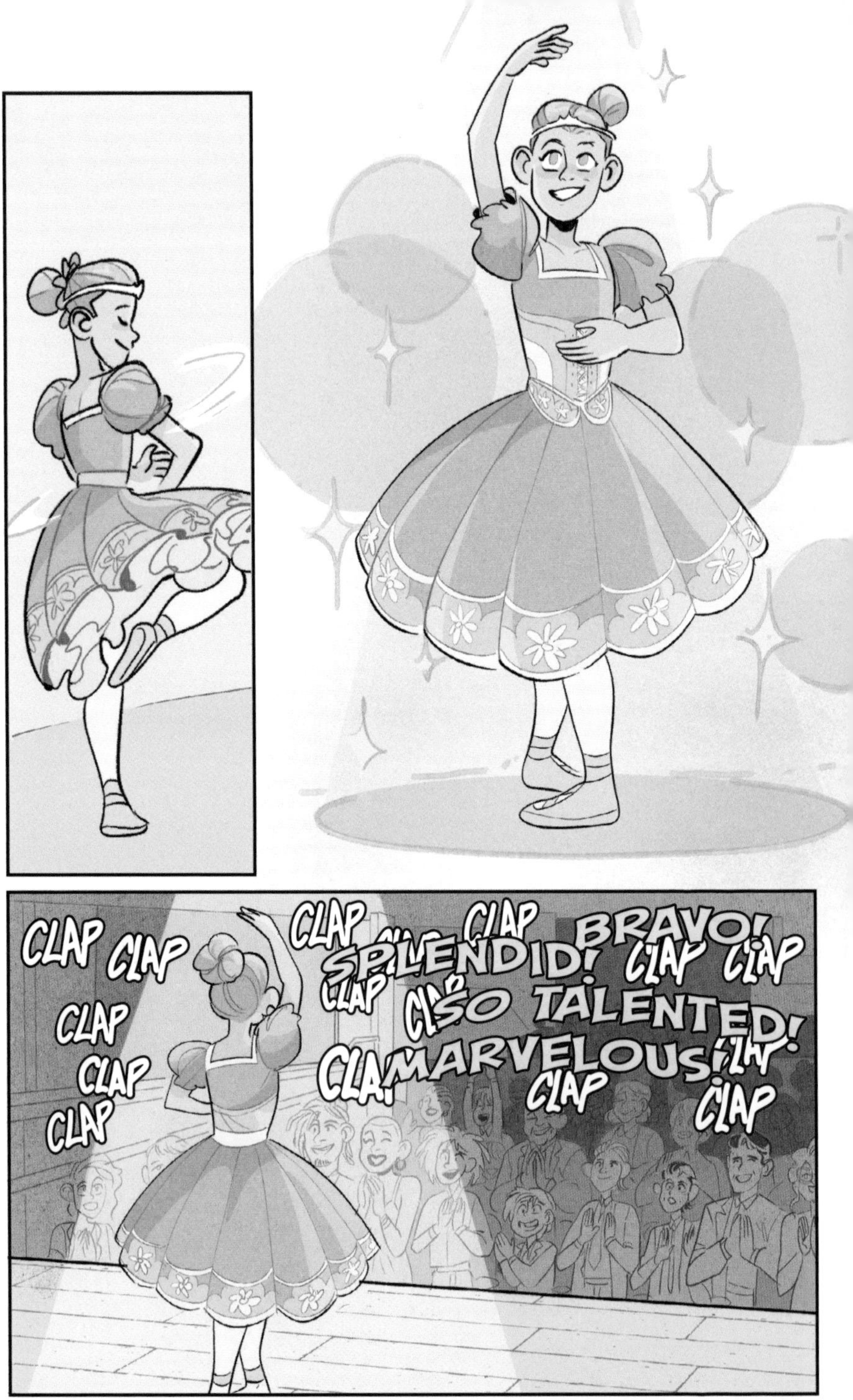
CLAP CLAP
CLAP
CLAP
CLAP
CLAP
CLAP
BRAVO!
SPLENDID!
CLAP CLAP
CLAP
CLAP
SO TALENTED!
CLA
MARVELOUS!
CLAP
CLAP

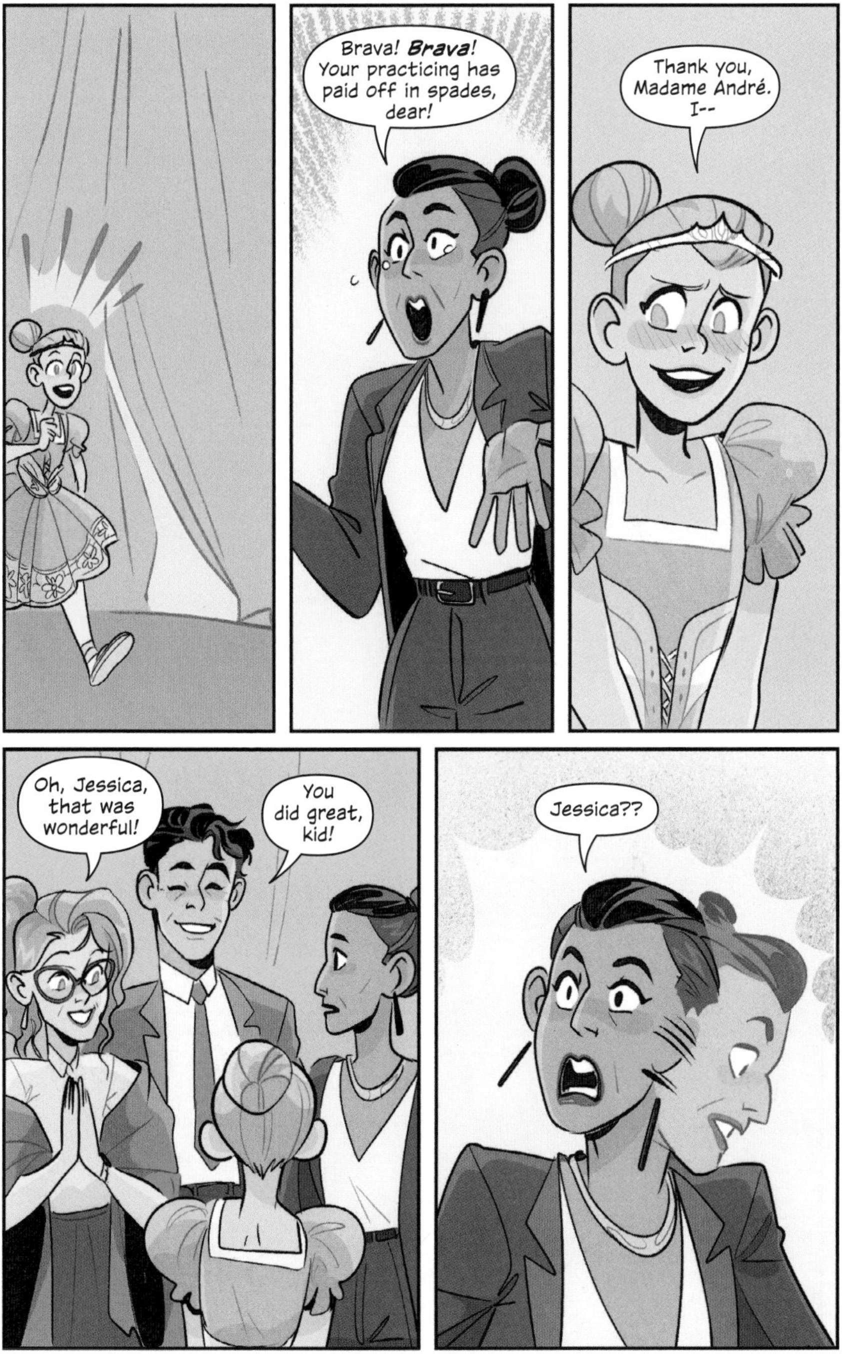
Brava! **Brava!** Your practicing has paid off in spades, dear!
Thank you, Madame André. I--
Oh, Jessica, that was wonderful!
You did great, kid!
Jessica??

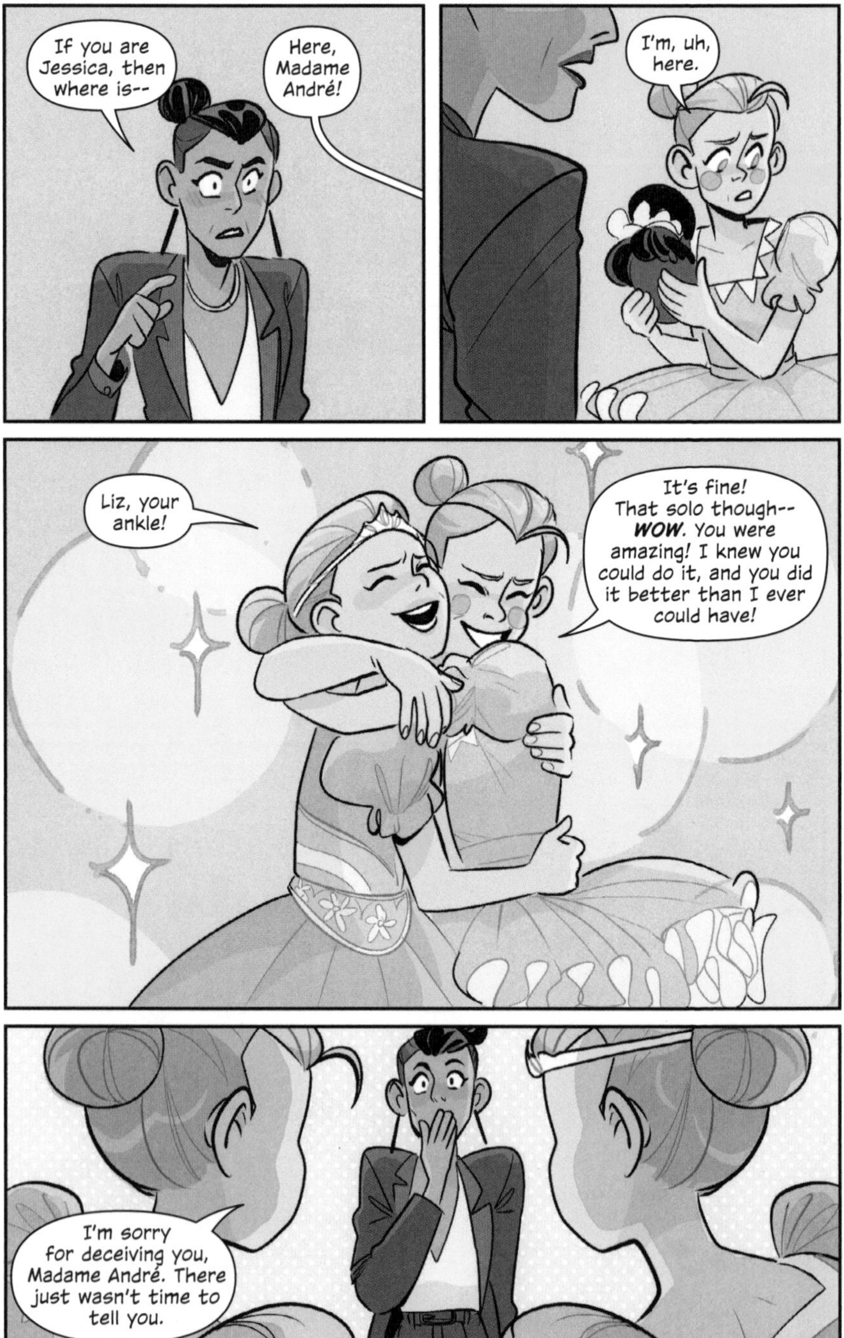
If you are Jessica, then where is--
Here, Madame André!
I'm, uh, here.
Liz, your ankle!
It's fine! That solo though-- **WOW**. You were amazing! I knew you could do it, and you did it better than I ever could have!
I'm sorry for deceiving you, Madame André. There just wasn't time to tell you.

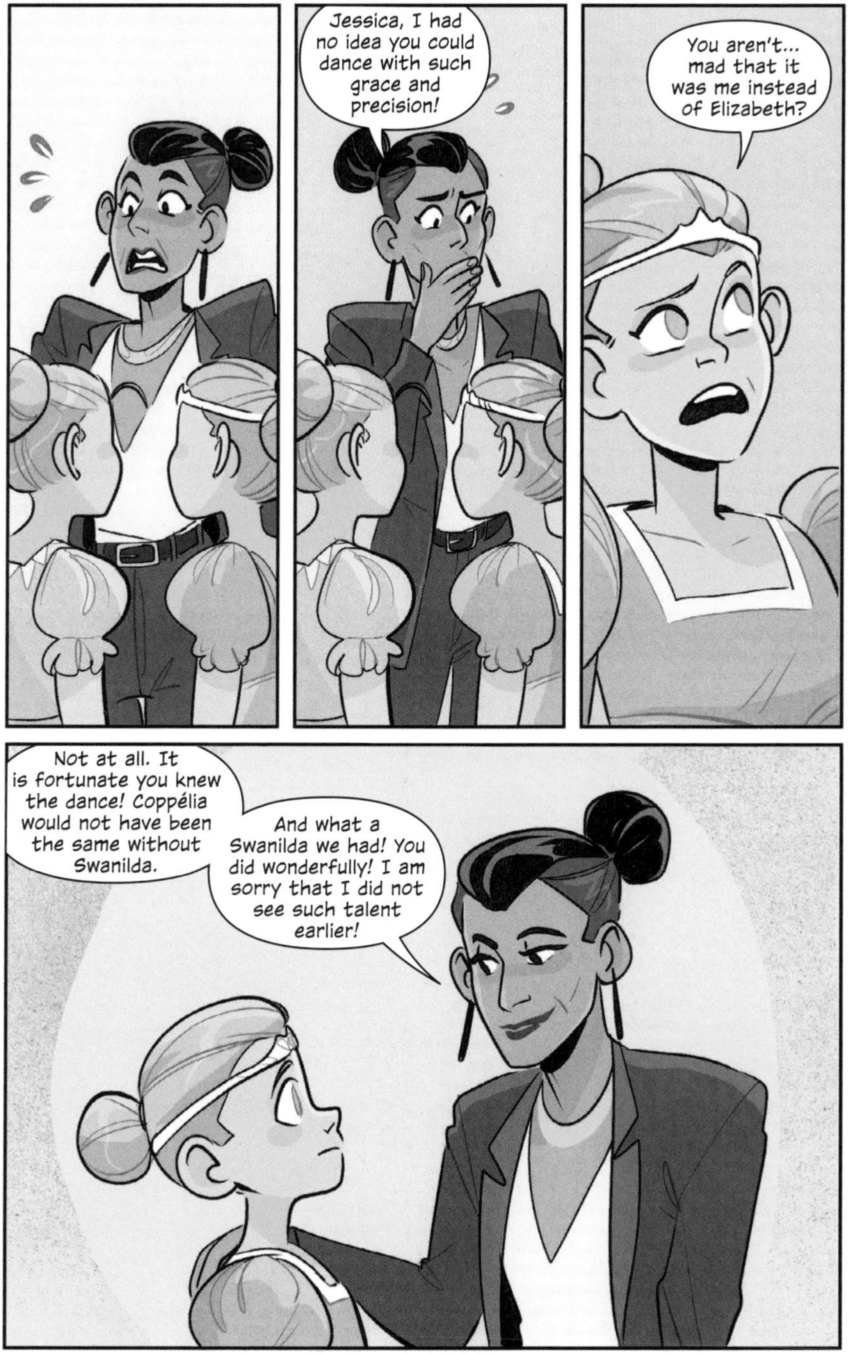

Jessica, I had no idea you could dance with such grace and precision!
You aren't... mad that it was me instead of Elizabeth?
Not at all. It is fortunate you knew the dance! Coppélia would not have been the same without Swanilda.
And what a Swanilda we had! You did wonderfully! I am sorry that I did not see such talent earlier!

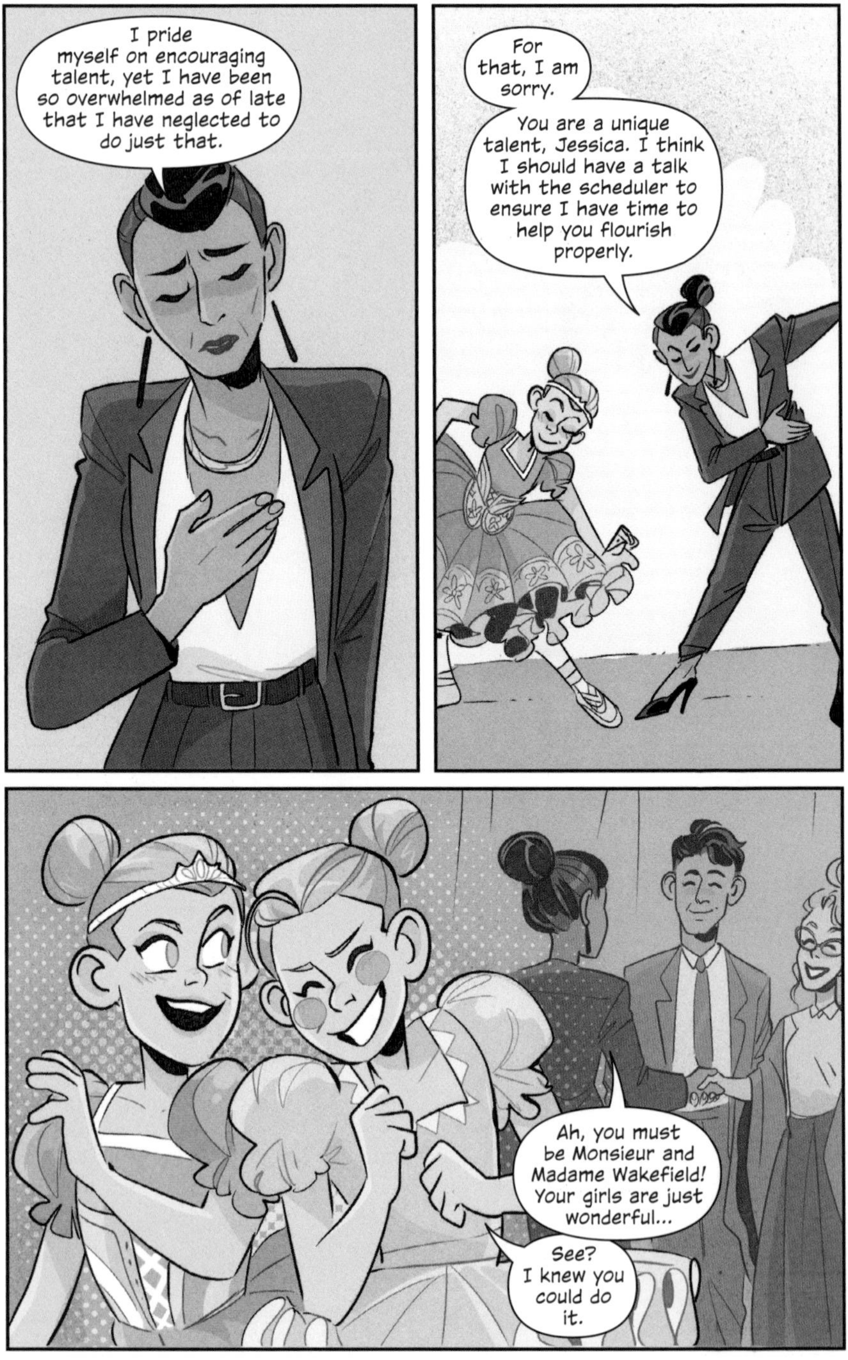
I pride myself on encouraging talent, yet I have been so overwhelmed as of late that I have neglected to do just that.
For that, I am sorry.
You are a unique talent, Jessica. I think I should have a talk with the scheduler to ensure I have time to help you flourish properly.
Ah, you must be Monsieur and Madame Wakefield! Your girls are just wonderful...
See? I knew you could do it.

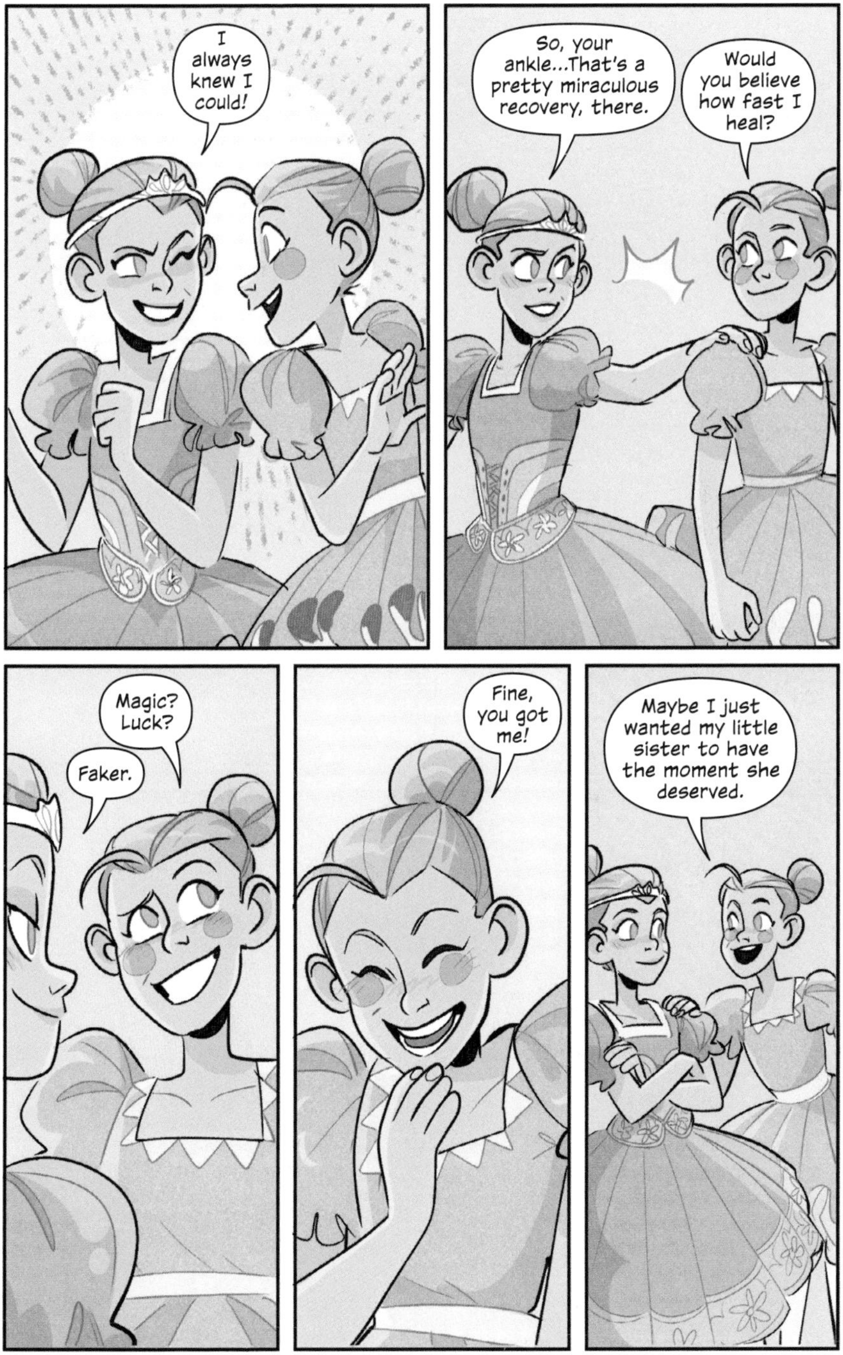
I always knew I could!
So, your ankle...That's a pretty miraculous recovery, there.
Would you believe how fast I heal?
Faker.
Magic? Luck?
Fine, you got me!
Maybe I just wanted my little sister to have the moment she deserved.

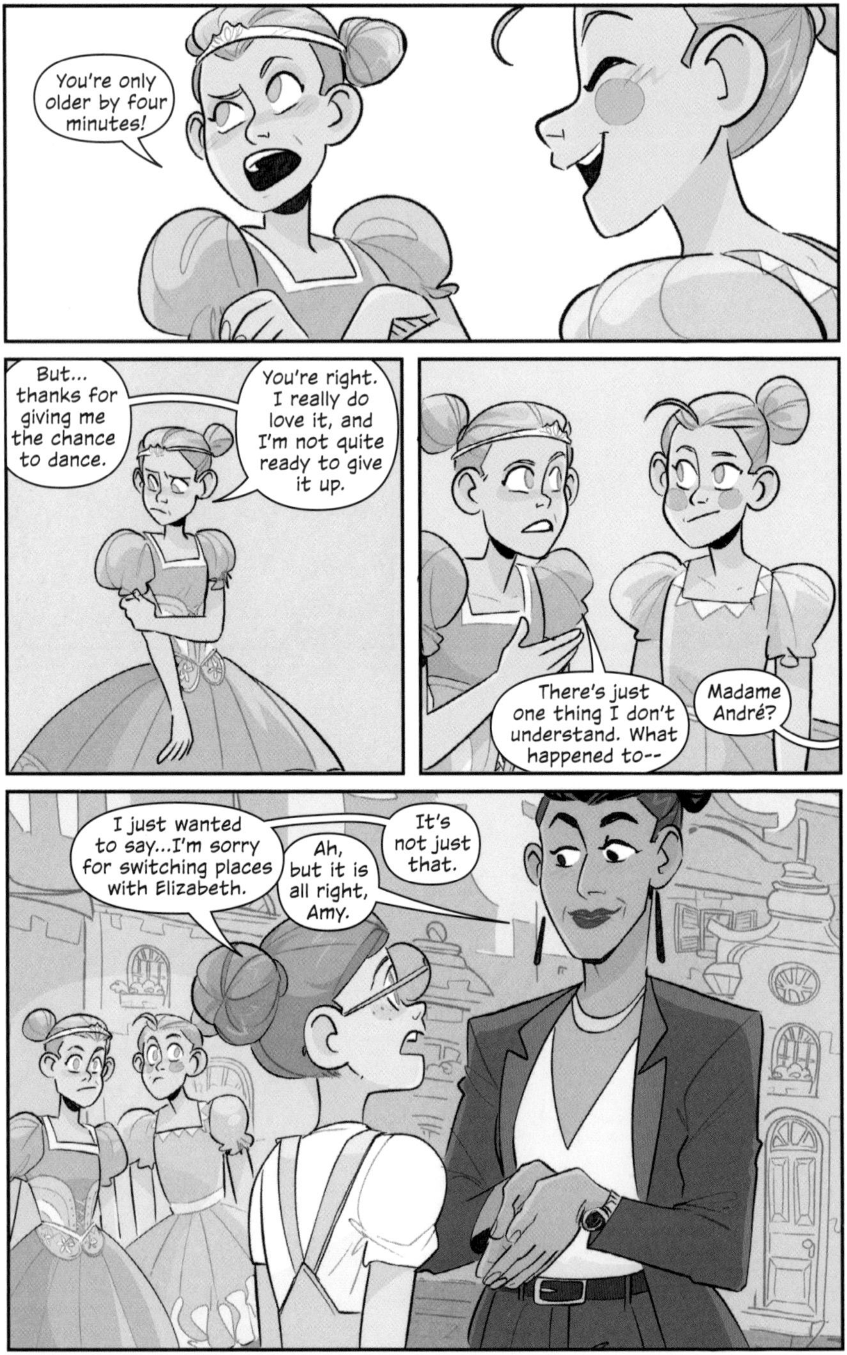
You're only older by four minutes!
But... thanks for giving me the chance to dance.
You're right. I really do love it, and I'm not quite ready to give it up.
There's just one thing I don't understand. What happened to--
Madame André?
I just wanted to say...I'm sorry for switching places with Elizabeth.
It's not just that.
Ah, but it is all right, Amy.

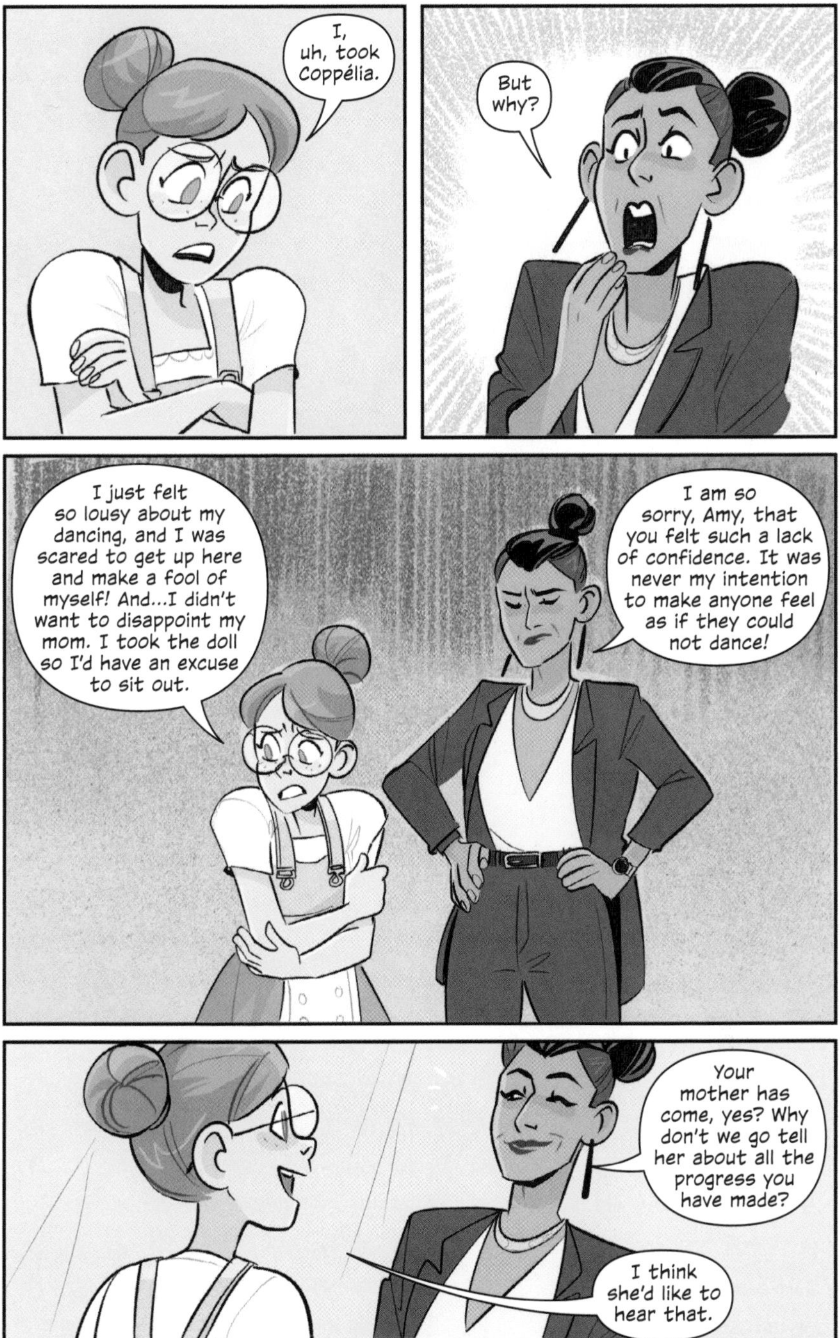
I, uh, took Coppélia.
But why?
I just felt so lousy about my dancing, and I was scared to get up here and make a fool of myself! And...I didn't want to disappoint my mom. I took the doll so I'd have an excuse to sit out.
I am so sorry, Amy, that you felt such a lack of confidence. It was never my intention to make anyone feel as if they could not dance!
Your mother has come, yes? Why don't we go tell her about all the progress you have made?
I think she'd like to hear that.

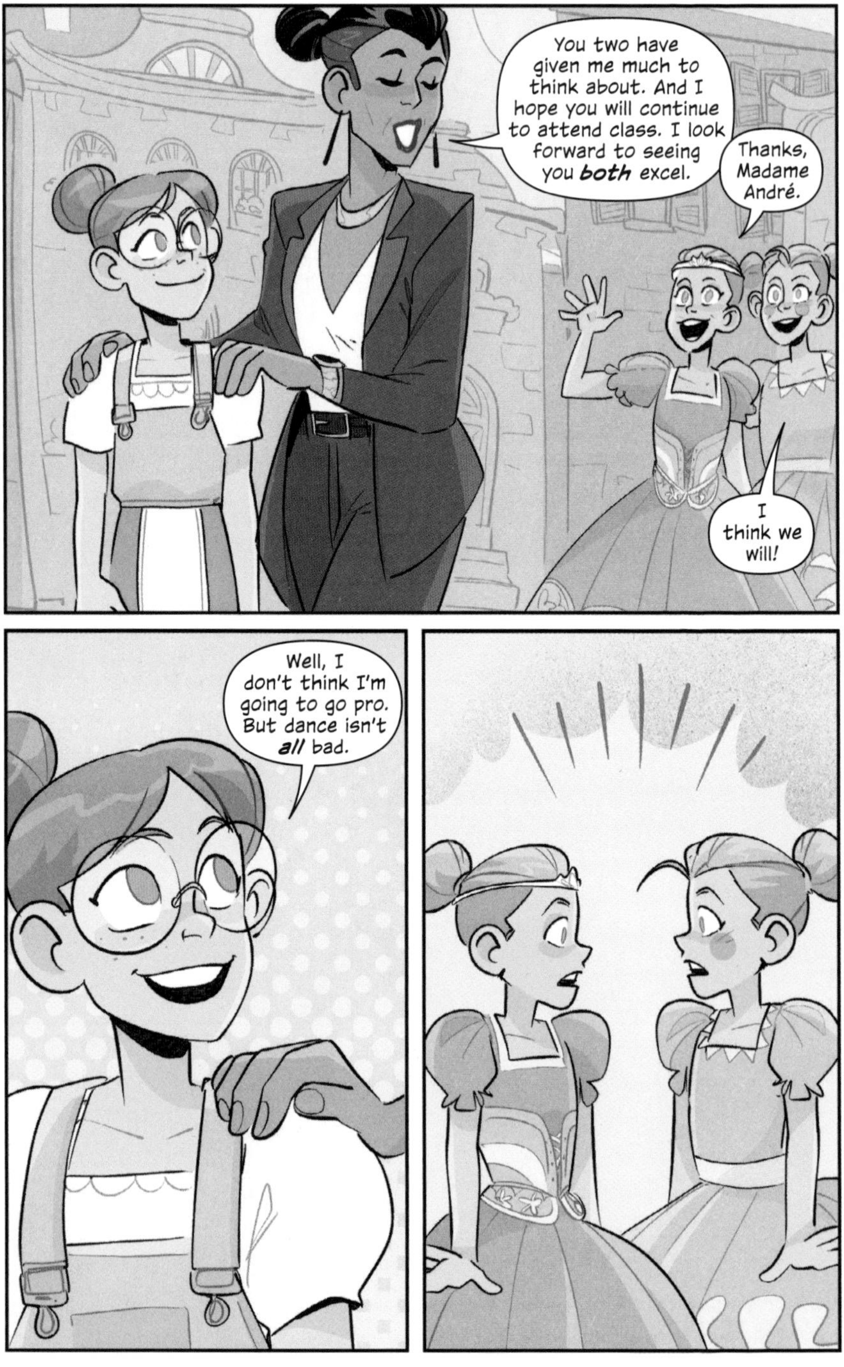
You two have given me much to think about. And I hope you will continue to attend class. I look forward to seeing you *both* excel.
Thanks, Madame André.
I think we will!
Well, I don't think I'm going to go pro. But dance isn't *all* bad.

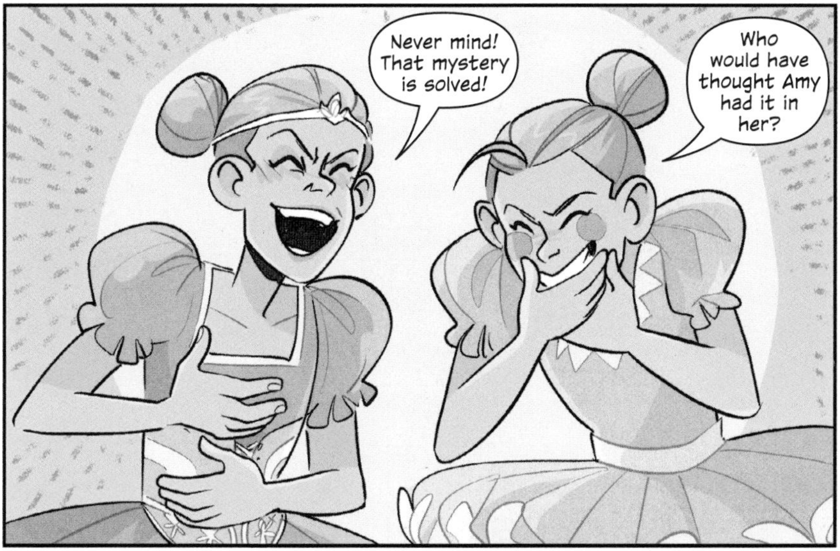
Never mind! That mystery is solved!
Who would have thought Amy had it in her?

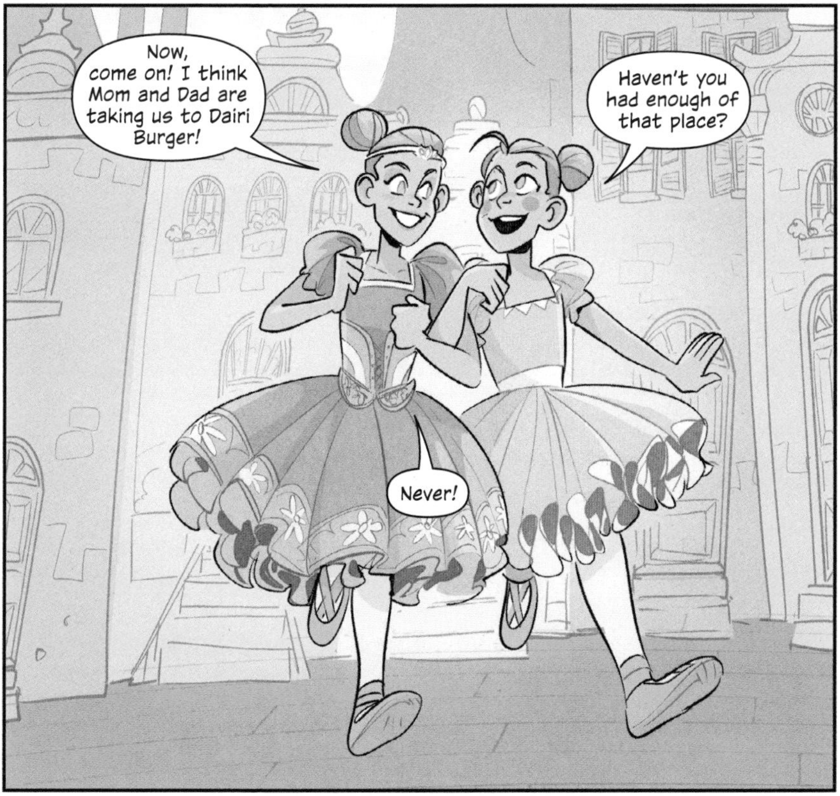
Now, come on! I think Mom and Dad are taking us to Dairi Burger!
Haven't you had enough of that place?
Never!

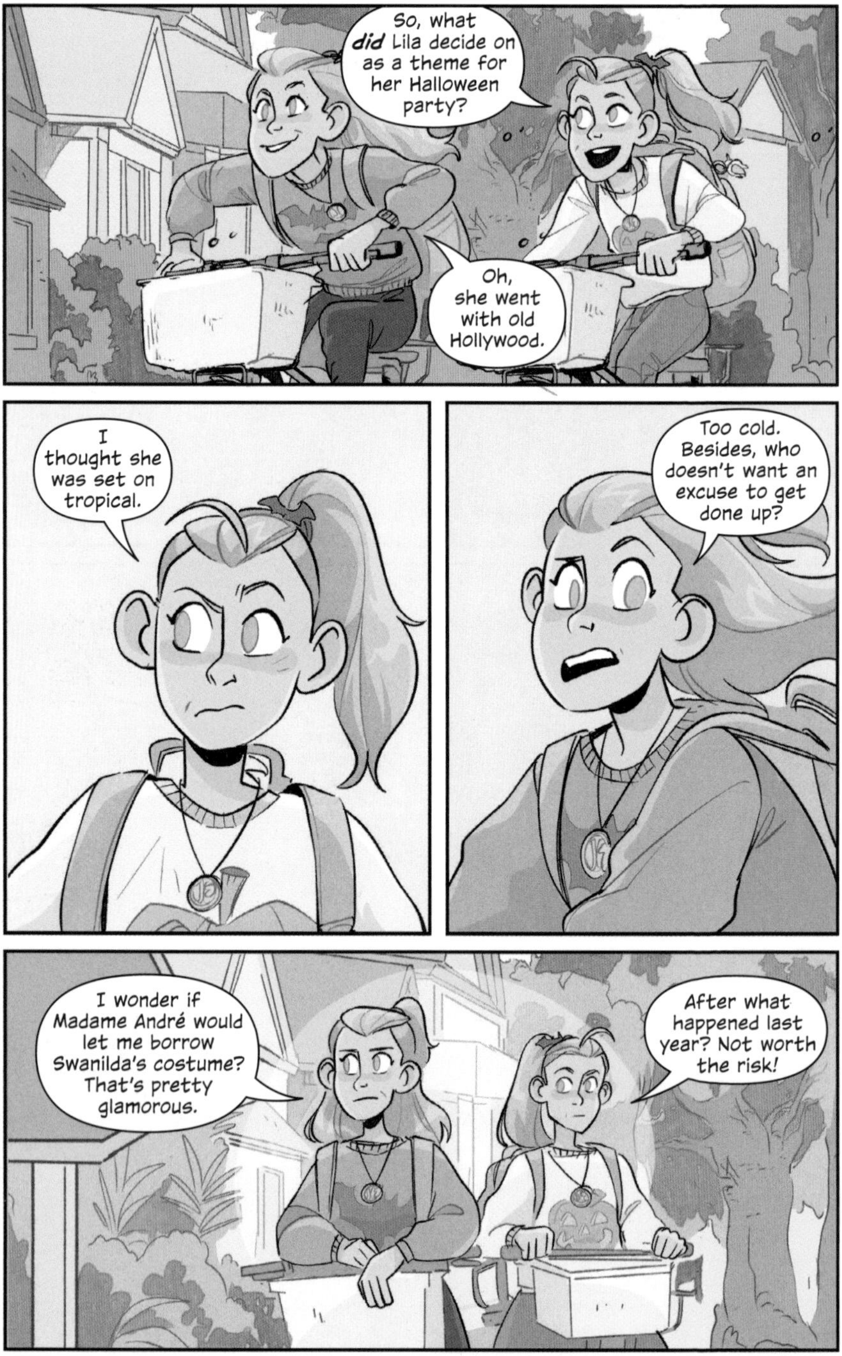

So, what *did* Lila decide on as a theme for her Halloween party?
Oh, she went with old Hollywood.
I thought she was set on tropical.
Too cold. Besides, who doesn't want an excuse to get done up?
I wonder if Madame André would let me borrow Swanilda's costume? That's pretty glamorous.
After what happened last year? Not worth the risk!

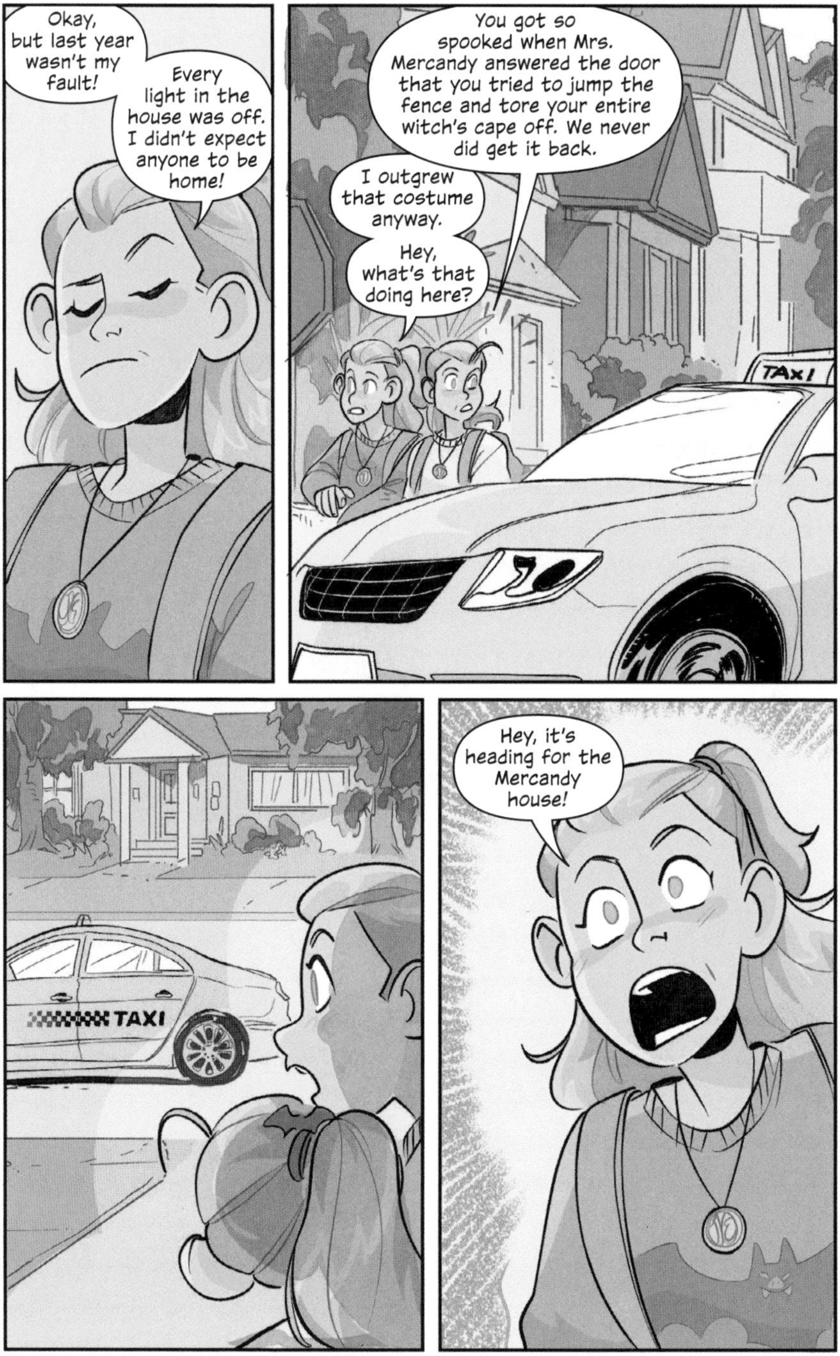
Okay, but last year wasn't my fault!
Every light in the house was off. I didn't expect anyone to be home!
You got so spooked when Mrs. Mercandy answered the door that you tried to jump the fence and tore your entire witch's cape off. We never did get it back.
I outgrew that costume anyway.
Hey, what's that doing here?
TAXI
TAXI
Hey, it's heading for the Mercandy house!

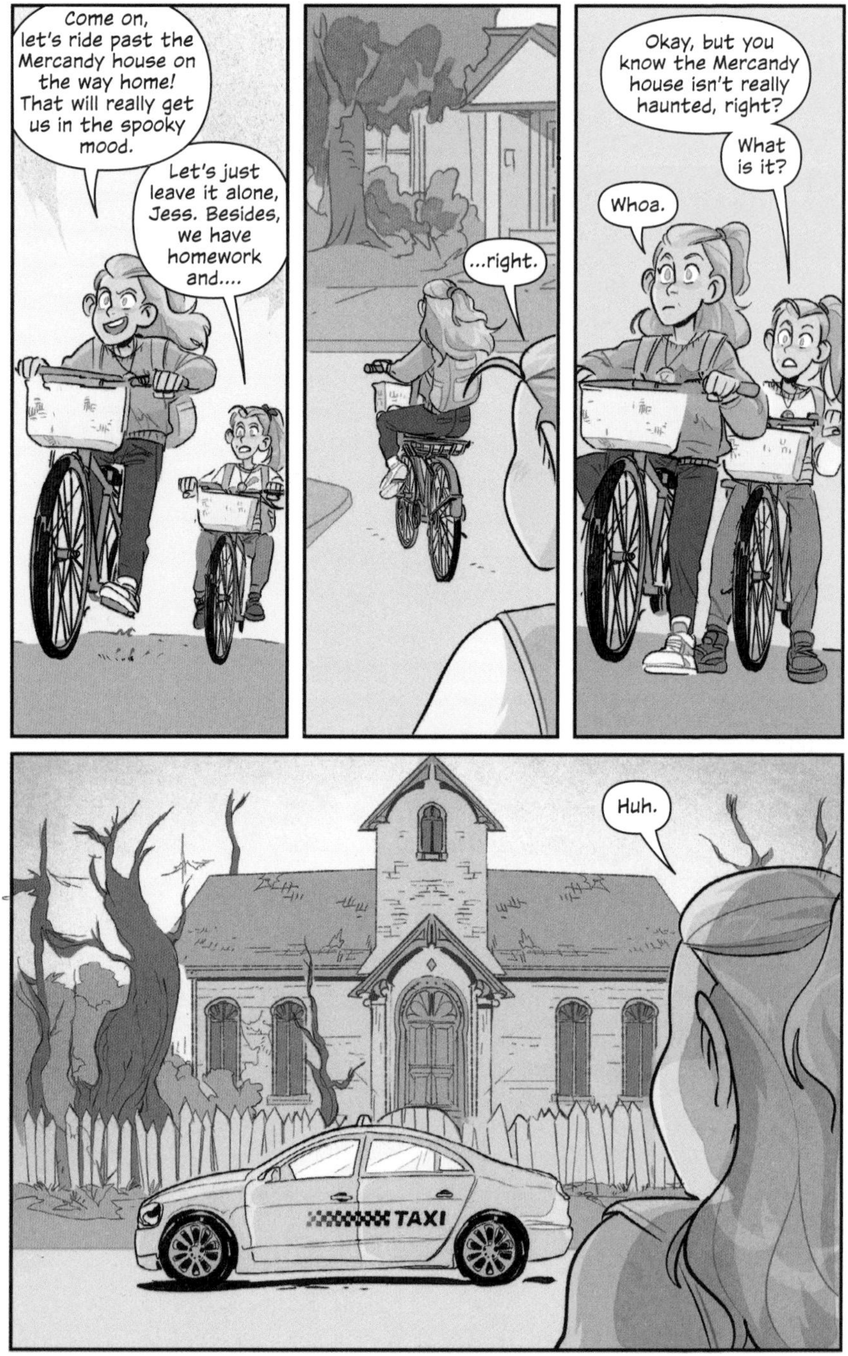
Come on, let's ride past the Mercandy house on the way home! That will really get us in the spooky mood.
Let's just leave it alone, Jess. Besides, we have homework and....
...right.
Okay, but you know the Mercandy house isn't really haunted, right?
What is it?
Whoa.
Huh.
TAXI

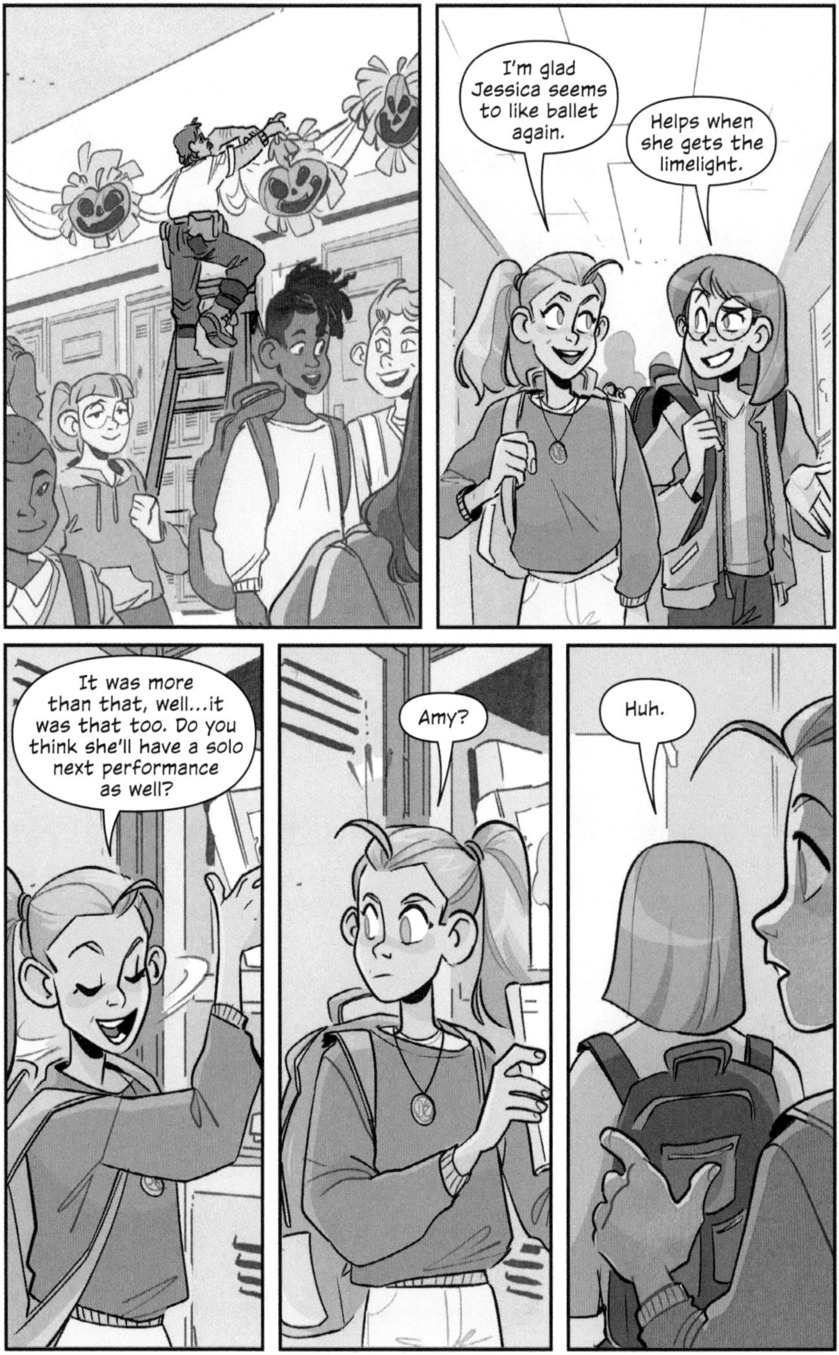
I'm glad Jessica seems to like ballet again.
Helps when she gets the limelight.
It was more than that, well...it was that too. Do you think she'll have a solo next performance as well?
Amy?
Huh.

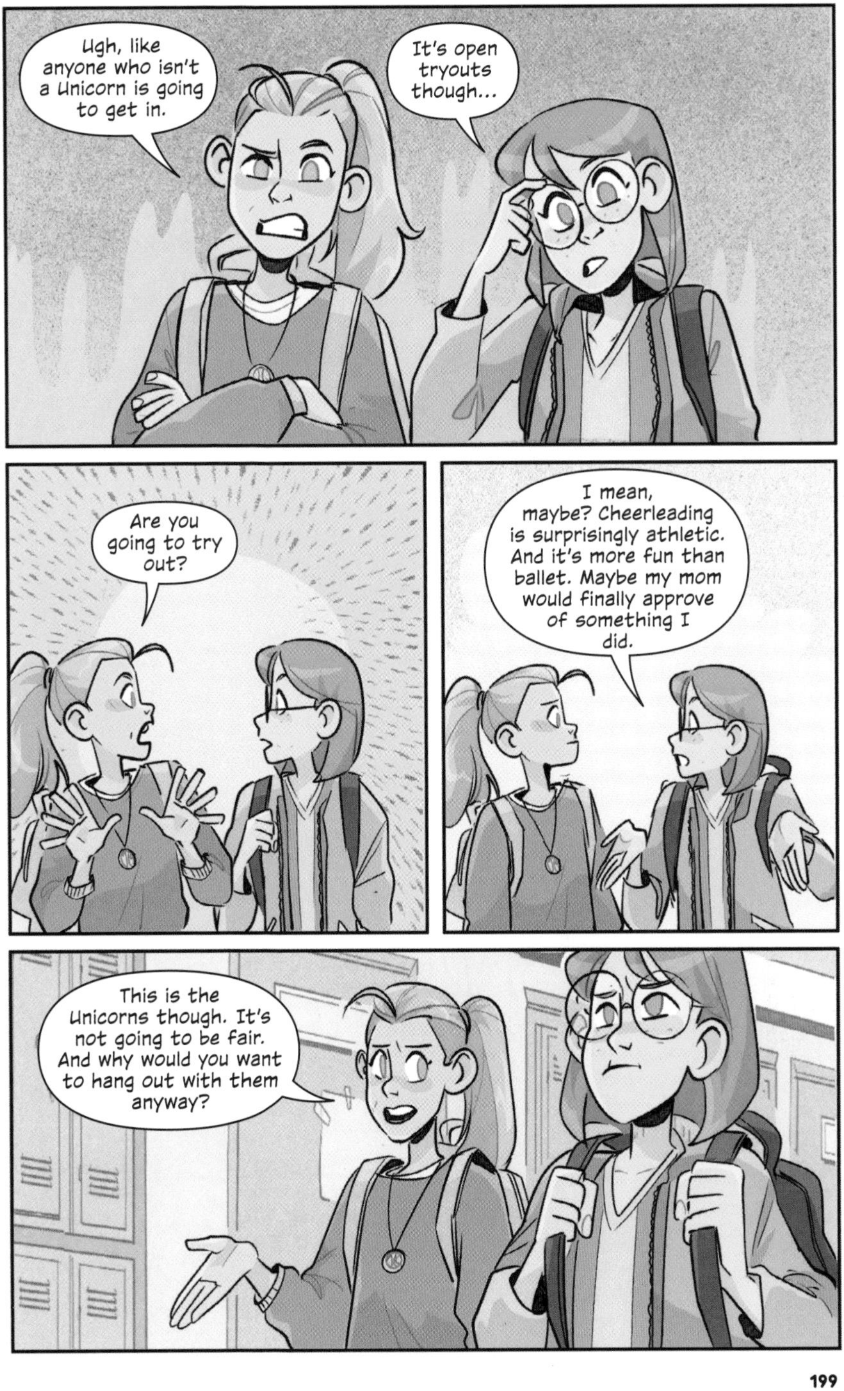

Ugh, like anyone who isn't a Unicorn is going to get in.
It's open tryouts though...
Are you going to try out?
I mean, maybe? Cheerleading is surprisingly athletic. And it's more fun than ballet. Maybe my mom would finally approve of something I did.
This is the Unicorns though. It's not going to be fair. And why would you want to hang out with them anyway?

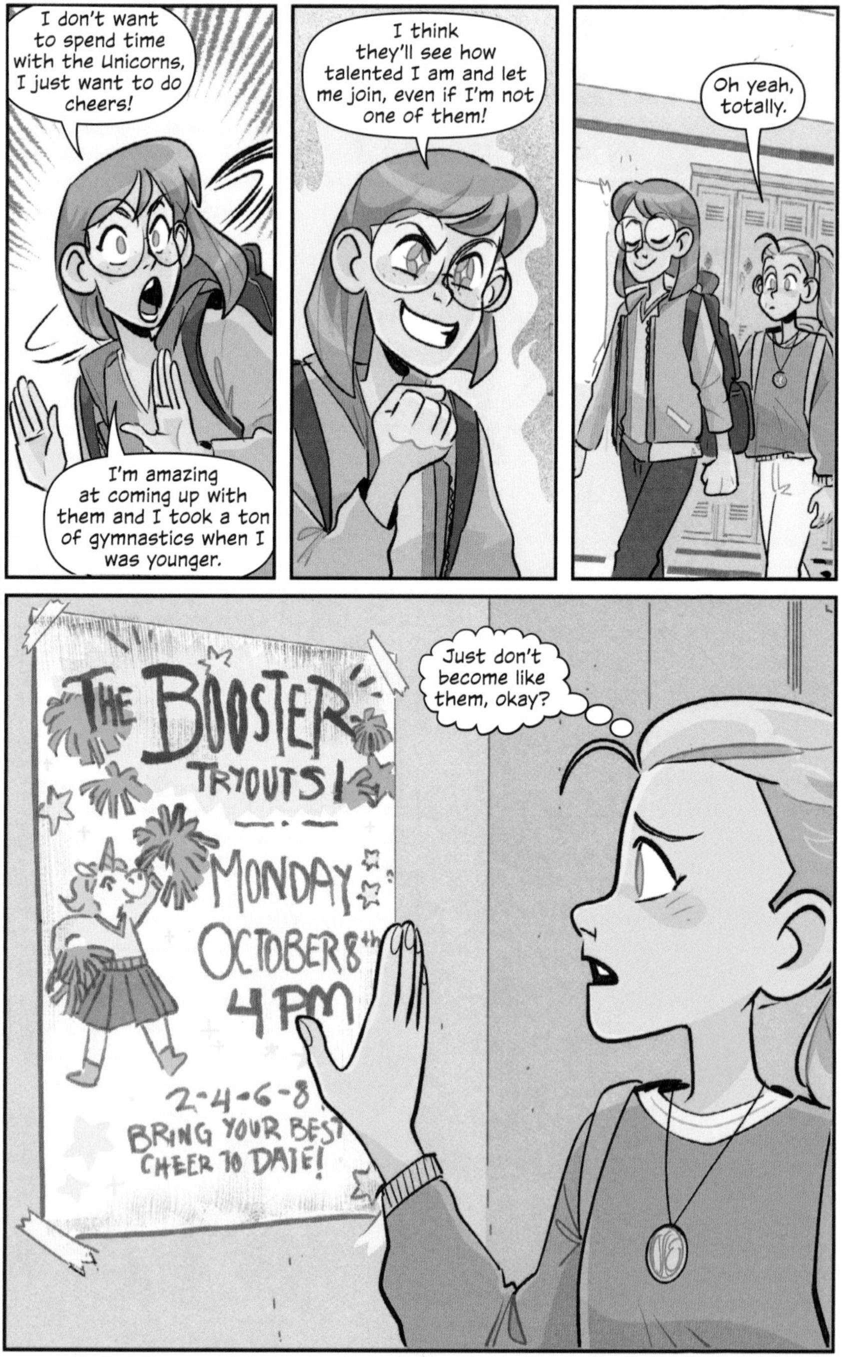
I don't want to spend time with the Unicorns, I just want to do cheers!
I'm amazing at coming up with them and I took a ton of gymnastics when I was younger.
I think they'll see how talented I am and let me join, even if I'm not one of them!
Oh yeah, totally.
THE BOOSTER TRYOUTS!
MONDAY OCTOBER 8th 4PM
2-4-6-8
BRING YOUR BEST CHEER TO DATE!
Just don't become like them, okay?

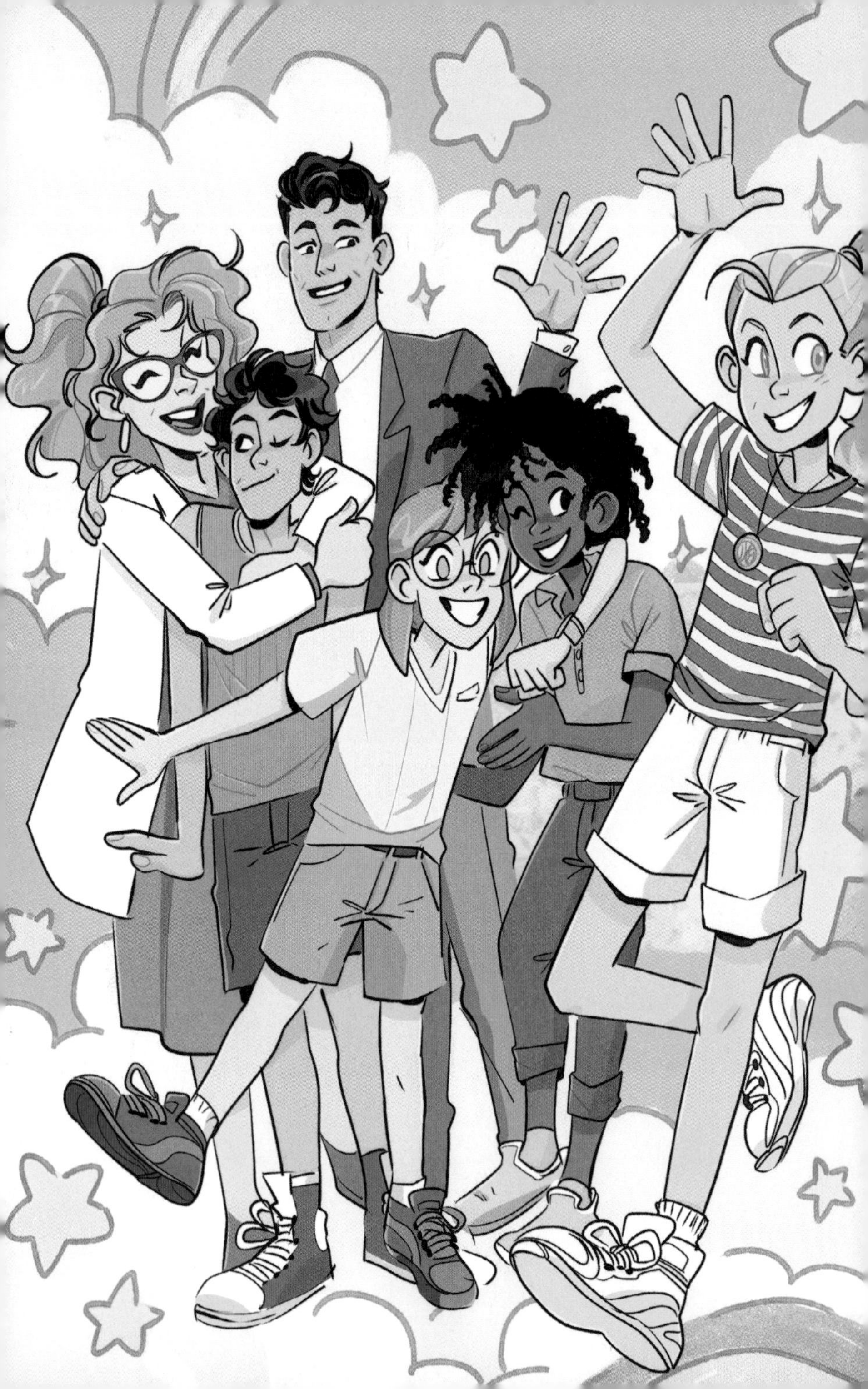

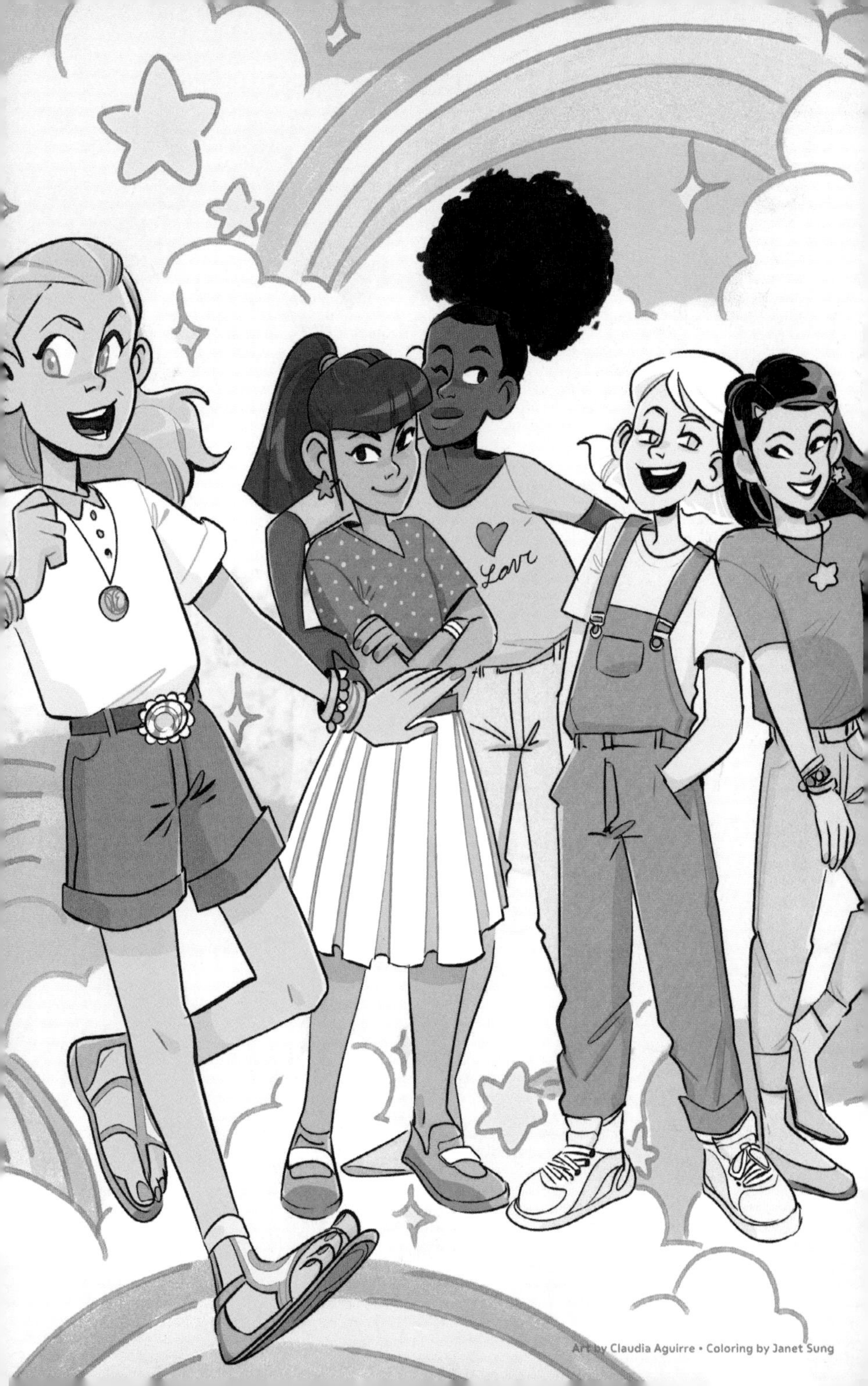
Love
Art by Claudia Aguirre • Coloring by Janet Sung

JESSICA and ELIZABETH RETURN in

FRANCINE PASCAL'S

SWEET VALLEY

Twins

CHOOSING SIDES

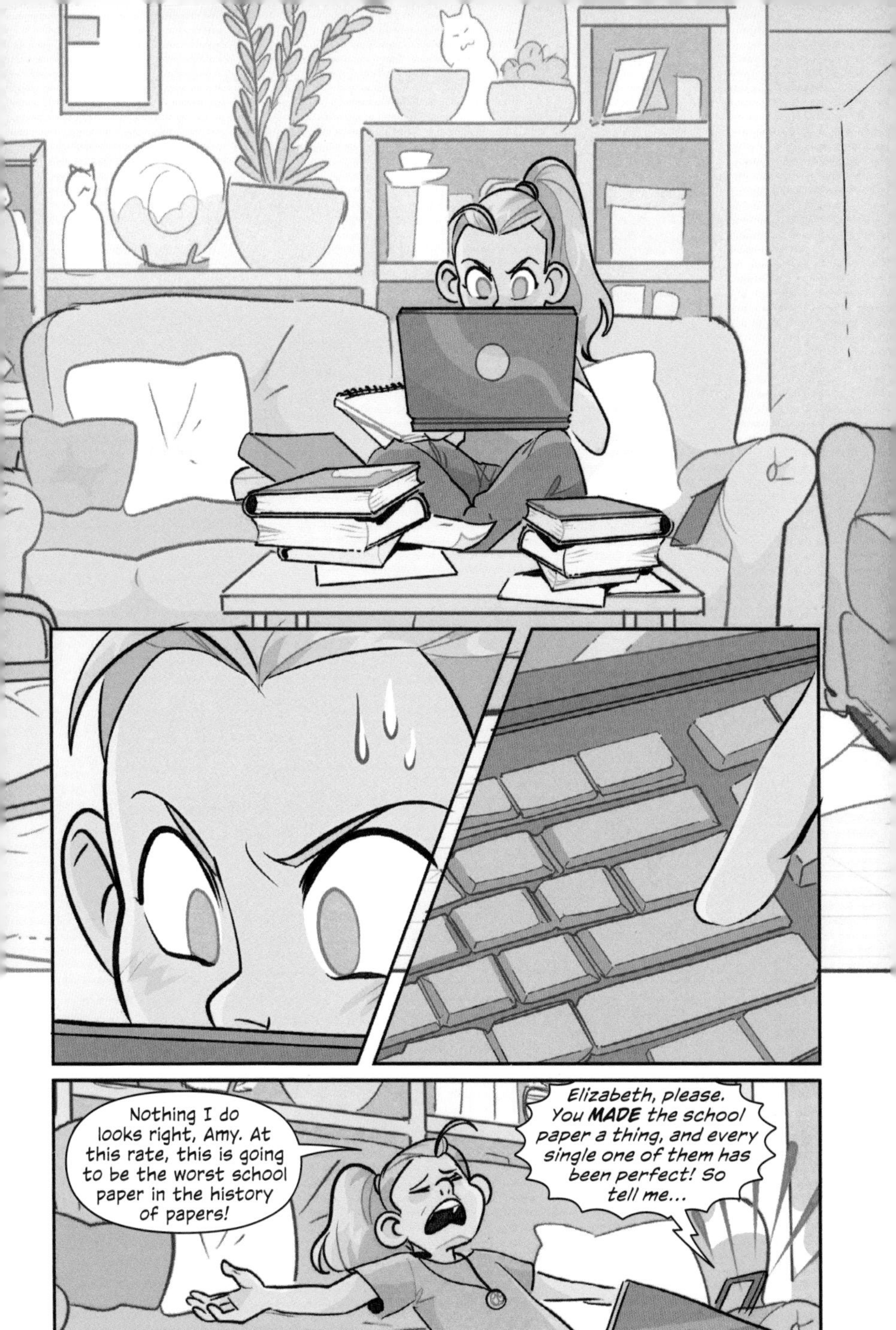
Nothing I do looks right, Amy. At this rate, this is going to be the worst school paper in the history of papers!
Elizabeth, please. You **MADE** the school paper a thing, and every single one of them has been perfect! So tell me...

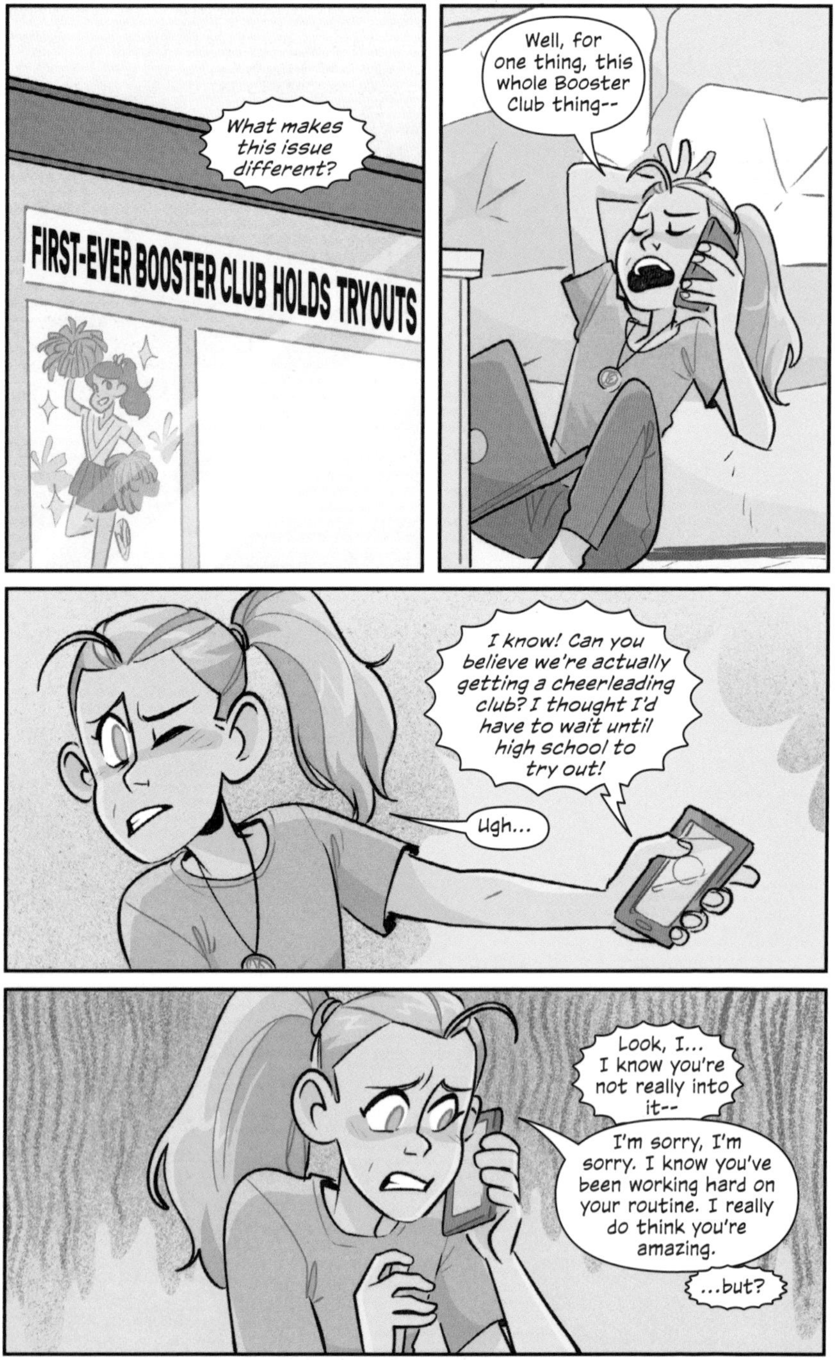
What makes this issue different?
FIRST-EVER BOOSTER CLUB HOLDS TRYOUTS
Well, for one thing, this whole Booster Club thing--
I know! Can you believe we're actually getting a cheerleading club? I thought I'd have to wait until high school to try out!
Ugh...
Look, I... I know you're not really into it--
I'm sorry, I'm sorry. I know you've been working hard on your routine. I really do think you're amazing.
...but?

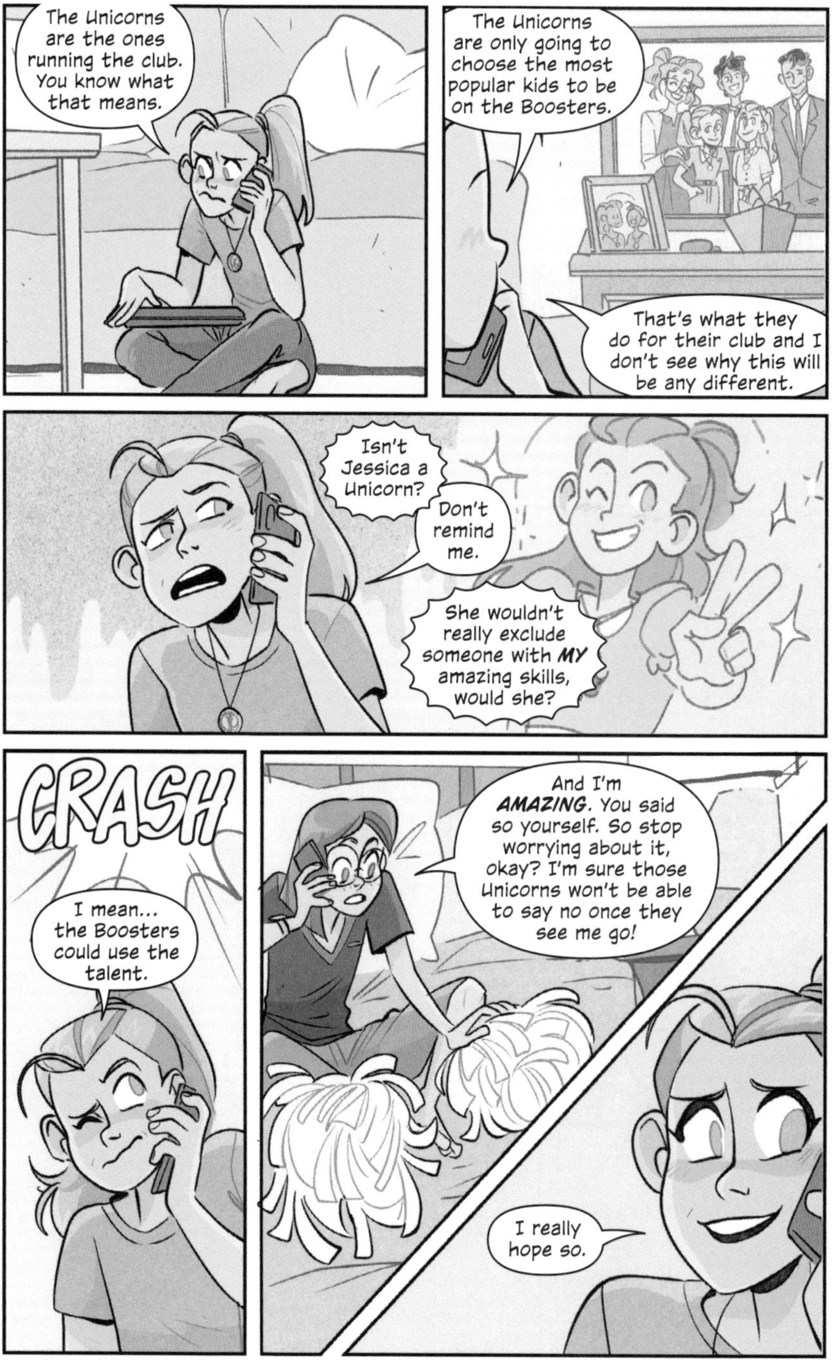
The Unicorns are the ones running the club. You know what that means.
The Unicorns are only going to choose the most popular kids to be on the Boosters.
That's what they do for their club and I don't see why this will be any different.
Isn't Jessica a Unicorn?
Don't remind me.
She wouldn't really exclude someone with *MY* amazing skills, would she?
CRASH
I mean... the Boosters could use the talent.
And I'm *AMAZING*. You said so yourself. So stop worrying about it, okay? I'm sure those Unicorns won't be able to say no once they see me go!
I really hope so.

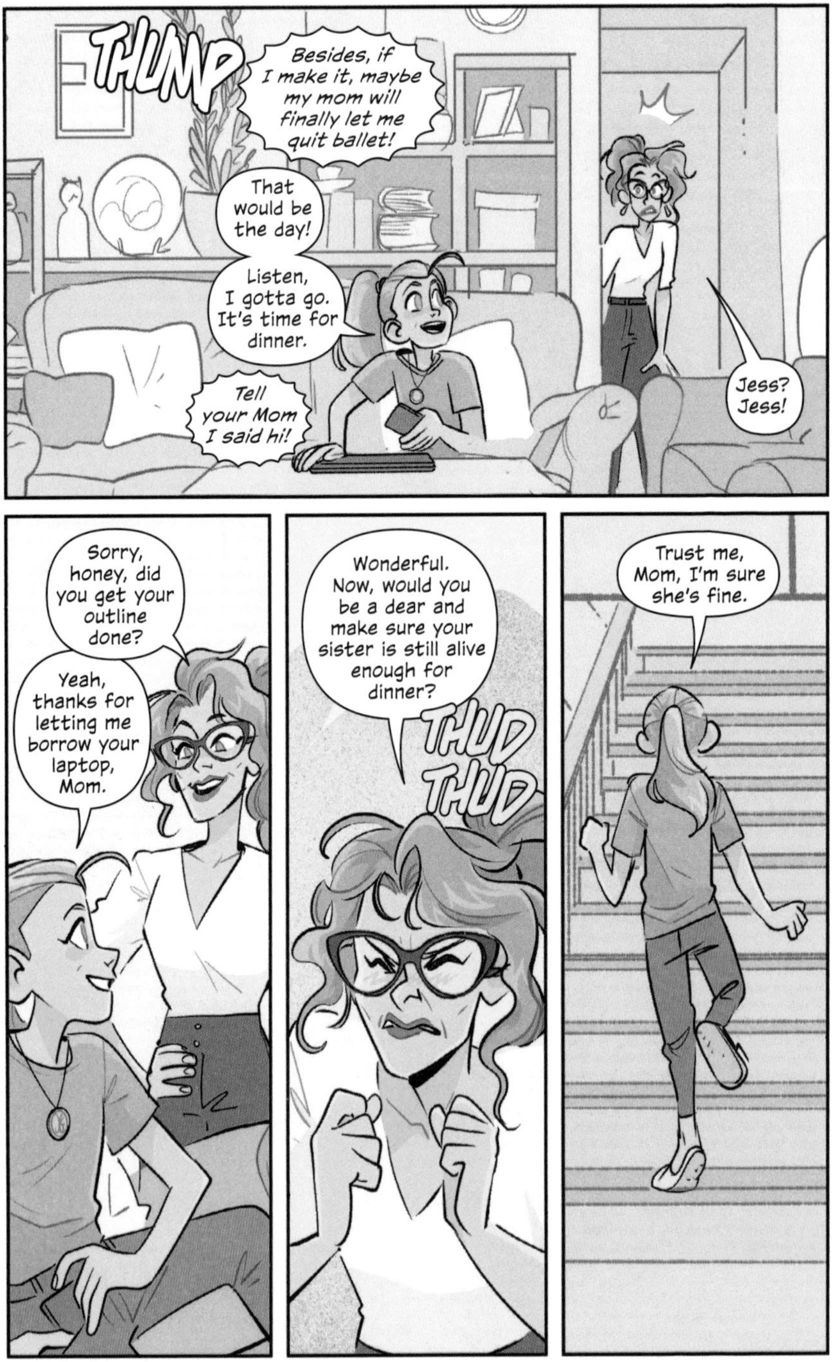
THUMP
Besides, if I make it, maybe my mom will finally let me quit ballet!
That would be the day!
Listen, I gotta go. It's time for dinner.
Tell your Mom I said hi!
Jess? Jess!
Sorry, honey, did you get your outline done?
Yeah, thanks for letting me borrow your laptop, Mom.
Wonderful. Now, would you be a dear and make sure your sister is still alive enough for dinner?
THUD THUD
Trust me, Mom, I'm sure she's fine.

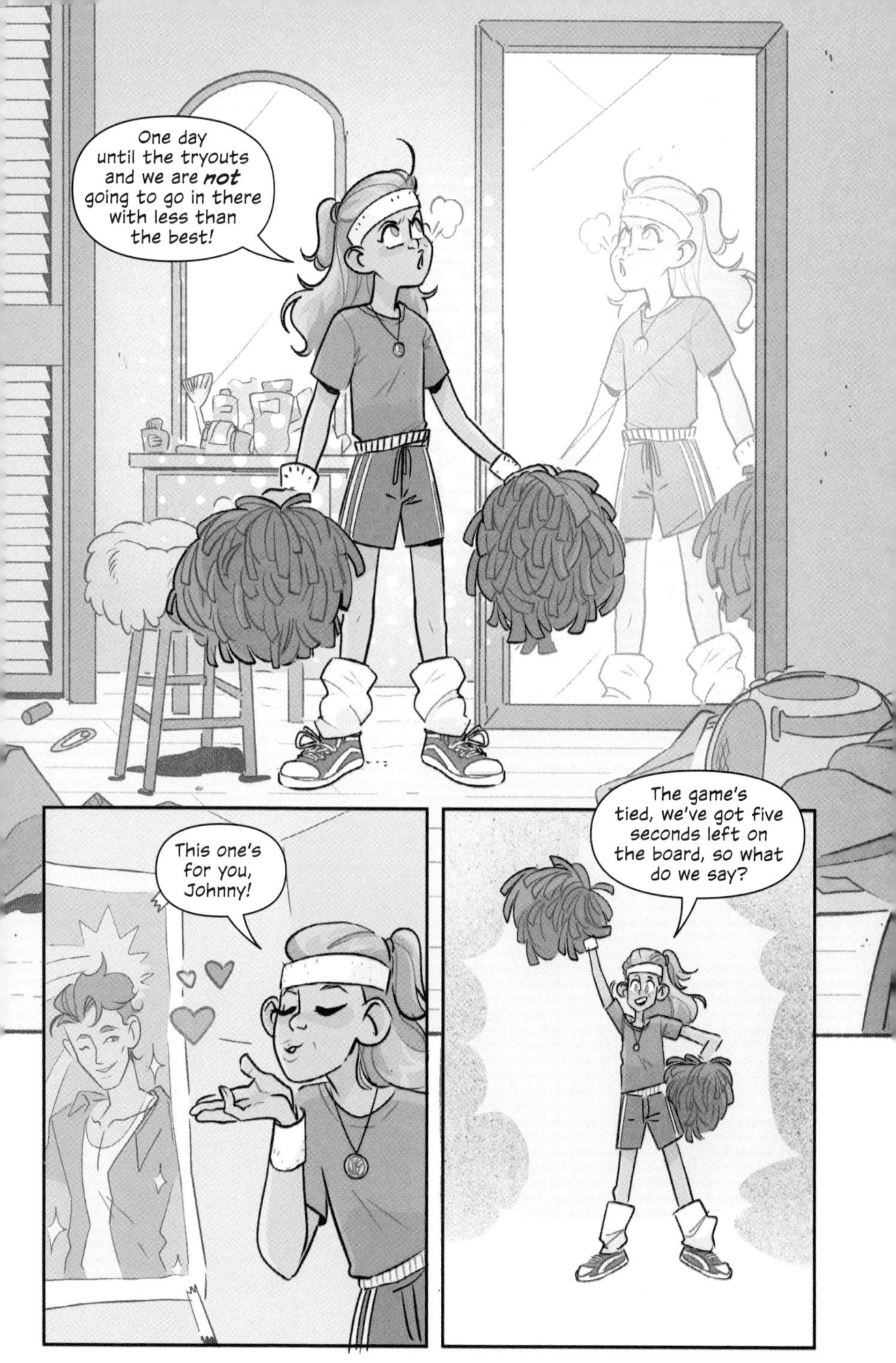
One day until the tryouts and we are ***not*** going to go in there with less than the best!
This one's for you, Johnny!
The game's tied, we've got five seconds left on the board, so what do we say?

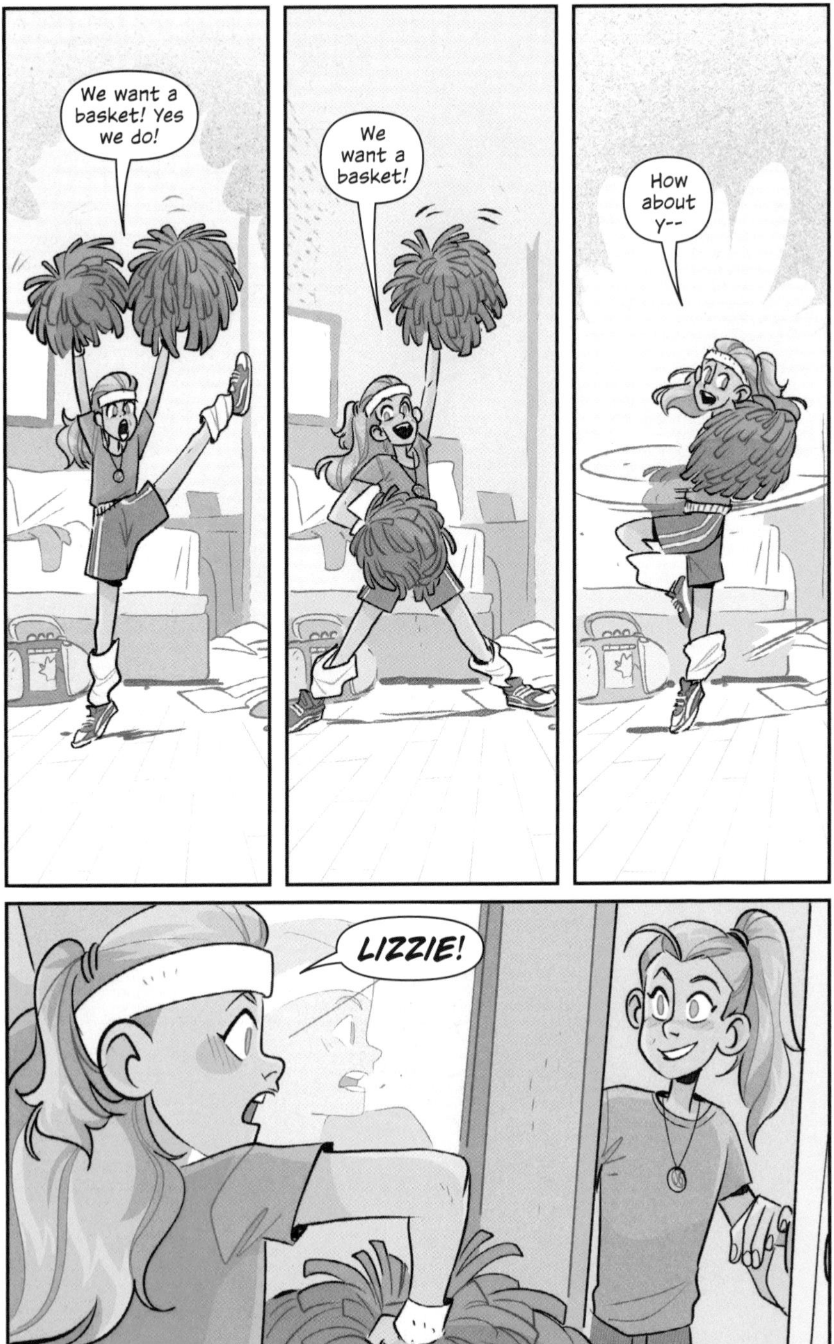
We want a basket! Yes we do!
We want a basket!
How about y--
LIZZIE!

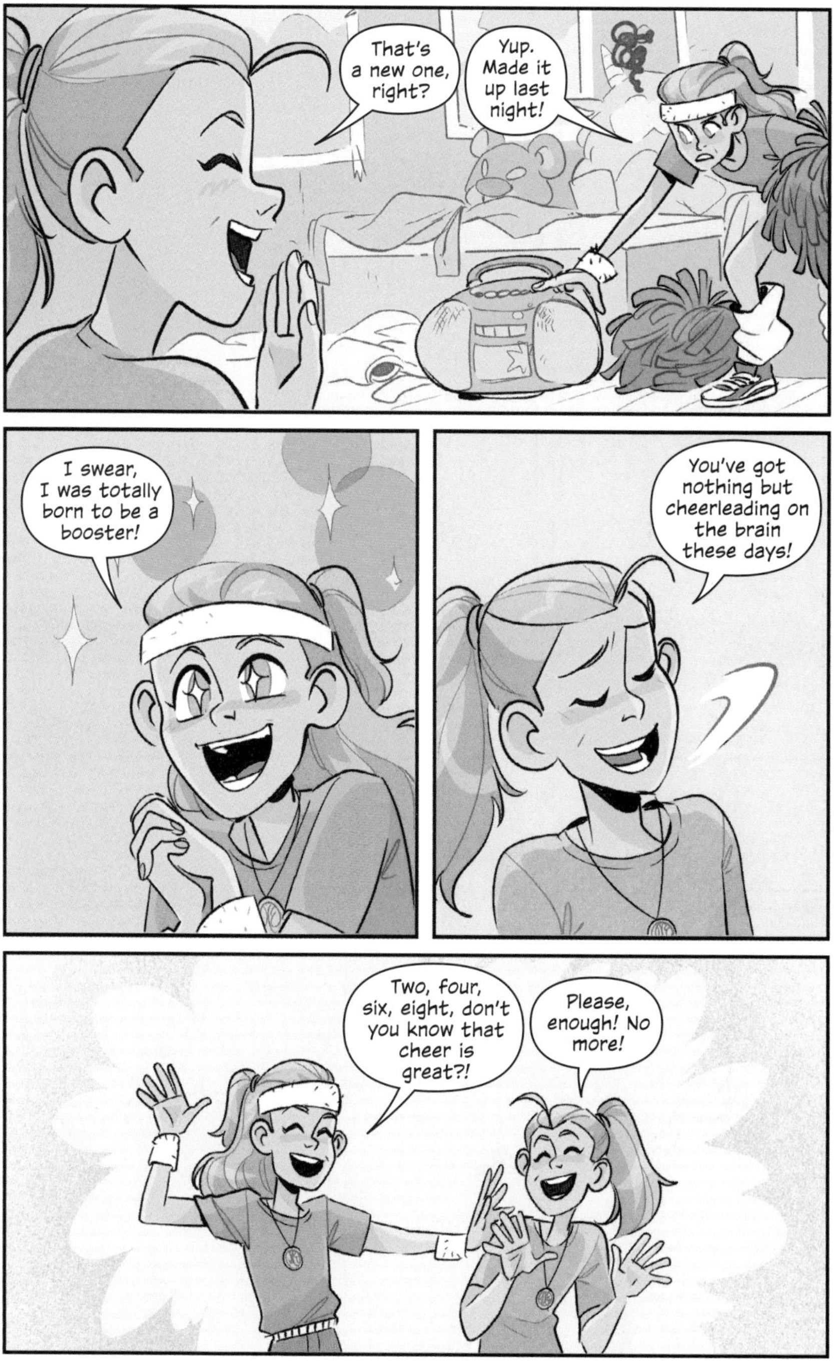
That's a new one, right?
Yup. Made it up last night!
I swear, I was totally born to be a booster!
You've got nothing but cheerleading on the brain these days!
Two, four, six, eight, don't you know that cheer is great?!
Please, enough! No more!

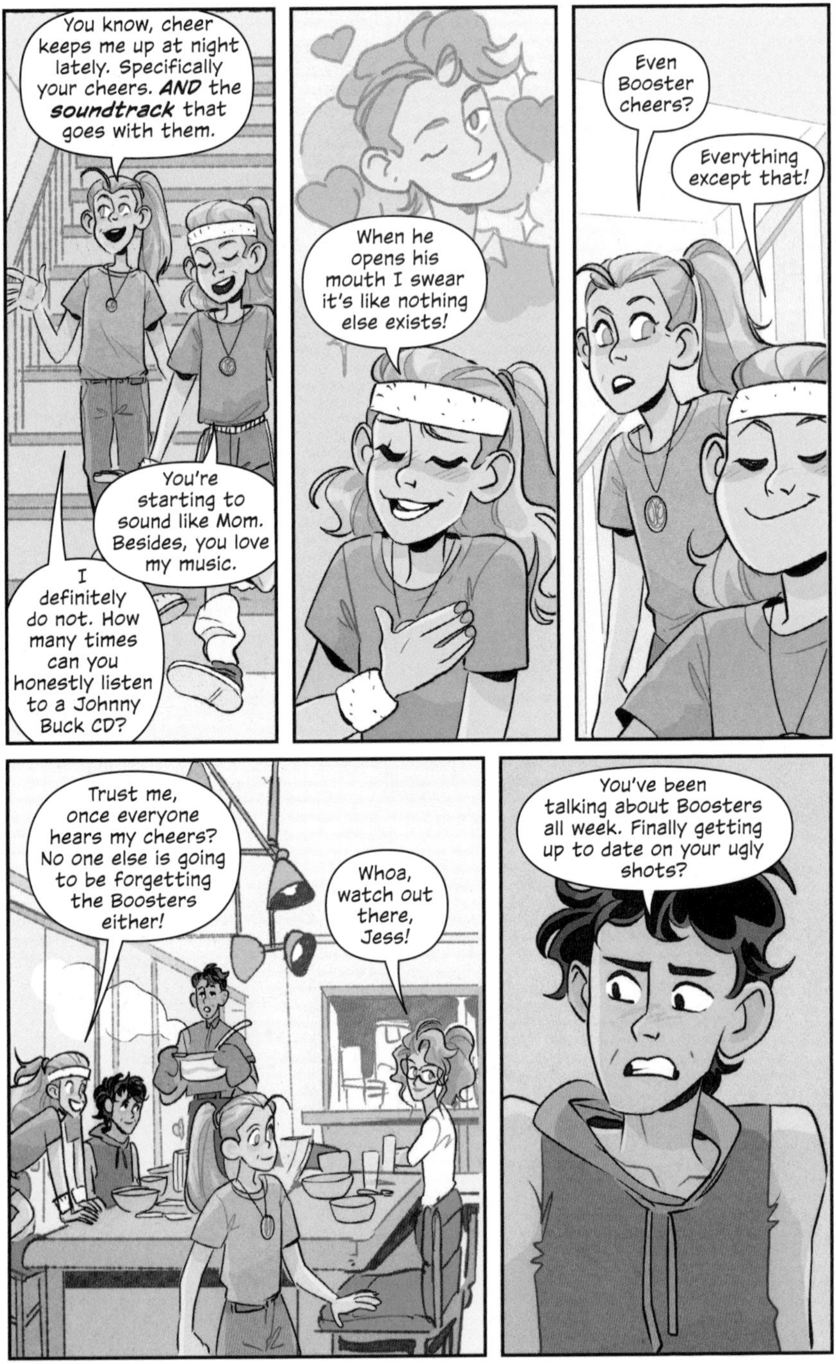
You know, cheer keeps me up at night lately. Specifically your cheers. ***AND*** the ***soundtrack*** that goes with them.
You're starting to sound like Mom. Besides, you love my music.
I definitely do not. How many times can you honestly listen to a Johnny Buck CD?
When he opens his mouth I swear it's like nothing else exists!
Even Booster cheers?
Everything except that!
Trust me, once everyone hears my cheers? No one else is going to be forgetting the Boosters either!
Whoa, watch out there, Jess!
You've been talking about Boosters all week. Finally getting up to date on your ugly shots?

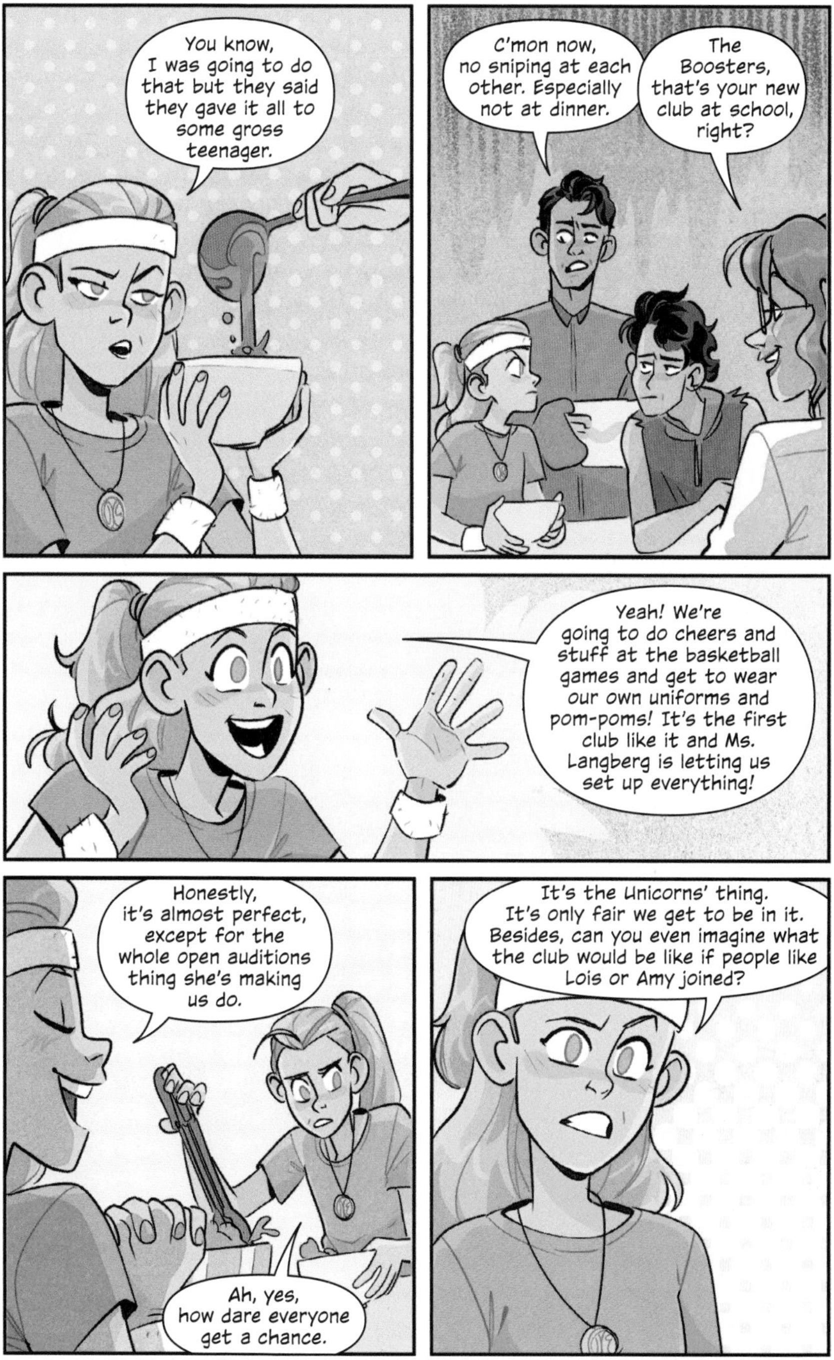
You know, I was going to do that but they said they gave it all to some gross teenager.
C'mon now, no sniping at each other. Especially not at dinner.
The Boosters, that's your new club at school, right?
Yeah! We're going to do cheers and stuff at the basketball games and get to wear our own uniforms and pom-poms! It's the first club like it and Ms. Langberg is letting us set up everything!
Honestly, it's almost perfect, except for the whole open auditions thing she's making us do.
Ah, yes, how dare everyone get a chance.
It's the Unicorns' thing. It's only fair we get to be in it. Besides, can you even imagine what the club would be like if people like Lois or Amy joined?

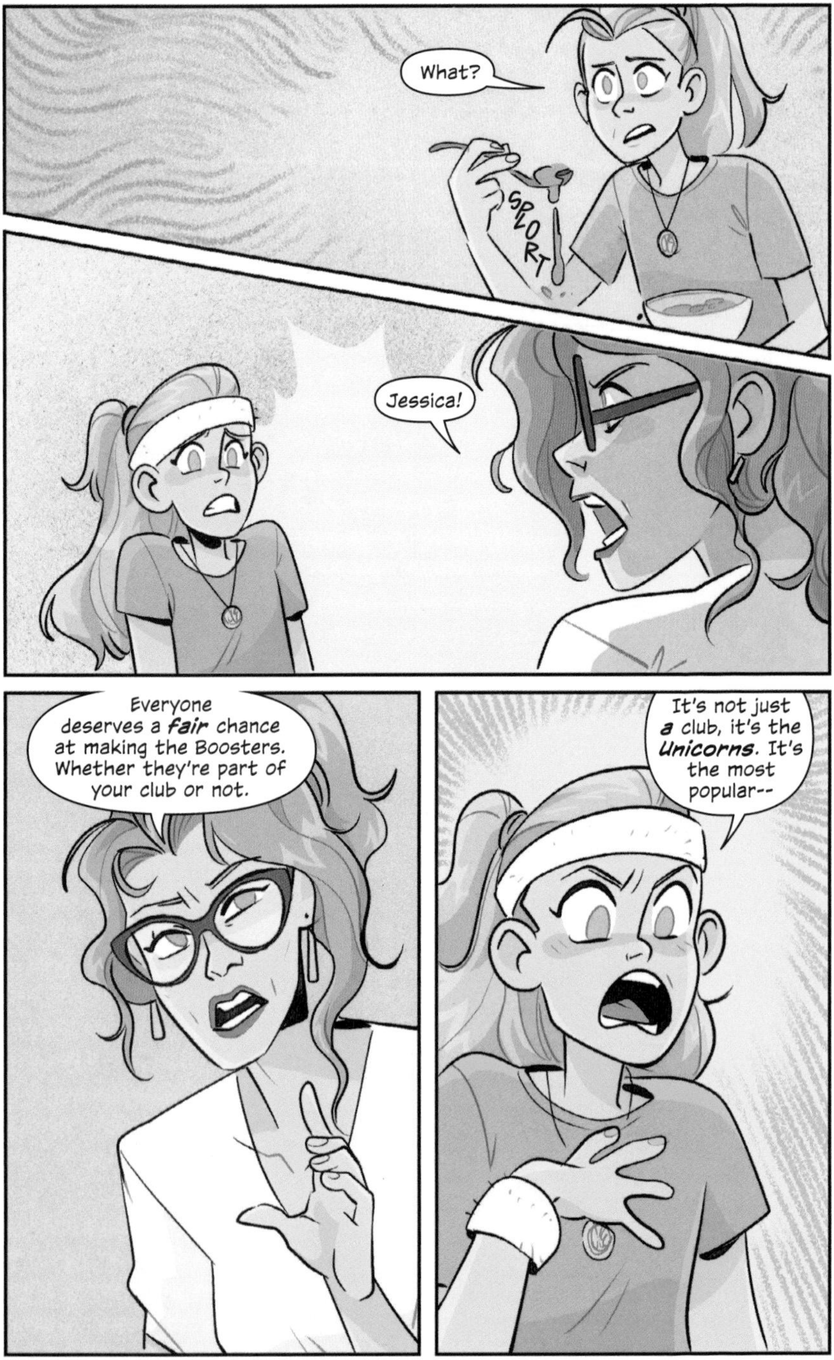
What?
SPLORT
Jessica!
Everyone deserves a ***fair*** chance at making the Boosters. Whether they're part of your club or not.
It's not just ***a*** club, it's the ***Unicorns***. It's the most popular--

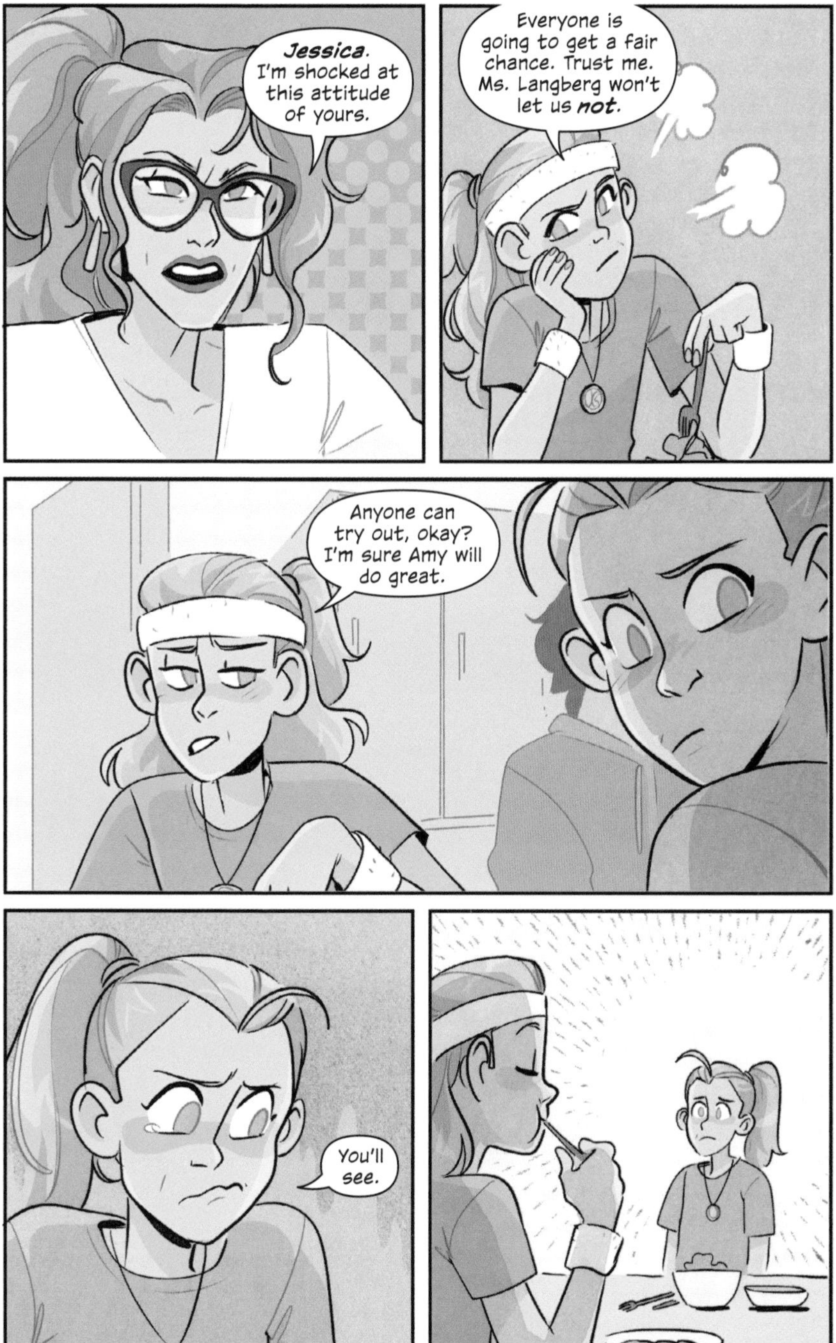
Jessica. I'm shocked at this attitude of yours.
Everyone is going to get a fair chance. Trust me. Ms. Langberg won't let us ***not***.
Anyone can try out, okay? I'm sure Amy will do great.
You'll see.

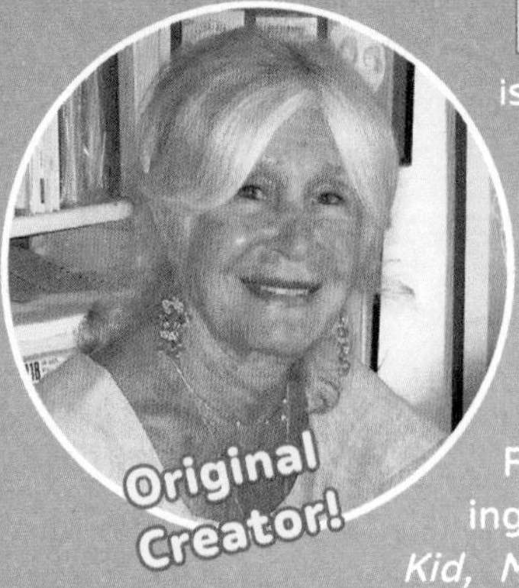
Original Creator!

FRANCINE PASCAL

is one of the world's most popular fiction writers for teenagers and is the creator of the Sweet Valley universe. This includes Sweet Valley Twins®, Sweet Valley High®, and Sweet Valley Unicorn Club. Over their lifetime, Sweet Valley books have sold millions of copies and have inspired board games, puzzles, and dolls. Francine is also the author of several bestselling novels, including *My Mother Was Never a Kid, My First Love and Other Disasters,* and the Fearless® series. Her adult novels include *Save Johanna!* and *La Villa* and the nonfiction book *The Strange Case of Patty Hearst.* She has collaborated with Michael Stewart on the Broadway musical *George M!,* and with Jon Marans and Graham Lyle she has written the musical *The Fearless Girl.* She is on the advisory board of the American Theatre Wing. Her favorite sport is a monthly poker game. Francine lives in New York and the South of France.

@francinepascal_

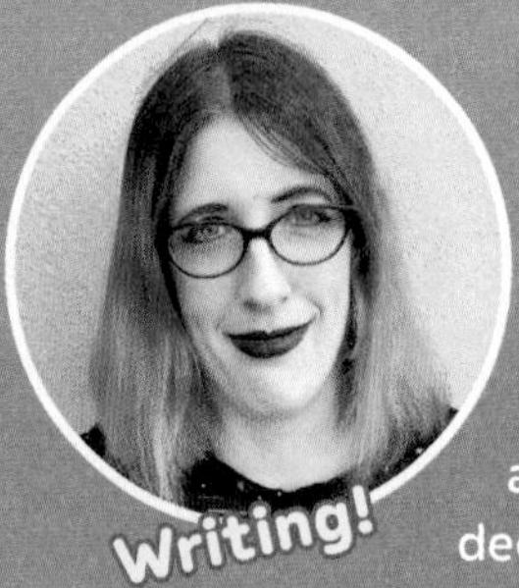
Writing!

NICOLE ANDELFINGER

was crafting stories as far back as when coloring in the squiggles on your composition book was considered cool. Since then, she's only continued to dwell in the realms of magic, monsters, and myth. She lives with her absolutely, most decidedly perfect cat in Los Angeles.

@nandelfinger

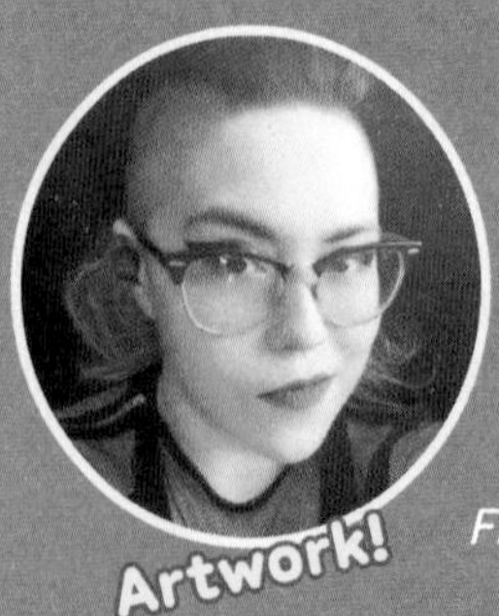
Artwork!

CLAUDIA AGUIRRE

is a Mexican comic-book artist and writer. She is a cofounder of Boudika Comics, where she self-publishes comics, and is a GLAAD Media Award nominee and an Eisner Award nominee. Her comic works include *Lost on Planet Earth, Hotel Dare, Firebrand, Morning in America,* and *Kim & Kim.*

@claudiaguirre